A GOOD MOTHER

PATRICIA DIXON

BLOODHOUND
— BOOKS —

www.bloodhoundbooks.com

Print ISBN: 978-1-5040-8548-9

For Tara,
With love, respect, and admiration.
Always.
x

ALSO BY PATRICIA DIXON

PSYCHOLOGICAL THRILLERS / SUSPENSE / DRAMAS

Over My Shoulder

The Secrets of Tenley House

#MeToo

Liars (co-authored with Anita Waller)

Blame

The Other Woman

Coming Home

Venus Was Her Name

———

WOMEN'S FICTION / FAMILY SAGAS

They Don't Know

Resistance

Birthright

The Destiny Series:

Rosie and Ruby

Anna

Tilly

Grace

Destiny

Little bird, I have heard
What a merry song you sing
Soaring high, to the sky
On your tiny wing
Jesus little ones are we
And he loves us you and me
As we share in his care
Happy we must be.

William H Parker circa 1881

THE PARISH OF ST MARY, LITTLE BUDDINGTON, CHESHIRE
PRESENT DAY

MORNING HAS BROKEN. I KNOW THIS BEFORE I OPEN MY eyes because outside the dawn chorus is in full song. I picture pale sunrays illuminating the sky while an array of little birds go about their business. No care for their sleeping human neighbours. Stubborn beaks and wings spread wide. Joyful in the new day.

I know each of them by name, not personally but wouldn't that be nice. I mean their song and species, their chirps and trills, whistles, and rattles. There was a poster on the wall in school and after listening to a tinny recording of birdsong, we took turns identifying them. I won a prize, a bookmark. I refused to use it, such was my pride and I still have it in my box of treasures.

I listen. Remaining motionless apart from my eyelids that open slowly, revealing where I am. Not in our bedroom. The reason why. Because I couldn't bear to sleep another night by my husband's side.

It's been torture. The close proximity to a person who's let me down so badly is oppressive, as though he's intruding on my personal space but, thankfully, not the forbidden area of my mind. My thoughts and secrets, my intentions, are known only to me.

I should've left the fug of our airless, soulless room before and I feel foolish for enduring it for so long. Especially the pig-like grunts that make me think of the petting zoo at the local garden centre.

Here, at least I've been able to leave the curtains and the window open. Greet each new day as it begins or ends. Sun, moon, stars. An unexpected pink sunset and all the elements in all their glory.

I hate the dark. Claustrophobia's ally. When I am exhausted or in a low mood the sheath of gloom is like a blanket. It smothers me and brings on a panic attack. Invisible fingers wrap around the sinews in my neck. Thumbs press on my windpipe and then the drum of my heart beats Morse code for help as my lungs beg for oxygen.

I spent most of last night in such torment. Baited first by my conscience and utter, lip-numbing fear but considering what lies ahead of me today, it was expected. Then slowly, as I became resigned to it all, calmness settled and left me cocooned in a wonderful sense of peace.

Anyway, it's here now. Morning. And once it begins this day will change my life, and that of others forever. Some more than most. Lives will end and lives will begin.

It's 6.30am. I know this because I heard a motorbike engine as our neighbour rumbled off on his way to work. Regular as clockwork Joe is. Same as the milkman. He'll be here at 7.30am on the button, making the last few drops on his rounds of the village.

Today is Sunday. One pint of orange, two of milk, fresh bread and six eggs. Maybe I should have cancelled, but Bobby needs the custom so it's all good.

I hate Sundays, have done for so long; yet today, I welcome it and what it will bring. Usually, the hours stretch on and on until my shift is finished. That's how I see life, as a shift. Rinse and repeat. Another day ticked off the calendar. But it's never truly over, not really, because even when the body gives in, the mind carries on. I'm a mother and they never clock off. There's no handy sign to hang on the door saying, 'Sorry. We are closed.' Mothers never flip the sign, not really.

Perhaps that's added to it all. To today. The humongous responsibility that's fallen on my shoulders ever since the children arrived. Since then, it's been down to me. No matter what anyone says, the buck stops here. It doesn't matter if you've just sat down with a cuppa, resting your achy feet and frazzled mind, or your favourite programme has started. If they call, you answer.

I wouldn't change it though, not for the world because my children are what makes mine go round, or they did until it all changed. My hand has been forced and I have to make a choice. One I don't relish, and never wished for, and I don't think I deserve. Nevertheless, it has to be done.

To look at me, sitting here, you wouldn't know what was going on inside, the churn of my stomach that disturbs the butterflies. You'd think I was completely composed, or dead. Not decomposed. Although there have been moments when I've felt rotten to the core and wished I could escape my own mind. One that is riddled with hate, such terrible anger that bubbles inside, telling me to do things I never would've considered before. Like the thing I'm about to do.

Calm returns, and I tell myself there's no rush and I obey because once I push back this duvet, place my feet on the carpet, it will start. No going back.

I can't allow my resolve to weaken, but I can delay the

inevitable. So, I'll listen to the birds beyond the window, and hold on to the last moments of 'before'.

One more hour. One more chance to think it through, so it's all straight in my head. Then it will be 'after'. This is the part that makes my tummy flutter the most and makes my chest contract because 'after' means stepping into the unknown.

What I will do, how and when I will do it I am sure of. And I hope that when it's done, my actions will be deemed justified, for the greater good. Or at the very least, I'll have spared my family more heartache than is necessary.

So, until I hear the hum of the milkman's float, the clink of bottles and the creak of the gate, here I will stay. Go over it all. Everything that led to today.

I need to walk it through in my mind, just one more time.

BEFORE

1

MARCH 2020

GINA

GINA SAT IN SILENCE, PRETENDING TO WATCH THE television when in truth she was forcing herself not to look at Jimmy, her husband. He was slumped in the armchair opposite no doubt trying to take in the ramifications of the prime minister's landmark speech.

It wasn't as if they hadn't seen it coming. The press were always one step ahead of the public thanks to leaked memos and inside contacts hence Sky News had been pre-empting something big for the past twenty-four hours.

Hearing it from the PM himself was still a shock, though. The camera had zoomed in for maximum effect while his familiar bumbling manner had been replaced with a more statesman-like approach as he addressed the nation. It was just a shame he hadn't bothered to brush his hair.

Boris got on Gina's nerves full stop, but his shabby appearance and double standards were the least of her concerns. Top of the list was the fact they all had to stay at home and a new term, 'lockdown', now applied to the UK, which had followed in European footsteps. While the press fired questions at the PM, Gina's brain pinged over its own list of what-ifs and what-nows.

All she knew for sure was that if they stayed at home, safe in their little haven, it might all be okay. And by that she didn't just mean germ free.

For a start, if you had to be locked down, Swallow's Nest Cottage was as good a place as any. The envy of many villagers, the chocolate box exterior was double fronted, with whitewashed walls and a thatched roof, set back from the road on a quiet lane with only two neighbours, one either side. Far enough apart to give them privacy, near enough not to feel isolated. The front garden was enclosed by a low picket fence and the lawns on either side of the central path were bordered by flowerbeds, tended by their gardener and about to come into bloom. But it was once you went inside that the cottage truly blossomed.

Despite the cottage's age and attractive appearance, they'd swerved a graded listing. After three rounds of planning applications, Jimmy had been given permission to bring Swallow's Nest into the twenty-first century. The two front rooms of the house had been transformed into a stunning lounge and dining room, thanks to Gina's skill as a lapsed interior designer. It was when you went through to the rear that Jimmy's undisputed talent was fully on show.

Courtesy of a two-story extension, the cottage now boasted four spacious en suite rooms; the fifth had been transformed into Jimmy's home-office that overlooked the garden. Below, the kitchen-snug-diner expanded outwards where the vaulted glass roof and bi-folding doors allowed the outside in. The manicured lawns boasted a decked dining area with barbeque and in the corner was a wood-clad summer house and the children's play area. Home.

It was their haven, designed by Jimmy for his family, to his wife's specifications so that every box on her wish list was ticked. Whenever praise was heaped on Swallow's Nest, he always insisted it was a joint effort, their design skills combined. Gina, however, saw her input as embellishment. He was the diamond who sparkled, and her jewel attracted a lot of attention. Too much, in fact.

While Jimmy appeared to be absorbed by the press conference, Gina watched Max and Mimi playing tig. At least they were oblivious, but the whole thing would take some explaining in words that a five-year-old would understand. Their three-year-old wouldn't really care.

Ironically, though, Gina considered lockdown to be a positive. The conversation she'd imagined having with her children, as she lay in bed, riddled with anxiety, might not happen. All those hours – three months, one week and four days of driving herself insane might have been for nothing because the dreadful virus that was rampaging across the world had actually bought her some time.

Jimmy's voice cut into her thoughts and her head snapped in his direction. 'Babe, can you turn that off. It's going to be on a sodding loop all night and the whole thing's doing my head in.'

Picking up the remote by her side, Gina muted the sound. It was quickly replaced by her children's voices on full volume as they played in the garden. They looked happy enough and that's how she wanted it to stay: their lives untouched by trauma, not blighted by a disease or the failures of their parents.

There was so much to think about, a new way of life to navigate, face masks and frenzied handwashing. Banalities like making another trip to the supermarket that only the day before had been pillaged by selfish lunatics. For now, toilet roll was the least of her worries. What Gina needed to know was that what was going on in her husband's head outweighed everything.

Ignoring the swirling in her stomach and the wave of

anxiety that threatened to crush her sternum, Gina grasped onto a life-raft named hope. Modulating her voice so as not to betray her inner turmoil she offered up a question. 'So, that's that. The rumours came true. Are you okay, love? You look really mithered. Are you worried about work?'

Jimmy didn't answer, he seemed lost in a world of his own and it set alarm bells ringing, causing her default setting to kick in – desperation veiled by enthusiasm.

'I'm sure it'll be fine and the whole team will get used to functioning from home, and you've got the office here. And best of all you'll have me. I can be your dedicated personal assistant. I'll even go on the butty run, to the kitchen... and keep you topped up with coffee.' She smiled, the special one that she used on Max when he hovered at the classroom door, or when she needed to pretend that needles didn't hurt, and that granny's sloppy stew really wouldn't poison them.

Jimmy brushed a hand over his face and sighed. 'I'm not too worried. My contracts are long-term projects, and I can still do my bit from here. And I'm used to remote meetings so it's no big deal in that respect. The only thing that concerns me are the sites where the build's about to start. Delays mean money lost across the board, not least to the construction teams who'll be stood down.'

'That'll be a worry financially, for workforce and the firms that employ them. Let's hope it's only for a few weeks and we'll get back to normal soon as. Trust this to happen now, when the weather's good, the best bloody time to build.' He shook his head and stood.

'Do you fancy a brew? And some cheeky biscuits while the monsters are occupied.' He looked outside to where Max and Mimi were playing on the grass.

Gina nodded, watching him intently as he headed over to

the kitchen, knowing he needed something to occupy his mind and hands. That was Jimmy all over. Apart from being a workaholic, he always saw the whole picture, taking his responsibilities seriously. To Gina and their children, his mum and dad, his friends, his work colleagues on each rung of the ladder but more so, those on the lower section with whom he would always have an affinity.

Yes, he'd done well. His family wanted for nothing. They lived in a spectacularly beautiful home. He drove a car that turned heads when he pulled up at the golf club. He moved in professional circles, rubbing shoulders with the Cheshire set in between jetting off to Europe and beyond for work.

He could hold his own in the board room, at sportsman's dinners, in the company of demanding millionaires or town planners with bees in their bonnets. Then again he was just as happy in the village pub or round at his parents for Friday chippy tea. At the core of Jimmy were his working-class roots and he clung on to them with a passion.

Jimmy's dad was a builder, a self-employed grafter and as a child, seeing the homes his father created brick by brick, fuelled a dream. From solid foundations of hard work and a close-knit family, Jimmy followed in his father's footsteps albeit at the creative end of the process.

His talent as an architect aside, her husband shone, stood out from the crowd. He was her vision of perfection. Even in his tracksuit bottoms and T-shirt that was splattered with some of Mimi's lunch, he still made her heart... ache. For so many reasons.

As he flicked on the kettle, grabbed milk from the fridge and then rummaged in the cupboard for biscuits, eating as he moved, dropping crumbs everywhere, Gina tried to banish her aches and worries. He made her smile and wonder how a man who was obsessed by ordered lines, ruled by accuracy and precise angles could create so much mess in such a short space of time. And Jimmy had made such a mess, she was sure of it, and not just in her high gloss kitchen.

CHAPTER TWO

JIMMY NEVER STOPPED EATING AND IF THE KIDS CAUGHT him raiding the cupboards her 'no snacks before dinner' rule would crash and burn, but how could she resist him? How could anyone?

Don't go there. Focus.

She could feel herself descending again, her mood dipping, her mind switching up a gear into overdrive, reminding her of the task at hand. The need to claw back some sense of order. As her tummy rumbled, the threat of failure and lack of food began to overwhelm her. She didn't need to eat, though. The answer wasn't in a biscuit, or a bar of chocolate. Instead, she ignored hunger – that was the easy part – and homed in on the present, where they were at. Not how her life might turn out.

Jimmy also vied for attention. 'Earth to Gina... do we have any chocolate? I promise I won't tell the kids. I know you've got some stashed somewhere, my little Mars bar muncher.' He winked, still chewing a Jammie Dodger, his blue eyes fixed, smiling. She loved that, when his smile was just for her, even for a second.

'Top shelf inside the box of All Bran.' Gina revelled in his look of joy, a grin spreading across his face followed by a grimace.

'Urgh, who in their right mind eats All Bran?'

'Well definitely not the kids, which is why I hid it there and DON'T you dare eat all my stash. Save some for me.'

He raced over to the cupboard, rubbing his hands together in delight at the prospect of a treat. How she loved him, this disappointing man whose normally groomed fair hair, currently left to its own devices, now flopped in unruly waves as he delved inside the box. Yes, his trendy beard needed a trim and the 'just got out of bed' look might soon wear thin, but nothing could disguise his charm or smother his wicked sense of humour and caring nature. Of all his glowing attributes, if you took away the fancy trimmings, in looks and life, he was still the guy she'd met at a rugby do, a people person. A decent bloke. Or that's what she'd believed.

No, she couldn't go there. It was too much to even peep at the pictures she'd painted in her head. She had to deal with the present, smooth the crinkles out of their life and in turn, ease the ones etched across her husband's brow. Even though he'd been worried about the economy, at that moment she suspected the difficult choice between a bar of Galaxy, or a Flake was currently his greatest concern.

'Have the Galaxy; you make too much mess with a Flake.'

Jimmy nodded, knowing his own limitations and stuffed the second choice back in the cereal box while she delved into his mind.

'I reckon lockdown is going to be a huge challenge for any employer, but if the government helps out, you'll just need to focus on motivating your team and keeping that side of things on track... for when it's over and everyone can get back to work.'

How bizarre, that even though it had just begun, the

mention of lockdown ending caused something inside her chest to flutter and Gina knew why. When the kettle clicked, she decided to test the water.

'Do you think it's going to drive you mad, being here with me for days on end?' She'd purposely omitted the children because they weren't the problem; she was. It was she who lacked, just like always. She held her breath, watching his eyes concentrating on spooning sugar into his mug because it drove her mad when he sprinkled granules on the worktop.

When he looked up, he wore a quizzical expression. 'No, not at all. In fact I think it'll be fun, having some time with you and the kids especially in this weather. We'll just have to make the best of it.'

Gina bridled yet forced a smile and turned her anger into a jokey retort. 'What, make the best of a bad job? Being trapped at home with the wife. Deprived of your interesting colleagues and friends. Ah, I get it. I'm the booby prize.'

A flicker of something crossed his face, he looked troubled, suspicious before turning her comment on its head. 'No, I don't mean that, Mrs Touchy. I meant that it's a situation we didn't expect but could turn to our advantage. When am I ever going to get this chance again? Not to be up at stupid o'clock to avoid the rush-hour drive into the city. To have breakfast with the kids, be home before bath-time, read Mimi the same fairy story a hundred times or play football with Max. It'll be nice not having to pack family time into just the weekend. For however long it lasts we can pretend the weekend happens every day. *That's* what I meant.'

And even though his words should've brought comfort, they hadn't. Because he hadn't mentioned her, not really. He hadn't singled her out. He'd lumped her in like she came with the deal, part of the package. And it stung like nettles, the blisters of hurt blooming below the surface, out of sight in the place she kept her secret, or – more to the point – his secret.

Swallowing her disappointment Gina chose to rally. 'Well, it's not going to be all fun and games because you still have work to do. And Max will need to be home-schooled, but I can take care of that. Mimi probably won't even notice but I think they'll miss their friends.'

Jimmy brought over their mugs and sat opposite at the kitchen island. 'I'll do my bit, don't worry about that. I've been saying you look tired lately and you've lost weight again. Don't think I haven't noticed.'

He gave Gina a look that meant, *do you want to talk about it?* And in truth she did, but couldn't because then it would all come out. Like when you opened the fluff-filter in the washing machine and all the gunge and grime dribbled out. And then they'd be finished. So instead she responded with a vacant expression, one that meant *move on.* So he did.

'Maybe we'll need to have some kind of daily timetable, you know, to keep the monsters in check, so Mimi doesn't go feral, and Max does his lessons. If I set aside part of the day for working, I'm sure there'll be plenty of time to do family stuff. After all, I won't be commuting or entertaining clients or wasting an hour for lunch because we can have it here, together. See, I'm liking lockdown more and more with every minute.'

Jimmy took a swig of tea then stood, his attention drawn to the garden where Max was attempting keepy-uppies and Mimi was having a conversation with her dolls and teddies who she'd gathered in a semi-circle around her.

Gina followed his gaze and took in the scene and held in her mind a moment of childhood bliss. An afternoon cocooned in ignorance of everything that was going on in the world, on the other side of the perimeter fence, or in their parents' marriage.

The thing was Gina wasn't even sure what was really going

on there either, although she had a very good idea and it had been killing her for too long. Slowly and surely like a disease eating her mind and body.

'Come on, let's go outside and get some sun on our faces, and I'll show Max my superior keepy-uppy skills. Let's stick the barbecue on and eat outside. Have we got any sausages?'

'What?' Gina was miles away and dragged her eyes and concentration back to Jimmy.

'Sausages, do we have any?' Jimmy drained the last of his tea and placed the mug on the island.

'Yes, we have loads, some in the fridge and more in the freezer. I'll get them out and wash these up. You go outside. I'll be there in a minute. We'll discuss timetables and navigating lockdown later when the kids are in bed.'

He didn't need to be asked twice, mainly because washing-up wasn't on Jimmy's radar and he was useless at loading the dishwasher. His mum said it was a ploy he'd perfected at thirteen and Gina was a fool to fall for it. Yes, Gina was a fool all right, no doubt about that.

Dumping the mugs inside the dishwasher Gina slammed the door shut and then rested her hands on the cool marble, closing her eyes and taking a moment to compose herself, go over the rules that would govern their lives, that would keep Jimmy at home with her and well away from that woman. The bane of her life.

She'd been given another chance and finally, after all the years of saying her prayers, believing, clinging on to her faith like a talisman, just as she was about to throw the towel in and tell God that he was a big let-down, there was hope. Not that she'd asked for a pandemic. But as an answer to a prayer for the woman who was having an affair with your husband to drop dead, it wasn't far off the mark.

As she engaged her slow-breathing technique, Gina also

admonished herself, taking the blame for allowing a charmed life to lull her into a cycle. Rinse and repeat. She'd just stood back and let it happen, been complacent and the buzz they once had was barely audible, the spark intermittent like a dodgy pilot light.

Tutting, she moved towards the window and watched her family at play. Jimmy had Mimi on his shoulders. She was screeching with delight as they dribbled the ball around Max who'd resorted to cheating, clinging on to his dad's legs as they ran.

'Oh, Jimmy, what have you done?' She said to the crazy man in the garden, the one she'd trusted implicitly, loved unreservedly.

Then she asked herself a question. Was there a chance she'd got it all wrong?

If she had, she vowed never to be in this predicament again. If she hadn't, there was still a chance she could reverse everything, save her marriage, prevent Max and Mimi from the heartbreak of a broken home.

It was up to her. Her job to protect them and their future and while she had breath in her body, that's what she would do. And while everyone was terrified of a hidden enemy, Gina knew exactly who hers was. Most people were probably in a state of shock at going into lockdown, dreading being trapped in their homes but secretly, Gina was rejoicing.

CHAPTER THREE

BABS

DROPPING HER PHONE INTO THE BAG-FOR-LIFE THAT rested by her side, Babs relaxed on her favourite bench to enjoy the early evening sunshine and a spot of bird watching – ducks to be precise. It was lovely and peaceful on the green and from their vantage point she and her feathery friends could watch the residents of Little Buddington go about their business.

She was blessed. Babs always thought that when she took a moment to appreciate her surroundings and today was no exception. Spring was getting itself into gear. The first green shoots were tentatively peeping from the soil in flowerbeds dotted around the grassed area, lining the cobbled path along the edge of the pond.

Soon the whole village would burst into life, spring and summer were packed with sports days, village hall bake-offs, the July fete, and lots of weddings up at the church.

During the warmer months the scent from hanging baskets which adorned the lampposts, abundant with colourful blooms, was heavenly. She'd lost count of how many times they'd won accolades, but their victories were well deserved because

'Budders' as it was affectionately known, prided itself on looking pristine.

This was all thanks to the indefatigable spirit of the Budders Resident's Committee, whose competitive streak never waned, and their determination to get into the 'Best Blooming Village' category in the local paper.

Thinking of past glories made Babs wonder about the future, because it was already a lot quieter than normal. Most people were at home, glued to the news channels, keeping up with the evolving lockdown situation. Babs had watched the PM's speech on her phone and as a consequence, had no intention of hurrying, determined to make the most of her freedom and solitude.

That was why she'd left her little Fiat in the Co-op car park and after passing the cenotaph that stood proud in the centre of the green, wandered across to the duck pond. Her excuse for being late would be the humongous queue she'd had to wait in. Right out onto the street it was! In truth, there'd only been three people up ahead.

After nipping into the mini-market she often stopped by the pond to rest her aching feet and body. Sometimes, she'd even treat herself to a meal deal. Pete would moan if he knew, saying it was an unnecessary extravagance, all £3.50 of it. Well he could sod off because it was nice to eat a sandwich or a fancy poke bowl, the name of which made her chuckle.

It was weird, but due to the fact that someone else had made it, the meal deals always tasted much better than her own packed lunch. Her favourite sandwich was prawn mayonnaise, but Babs studiously alternated to add a bit of variety to life. She always had fruit for her snack, though. Part of her five-a-day. And she stuck to water, staying hydrated and fending of the dreaded middle age spread.

The church clock said 6.45. Babs knew it was a bit too late

for a treat and she'd done well to resist buying a cheeky Snickers even though she was starving. She was always bloody starving lately. Her thoughts turned to the three big pizzas she'd bought from the reduced section. Monday's meal was always a quickie, basically because Babs hated them. Mondays, that was. Not pizzas.

She hated Sundays even more. They were dreary, and still reminded her of school and that horrible feeling that lessons loomed. The day would drag. Nothing on the telly, then bath, hair washed and ready for bed. Now she was an adult, she'd swapped maths and English and instead, was starting to dread the whole week!

Babs cleaned for a living and took great pride in her little business but lately it was wearing thin, that and the daily grind of life in general. She'd worked out that over thirty years of marriage, she must have made around 10,000 evening meals. 10,000! And Pete must have complained about half of them.

That's why she'd bought pizza, nice and quick. She would have salad with hers, which in her book made it a healthy choice. Pete would definitely moan. According to him it wasn't a proper meal, so she'd probably end up doing him egg and chips. In fact, she wasn't even sure the three gannets would even eat spinach and ricotta which meant a fight for the meat feast and the spicy chicken ones. Which then made her wonder why she'd even bothered buying the pizzas in the first bloody place!

Maybe the shop would take them back, or she could stick them in the freezer, and they could all have egg and chips. And a bit of salad on the side for her, to show willing. 'And this, is my wonderful, scintillating life.' Barbara muttered to the ducks who completely ignored her. She was used to that, being ignored.

Sighing, Babs awarded herself five more minutes, then she'd head off. She wasn't really avoiding going home it was just that she deserved some me-time before what she referred to as the 'evening shift,' began. And anyway, she loved the solitude and fresh air, feeling the breeze on her face as it cooled her cheeks that were often on fire.

Sometimes she'd sit there on her favourite bench even if it was pouring with rain, brolly up, her and the ducks enjoying the downpour. Rumour had it that after the war, one of the villagers had taken their own life, right there in the pond. Babs thought that was sad and couldn't ever imagine life being so bad she'd do that. Perhaps she needed to stop being a grumpy sod, like Pete said she was. Charming!

But to be fair, all the virus and lockdown business wasn't helping. It was the only thing everyone talked about, and the news channels were relentless, her lot included. Babs was in no mood to listen to them going on and on about it, face-maskers versus non-face-maskers. Conspiracy theorists boring the crap out of the equally dreary doom-mongers.

The Finch family debating team was split fifty-fifty on the ramifications and regulations regarding the virus and therefore Babs' ten-pence-worth was eagerly sought after. That was actually a bit of a turn-up because usually nobody gave a rat's arse what she thought. Babs wouldn't be drawn and instead, would stick to Boris's rules, keep her counsel from her place on the fence, and revel in her moment of petty revenge.

She'd found she was doing that a lot lately, thinking wicked thoughts, plotting against people who'd crossed her and hating on random folk who got on her nerves by merely existing. Anything really.

Strangers in the street, neighbours especially, people on the telly, daft endings in books, stupid adverts and jingles, Boris and his goofy girlfriend, the wallpaper in her hallway – Babs' house, not number 10. Her hit list was endless. Her family were especially irritating even though, knowing them as well as she did, they'd be oblivious of any wrongdoing.

Bald Eagle was the worst. That was her semi-affectionate name for her husband, Pete. Now he really did boil her blood, just by being in the same room. In fact, she couldn't actually think of one good thing to say about her husband lately, and he'd probably say the same about her.

They weren't getting on. She could feel they were drifting further and further apart. Lost at sea. That was a good way to describe them, and it seemed like neither had the inclination to pull their very separate boats ashore, tie them back together and find a way to anchor their lives.

Babs sighed. She knew that the fault lay with her because she was perpetually in a bad mood and was turning into a sour-faced old grump which at fifty, wasn't a great look, but she simply couldn't help it. Her face seemed to wear a permanent frown, like she was cross with everyone and everything. And now, Lord help her, after being stuck at home she'd look like the moody gargoyles above the vicarage door.

Even thinking of that place made Babs seethe. She cleaned there once a week, and the church, so seeing as both places brought in regular money, she had to grin and bear it. That vicarage had bad vibes and she knew exactly why.

This train of thought only added to her woes because thanks to the bloody virus they'd be down a wage and it'd cause problems at home. She was in great demand in and around Little Buddington so her small business helped pay the bills. But to Babs, it was more than the money. Even though it wasn't rock and roll, her job was her independence. Her clients were mostly lovely and relied on her. She'd miss them.

The only saving grace was that Bald Eagle and their eldest, Isaac, were classed as key workers and therefore *should* be out all day. One driving a recycling truck for the local council, the other driving a bus in and out of the city. As for her two daughters, that would be interesting to say the least.

Demi, the youngest at fifteen, hated being off school. Babs understood her moody-mare's hormonally-induced personality disorder but at least for a few hours a day she was the teacher's problem child. Not hers. She was now!

Sometimes, nice Demi went to bed with a cup of tea and her latest book and then overnight, she'd be possessed by an eye-rolling she-devil. Nobody ever knew which version would come stomping down the stairs for breakfast and as the kitchen door opened, Babs hoped it wasn't the girl who could chill the atmosphere with her presence and freeze your blood with a frosty glare.

For the most part though, Demi was a good kid, extremely bright and hard-working. A regular mother's little helper and ally, which was why Babs often forgave the mood swings – after all, she knew exactly how it felt.

Then there was Sasha. What could Babs say about their middle child that didn't make her sound like the most critical mother in the world? That she was lazy, scruffy, lacked direction, needed to get off her arse and get a proper job, was man-mad, and an all-round let-down.

Yes, that summed Sasha up nicely. She'd graduated from university with a 2:2 in Media and Journalism and had spent the last nine months going from one job disaster to another, none of them remotely to do with her chosen field of very costly expertise.

She'd started off at the garden centre until it got too cold. At Frankie & Benny's the piped music sent her mad. At KFC the sight of raw chicken made her heave, as did the fumes at the petrol station, where to be fair, she lasted for a whole miraculous month. She endured one full day at Asda where unfortunately the check-out manager was Jodie, Sasha's arch-enemy from school. It kicked off during training and Sasha was escorted from the building. And finally, a barmaid at the local pub, which, thanks to the bloody virus, was now closed.

Babs was convinced that Sasha's student loan would never get paid off, unless the bank waited till she drew her state pension then they were in with a chance.

The sound of a bird chirping very loudly had Babs delving into her shopping bag and after a quick rummage, she located her phone and glanced at the screen, tutting as she swiped to accept the call.

It was Demi. 'Mum, where are you? I'm starving and there's nothing nice in.'

'I'm in the check-out queue at the Co-op, love. Shouldn't be too long now. Drink some water or make yourself a sarnie.'

An exasperated voice replied. 'I can't because Isaac's had all the bread, the fat basta... greedy pig.'

Babs raised an eyebrow and uttered the words all her kids hated to hear. 'Have an apple. I'll be there soon, look, I have to go. It's nearly my turn.' Chuckling, Babs disconnected and imagined the look of disgust on Demi's face as she sloped off to the fruit bowl.

Sighing, Babs got to her feet. There was no point in stalling, so she said goodbye to the ducks and made her way back to the car. After loading her bag onto the passenger seat, Babs sank behind the wheel and resignedly started the engine, nudged her way out of the car park and wished there was a long way home.

CHAPTER FOUR

APART FROM A LONE DOG WALKER, BUDDINGTON WAS deserted, and it felt quite eerie. She'd lived there all her life and it hadn't changed a bit. The tiny Cheshire village wasn't affluent by any means, merely well cared for by the stalwarts. Apart from the retirees and the old guard who like herself, were born and bred there, most of the inhabitants commuted to the larger outlying towns to work, now that many of the farms in the area had scaled down or shut down.

Budders had only three main roads shooting off the roundabout, with the green and duck pond at the centre. On the imaginatively named Main Street, on the village's periphery, stood the Co-op supermarket, taking up one third of the circumference. It had been built in the early twenties with a few face-lifts since then, and Babs had fond memories of shopping there with her mum and Nan.

In the next third was The Carters public house, a popular hostelry with a thatched roof and quirky, twisted walls held up from the inside by centuries-old timber. And then came the school which was slightly set back in the final section of the roundabout.

St Mary's Primary was the true heart of the community. With its village hall, sports field, and tennis courts, it not only served the residents of Buddington, but pupils from the nearby village of Gawsworth. All of the Finch children had gone there, as had Babs and Pete before they headed off to the secondary modern on the outskirts of Macclesfield. That had been such an adventure. Catching the bus each morning, leaving the picturesque village behind and experiencing a few hours in a new school with new faces.

She hadn't appreciated it back then, how perfect, and peaceful village life was, how fortunate she'd been to live there. Dotted along the three roads out, were thatched cottages, beautifully preserved with whitewashed walls and neat gardens, as were the quirky higgledy-piggledy rows of farm terraces that were once inhabited by land-workers.

Nestled safely amongst the lush, rolling Cheshire countryside, Buddington had a crime rate of almost zero. This was due perhaps to its isolated location – if a roaming burglar blinked, he might miss the turning – or perhaps it was the very zealous but mostly redundant neighbourhood watch? Anyway, the residents felt safe and secure in their rural idyll.

Taking the Gawsworth Road, Babs headed out of the village and towards home, which was in a less picturesque setting, behind a purpose-built row of shops on a small estate of houses. A five-minute walk from the chippy, off-licence, launderette and sub-post office, The Willows had been built in the late seventies. Community homes they were called back then; the countryside equivalent to social housing.

She had no idea how the local planners managed to swing the development or who designed the very average set of ten identical cul-de-sacs that held an assortment of properties to suit the nuclear family, one of them being her three-bedroomed detached.

Years later, they'd jumped at the chance to buy their house from the council but deep down, Babs had begun to hate her red-brick, bog-standard home with a passion. It was her prison, that's how she saw it. No longer a cosy family home to put down roots in. It was tired, far too small for purpose, unless their Isaac finally got a place of his own with his girlfriend Fiona. Demi and Sasha needed a room of their own. Even better, if Sasha managed to keep a job long enough to pay rent and buggered off, Babs could nab the box room and escape Bald Eagle's snores. Bliss.

She'd had big plans for their family home but none of them had come to fruition. Like new double-glazed windows. Some of that nice woody decking that Gina Morgan had, and a conservatory with one of those rattan furniture sets. There, she would sit and read, well away from the blare of the telly and endless squabbles about the bathroom or whose turn it was to wash the pots. That made her think of the dishwasher.

Don't even get me started on the dishwasher.

Of course, none of it was going to happen, not while Pete had a hole in his arse because his agenda, his wants, his acceptable extravagances came first, always had.

Like his season ticket to Macclesfield Town – *it's a family tradition, love.* Just like the pool team coach trips, and those sly little bets she knew he had at the bookies, not to mention the reason his beer belly looked like he was seven months gone.

There was always enough spare for the things Bald Eagle wanted. Not a meal deal from the Co-op, though.

And it wasn't just a case of money, either. She was a saver, and they could afford bits here and there. It was the lack of motivation that hindered her plans. And the excuses of course. Like his bad back – that meant decking was a no-no. The leaky windows *still had a bit of life in them yet,* and *sorry love, there's not enough room in the garden for a conservatory...*

Babs had tuned out his excuses long ago then just gave up asking. It also saved having a row, so instead she enjoyed the moments she spent in other people's lovely homes. Admiring their tasteful nick-nacks as she dusted, hoovered their plush carpets with the twinkly bits of glitter in, or loading their state-of-the-art washing machines that played a tune when the cycle finished.

Best of all, was sitting on classy rattan furniture on the woody deck and having a cup of tea with her favourite client, and friend Gina. Babs had a soft spot for the young mum who she'd known all her life because she hadn't had an easy time growing up. It had all turned out fine when she found Jimmy, who was dedicated to giving Gina all the things she'd missed out on. And with a mum like hers, Gina had missed out on a lot, including love.

They often had a catch-up after work, in nice weather sitting on the lovely patio with a cup of tea and a biscuit, or otherwise in the beautiful kitchen that Babs coveted. Actually, it was mostly Babs who ate the biscuits, posh ones from M&S. To hell with her diet.

Gina didn't eat biscuits. In fact, lately she looked like she hadn't been eating much at all. Babs had intended having a tactful word with her because she didn't want Gina falling back into her old ways. The little chat wouldn't be happening any time soon, but there was always the phone. Babs would keep in touch that way, just in case.

Babs huffed loudly as she pootled onwards. It was that bloody lot in China that she blamed, especially after she'd seen the photos of the wet markets on the news. It had made her gag and put her right off takeaways. She wasn't going to ban them though, but only because it meant she didn't have to cook.

Babs was lost in thought as she left the quaint section of the village behind, mentally going through the menu at the Golden

Bridge Chippy as she followed a short expanse of country road. And there, up ahead, set at an angle was the yellow sandstone edifice of St Mary's Parish Church.

It loomed high over the village. The square clock tower and steeple could be seen from most locations and as far as Babs was concerned it was a blot on the landscape. It was nothing special, as churches go, the kind that little kids drew in crayon, simple in design, oblong, wide arched doors to the front, with a flagstone path to the porticoed gateway. It was surrounded on all sides by gravestones dating back to the 1800s when it was built and to the rear, the drystone walls separated consecrated land from the farmer's fields. To the right, almost obscured by the mature trees that lined the perimeter stood the vicarage.

From the outside, parishioners had no reason to believe it was nothing more than their dear vicar's family home. The sandstone façade was adorned by a yellow climbing rose that gracefully wound its way along the archway above the front door and in bloom, its beauty belied the ugly misery of what was going on behind it. And Babs knew who to blame for that.

Again, she felt a swell of rage, this time directed at one person in particular. The Reverend Edmund Hilyard, vicar of the parish. Babs despised him. As far as she was concerned he was a bigoted fake and if it hadn't been for two things, she'd have told him where to stick his cleaning job. Not just that, she reckoned his boss, not the Archbishop of Canterbury, the one upstairs, would agree. But she needed the money.

And no way could she leave Robin, his lovely wife in the lurch, not under the circumstances when the poor woman needed all the support and friendship she could get. Which was why Babs bit her tongue, averted her eyes, and got on with her work whenever he was around.

Leaving the spectre of St Mary's behind, Babs put her foot down and zoomed along the country road and then, after a gentle bend and another patch of greenery she passed the shops. The Golden Bridge chippy and the bus stop with the concrete bench that held the usual gaggle of bored youths.

Maybe lockdown will keep the little buggers on the straight and narrow for a while, thought Babs as she indicated left and took the narrow road which led to The Willows.

This thought led to another. That even though it had been a sobering moment when the PM made his announcement, money worries aside, there might actually be some benefits to her situation. For a start she wouldn't be up at the crack of dawn to start her early shift, so for the first time in ages she'd have a big lie-in, every day if she wanted.

The forecast said it would be a scorcher of a week, so she'd get Isaac to cut the grass, unless it was Pete's turn. Oh Lordy, another row was on the cards... Sod it, she'd do it herself, and then she could get the deckchairs out, sit in the sun and read, maybe get a bit of a tan.

Then another thought pinged, and this was the best... if they had to cancel the summer holiday that she was dreading, then the money they'd save could be used for some home improvements. And now Pete couldn't go to the football, or pool, or the pub or anywhere apart from the cab of his bin-waggon, he'd have plenty of free time on his hands. Same as Isaac.

Chuckling at her own cunning, and with her mind still ticking, Babs smiled as she walked up the side path, ignoring the fact that nobody had bothered to bring in the washing she'd hung out at 5.30am that morning. It just made her even more determined.

Things needed to change at Finch Towers and while she had plenty of time on her hands, not only was she going to take some well-earned rest, she was also going to give them indoors a much-needed kick up the arse.

CHAPTER FIVE

ROBIN

ROBIN WAS MAKING HER WAY ALONG THE FLAGSTONE PATH that skirted the church walls when she spotted the little blue Fiat as it sped by and even though she'd raised her arm and waved, Babs hadn't noticed her. The sight of the car disappearing into the distance had made Robin sad and she knew why. It was the notion that had Babs stopped, it would have been Robin's last chance to talk to someone on the outside, a cheeky catch-up, a cheery smile, a problem shared.

Never mind. Banishing the maudlin, she continued on her route to the sunny side of the church because today of all days she needed some light in her life. Robin checked her wristwatch, awarding herself thirty minutes of fresh air and solitude before heading back to the vicarage.

She'd been desperate to escape the confines of her home that since early morning had echoed with the monotonous sound of her husband's droning. And it really did drone, like one of those flying camera things hovering above your head, the buzzy vibrations invading your ear and burrowing into your brain.

Edmund utilised the same tone for every conceivable

situation and event where his colourless vocabulary was accompanied by the actual sound of tedium. It was bizarre but true. Edmund had canned the art of conveying misery, distorting words into uninspiring, flat sermons that he would project right to the back of the nave.

And it didn't matter what the occasion. Sunday service, prize-giving at the summer fete. Even on happy occasions Edmund nailed it. A wedding would seem more like a death knell. A baptism an ominous portent of a life not yet lived. He was a bloody natural at funerals.

There was an exception. Because when he was angry, Edmund miraculously made full use of his range and vocal cords. He loved a good old rant and was in his element condemning the sinner to eternal damnation, advocating repentance, serving the threat of divine punishment as a side dish. Edmund was a natural and could put any fire-and-brimstone Methodist to shame.

It had happened many times, not necessarily in the pulpit. Most notably when someone stole the lead off the church roof – he was incandescent and actually drove to the traveller site in the next town to accuse them. Stupid move because a week later someone pinched the wheels off his car. Oh, that had really made Robin smile, seeing his Honda Civic on the drive, on bricks.

Then they'd had 'the trouble' with their son Cris and Tom, Babs' younger brother. An awful time. Just thinking of it made Robin shudder. There was no mirth to be found in that situation but at least she and Babs had managed to stay friends, despite how Edmund had behaved.

She should be used to it by now, after thirty-three years, and realised that marriage, hers anyway, was merely a form of earthly torture that she'd just have to live with. A penance for a sin she had willingly committed.

Now and then, in her more rebellious moments – usually after a bottle of red and a sneaky ciggie in the company of old Martha Nottingham – she did wonder, if she ever plucked up the courage to leave and divorce Edmund, would this and her deepest secret, be worthwhile mortal sins? Worth being locked out of heaven for, and spending eternity in purgatory's waiting room.

But Robin would never leave Edmund. She knew it. He knew it. And she hated that. His power over her was supreme, at one time aided and abetted by her faith, instilled, and nurtured since an early age. Her belief was a gift from God and had brought her great comfort.

What hurt Robin deeply was not so much her predicament; it was how *he* had tainted something that was part of her, something that had filled her heart with comfort and joy. She had never resented it, or her parents for the Christian life they led. Her kind and loving father, also a vicar, had been the polar opposite to Edmund. He had been enlightened and progressive, where her husband upheld and followed the doctrines of the church to the letter. There was no middle ground with Edmund regardless of who he hurt, even his own wife and children.

So, it was no surprise, all things considered, after 'the trouble' and the worries over their daughter, Willow, that Robin had questioned everything she had ever known. Whether it was to spite or punish her husband, be it borne from rage or regret, despair and immense sorrow, or simply the need to do something of her own accord, she'd turned her back on God, and Edmund.

Sod him, thought Robin as she picked up her pace and headed towards where Martha would be waiting for her. But tonight, there'd be no time for wine and ciggies.

Robin only imbibed if she knew it was safe for her to do so, when Willow had someone to watch over her. Nate, her son-in-law was going out soon, so she had to be quick.

As she rounded the north-east corner of the church, Robin was caught in the mellow glow of the evening sun and the warmth of its rays lifted her instantly, causing her to smile and tilt her chin a little higher. It had been another beautiful day, hence her floral maxi skirt and yellow vest top that exposed her lithe arms and fair, freckled skin. She'd always had to be careful; redheads and the sun weren't a match made in heaven.

But Robin loved the outdoors, gardening especially because it was a release, her escape into a world of colour and glorious scents, finding calm in ordered rows of vegetables and borders of flowers that when they burst into life, brought joy into hers.

Yellow was her favourite colour, her go-to preference in clothes and furnishings, including the feature wall in the vicarage kitchen, brightening what was essentially a draughty, austere abode that had desperately needed a dose of the twentieth century. B&Q had helped her with that, and her trusty paint roller.

Yellow was also her choice of rose which she'd planted under the vicarage windows all those years before, when she and Edmund arrived in the village. A gift to the house, the laying down of roots, and in some ways a putting to bed of things that could never be, burying her deepest desires and secrets under a layer of topsoil.

Robin didn't like to think of that time too much, but she remembered kneeling on the path as she dug deep then lowered the sapling into the hole. Tears were running down her cheeks as she prayed for divine guidance, strength, anything God could spare so she might find the courage to honour her wedding vows and navigate married life. Thankfully, that day, he'd been listening.

For many years, with the birth of her two children, Robin's

cup had, for a time, overflowed with love and gratitude for such wondrous good fortune, right up until 'the trouble' and then the tragedy that led to Willow's rapid decline.

God had held her up, been her rod and staff, guiding her through death's dark veil and the searing pain of loss. He'd taken his share of the burden when the weight of duty was too much to bear, held her hand tightly when the one she reached for let her down.

It was God, not Edmund who'd done these things.

In the past thirty-three years, Robin would say her husband was the most terrible disappointment of all. But worse than all the things she attributed to him, was the loss of something she'd held so dear, equal to the love of her parents and children. Her faith.

Striding along the worn pathways that criss-crossed the gently sloping graveyard, Robin was aware of the familiar ball of anger burning like a comet inside her chest. But she forbade it to ruin her moments of freedom. Reaching the far, deserted corner she stepped around the leaning headstones, exhausted not from daily toil, more from allowing her memories headspace. There, Robin sat and rested her back against the bumpy wall, stretched out her long legs and once she was settled, said hello to dear Martha.

'Well, what a day it's been here! But I'm sure you know what's going on, so I won't bore you with the details... although Edmund is in a bit of a lather about it all. I suspect it's more to do with him being forced out of his comfort zone and I did have a bit of a giggle when I heard the bishop – they were on loudspeaker you see – mention setting up a Facebook group so they could conduct Zoom sermons. I could only see the back of Edmund's head and tensed shoulders, but I knew from the fervent finger tapping he would be puce with anger. Imagine, him on social media.'

As always Martha just listened. She never interrupted but how could she, when she was six feet under? So instead, Robin imagined her reply.

Dear sweet Martha always agreed.

'I know what he'll do, though. He'll get Nate to help him set it up, and then rope in some poor unsuspecting parishioner to do all the legwork, you know, posting stuff. Then he'll take the credit.'

Another thought occurred to Robin, that at least with Zoom, the parishioners could switch the old bore off when he started banging on.

'I quite fancy having a Facebook account, you know. So that I can have a gander at what's going on in the village and in the big wide world and get in on the gossip. Babs has one and she loves it and tells me all sorts. I think it would be fun.'

Martha agreed and said she should go for it, what was there to lose? And it'd piss old Eddie off for a start. Robin smiled because when Martha spoke her voice belonged to a raspy, forty ciggies a day kinda gal who coughed when she laughed. And she had a cockney accent, definitely not from Cheshire.

'And Babs says there are a lot of support groups on there, you know, where I could chat to people in the same situation as us. She thinks it would do me good... but then again I don't think I'd like strangers knowing all my personal business. I get it's a positive thing, for people to have a place where they can reach out, share their innermost feelings or worries, ups and downs and on their worst days know someone is there, listening.'

She smoothed her skirt and contemplated social media.

'I think I'm a good listener but I'm not so good at sharing. Not like Babs. There's always something happening at Finch Towers as she calls it, bless her. She loves them all really, even Pete although she calls him rotten. It's just bluster because she'd do anything for him and her kids. Whereas in my case, when I say I cannot bear Edmund and if he fell into an open grave I'd fill it in there and then, I really do mean it.'

Robin paused on her last statement which was a rather murderous or manslaughtery fact. And where her two children were concerned, she too would do anything for them. They were her life, and she would lay hers down in an instant to save either one of them. But that wasn't how it went, she knew that.

Nobody got to do a deal with God, swap one life for another, theirs for someone they loved. Not in her world, the real world that was completely and utterly shit.

'LIFE IS SHIT!' Robin said it out loud, making two blackbirds who'd been pecking at the base of a headstone flap and flutter away.

'Oops, sorry little birdies. I didn't mean to scare you. And I can hear you laughing, Martha Nottingham, at me, the upstanding vicar's wife, saying a naughty swear word. Well, I can tell you now, I say worse than that, think them too. Words so bad I make myself blush purple, like the bishop's cassock. But you know what? I don't give a fucking fig, not anymore.'

Robin uncrossed and re-crossed her legs so her ankles wouldn't swell and listened to Martha who'd found her outburst very amusing. Martha said that back in her day, in the fifties when she was the landlady at The Carters, she'd heard it all and nothing shocked her. Robin therefore had permission to turn the air blue if it made her feel better.

This made Robin smile. She could picture her silent friend so clearly, thanks to a black-and-white photograph on the wall of the village pub, a kind of rogues' gallery of landlords past and present.

It was such a strange thing, that a snapshot taken in the fifties could have such an impact and had kick-started a friendship borne from a mutual understanding of loneliness. It was their special story, the tale of Martha and Robin.

CHAPTER SIX

THEY'D MET AT A WAKE. IF YOU COULD CALL TALKING TO A photograph actually meeting someone, but it would turn out to be a lasting friendship of mutual respect, albeit one-sided and from the grave.

Edmund had conducted his first funeral since moving to Buddington, and they'd both shown willing and accepted the invitation to The Carters for the wake. Nowadays they'd call it a PR exercise whereas back then it was called being polite and paying your respects to the outgoing, celestial-bound headmaster of St Mary's Primary.

They'd been in Buddington a matter of weeks. Robin was eight months pregnant at the time, missing her parents and very lonely. In between making a home of the dismal vicarage, she hadn't had time to make new friends, not ones of her own age or whom she'd chosen herself.

The only people she'd come into contact with were the parishioners on the church committee and making pleasantries as she shopped in the Co-op, so Robin spent much of the day alone, lost in thought as she paddled her way through homesickness. She wasn't about to drown exactly, but on really bad days she swore she could feel the water lapping at her knees and that had worried her.

Edmund had been busy shaking hands and commiserating while Robin occupied herself with the paintings and photographs on the wall. The moment Robin clapped eyes on the lone landlady, and read the name plate below, the hairs on the back of her neck prickled.

Martha had been the proprietor from 1931 to 1952 and her cheery smile beamed from the frame, her laughing eyes crinkled at the corner so her crow's feet rested on the bone of her cheeks.

When a voice by her side interrupted Robin, she turned and looked down onto the kindly face of a mourner. 'That's my Aunty Martha, on my old dad's side. My names Hilda, by the way, and I know you're Robin. Pleasure to meet you at last. Shame it's under these circumstances, though.' Hilda gave a jerk of the head towards the grieving family who were sipping tea at a table in the corner.

Robin accepted the dainty handshake and smiled, glad of someone to talk to at last. 'Pleasure to meet you, too, Hilda.' Turning her gaze to the photograph she delved a little. 'Your aunt looks like a lovely lady... do you remember her by any chance?' Robin was being tactful because her companion couldn't possibly be a day under seventy.

'Oh yes, like I last saw her yesterday. Had a tough time did Aunty Martha, leaving her family in London to move up here with my uncle Jack. They met at a wedding, a second cousin I believe. She missed her old mum like mad, she did. But her and Uncle Jack were in love, and she was determined to make a go of it, the pub and married life. Took to running this place like a duck to water she did, always wore the pants my mum said. An independent woman before her time, I reckon.'

Something inside Robin's heart twanged, knowing precisely how it felt, to miss your mother. Not the independent woman part. 'Oh, that's sad. I miss my mother so much especially with a baby on the way.'

She rested her hand protectively on her stomach as Hilda smiled at the bump then chatted on.

'And then there was the war, that's what broke her in the end, so my dad used to say.'

Dread swept over Robin and for a second she hadn't wanted to ask the obvious, but she did, totally invested in Martha by then. 'Why, what happened in the war?'

A sigh, a wistful look and the hint of a tear preceded the answer. 'Her parents and younger sister were killed in the Blitz, while her Jack and only son, my cousin Tommy, were away fighting. Shouldn't have been allowed in my opinion, father and son sent off to war like that, Hitler, or no Hitler.

'On the day they left the whole village gathered on the green to wave the menfolk off. They all went together, even my dad, but my uncle and cousin never came back. Nearly killed Aunty Martha, it did. My mum reckoned Martha wanted to die, to be with them both and in the end she got her wish, I suppose.'

Robin was clutching her neck, something she did when she was anxious or shocked, and her cheeks were aflame, another subconscious reaction that always left her even more flustered. 'Why, what happened?' Robin looked at the photo. 'She looks so happy in the picture.'

'Agh, well, that's the thing, isn't it? Nobody knows what's really going on inside folks' heads, or what pain hides behind their eyes. From what I know she struggled to keep going, putting on a brave face for her customers when Jack and Tom went to war. Then afterwards, when she'd lost them both, Martha carried on as best she could, hiding her grief, putting one foot in front of the other for seven long years. Then one night, there was a terrible accident.' Hilda paused and moved closer, lowering her voice a notch.

'The last time she saw her boys was the day she waved them off from the green, where the cenotaph is now. My mum said she'd often find Martha there, sitting on the bench late at night, a bit worse for wear, if you get my drift.'

Robin nodded.

'Well anyway, after a few too many gins, Martha often told my mum that she was waiting for her boys and that one day, Jack and Tommy would come back for her... poor bugger. That's why she sat there, watching the road for ghosts. The night she died; she must have gone over there after the pub closed.'

Robin suspected and dreaded what came next.

'The coroner's report said it was a tragic accident, that she tripped and fell, landed face down in the pond and drowned. The milkman spotted her the next morning. There was a rumour, and mind you take no notice if you hear it, that Aunty Martha took her own life. But I don't believe that. Some did, busybodies and the churchy lot,' Hilda paused, as though realising her mistake, 'sorry, dear, but I speak as I find. No offence meant.'

Robin felt her lips twitch, amused by Hilda's faux pas. 'None taken, I promise.'

'It was still a crime back then, to take your own life and a sin in the eyes of the church. But thankfully the Reverend at the time was a nice chap, had a good heart and was a regular here at the pub and he stood her corner. Wouldn't listen to all that sinner nonsense and didn't believe Martha had taken her own life so made sure she got a nice service and burial up at St Mary's. Otherwise, she'd have ended up on the other side of the wall, with all of them sinners from the old days.'

Silence fell on Robin and Hilda as they stared at Martha. The only sound came from the mourners, respectful murmurs honouring the deceased, china cups clinking on saucers and the odd out-of-place ripple of laughter.

Robin sighed. 'That's such a sad story, but I'm so glad that the vicar stood up for her. Has she any family buried close by, at the church?'

Hilda shook her head. 'No, she's on her own. Jack and Tommy fell in France, her parents and sister were buried in Hackney and my parents were cremated. But I do go up there now and then, not as much as I should, but my knees aren't what they used to be. That's by the by though, because Martha won't care if I go or not. She's with her boys now, and that's what matters. It's how I think of her, and my parents. Free at last, happy, and together forever.'

Movement from behind distracted them for a moment as the barmaid announced that refreshments were being served, which signalled the end of their chat.

Hilda smiled. 'Right, I'm off to get some food before it all goes, and I might treat myself to a large sherry. All this nattering's given me a thirst.'

'Yes, you go, and I'll get my husband to bring you a sherry. You sit down and relax. And thank you for telling me about Martha.' Robin placed her hand on Hilda's arm and received a smile and a gentle pat in return.

Once Hilda had shuffled off to the buffet table, Robin stepped forward, drawn in closer, overwhelmed by the sudden urge to say hello and touch the face of a woman she'd never met, on an image taken long ago.

Peering at Martha she whispered, 'Hello, my name's Robin and I'm new here.'

In return, an imagined voice from nowhere replied, *'Ello darlin', nice to meet yer.*

It had played on Robin's mind all night. Martha's story had touched her soul and first thing the next morning, she'd gone to Edmund's study and searched the records of names and plot numbers of everyone buried in the graveyard. It was easy enough to find Martha, and once she had, Robin raced, as fast as an eight-month pregnant woman can, to Martha's resting place. It was the beginning of their most special friendship.

Robin looked at the inscription on the headstone and then down at the plot which she'd fastidiously kept tended and brightened up with flowers all year round. 'What would I do without you to talk to, eh? We've been through some stuff together that's for sure.'

In Robin's mind, Martha nodded, then took a drag of her ciggie. She was exactly as the photo in the pub portrayed her. White-blonde hair that always looked lovely. A kind of fluffy Doris Day style, backcombed on top and the side tucked neatly behind her ears, set under space helmet driers at the salon during her weekly appointment.

She was captured in time and Robin's imagination, wearing a flowery dress, a riot of summer colours, the New Look that became popular after Dior put a bit of oomph back into women's clothing in 1947. The style, three-quarter sleeved, boat necked and nipped in at the waist emphasised an hourglass figure. Having no idea what Martha wore on her feet Robin improvised and chose pale pink kitten heels, sling back, a hint of glamour but sensible enough for working behind the bar all day.

Looking down at her own sandalled feet, size 8, definitely not kitten heel dainty, Robin imagined her and Martha side by side. She tall and gangly, reed thin and rather bohemian in her choice of attire, whereas her friend would be petite yet curvy, and about two feet shorter. Oh, how she wished she could have met Martha in life.

Lifting her face to the sun, Robin was jolted by the sound of a car, louder it seemed than normal as it sped past, and it caused her to check her watch. Seeing that she'd overstayed, her thoughts moved from sleepy Martha to dinner duties so with a sigh and a tut she stood. Brushing dust from her skirt, she bade goodbye to her friend. 'I'll no doubt pop by tomorrow, but if not, soon as. Be good, and don't do anything I wouldn't.'

As she headed along the path deep in thought, Robin was aware of being followed. The shadow of gloom lurked only a few inches behind her, stealthy, patient and by the time she'd reached the vicarage it was ready to pounce.

She never looked at the gargoyles above the lintel; they reminded her of Edmund and instead closed her eyes. Before she stepped inside, Robin rested her hand on the front door in preparation for the hours ahead, avoiding Edmund and focusing her devotions on someone who deserved it. Willow.

Just like dear Martha had been trapped in a world of sorrow, her pain hidden behind eyes that yearned to see their loved ones once again, Robin's daughter was locked in the prison of her mind. And as much as Robin had tried to find the key so she could open the door and get Willow back, or set her free, it was nowhere to be found.

Edmund failed to see that prayers weren't going to work, and she sensed that Nate was slowly pulling away from the wife he'd promised to love in sickness and in health. Robin would never give up, though, not on her child. So, it was with a deep sigh that she pushed open the door, and leaving Martha and the sunshine behind, she and gloom stepped inside.

CHAPTER SEVEN

GINA

I bring it on myself, I know I do. I'm my own worst enemy. If only I had a tenner for every time someone has said that to me. For a start my best friend Willow would be quids in.

You see, no matter how good life is, I find a way to ruin it by giving in to the overwhelming fear that it's all going to go wrong. And yes, I know exactly where it all started, why I do it. The way I cope with it isn't ideal either. The fact is, eventually bad luck always turns up and bites me on the bum.

42 Lily Lane. That's where it began on the day my dad, Don, came home and caught my mum, Debbie, in bed with the man who drove the road sweeping cart. Apparently she'd been at it with the bin man, too, and the bloke who came to fit a new bulb to the streetlamp outside our house. I reckon she had a thing about council workers and high-vis vests. She did buck the trend with a taxi driver who brought her home from the pub, which proves my case: he was easy, like her.

It was a Thursday, almost the end of the summer term. I was six and we were due to go camping that weekend: two weeks in Tenby and I'd been looking forward to it for months.

Apparently after Dad thumped the road sweeper, Mum

threw all Dad's clothes out of the bedroom window onto the front garden, then rang the police. By the time I got home, Babs once again swooping in when she saw me waiting at the gate alone, Dad had been locked up and Mum was well into the role of the victim. I remember being so embarrassed because a pair of Dad's Y-fronts were tangled in the privets and the parents and kids who passed by were laughing.

While I cried myself to sleep that night, all I could think of was Tenby, our holiday, and how it had all gone wrong.

Life went downhill from there really. I became that kid who was pulled apart by warring parents because while Dad made a big show of wanting me to go and live with him, it was never going to happen. He might have been the more capable, sensible parent but working continental shifts and living in a bedsit miles away meant he became Weekend Dad. You know the score, bad atmosphere, sarky comments when he picked me up. Then the tutting and door slamming when we were five minutes late, her threatening to ring her solicitor. Like she even had one.

Mum never worked again after Dad left. Said her nerves were bad and we lived on benefits and the kindness of strangers, friends really, like Babs and Robin. They both took me under their wings thank the Lord.

Mum struggled to get out of bed on time to walk me to school and I was always late, so seeing as she knew my mum of old, Babs stepped in and offered to take me. She lived next door but one in those days, so each morning as she passed by with her son Isaac, two years younger than me, she'd wait at the gate and I'd rush down the path, cling on to her pram that contained baby Sasha, and off we'd go.

One day, as I skipped along eating a slice of toast – Babs always wrapped something in tin foil for me, a crumpet or a potato cake which I loved the most – I passed on a worldly-wise thought to my guardian angel.

'I'm so lucky, Babs.'

As she pulled the blanket up over Sasha's legs, she asked why.

I was happy to explain. 'Cos I've got two little birdies to look after me.'

Babs looked down and ruffled my hair while Isaac marched on ahead, clearly not wanting to be seen with a girl. 'What do you mean, birdies?'

'I saw a picture in a book at Sunday school of a bird and under its wing was a little chick and it made me think of you and Willow's mum. You're Mrs Finch and that's a bird, and so is a Robin. I think Jesus has sent you both from heaven to put me under your wings and take care of me, because Jesus is kind and good and loves everyone even little girls with naughty mummies.'

At this, Babs stalled for a second and looked at me in a strange way, like I'd made her happy and fed up all at once. 'What makes you think your mummy is naughty?'

'Bella Young told me. She said her mummy won't let her play with me cos my mummy is a dirty lady and has been naughty with lots of men. I'm not bothered cos I don't like Bella. She's nasty, and I s'pose Mummy is a bit dirty cos she never washes the pots and swears at my dad down the phone which is *very* naughty. But she's still my mummy and I love her. Like Jesus tells us to do.'

Babs didn't reply straight away, and instead put her arm around me and gave me a squishy hug then said, 'Well, me and Robin are here anytime, so if you're a bit fed up, or anything like that, all you have to do is ask us and we will pop you under our wings, just like this.'

Babs kept her arm around me all the way to the gate and has done ever since which is why now it's my turn to look after her, and Robin too. Because in their own ways they both need as much help as they can get.

When we moved in here and I was six months pregnant, I thought it was a sign – that the name Swallow's Nest Cottage was telling me I'd found my place. I was a little bird and here, I could make my nest.

Babs came round and helped me get it all spick and span. I loved it, having her here, yakking away while she wiped sawdust from inside the cupboards, then helped me stack the new pots and pans, and basically showed me how to look after a home.

I'd only ever lived in halls at uni, or in shared student houses so I had no clue where to begin in a huge house. My mum is still a waste of space and wasn't the best role model so Babs is my surrogate parent. I adore her.

I remember telling her she should write a book, for dorks like me but that bloody Mrs Hinch beat her to it which is really annoying. It was my idea to take her on as my housekeeper and we pay her well over the odds. I refuse to call her my cleaner because she's much more than that and was a godsend when I had Max and the baby-blues gripped me. And again when Mimi came along.

See, that's what I mean. There's always been something, some bloody issue in my life that I couldn't cope with, things that most people breeze through but oh no, not me. And as much as Babs and the doctor assured me it wasn't my fault, I blamed myself, my past.

I loathe me. Flaky Gina Morgan who has to have a meltdown, make a bloody mountain out of a molehill. God, I annoy myself so much.

I totally get why I'm this way. It's because I have never felt worthy, that I'm from an underclass. Each time I achieve something or find a happy place, I expect the worst. For it all to go wrong. Which is where the control thing comes in.

You see, while I was at school, St Mary's to start with, Babs was a dinner lady and managed to spread her wings across the canteen. She always made sure I got seconds. Food wasn't a high priority for Mum – lager was – so I developed a cunning way of never being hungry. After school, I'd scavenge something at home, and then wander round to see Babs or call for Willow and if they asked had I eaten, I'd say no. I always got a proper tea there.

When me and Willow went to secondary school, Robin always sent plenty in a big butty box for us to share. Even when Willow struggled with her maths and they got a tutor in to make sure she passed her GCSEs, guess who was sitting opposite, soaking up what I could, making the most of another freebie.

Yes, it did make me feel ashamed, and as I got older I had to put up with bitchy comments from people like Bella Young and her cronies about me being a bit tubby – my devious ways were starting to take their toll. Otherwise they'd mention my slutty mum, our tatty house, or my shoes that lacked the correct label. Bella always found something to shame me with.

Bella was one of those girls who had it all. Lived in a gorgeous farmhouse on the outskirts of the village, had two ponies, a holiday home and parents who were able to indulge her every whim. That girl followed me through life like a curse and whenever I turned round she was there, all through school and then college.

I thought I'd never shake her off, but I did because I had something she didn't. Brains and ambition.

I also had Robin and Babs, and their charity, because that's what it was, but given kindly in a way that made me feel loved and welcome, especially when I stayed at the vicarage, which in my teenage years was a lot.

Willow and I were inseparable. Days out with my dad dwindled when he found himself a girlfriend, and Mum spent her weekends 'entertaining'. I couldn't wait to get out of our scruffy, smelly, pit of doom house.

I loved being in the vicarage because the kitchen walls were painted yellow, and everyone sat around the table to eat and talk. Even Willow's older brother, Cris, was nice, very shy, and especially timid around his dad who insisted on calling him his full name, Crispin. Poor sod. Thank goodness Robin got her way naming Willow.

I was a bit scared of Edmund at first as I was never really sure where him being the vicar, who often looked solemn and ever so important, ended, and a dad and husband began. He was always pleasant enough to me in front of people, even though after hearing a hushed conversation I realised he was being fake.

'Are you sure she's not going to be a bad influence on Willow? We all know about her mother and how *she* behaves.'

Robin tutted. 'She's seven years old and very sweet. She couldn't possibly be a bad influence; and anyway, where's your Christian responsibility? Really, Edmund, what would the boss think? Now wash your hands for dinner and be nice to our guest. Humility won't kill you.'

Tears stung my eyes, and I hated my mum so much. From that moment on I was determined to prove to Edmund that I was a good girl.

Now I look back I think he tolerated the intrusion because it suited his job description, made him feel benevolent. I was the lost sheep that he allowed into his home, but it was Robin who was the true good Samaritan. It's weird isn't it, how as you get older you start to see someone differently and a person you kind of worshipped, you grow to despise.

Putting The Reverend Mr Hilyard, practised narcissist and fake, aside, I always think fondly of my time with Willow at the vicarage. And being a member of the church community, being part of a clan, having somewhere to go and belong was a gift. Me and Willow kept the Brownie-Guide law, helped arrange flowers at weddings, rose through the churchy ranks and got our own cake stall at the summer fete. We even helped Robin tend the graves of people who didn't get visitors anymore.

We were totally invested in Jesus. We loved him in every way – even if we'd got the wrong end of the stick and had no concept of monogamy. Me and Willow thought Jesus was very good looking, with his lovely long hair and trimmed beard, those smiley blue eyes and lovely smile, and agreed he'd make a great husband. He had all the best qualities. When you're eight you see life in a much simpler form, especially as we were going to share the son of God and would take turns being his wife. Oh, happy days.

We treated St Mary's like it belonged to us, and spent hours in the church, taking one pew each where we would sit with a picnic, reading Enid Blyton and Jaqueline Wilson. Our grand plan involved going to boarding school together, then later we'd become brides of Christ and take holy orders – this confusing phase was due to watching *The Sound of Music* on a loop. We knew all the songs and would pretend we were nuns, gliding around the nave clasping Bibles to our chests singing 'Ave Maria'.

It was so wonderful living in our fantasy world, cocooned in the knowledge that Jesus was our friend and people like Edmund never lied or did bad things and then, poof, just like that it all changed and once again, like with Mum and Dad, it all went wrong.

CHAPTER EIGHT

IMAGINE IT LIKE A PERFECT SHITSTORM OF THE MIND. I'd managed to separate my home-life from the one I'd latched on to with Willow's family, and Babs, who always invited me to family dos or for a glass of pop and a biscuit. All was good in the world and then at seventeen, it dawned on me that the path I'd trod, getting good grades in my GCSEs, and predicted Bs in my A levels meant that eventually, I was going to have to move on, move out and go to uni.

Worse, Willow had applied to Cambridge and no way was I going there. It was out of my price and brain range and anyway, my choice of career wasn't on their curriculum.

Freedom came at a cost, but I was prepared to go into debt and get a student loan, knowing I'd have to work to feed and clothe myself, seeing as I'd get no help from my parents. But the thought that me and Willow would be parted, that my safety net would be gone, was the most terrifying thing, ever.

I had two options. Be brave and strike out alone or forget university, stay put and get a job. I chose uni and it was hard, because while Willow had backup, I was a one-woman-team.

And then, when I was teetering on the edge of the rug, grasping on to the notion that Little Buddington, the vicarage and my faith would always be something solid that I could cling on to, Edmund yanked it from under me.

It was a dismal, rainy Saturday evening one week before I went to uni. Robin had gone to visit a parishioner in hospital and Willow and me were watching *Charmed* in the lounge. During the ads, she nipped upstairs to the loo just as the vicarage phone began to ring.

It was the bishop, that's how he introduced himself and you'd have thought I was speaking to the almighty himself the way my heart raced. He needed to speak to Edmund as a matter of urgency so I, always wanting to help, said I'd nip down to the church and see if he was there. Willow was on her way back downstairs and when I relayed the conversation she rolled her eyes and said she'd get us some snacks while I delivered the message. Off I went.

I've never been scared of the church grounds in the dark. The pathway was illuminated by the streetlamp on the corner, enough so I could see my way. I knew the main doors would be locked so I went around the back. It's a bit eerie in the graveyard but the dead can't hurt me, and it was too early for the cider-drinking teens to play chicken amongst the headstones.

I reached the small door that led into a hallway of the vestry where I expected Edmund to be, but it was locked. Thinking that he wasn't there I turned to go, just as on the other side I heard voices approaching. I recognised them both immediately.

'When can I see you again... I hate waiting so long. And from that performance I can tell you miss me too, my little tiger. Let's do it one more time. Come on. I'll be lonely at home, all by myself.' I cringed at my mum's pathetic wheedling as I listened, sick to my stomach but unable to tear myself away.

'Debbie, you know I'd love for you to stay but I have to get on... and you've been very naughty coming here. Next time we'll meet on the lane like before.' Edmund sounded weird, softer, huskier, like some crap actor and had I not been so horrified, I'd have laughed.

'Come on, Eddie, you can't resist this.' Silence then a giggle. 'See, you naughty boy, I knew you needed more.' A few moments of Mum giggling and then it sounded like they both thudded against the door. I dreaded to think what was happening on the other side, but it seemed Eddie had managed to control the tiger in his tank and my mum, so when I heard the key rattle in the lock I turned and ran.

I'll never forget how I felt that night. Tormented by the sins that Eddie had committed – that's how I always thought of him after that. Common, normal bloke Eddie who was once a beacon of... virtue, I suppose.

In my mind he'd fallen from grace and the pulpit, smashing his pious, smug face on the floor of the nave and when he got back up, he was unrecognisable. Disfigured body and soul, a hypocrite, an adulterer. I didn't care about my mum because she was a lost cause and I'd morally washed my hands of her long before, but him... How could he?

And worse, he made me commit a sin, too. Because I lied to my best friend when I said I couldn't find her dad. And to dear kind Robin when she asked me if I wasn't well when I couldn't eat the Chinese food she'd brought home. No matter how much I knew it was wrong, all of it, I couldn't tell them what I'd heard because it would ruin their lives.

I so wanted to get out of that house but where would I go? Home to dirty Deborah Watson, local bike, and vicar shagger. Instead, I stayed. Averting my eyes when Eddie came home, and as he nipped upstairs for a quick shower. Urgh, it made my skin crawl the thought of what they'd been doing and poor oblivious Robin having to stuff his undies in the washer.

I was so confused, shocked. Disappointed, too. It took me days to process it and as much as I'd been nervous about going to uni, I suddenly couldn't wait to go. In temper, I'd vowed never to step foot in church again because one of God's own was a baddie. I took my rage out on him and his one and only son even though it wasn't their fault Eddie was a sicko. But I was torn and confused and that's not a good place for me to be.

Looking back, I think being let down like that must have all been too much, so I bottled it up inside.

Moving away, into halls, enrolling, meeting new people, plus a bout of homesickness that I knew was for my village and a few people in it, certainly not my mum, didn't help. Nor did the worries about how much textbooks cost, food, bus fares, joining in. I went through the motions in a trance at first, then threw myself into the course which I began to enjoy. I settled in, made friends, got on with it and then a few months later, boom.

As I walked to my first lecture of the day, it hit me. I was happy. I smiled and laughed. Life was good and no sooner had I thought it, this slimy horrible hand slid around my heart and reminded me not to get too comfortable because at any moment, it could all go wrong. I crumbled right there on the pavement, swallowed whole by a panic attack, unable to breathe, walk or talk until I was rescued by one of my friends.

It happened frequently after that and I knew I had to take control of my life, find some order, and not allow a descent into chaos. That would waste everything I'd achieved; throw away all those crumpets and potato cakes; and disrespect the kindness and love that helped me to get to that point.

I also realised I'd let Edmund rock my faith because, just like one of my favourite childhood stories, one bad apple had spoiled the lot.

I was so angry, with him and myself. So, I went back to church, my place of comfort, allowed myself to believe, in my mate Jesus and the lady reverend at the university chapel, that they would be my rod and staff, and see me through.

It may have been a coincidence, or part of my quest for mental stability but being a very skint student who was terrified of living her post grad life in massive debt, led to another form of control. Food. Or should I say the lack of it.

I truthfully can't remember when it started, perhaps somewhere deep in my subconscious were strains of nasty Bella making fun of my weight when my two-teas habit began to take its toll; or maybe I caught a glimpse of myself and did not like what I saw.

So, I binned the bus and walked everywhere, and existed on a four pack of apples a day, or a couple of bananas, a tin of soup – the cheaper the better – and whatever was on the reduced shelf at Spar. Losing weight, saving money, being in control. It was my thing, my challenge. Best of all, my hero had fasted for forty days and forty nights so he couldn't chastise me. My mate Jesus was no hypocrite. The thing was, I took it to the extreme.

And that's how it's always been. It's like I have the power to be kind to myself or be ruthless when I feel I don't deserve it. I apply the pressure or take my foot off the brake in my own haphazard, quite frankly self-destructive way. But I've never succumbed in a way that put me in danger, not like so many poor souls do. I have peaks and troughs.

I'm happy when all is well in my world, but the minute life throws me a curved ball, if I'm stressed, or my equilibrium is threatened in any way I panic and convince myself it's all going to go wrong. I have to take control the only way I know. When I got my first job. Met Jimmy. When he proposed. Planning the wedding.

The only time I didn't succumb is when I had the kids

because that was a good time and I put them before me, and I always will. My family is my life.

Anyway, back to Robin and Eddie. When there were homecomings, I'd endure my mum, and spend time at the vicarage playing let's pretend because I felt I owed Willow and Robin that. And then there was the trouble with Cris, and once again I saw the face of the devil reflected in Edmund's and the urge to set Robin free was immense.

All I had to do was speak up, let that cat out of the bag. I was too scared, in case it was the wrong thing to do, and I made it all worse. Instead, I used my hate for Eddie as another form of stubborn control and clung on so hard to my secret about him, about me. I also clung to my faith because I refused to let him take that from me again, ever.

I kept quiet and Willow was allowed to love her dad like she'd always done but my heart hurt for Robin because she was stuck in a sham marriage. I could see that then and I still can now – more than ever since Willow's tragedy.

And now, just when I thought life couldn't get any better, this awful virus is sweeping across the world. But it's not that I really fear. It's the thought of losing Jimmy. A face from the past has come back to haunt me and now it's like that perfect mind-fuck shitstorm is hovering offshore and when it hits, it'll swallow me whole and I can't bear it.

And that's why I've begun to take control and Jimmy has noticed, he always does. That's another reason why I love him so much.

I was his world, he said it in our vows, and he is mine, my everything. It is also why I'm going to embrace being shut in this house. Lockdown has given me double control and will, for a while, enable me to keep him away from her, Bella Young. She's not going to ruin things for me. She will not take my husband.

She will not separate a father from his children and if she thinks she can, she is wrong.

And as God and my mate Jesus are my witnesses, if she tries, I will make her sorry.

CHAPTER NINE

BABS

I AM ABSOLUUUUTELY FUMING! I MEAN THE CHEEK OF IT. And as for Pete, he is well and truly in the doghouse. But what's new? Him siding with our Isaac. I couldn't believe it when I walked in last night and saw the leopard print suitcase at the bottom of the stairs and Fiona sitting at the kitchen table painting her nails.

I knew without even having to ask what was going on, but I did anyway, just for the hell of it.

'Is that your suitcase in the hall?'

She looked up and gave me a nervous smile. 'Yes, but I left it there until you came home because I insisted we check with you first, that it was okay even though Pete said you won't mind.'

I played dim. 'Check what's okay... are you both going on holiday? Because I think you're going to be disappointed. And even if you could jet off, you don't actually need my permission for a jolly, seeing as Isaac's supposed to be an adult even if he doesn't act like one.'

She had the grace to blush at this point and as her eyes searched along the hallway Fiona was saved by a thudding on the stairs that heralded the appearance of daft-and-stupid in the flesh. My man-child, Isaac.

'Ah, Mum, you're back. We wondered where you'd got to. Has Fi told you she's moving in? It's the sensible option, otherwise we won't be able to see each other. It's okay, isn't it? Dad said it would be.' Then a glance at my shopping bag. 'Ooh, pizza. Nice. I'm starving.'

I watched, gobsmacked as he began to unload my bag-for-life and that cheeky mare got up and put the oven on. My oven, in my kitchen. Well, I was furious, and I wasn't going to be walked over like that. I knew it was a done deal and she'd be staying because I really couldn't be arsed with the drama of booting her out. Then again, I wasn't going to take the intrusion lying down.

'Er, excuse me, but why can't you go and stay at Fiona's house?' I refuse to say Fi because it's annoying, like her.

Isaac paused, mid-rip of the plastic that covered the spicy chicken pizza. 'Fi's mum and dad are properly isolating because of their health issues and it's too dangerous, you know, if me and Fi keep coming and going. We could infect them. So it's best we stay here, in this bubble.'

'What health issues?' I turned my attention to Fiona who was getting plates out of my cupboards. 'I didn't know your mum and dad were poorly.'

She didn't miss a beat and delivered her lines deadpan. 'Oh, yes. My dad has angina and Mum has anxiety issues so they both struggle. I'm sure I told you. Anyway, having a houseful will only make them worse so it's best we stay here.'

I looked from one to the other. 'Have you both lost your minds? A houseful! It's not like this is a bloody mansion you know! There's loads more room at yours. You even have a conservatory *and* a downstairs loo.'

At this Isaac had the cheek to laugh and directed his next

quip at Fiona. 'Oh, oh. Here we go, Mum's going to remind us that Dad's never built her a conservatory.'

I ignored Isaac, not wanting to remove the head of my eldest child in front of a witness and before tea, so focused on Fiona. 'And I'm sorry, but I don't think "anxiety" and "angina" are up there on the danger list for people who should totally isolate.'

'I know, but it's already affecting them both, the stress of what's on telly. Dad's been having chest pain and Mum's staying in bed because she's scared...'

Her voice trailed off to a whisper and I noticed the lip wobble. That was all I needed. Crocodile tears. Placing the plates on the table, she let out a big sigh. At this point I had to force my eyes to not roll into the back of my head as I listened to Fiona fake it. Her voice was wobbly, and so, so sad.

'Your mum's right, Zac. It's too much of a squash here and I can tell she's not keen, so I'll get my case and go... I don't want to be in the way.'

It really annoys me that she calls him Zac. His name is Isaac. Regardless of my very sensible point, daft-and-stupid took Fiona's bait. 'Mum, tell Fi she's welcome. Fi, Mum *does* want you to stay, don't you, Mum?'

He looked at me like he did when he conned me into lending him the deposit money for that stupid boy-racer car that takes up half the drive. And you know what? I just couldn't be bothered. Arguing, pandering, standing up on my aching legs for one second longer, so I gave in. Owt for a quiet bloody life. And I also had an idea.

'Of course, she can stay... I'm only teasing, but you'll need to sort out some kind of rota for the bathroom.' I turned to Fiona. 'And you'll have to do your bit with the housework, too. In fact, from now on, you can be responsible for Isaac's laundry. It'll give me a break and good practice for whenever you both finally -bugger off and get a place of your own.' I added a cheeky wink and a smile, the same one that Pete does when he thinks he's being funny, when he's really not.

You can get away with anything if you make out you're being jovial, and Fiona fell for it. 'What are you like, Babs. You do make me chuckle and of course, I'll do my bit. You won't know I'm here.' Fiona had perked up and the tears had miraculously dried, so while I was on a roll...

'Tell you what. Let's start as we mean to go on. You can do the tea, Fiona, and you'll need to put some oven chips in as there won't be enough pizza. And will you do me a nice side salad while I go for a quick shower.' I'd already decided that Pete was not getting eggs and chips. He could suffer and eat the same as everyone else or lump it.

And my final demand, 'Oh, Isaac, be a love and bring that washing in, will you.' And with that, I left them to it and headed upstairs, the word touché accompanying a very satisfied smile.

That was yesterday. Today is the first day of my new way of life. The one I came up with while I ate the biggest slice of spicy chicken pizza, and then watched everyone else grimace through the spinach and ricotta, then argue about washing the pots. I'm still ignoring Pete.

Now don't get me wrong, I'm totally crapping myself over this virus and I hate watching the news because of the horror stories on there. Then again, this is the first time in bloody ages I've not been up at stupid o'clock to make packed lunches and drop Demi at school before I go to work. Sunday is my only real day off and now I have six more.

To add further to my silent enjoyment, if that's the best word for this strange phase in our lives, the rent money from Fiona will compensate a bit for my loss of earnings. You see, there is an upside to being married to a tight arse, and that's the fact that Pete has told Isaac that his live-in-lover has to pay her way. I heard this thirdhand from our Sasha who isn't best pleased about our new housemate, I can tell you.

I know I'm going to get earache from Pete, about me not bringing in a wage. It's not like I make a fortune because Pete always preferred me to work part-time, so I was here for the kids when they were little. And he likes his tea on the table at 6pm and the house to run nice and smooth. What I bring in pays for the extras, like our family holidays, Christmas and birthdays, stuff like that. Not a dishwasher though!

I've been thinking a lot, over the past few days and this morning as I had a big lie-in and listened to the kerfuffle for the bathroom, about life, my life really.

Let's face it, you can't help but take stock when you see what's going on all over the world. Maybe on some deeper level – and yes, despite what my lot say I *can* think beyond Finch Towers and the goings on in *Emmerdale* but I realise I've been unsettled for a while.

I haven't had time to analyse it, so I pushed it to the back of my mind rather than face facts. However, last night during another bout of menopausal insomnia and a hot flush, I allowed my thoughts out of their cage, to roam free. Talking of cages, as Pete snored away, I was reminded of the petting section at Appleton Garden Centre and that smothering someone in their sleep is a crime. I was sorely tempted though.

Now, where was I? Oh yes. First, I need to stop blaming everything on the menopause and accept that I'm unhappy; but that actually makes me feel sad. Are they the same thing? I'm not really sure but it's the only way I can describe it.

I've realised I'm not happy with my life that consists of a decent if annoying husband, and three kids who are basically good, but can also be very bloody annoying in their own way. And that I'm not sure if I love my husband anymore, although I am sure, if not positive, that I love my kids.

And this has kind of rocked my world.

Then another shockwave hit.

Is it possible you can be too good at being a mum?

Because I am good at it; those kids are my whole life and I threw myself into being the best mother, albeit in limited circumstances.

What I couldn't provide them in a material way, I made up for in love and attention, always being here. In some ways my kids wanted for nothing, not where being cared for and nurtured is concerned. In fact, I overdosed them emotionally and now I realise I might not have done them a favour. And...

Have I made a rod for my own back?

Am I the reason why Isaac hasn't the merest inclination to move out – I mean why would he? And I know he's stalling, using saving up for a mortgage deposit as an excuse. Renting is dead money you see, but seriously, he's a grown man!

Okay, so I was never forced into having three kids. Or being a nursery nurse. It was easy and paid enough for a nineteen-year-old to have fun. I loved the little ones and my colleagues. But I was coasting, until my best friend Lynda burst into work one chilly February morning with the most exciting news, *ever*.

Her last name was Checkley, so we called her Cheeky Checkers because she was such a laugh and always up for a bit of mischief. I was Bubbles, Bubbly Babs. I know – kill me now!

I didn't mind the name back then, it was between us girls, until last year, at Pete's Christmas do he introduced me as his other half, the one and only 'cuddly bubbly Babs'. I excused myself and cried in the toilet, hating myself and my stupid party frock that was three sizes bigger than my size ten wedding dress. So, if anyone dares call me bubbly again, I swear I'll punch them. Anyway, I'm wandering. I do that a lot.

So, Lynda's aunty had opened a bar in Costa Blanca and offered Lynda a job for the summer season and, this was the best bit, she could bring a friend. Imagine. March through to September. Free lodgings. Getting paid to serve beer and cocktails in the sun. Then spend our days off on the beach. And the best bit – there would be hot, sexy men *everywhere*.

How could I resist the chance of a lifetime? Swap changing nappies for sun, sea and sangria. That lunchtime we raced to the travel agent on the high street to check out flights and grab some glossy brochures so we could gaze at Playa Flamenca. The name alone made us giddy never mind the photos of miles and miles of beaches and the bluest skies you've ever seen.

There was only one problem, my boyfriend, Pete.

CHAPTER TEN

ME AND PETE HAD BEEN GOING OUT FOR FIVE AND A HALF months and I did like him. I liked having a boyfriend and saying, 'Pete's going to pick me up in the van after work,' or 'I'm going to Pete's for tea.' I liked to fit in.

So, after kidding myself that honesty was the best policy and that he'd find someone new once I was gone, I plucked up the courage to end things, nice and gently, then leg it to Manchester Airport with Lynda – until I realised I'd missed my period and you don't have to be a rocket scientist to guess what happened next.

I wasn't in love with Pete, I kind of grew to love him but what choice did I have? I mean easy choices, not one that would mean a visit to a clinic or being a single mum. Either way I wasn't that brave so, as my parents reminded me, I'd made my bed and I lay in it.

I bloody hate that stupid saying and Christ, those two wore it out!

I cried so much when Lynda said goodbye because I was losing my best friend and my dream. She never came back, not to live here permanently. She married a Spanish guy, and they live in a lovely villa that looks out across the Med. I'm pleased for her, I really am. She used to invite me – us – to stay but family life always had a way of scuppering that and now we're just Facebook friends.

At least we reconnected once the internet revolution arrived, and that's nice, and sometimes it's not. It's a constant reminder of what I missed. It's not Lynda's fault I messed up and I was chuffed she still wanted to be friends with someone as boring as me.

Thinking about Lynda makes me wonder about our summer holidays this year and what I say next will sound so bad and ungrateful, but I won't care if we don't go. Honestly. I'll be over the bloody moon.

I used to love our summer holidays when the kids were little. We'd go to a static caravan in Whitby and have the best time on the beach, or walking along the prom at Scarborough. In the evening we'd get dressed up and go to the club and watch the acts. Just the four of us at the time.

Demi was our surprise baby. And although having a newborn as your eldest comes of age and your middle one hits puberty isn't ideal, we muddled through and embraced being a unit of five.

We still went to a caravan, but money was getting better, so we ventured south to Cornwall, or Devon. I loved it there so much, like another world it is. Everything changed around the time Demi was eight. Pete got promoted and met Calvin his new counterpart.

Calvin is a flash knobhead. Penelope is his flashier wife, Penny to her friends like me. Although she's not really my friend, it's just a tag that I wear to keep the peace. A friend is someone you can confide in, who gets you, makes you laugh and feel at ease. Penny does none of these things and neither does Sheryl and her husband Barry, another member of the bin crew.

Unfortunately they've become our circle of friends, who Pete thinks are the bees' knees and that's why for the past few years they have been our social and holiday companions.

Calvin is head honcho, and he basically picks the location for our holidays. He books it all, days out, hire cars, the bloody lot. Sheryl and Penny spend the spring months preparing – and by this I mean buying new outfits, getting bits plucked, fake tanned, false nailed and in Penny's case a syringe or two of Botox.

I can't compete with them, and nor do I want to. The whole fortnight exhausts me. Yes, I sound so ungrateful because a lot of people would love to go all-inclusive to Tenerife, or any of the other destinations I've endured. But all I can think about is the hours and hours I worked all year, the big fat chubby envelope of hard-earned cash that paid for it. And I wouldn't mind if I got a choice, but I don't.

Sasha does her own thing now, like Isaac, but I still have my Demi who loves it because she has ready-made friends in Sheryl's two daughters. Pete loves it because he gets to hang with his workmates 24/7 and even though he drives me mad, I remind myself he works hard, too, and deserves a holiday. Who am I to ruin all that?

So I fake interest in Penny's strappy maxi-frocks from Primark, and her tacky accessories, although I could do without seeing how smooth her Brazilian is. She's very gregarious, is Penny, and uninhibited especially when drunk. Life and soul of the party she is, they all say it, like it's a badge of honour to be carried home on a deckchair by Barry and Calvin cos you're too pissed to walk.

I did ask Pete once, if we might go away, just the three of us. It was last year, as the spectre of holiday number six loomed. His response stung. The hurt lingers still.

We'd been to a curry night, to celebrate Barry's birthday,

and the subject of holidays had come up. My heart had plummeted, and I refused to join in the discussion and decided there and then that I wasn't going.

Later, as I drove us home, I took a deep breath and broached the subject. I had Pete to myself, strapped into his seat so he couldn't wander off mid-conversation like he always does when he's put on the spot.

'Pete, hear me out on this before you say no. It's just an idea but it's been on my mind for ages.' When he remained silent I took it as a sign to continue. 'The thing is, I really fancy a change so next year I'd like to go away on our own, with Demi of course, but have a break from the others. We see them all year round and I'm tired of doing the same thing every summer.'

Usually his eyes are glued to the road ahead, a terrible passenger even when he'd had a few but that night he swivelled to face me, his voice incredulous. 'What? I don't get it. Why do we need a break from our friends? What's wrong with them? They're a good laugh, we're a gang, and we've had some brilliant holidays together. And you know what they say, if it's not broken...'

I interrupted, snappy and annoyed. 'Yes, Pete, I know the saying and it's crap. And you might enjoy seeing Calvin and Barry day in, day out, but I think it's time we pulled away and did our own thing. It won't kill you or them. And I'd like to choose where we went, something a bit different. Not all-inclusive or non-stop entertainment. We could go to Lynda's villa. She's always asking and has a separate annexe we can stay in. I'd love that.'

'But it's Calvin's fiftieth. Turning fifty is a big thing.'

'What, like my fabulous fiftieth? When we had a family meal at a Brewers Fayre! Not a big bash. Why? Because you couldn't be arsed to organise anything, and I was *not* going to throw myself a do. So, tell me, why is Calvin's big birthday more special than mine?'

I was livid, all the hurt I'd buried deep, the sense of embarrassment, because that's what it was. After all the parties I'd thrown for him and the kids, nobody could be bothered to do one for me. Well, it had festered like a big yellow pus-filled boil, and I'd just given it a good squeeze and splattered it over the windscreen. It was either pus or Pete's blood.

'You're not even a party person,' he blustered, 'and you never said you wanted a do, so that's not my fault. I wanted a weekend golf trip with the lads for my fiftieth and that's what I got because I spoke up. So if you'd wanted something special then you should have said, so don't go blaming me. I'm not a sodding mind reader, Babs.'

I gripped the wheel. 'Yes, you always get what you want, don't you, Pete. So now it's my turn and even though I can't think of anyone more annoying to go on holiday with, I want to go with you, and Demi. Not with that lot. OKAY!'

And then it came, the thoughtless comment, a damning indictment that said more about our marriage than the fact I'd had the audacity to suggest breaking free.

'Have you gone mad? It would be boring, just the two of us. I mean, what would we do? And our Demi wouldn't have any friends of her own, so she'd be stuck with us all day. Nah, no way.

'And I'm not going to see Lynda, either. She's your friend not mine. I like all-inclusive and being entertained, it's what I look forward to all year. Anyway, they'd take the huff if we even suggested it. It's like a snub.' After his big speech he folded his arms and stared ahead. His body language telling me loud and clear the decision was made.

Everything he'd said was like a slap, one of those that make a cracking sound, and sting but I swallowed down the tears and squeezed the steering wheel because if I'd let go, I reckon I'd have smacked him in the gob.

I couldn't speak at first. Even though I hadn't expected him to be quite so honest and whether it was the beer that had loosened his lips, they'd spoken the truth and told me exactly who he'd rather spend a fortnight with. When I finally gathered my emotions, my voice was calm, my thoughts collected.

'So, what you're saying is that you'd rather ignore the wishes of your wife, than offend that lot. You're happy to put your idea of a perfect holiday before mine, not even prepared to compromise.'

I could hear the anger in my voice, and it was one of those situations where that rage could easily turn to tears and hysteria, so I forced both back and waited. When Pete spoke, I wasn't prepared for the sarcasm, let alone his words.

'Oh, stop being a drama queen! I'm sick of your mood swings and the snappy way you talk to me and the kids. It's like living with Jekyll and Hyde. It's like tonight, you were in a mood, and everyone could tell. You need to sort yourself out...'

I'd heard this little speech so many times before, telling me I needed to go to the doctors and get some pills, and seeing as I'd pulled onto the drive I didn't even bother to listen to the rest. I got out, slammed the door, and went inside leaving him to turn off the engine and lock up. Then I slept on the settee. For a week.

And you know what it was, it was the memories of our family holidays that did it, when we scrimped enough to go away and bundled into an old banger loaded to the roof, with more on top.

Yes, at the beginning it was a rough and ready holiday then slowly, we were able to afford a bit more and once Pete was promoted and I started my little cleaning business, we took our first holiday abroad. I'll never forget how excited we all were, going to the airport in a minibus, and then on a plane and even Isaac came along. It was a lovely time.

I'll also never forget, how, that night in the car, Pete didn't give me a chance, to tell him what my idea of a holiday would be, to listen to my imaginings. Because it wasn't just for me that I wanted us to break free of 'the gang'. It was for us.

I thought maybe, if we had some time together, took a walk hand-in-hand along a beach at sunset, hired a jeep and drove to the mountains to watch the sunrise. Or sat opposite each other at a small round table in a little Greek taverna, looking over the ocean, we'd reconnect.

It didn't have to be abroad either. I'd have been happy with a beach hut in Skegness as long as we talked, laughed, remembered. Found our way back to a point in our marriage where even if it wasn't perfect, we had enough in the tank, some shared dreams, and interests to see us through to the end, the last leg of our lives together.

But he didn't and while I have somehow managed to smother the many disappointments and regrets along the way, when I think of that conversation, the anger reignites.

And it's not the menopause, because everybody blames bloody everything on that.

It's us.

We don't fit anymore. I don't fit. Into this life I'm leading, even my sodding clothes, and – this is the worst bit – what hurts the most, is that sometimes I don't feel like I fit into our family, either. It's like I'm on the edge, looking in, surplus to requirements but still required to perform motherly tasks, even wifely tasks every now and then, and that's not right. Thinking these thoughts isn't right either and I hate myself even more because of it.

So, I've decided, during the long and lonely hours since 4.27am, that I'm going to use being in lockdown wisely, while I have time to breathe, think, and take some time for me. First priority is staying alive. Keeping my family safe but after that, I need to formulate some kind of plan. If I don't, I fear the chemical reaction that's going on inside my body, plus being married to an insensitive knobhead, and this very unnerving sense of time running out, will do for me.

And I'm not done yet. Bubbly Babs Finch is down, but she's certainly not out.

CHAPTER ELEVEN

ROBIN

Do you know what it feels like to be trapped? Not down a hole, or backed into a corner down a dark alley, squished against passengers on the Tube or stuck in a lift between floors. I mean by upbringing, loyalty, love, and faith.

I'm held prisoner by all of these. Well I was until something had to give and in order to stay sane, I've abandoned the one thing that was as natural to me as breathing. Turned my back on God, my beliefs, and everything I held dear because the crippling rage that exists deep inside me had to be exorcised. The hate and revulsion I have for my husband, the Very Reverend Edmund Hilyard.

I cannot bear to look at him, or hear his voice, his preaching, the sound he makes when he eats, so I took revenge the only way I could. I withdrew from his life, our marriage and I suppose one could say my job, one that I truly loved in spite of my wobbly start.

It was the role I felt destined for, seeing as at the time there was no route into the priesthood for women, not in our Church of England, anyway. That didn't happen until 1994 and by then I was invested in my marriage and motherhood. Instead of following my vocation, I followed in my darling mother's footsteps and became the vicar's wife.

I was so good at it. Gave it all I had. Wiped the slate clean and put my desires and regrets, all that fanciful stuff to bed. Got on with looking after our beautiful baby girl, making a home, answering the phone, organising *his* diary and church events. Teaching at Sunday school – was my absolute favourite, best day of the week especially when Willow and Gina joined the group. Oh, how those two made me laugh. Jesus's very own dedicated disciples, my little helpers.

Being the best vicar's wife ever helped me through the days; years, I suppose. It diverted my attention and back then I told myself it wasn't Edmund's fault, or God's, that I had succumbed to temptation. It was my weakness and if I focused on priorities, repeated my wedding vows like a mantra, I'd be forgiven. I'd be okay.

And it worked. For half of my married life, I convinced myself I was happy, that I'd made the right choice and then, when I was least expecting it, he came back. Not God, or Jesus, in case you're wondering if I'd had visitation from the almighty.

Arty came back.

I'm sorry, I haven't explained it all properly, have I?

I was an only child and totally enamoured by our happy, loving family way of life. My father's parish was in a semi-rural Gloucestershire town and, as I had no desire to go to university, once I'd finished my A levels my father arranged an administrative job at the diocese headquarters in Tewkesbury. Around a year later, I met Edmund at a garden party hosted by our bishop.

I was instantly taken with this newly anointed, earnest man who'd followed his calling and taken his first appointment in a rougher area of the city. He was only five years older than me, yet seemed so worldly wise, well-educated, tall, and handsome in a rather James Stewart, 1950s gentlemanly way.

On his part it was a slow burn relationship, whereas I was like a giddy colt who couldn't wait to get out of the stable and into the grown-up world of dating and all the bits and bobs that went with it. Yes, that's what me and my best friend Francesca used to call sex. We were so cloistered within our social circle, and we existed in a make-believe world, happy but so out of touch with reality.

Even now I feel such love for those two naïve girls who looked at life from the perspective of Sandra Dee, thoroughly lousy with virginity. But I'll come back to that in a minute, the rules and regulations around the bits and bobs and marriage. First I need to explain about Arty.

He was three years younger than Edmund, a teacher who worked abroad at a private school in Abu Dhabi. He came over for a holiday around the time Edmund and I started courting. Yes, that's what we called it!

Now, what can I say about Arty, short for Arthur? He was loud, confident, politically opinionated erring on the liberal, irreverent with regards to authority of any kind and, to my abject horror, an atheist. So basically, he was the polar opposite of Edmund, who, rather than be irritated by his younger brother, took Arty in his stride – the recalcitrant sibling he simply tolerated.

I couldn't understand how they could be so diametrically opposed and yes, I was offended by Arty's views and comments, his glib attitude to Edmund *and* my father's vocation. I also felt that while he didn't come right out and say it, he thought I was a bit of a stuck-up prig. Which was why I was glad when he buggered off back to Abu Dhabi and then took another post in Japan.

After that, communication between the brothers was via

letter, and I was glad, especially because he was on the other side of the world.

We didn't see him for two years but when Edmund finally proposed, and a date was set, Arty came home for the wedding. I suppose I was too wrapped up in the arrangements to be irritated by his imminent return, and my mother and Francesca kept me occupied on the run-up to the big day. So much so that when Edmund rang to say that Arty had flown in a couple of weeks earlier than expected, I was totally blindsided.

Being polite, I asked Edmund to bring him for Sunday lunch at the vicarage. I'd resolved to keep the peace and say an extra prayer at morning service, asking that Arty buggered right back off again, once the wedding was over.

I feel it's important to point out that whilst it was the eighties, not the Edwardian era, because of our faith and especially Edmund's job, sex outside marriage was strictly forbidden. And for a red-blooded young woman in her very early twenties, it was the first time that my beliefs were sorely tested. Unfortunately my fiancé was made of sterner stuff. However, it would only have taken a nod and a wink from Edmund, and I would've happily disobeyed the Lord, raced to my bedroom, and got down to some bits and bobbing. Sadly, it was not to be.

Edmund and I only ever held hands and shared kisses, and I admit to exaggerating our very chaste moments. In whispers, as we sat in our regular corner pew at church, I told Francesca the most ridiculous tales of fumblings in the back of his Vauxhall Astra and red-hot moments of passion in the parlour while my parents were at prayer meetings.

Privately, I built our wedding night up in my head to equal every single Mills & Boon and Rosamunde Pilcher I'd ever read. I was bubbling with nerves and excitement about finally knowing what all the fuss was about. Because Edmund was reserved in the passion department, I told myself he'd been saving it all up for me. As soon as the bedroom door closed and he saw me in my Janet Reger lace slip that I'd bought from Debenhams, blushing as I handed it to the assistant, he would explode.

I was on the verge myself when I clapped eyes on Arty again, at my parents' house, on the veranda that Sunday afternoon. He took my hand, an action I thought rather unnecessary yet sweet, and looked me in the eye. He said he was *so* pleased to see me again and gave me a smile that would melt ice. In that very odd moment, something changed, in me.

Over lunch I was astounded by the difference in a man who'd previously irritated me to the point of tears. Gone was the bluster, the quips and one-liners, the tendency to take over the conversation with banal or self-absorbed points of view.

And then the looks, not furtive. They were aimed, as if trying to tell me something. He listened attentively when I spoke, causing me to clam up, not wishing to attract his attention and fall under the gaze of those pale blue eyes. As I tried to swallow my food and concentrate on whatever the others were saying I told myself not to look at him, then dared myself to disobey. Each time I weakened his eyes found mine. They were waiting.

I was in such a flap. Asking myself was it a game, to amuse and pass the time? Then after he'd had his fun, would the real Arty show himself and disappoint me? But he didn't.

It was early evening and while father and Edmund were examining the rose garden and discussing sawflies, mother had asked me to check the veranda for empty sherry glasses. I found Arty sitting alone at the patio table, deep in thought. He looked up, smiled. He didn't say a word at first and held me in his gaze like he was lost in the sight of me and poof, just like that, I found myself lost in him.

Arty recovered himself first. 'Hello, you. I was hoping you'd come outside so we could chat. I couldn't get a word in over lunch, and I really have been looking forward to seeing you again.' He patted the chair by his side and like a mesmerised child I obeyed and took a seat.

I really couldn't think of one word to say so instead I waited for him to take the lead which he did with confidence, and it struck me that maybe, he'd been rehearsing what to say. At the time it was a hunch, but I soon found out I was right. Arty had been waiting for years to see me again.

'So, marriage. I have to say I wasn't expecting that. When I received Edmund's letter, it was a huge surprise.' He was watching me closely as he spoke and when I somehow found my voice, was surprised at my own response.

'What, that he'd asked, or that I said yes?'

A smile, and then the answer which sounded a bit sad and a bit annoyed all at once.

'Both. I didn't think Ed had it in him, to take the plunge and be prepared to share himself with a real life human when he's always been in love with God, and himself obviously. I'd hoped that you wouldn't fall under his spell, but you have, and it makes me a bit...'

At this point mother popped her head through the French windows and asked if anyone would like tea. Father and Edmund were out of earshot. Arty and I declined but mother was determined to feed and water us all. 'I'll just bring a tray out anyway. Back in a tick.'

When she'd gone I turned to Arty and asked a question. Probably the most astounding of my whole life. And you know something, I think I already knew the answer and wanted him to confirm it, right there and then, tempting fate.

'And exactly how does it make you feel? Me, being under his spell.'

A heartbeat, I saw his chest expand, his eyes narrow a touch and then he answered. 'Disappointed, cross, usurped, out manoeuvred, foolish, ridiculously hurt. Need I go on?'

I swooned, it's really a thing. Something I'd read about but never experienced until then. I struggled to breathe, take in the magnitude of his words, their meaning. It was only the sound of the hostess tray rattling along the hall and my father and Edmund approaching that saved me. Actually, it was Arty, who masterfully steered attention away from me, just for a moment.

He focused on Edmund who was taking a seat opposite me. 'I was saying to Robin that now I'm home, and seeing as it's only for a short time, I really need to get to know my future sister-in-law. Make sure she's suitable for my old fuddy-duddy brother and vice versa.'

'I think that's a splendid idea, don't you, Robin?' Edmund somehow made questions sound like a command.

I nodded. 'Yes, that would be lovely but I'm so busy with the wedding arrangements and work...'

'Well, you must get a lunch hour. What say I pick you up tomorrow? Would that suit?' With an encouraging smile and earnest eyes, Arty waited.

I was struck mute once again and looked to Edmund for a sign that he realised what was going on.

'Dearest, don't look so worried. Arty will be on his best behaviour, won't you?' Edmund gave his brother a look, like he was a five-year-old prone to naughtiness and off to a birthday party.

Arty's response was the epitome of sincere, to begin with. 'Why, of course, brother dear. Robin will be safe with me. You have my word.' Then he turned to me, mischief written all over his face, his eyes dancing with mirth. 'So, what time do they let you out to play? I shall collect you on the dot and treat you to something magnificent. Whatever you fancy, your every wish will be my command.'

I gulped, knowing full well that Arty did not mean an egg and cress sandwich and a cup of tea at the Bob-In Café. Even Sandra Dee wasn't that stupid. And yet while half of my brain was running around in a panic looking for an excuse, the other half wanted to go, so badly.

'I take lunch from twelve thirty. I get an hour, but I only work half-day on Mondays.'

Arty merely nodded. 'Perfect. Then I will whisk you to lunch and afterwards, perhaps we can stroll along the river, or maybe take in a museum. What do you think?'

'I think that would be very nice, thank you.' Nice! I cringed at my trite response as heat flooded my entire body because I didn't want nice. I wanted more.

After an almost imperceivable nod, Arty craned his head in the direction of the vicarage. 'Now, where is that tea we were promised?'

And as if by magic mother appeared with her trusty golden hostess trolley packed with handmade delights. The conversation soon flipped to the weather and our attention focused on cucumber sandwiches and Battenburg. As I passed Arty his cup and saucer his finger connected with mine, ever so slightly and unnecessarily. I left mine where it was, just for a touch, and in doing so, booked myself a room in hell.

CHAPTER TWELVE

It won't surprise you to know that the hours before I stepped out into the midday sunshine, to where Arty was waiting for me, were spent in a state. One that pinged me into the arms of terror, then twang, back into the grip of shame. I was buffeted by waves of sheer romanticism, feeding on lines from books that had been my guidebook to life.

I'd barely slept, averted my eyes from those of my mother over breakfast in fear she might see what lay behind them. At work I spent the morning making errors or lost in a daydream, jumping if anyone called my name, coughed, or slammed a door. I was guilty before the fact, and acting like it, too.

But nothing – nothing at all – would have prevented me from meeting Arty that day. Not the crucifix I wore around my neck; or the photograph of my parents on my desk; not even the one of Edmund tucked out of sight in my purse. Even though I knew it was wrong, I still went.

What was I expecting? An adventure, I think. A dance with the devil. To look temptation in the face and turn away. But not until I'd savoured an afternoon of life on the edge, of not being me. To dare. Nudge the boundaries with my toe.

I was so mixed up, bubbling with hormones and desire, dreamy notions of Grace Kelly wedding days and how wonderful doing bits and bobs would be, with Edmund of course. I had also, in the darkness of my room, allowed myself to imagine doing bits and bobs with Arty.

Oh the shame! So to assuage my guilt I assured myself that lunch with Arty, in public, was safe and I'd be fine. After all it was just a bit of fun. Our chance to bond and start afresh.

He was waiting for me on the pavement on the dot, as promised. When I reached the bottom of the steps he smiled and offered me his arm. 'Shall we?'

I giggled, Lord knows why because it was merely a polite gesture to which I replied, 'Yes, we shall.'

And, God forgive me, we did.

We ate lunch at Arty's hotel, the Tewkesbury Manor. He wasn't staying with Edmund. His aversion to all things Godly also applied to vicarages or so Edmund had quipped. However, it transpired that it was much more than that.

Lunch was, as I expected, a very polite affair where Arty showed me his best side, his wit minus the sarcasm I'd endured in our previous meetings. His enquiring mind focused solely on me. He wanted to know all about my job that was pure tedium to perform, let alone chat about so during our melon boat starters, I turned the attention to him.

'You seem different to the last time we met. In fact I'd say you're not the same person, so why the change? Has the Japanese culture rubbed off on you?'

That was bold, but it felt like playing a part. I was the leading actress in a film who hadn't rehearsed her lines, so I had to wing it. This panicked me because we only had a few hours, and I desperately wanted them not to be fake.

Realising that was almost as startling as Arty's response.

'Well, I'm glad you've noticed I'm on my best behaviour and

I'm trying very hard to be good. Now, would you like my cherry?' Arty held out the glacé orb that wibbled on his spoon. I blushed to match the fruit, reminded of one of Francesca's phrases and desperation to lose her virginity.

'Heavens no, they're terrible things. I was going to ask you if you wanted mine...' Oh dear God, I actually said that? What was I thinking?

When I dared to look from the cherry to his eyes, they were laughing at me but not in an unkind way. Then he saved me by lightening the moment. 'Shall I flick this one at sour puss over in the corner then, see if I get a bullseye. I was a cracking shot at school. Nobody in the refectory was safe from my aim.'

I relaxed, glancing at the portly man who slurped his Windsor Brown soup, then smiled at the image of a young Arty, dressed in his grey boarding school uniform, flicking bits of his dinner at unsuspecting teachers and prefects. Apparently Arty had been a challenge both to his parents and his very expensive school alike, but everyone agreed, apart from his masters, that it was worth every single penny.

'Well, normally I'd encourage you but I'm starving and don't want to be turfed out before I've had my Dover sole, or my Queen of Puds, so behave! And you still haven't answered my question. Who stole the real Arty?'

Lowering his spoon he sighed. 'Well I hate to disappoint you, but he's still right here, however, since we last met I realised the error of my ways and spent the last two years regretting being a complete arse. Which is why I resolved to show you a better side to me, this time.'

'Well, I'm flattered that you're going to so much effort on my behalf and rather taken aback, that I was on your mind because I genuinely thought you didn't like me enough to care.' Inwardly I was flattered and also astounded by my own honesty and the fact I was fishing, not necessarily for a compliment, more the truth.

When Arty rested back against his chair, his spoon clanging against the plate, his response was laced with exasperation. 'Robin, why on earth would I not like you? That notion is so far from the truth, and why I'm here today, to show you that's not the case and...'

The waiter had returned to remove our plates and once he'd scooted off, silence descended so I filled it with words, ones that would alleviate the tension.

'So, now we've sorted all that out, why don't you tell me about Japan, and your job and the children. I've never met anyone who's been there, and it sounds like such a fascinating place.'

Arty leant forward and rested his clasped hands on the table, regarded me for a second or two and then indulged me in my request, and for the next hour I learned all about his life on the other side of the world, and about a man who I'd misjudged quite badly, and one I wanted to know so much more.

The riverbank was mostly deserted as we strolled along in the afternoon sun, walking off our lunch, pointing out birdlife nestled in the bank opposite or peering into the nets of the occasional fisherman we passed by. It was a glorious day in late June, the sky clear, the occasional cloud too small to obscure the sun even for a second. Thankfully, children were still in school otherwise the shallows would have been full of paddlers, their parents keeping a watchful eye from the grassed borders.

Arty had taken off his suit jacket and slung it over his shoulder and I noticed his tanned forearms glistened with fine, golden hairs. Every now and then he came too close, and I skilfully avoided a clash of limbs, not wanting to feel his skin on mine, acutely aware that it would have been too close and personal.

I was enjoying the peace, though, and being by the side of someone who didn't feel the need to fill the silence. It was comfortable and companionable, and I realised that I hadn't experienced anything like that with Edmund and it bothered me. I didn't even like that it had occurred to me, not days before my wedding when I should have been sure about it all. The future, me, and Edmund.

When we were together, he talked all the time. About work, his sermons, discussions he'd had with his peers, parishioners that were thin on the ground at his church. And when he was in the company of my parents the talk was much the same and up until that moment on the riverbank I'd accepted it as part of who he was. What our life would be like together.

Yes, we'd chatted about other things when I pushed the conversation in a certain direction. About Edmund's private education, his wealthy parents who were pillars of the church, now deceased. His two missions to Asia and Africa, his willingness to go wherever the bishop sent him although he rather hankered after a country parish. Edmund didn't feel suited to the inner city and thought his talents would be served better elsewhere.

Nowadays, I know he's lazy, and that the suburbs were too much of a challenge, the parishioners not his kind. For Edmund, the archetypal all-encompassing snob, God's work didn't involve getting his hands dirty.

In the hour or so I'd spent with Arty, I'd heard all about his life so far and dreams for the future – to travel the world teaching, learning about each country and their cultures, broadening his horizons and those of his pupils. He wanted to holiday in South America, drive a Mustang along Route 66, whale watch in Alaska, rent a cottage on the Isle of Mull and live like a hermit, just for a week or two. One day he would settle in Blighty, find a house by the sea, teach at a local school, write a book, learn to play the guitar.

Edmund wanted to be a vicar, to serve God, rise through the ranks and have a wife and two children. The End.

Had I asked Edmund where he would like to go on holiday each year? Probably not. Did I complain about his choice of honeymoon destination – a walking holiday in the Brecon Beacons, a perfect place for meditation and bird watching? No. That was my fault. It all was. Edmund was my pick, my doing. A crowd pleaser, just like me. What had I done?

Up until that moment, the future had seemed so sure and perfect. So why was there this niggle of doubt? Unhelpfully accompanied by a frisson of something alien every time I looked at Arty or imagined his body beneath his white shirt and what lay behind the zip of his trousers. I was losing my mind right there on the riverbank as temptation beckoned. And I desperately wanted to follow.

I'd been locked in thought while Arty smoked a cigarette, nodding politely to passers-by as we walked in a loop and found ourselves back in the grounds of his hotel. I watched as he flicked the stub into the bin, paused a moment then looked me in the eye, the meaning of his next question not lost on me. In that very second, I grew up. That's when I actually became a woman, making a choice that was just for me.

'So, what would you like to do now? Time's running out and I'll have to return you to Edmund soon.'

I faltered, unsure how to verbalise my deepest desire so I held his gaze and threw the ball back to Arty. 'What do you suggest?'

He looked upwards and for a second, imagined he was asking for divine guidance but no, he was merely looking for the perfect excuse. 'Well, it's a bit of a scorcher so why don't we head to my room. I'll order us a bottle of something cool and fizzy and we can sit on the balcony and chat, or whatever you want. How does that sound?'

Without a beat of hesitation, knowing exactly what I wanted, knowing that I really had lost my mind and not caring one bit, I replied. 'It sounds lovely.'

Then we headed inside, leaving Sandra Dee at the door.

Apart from the weekend when I was tied to home and my mother's constant fussing, we met every day, during my lunch hour, where I almost ran to his hotel room and there, Arty would be waiting.

A five-minute dash through the streets, forty-five minutes of joy, ten minutes to tidy myself up and race back to work. It was bliss. It was torture too, because we both knew it couldn't last or go anywhere and come hell or high water, I would be marrying Edmund. How could I not? How could I break my parents' hearts, shame them, rock their world?

And the strangest thing is neither I nor Arty spoke of it, the looming wedding and what it signified. Nor did we discuss the fact we were betraying Edmund. It was as though we were facing the end of the world and had to grasp every last moment until the planet went boom.

It was the Thursday before the wedding, our last meeting because I had the Friday off to prepare. I was dressing hurriedly, forcing myself not to cry, into my tights, shrugging on my dress, slipping into my shoes. I was ready to go back to work and face the rest of my life without Arty when he broke his silence.

I can see him now, pulling on his trousers and rushing to my side, his hand taking mine, his voice a whisper.

'I'll only ask you once, because I have to, otherwise it will send me insane not knowing.' He paused and I was touched by his nervousness, but not swayed because I already knew the question and answer after imagining it for nine days and nights.

'Will you run away with me? We could go today. Start a new life in Japan. I can make you happy, Robin, if you give me a chance, if you're brave enough to set yourself free.'

I knew he'd ask me. Arty had toed the line in order to show me his good side but that naughty boy, the rebellious teenager, the determined independent adult was always in there waiting to show himself, because that's who he was, and I'd come to love him for it. Which is why I forced out the lines I'd rehearsed, knowing that if I wasn't prepared I would capitulate and do something that I'd never be able to live with.

In that hotel room, standing on the blue Axminister, between four beige walls, beside a bed of crumpled sheets, a battle commenced – faith versus Arty.

The victor was never in any doubt.

CHAPTER THIRTEEN

GINA

Jimmy appeared on the decking with a bottle of wine and two glasses, barefoot and smiling like the cat who'd found the fridge door open and glugged a carton of cream. The evening was still warm, the sky a dusky blue. And for a reason that neither of them could adequately explain to Max before his bath and bed, to the right, Sammy Sun and to the left, Billy Moon hovered in a planetary face-off, both determined to light up the earth.

Gina was going to google it later, because even she was intrigued by the sun-moon phenomena. Her attention soon turned to her husband, and she smiled at the sight of him as she enjoyed another night off from being soaked in bubbles.

'What are you looking so pleased with yourself about?'

Jimmy flopped into the chair opposite. 'Because *I* am a natural at this bedtime malarkey. I've even cleaned the bathroom after the slippery dolphins trashed the place. You'll be most impressed when you see. In fact, you'll think Babs has been in with her Flash and trusty mop.'

At this Gina raised an eyebrow because never, in all the years she'd known him, had Jimmy been able to clean anything properly but, there was a first time for everything, and the last few days had proved it.

Seventy-two hours after they were confined to barracks, Gina was astounded that her gad-about, workaholic husband had slotted into home-life and seemed to be revelling in their new order. Still, she wasn't going to get her hopes up or let her guard down just because Jimmy had turned into a domestic god. He would get bored soon, like he had of her.

She watched as he poured them both a drink and thought it best to stroke his male ego and make the most of a nice moment. 'I'll go and examine your cleaning prowess in a bit, while you serve dinner that, I have to say, smells lovely.'

Jimmy raised his glass. 'Only the finest oven chips for madame and yes, that pie from M&S was lovingly removed from its packet by yours truly and will be served with a generous portion of peas, or beans, whatever your heart desires. I will even rustle up some gravy if you're good.'

'Okay, stop. You're getting a bit weird now. Please can I have normal Jimmy back?' That was a lie because Gina liked this version of him and wished she'd not said it in case it tempted fate. Telling herself it was ridiculous to be superstitious about casual remarks she sipped her wine and realised for the first time in ages she was looking forward to her meal.

'Is Max watching a DVD?'

'Yes, that one about the cute dinosaurs. I said you'd go up and turn it off in an hour.'

'*The Land Before Time*, and telly-off-time is in half an hour as well you know!' Gina raised her eyebrows.

'So, amaze me. Which story did Mimi make you read?'

A loud tut from Jimmy, 'That bloody bear hunt one. I'm *so* sick of it and no matter how many others I showed her she insisted on that. I told her I'm not reading it tomorrow. In fact, you can... it does my head in.'

Jimmy stretched out his legs and tipped his head back, eyes closed against the fading sunlight, and changed the subject. 'Don't you think it's nice, the peace and quiet? The only thing that spoils it is those birds! They're so loud. I wish they had volume control, just to turn them down a notch.'

'Stop complaining. The birdsong is lovely, and you sound like your dad when he moans about people cutting their lawns.'

He smiled because she was right. Gina loved, George, her father-in-law, but Lord, he was a grumpy sod. He drove Alma, his long-suffering wife, mad with his world views, general untidiness, and propensity for losing things and blaming everyone else for pinching his stuff. George didn't mean anything by it, though. It was his way, rough and ready, salt of the earth and would do anything for his family.

Unlike her far-away mother and fickle father who she rarely saw. She didn't miss either and referred to them as Debbie and Don. They were neither use nor ornament and so far she'd managed without them.

Don lived in Liverpool with his wife and their two kids, none of whom Gina had any interest in, simply because they had no interest in her. Debbie had moved to Leicester with a lorry driver she met on Plenty of Fish. She'd done a flit before the bailiffs came, and hot-trained it to Leicester without telling a soul. Not even her daughter.

Consequently, Debbie only met Jimmy after he'd proposed to Gina, and it was impossible to avoid a trip to Leicester any longer. They met at Wetherspoons. Gina wasn't chancing a visit to Debbie's house, knowing what their old home used to look like.

So, it was a case of, 'Jimmy, this is Mum. Mum, this is my fiancé, Jimmy.'

Then awkward handshakes and fake smiles as they met Mike. 'Gina, this is Mike. Mike, get the drinks in, love.'

Chairs were pulled from under the table as Mike did as he was told, then an embarrassing silence was followed by small talk and clock-watching. It was the longest two hours. Long enough to not eat her salad and refuse dessert while Jimmy made a valiant attempt at building bridges.

To be fair Mike was okay, pleasant, seemingly hard-working, a keen gardener and on the cusp of retirement. Gina knew Debbie would stay put, an eye on his pension. In return, Mike would be grateful for a warm body and a regular shag when he got home after a continental run. Harsh but no doubt true.

What her bone-idle mother got up to while he was gone was anyone's gruesome guess, but it certainly didn't entail working. Debbie was still bad with her nerves.

Promises were made to ring, and an invite to the wedding would be in the post, followed by tactful reassurances that costs for the big day would be met by the bride and groom. With a look of relief, Debbie, followed obediently by Mike, made a hasty retreat, as did Gina and Jimmy.

In the past seven and a half years, she'd only seen her parents a handful of times. Don refused to be in the same room as her mum so didn't come to the wedding. Which was why Gina walked herself down the aisle. She hadn't even contemplated asking Debbie because that would have been a bluff too far.

As if reading her mind, Jimmy interrupted the birds and her thoughts. 'Have you still not spoken to your mum?'

'I texted. She's fine. Mike is stuck in Zeebrugge, and she's not best pleased because the sink is leaking. Of course, it went over her head that the poor sod is miles from home and sleeping in his cab in a queue from hell. And before you ask Don is okay too. He's been furloughed. That's all I know.' This and her tone signalled to Jimmy that the conversation was at an end. He was good at reading the signs.

A moment passed then Jimmy piped up. 'I've been thinking.'

'Oh, oh... bright-idea alert.'

Ignoring her sarcasm he continued. 'Now that I'm around in the mornings, well, all day really, why don't you do something for yourself. Now you've got the best hands-on-dad-and-husband in Cheshire at your service.'

Gina was flummoxed. 'Like what exactly?'

'You could start running again. You used to love that, especially in the mornings and evenings and since we've had Mimi, you don't go anymore. I think it would be good for you.' Jimmy's face looked pinched; a sure sign he was worried about how she'd react.

'Why? What do you mean it'd be good for me? Are you trying to say I've put on weight or something?' Gina's heart hammered in her chest while her stomach churned, the swell of nausea rising towards her throat.

It was true, he was going off her and in his own cack-handed way was giving her a hint. So when he leapt forward, kneeling in front of her, taking her hands in his, he caught her off guard, as did his words. 'Gina, *no*! Stop that right now. That's not what I meant at all.' His eyes were wide and full of concern as he released his grip and took her face in the palm of his hands. 'Please, Gina, you have to listen to me and believe what I'm saying because the last thing I want is you getting sick, and you know what I mean by that, *don't you?*'

He waited for her to nod, then pressed on. 'You're beautiful, and you haven't put weight on. In fact it's the opposite and that's why I'm worried. It was your thing, running, so I thought it'd be nice for you to start again, put some colour in those gorgeous cheeks and have some time away from here, that's all.'

Gina nodded, blinking back tears as she tried to compute what Jimmy was saying. Even though she wanted to believe him, she didn't and instead, translated his concern into something else: paranoia and suspicion. 'Why do you want me out of the house? Christ, Jimmy. You've only been home for three days and you're sick of me already... that's a great start, isn't it.' And even though she'd tried to put a humorous slant on it, keeping her voice light, she'd meant every word.

Jimmy sighed, kissed her forehead, and tenderly wiped away her tears with his thumbs. 'Gina, stop... you're reading this all wrong. I swear it's not that, because – believe it or not – I love being here with you and the monsters, but... it's just that if I'm honest, I'm worried about you. You've seemed distant lately, edgy I suppose. And we can't skirt around it, you have lost weight and I think I know why, what's on your mind and we need to talk about it.'

The panic, when it hit, made Gina swoon, because she *did not* want to hear what she thought he was going to say. She didn't want to go over all that again; say *her* name and have it taint the walls of their home and stick to the furniture. She couldn't bear to listen to his lies, denials, be put down in defence of that woman like last time. She'd snap. And all the loathing, for herself and for that fucking bitch Bella Young, would come pouring out. And worse, he might actually admit to it.

Then it would be over; the dream would become a nightmare.

Her lips wouldn't move, her voice was trapped by invisible hands that squeezed her throat. And even though she wanted to run, her legs wouldn't move so she just sat and stared. In doing so, Jimmy took it as an invitation to speak.

'I've worked it out, what's wrong and part of it is my fault, I know. I've handled things badly and should've realised that going back to work isn't easy when you've been at home for a while. It's natural to lose your confidence and you've always suffered with anxiety so no wonder the whole getting a job malarkey is stressing you out, but I thought it's what you wanted.'

Gina was dumbfounded so merely nodded.

'And that's why I've been encouraging you, when nothing would give me more pleasure than knowing you were always here for the kids – and me, of course. Yes, it's a bit 1950s but who cares. This is our life, and we can live it how we want to.'

Jimmy paused and tilted his head slightly to one side, as if to gauge how Gina was feeling and thinking.

'So what I'm trying to say is why not leave it a while, or forever, whatever. Get a full-time job or don't, it's fine by me. And who knows what's round the corner, but right now this bloody virus has put the brakes on a lot of things so please, stop stressing about your CV and poncy recruitment agencies. Stuff them, delete them, and look after you. Take some time off from being Mum and let me help, *okay?*'

Gina could actually feel her lips again, and her chest wasn't about to snap under the pressure of whatever was crushing her lungs and ribcage. A job... he thought she was nervous and worried about getting a job.

Oh, thank God, thank you, God. Thank you, thank you, thank you.

Finally, she got it together and in utter relief, flopped forward and wrapped her arms around Jimmy's shoulders, pulling him as tight as she could with arms that felt like jelly. When she'd totally gained control Gina pulled away from his embrace, kissed him softly on the lips then put him straight with a pack of lies.

'Thank you... you're right. I'm being silly and getting in a bit of a tizzy about it all, you know, finding childcare for the kids, missing them, meeting new people. I've played it safe, writing the online articles but getting back out there and actually designing is a bit daunting so yes, I was overwhelmed. Like you said, I'm not that great with the big, bad outside world at the best of times.'

Jimmy opened his mouth to speak but was interrupted by the voice of Max, calling down the stairs. 'Mummy, are you coming to say night-night? I've turned the telly off but you haven't given me a cuddle yet.'

Hearing his words, Gina laughed. 'See, and this is why I can't bear to be parted from them! How can I resist that?'

She stood, and Jimmy followed suit but didn't let her run to Max until he'd given her another gentle, reassuring kiss. 'Go see to Max then we'll have dinner and some "us" time, okay.'

Gina nodded and pulled away, unable to speak, utterly overcome with emotion and totally bemused. As she headed up the glass staircase and gripped the banister for support, Gina listened to the voice in her head that echoed her thoughts.

Maybe you've got it wrong. Maybe you've misread the signals, misunderstood what Babs saw, misinterpreted the text message. Or you're going totally mad. Or Jimmy is a very, very convincing liar.

As she reached the top of the stairs and swept Max into her arms, Gina could only pray that she was the one to blame. It might be extreme, but losing the plot was far better than the alternative.

CHAPTER FOURTEEN

SHE'D STOPPED BY THE SIDE OF THE ROAD, LEANING against a drystone wall while she took a breather and checked her Apple watch to see how far she'd run. Two minutes off. She'd beaten the previous day's time. This made Gina smile. That and the fact Jimmy had been right. After just one month, running had given her a new lease of life. She was energised.

The endorphin buzz carried her through the day and better still, rather than being annoyed by hunger pains she reminded herself that her body needed fuel to sustain and prepare her for another circuit of the village. Appetite was good, it wasn't the enemy. Not only that, she had her very own personal chef making her meals, very nutritious and balanced ones at that, so found herself counting the calories less.

But best of all, was the feeling she had when she ran. It was like nothing else, and she'd forgotten how much she'd enjoyed the sense of freedom. Just her and the road as her trainers pounded the ground below. Pushing herself harder, loving the trickle of perspiration between her shoulder blades. Swiping her forehead to remove the proof she was burning up every ounce of fat in her body.

Sometimes she listened to music but only when she passed through the village. When she hit the lanes on the outskirts she preferred the sounds of the countryside and also, it was best to be aware and alert because apart from the odd car or the odd cyclist passing by, the route could be quite deserted.

Jimmy made her promise to be sensible and stick to the routes she'd shown him, a deviation each day, in rotation so she'd be safe, just in case. Yes, they lived in a beautiful part of Cheshire, but it didn't mean they could let their guard down. Bad things still happened in the nicest of places and nutters still roamed free, despite lockdown.

It was 6.37am. The air was fast losing its chill and if the forecasters were correct another glorious day was on the cards, so Gina fully intended making the most of her exercise hour before the Morgan family bubble went into action. Jimmy had always been a morning person so was happy to deal with feeding the monsters while she ran. Then once she returned, showered, and dressed, Gina took over and he hunkered down in his office for the morning.

Home-schooling Max was fun, and Mimi floated between joining in with her colouring book then wandering off to play with her toys. Gina was in charge of lunch, and the afternoons depended on Jimmy's workload. If he had stuff to do, she entertained the monsters, and while Mimi had a nap she would work on her column for the online magazine.

If Jimmy was free then they'd all go for a walk along the lane and into the woods, even though technically she was pinching another hour of exercise time, they doubted anyone would notice, or care.

It was something of a miracle, but Gina actually found herself looking forward to each day, and even dinner! And if she tried really, really hard she could completely banish the gut-wrenching thoughts that had plagued her during the months before. While she had Jimmy all to herself, inside their glorious bubble, she could actually make-believe that Bella Young didn't exist.

Gina constantly scrutinised Jimmy's every facial expression and remark, searching for clues. In fact, she was becoming so acutely observant, she could be a body language expert. Like those who paid close attention to police suspects during interviews, or family members at news conferences as they plead for information. So far, there was absolutely nothing to report. Jimmy was just being Jimmy.

He'd not stepped foot out of the house unless it was with her and the kids. He was his usual daft and funny self, and nothing was too much trouble. He didn't appear to be pining for his lover and was most attentive, extremely so when they were in bed which was another surprise. Unless he was making the best of a bad job until he could see Bella again.

Regardless, her heart fluttered when she saw him on the phone, looking serious and in deep conversation or laughing and smiling. Gina behaved like a covert agent, listening at doors, peering through the sheets as she hung them on the line. She could see him through the huge pane of glass that separated his upstairs office from the garden and whenever the opportunity arose she checked his phone for messages and recent calls. While he was in the bath she'd searched his desk, even his pockets and the recycling bin for notes. Nothing.

It was doing Gina's head in because she'd been so sure he was up to something, and the clues added up. Three wrongs made her right.

The lie had come first.

Then the text:

> I've left the key under the pot. Let yourself in and make yourself at home until I get there.

He must have deleted it soon after she saw it and that was a sure sign of guilt.

Then the voice note – *I have to go away, bit of an emergency with the parents, but we can pick up where we left off when I get back, if you still want to. Sorry I missed your call, don't be a stranger.* Delete, delete, delete. She could imagine Jimmy erasing Bella's words and being downcast because his bit on the side had buggered off. It made her sick, actually physically sick.

Maybe Bella had been visiting her parents in Italy and had got stuck there, unable to get a flight back. That's why there'd been no more messages. No point in texting if they couldn't meet up so he was making do with her while his lover was away. Unless he was being extra vigilant, extra sly. What if he had a secret phone, a cheat phone... Wasn't that what they were called? What a mug!

She bent down to re-fasten the laces in her trainers, telling herself to stop driving herself mad and if she wanted to know the truth all she had to do was ask Jimmy or even Bella, and have done with it. She was a coward, though. That's why she hadn't punched Bella's lights out long ago. Then she'd have known never to set foot in her house or even glance in Jimmy's direction.

Instead, she'd let a vicious bitch get away with it all through her childhood and as a result, Bella thought she'd make Gina's life a misery again, by ruining everything she held dear.

It had started at a pre-Christmas party Gina and Jimmy had hosted for family and friends. Gina wanted it to be a sedate kind of gathering, focusing on serving gorgeous food and wine and having a laugh, not a raucous late-night bash where her beautiful home might end up the worse for wear. They'd got the caterers in, with waiters to take care of the guests and – joy of joys – the clearing up afterwards.

They'd both been looking forward to it for weeks. Gina had thrown her all into turning the cottage into something you'd see in the Christmas edition of *Country Life*. She was still proud of the photos she'd taken before everyone arrived, of the decorations, the magnificent tree, the glowing fire, and the sumptuous festive feast.

Even Carmen was there, friend of the family and owner of Appleton Garden Centre where Gina had bought most of the adornments. Gina and Willow had worked there during school holidays and were close friends with Carmen's middle daughter, Violetta. That evening their bohemian buddy was resplendent in a flowing emerald creation that set off her auburn hair, piercings, and notorious fiery temperament.

Max and Mimi were settled in the snug with their cousins watching a DVD, so Gina took the opportunity to spend some time with Violetta. Weaving her arm around her waist, Gina was rewarded with a hug and a huge smile, followed by a clink of glasses.

'I have to say, Mrs Morgan, not only do you throw a fab party; you certainly know how to make four walls look next-level amazing. I thought my mum had the knack, but you've put her to shame... don't tell her I said that though, or I'll be in very deep poo!' Violetta gave Gina a cheeky wink just as the doorbell rang and Jimmy shot into the hall.

The lounge was almost full, everyone seemed to be happy and chatting away so, turning to Violetta, Gina smiled. 'Jimmy's in his element when he's entertaining so I'll just leave him to it. Right, stranger, tell me, how are things going at work, and how's

Leo–' She didn't finish the sentence because of the look on Violetta's face as she stared over Gina's shoulder, her mouth agape. Naturally Gina turned to follow her gaze while Violetta's next words were lost in a haze of a panic and utter disbelief.

'Well, she's got a nerve coming here, the cheeky cow! Who the hell invited her?'

Gina didn't respond immediately, too lost in a cold and clammy body that was rigid with shock, swiftly turning to rage. 'I have no idea, but it certainly wasn't me!'

Violetta moved closer and whispered. 'Bloody Nora, has she been on a sunbed, or does she live abroad? I'm sure someone said she went to Italy. And that hair... she was never blonde at school, was she? I remember her being mousey and I'd bet my next tattoo that those boobs aren't real, or those lips. She looks like a trout.'

Gina was struck mute, watching, hidden in the corner as Jimmy did his 'host with the most' performance and chatted with Bella and Guy, his old friend from university.

For some tragic reason, he'd left his boyfriend at home and in a warped quirk of fate chose to bring the evil bitch from hell as his plus-one. To Gina's home. Into her perfect life. And whether it was just memories of their schooldays or an actual portent of doom, she knew there and then that it was bad.

While Violetta nipped to the loo, Gina skulked from the room to avoid detection, scurrying off to the kitchen. There, around ten minutes later, Bella finally pinned her victim down just like the good old days. Gina was fetching cartons of juice for the children, keeping busy and avoiding the 'evil one' when a tap on the shoulder and a red painted talon heralded the arrival of Satan.

'There you are. I thought you might be baking sausage rolls or something tedious like that.'

True to form Bella immediately dispensed with niceties and

went straight for the jugular. But Gina was older, a bit wiser and not quite as scared and had no time for pleasantries either, so bit back.

'No, the caterers and staff will take care of all that, so if you'd like to ask the sommelier for a drink, he's the guy in the dark suit.' Gina pointed to a handsome man who was currently beguiling Carmen as he poured her a glass of red.

Bella was clearly going nowhere and instead, glanced around the room, hawk-eyed, taking it all in. The bespoke kitchen, the tasteful fixtures and fittings, Gina dressed in Armani.

Bella didn't appear impressed, smirking as she delivered her poison laced line. 'Well, I have to say it certainly looks like you landed on your feet, which reminds me... How's your mum? Is she here? Jimmy just introduced me to his parents, so where is dear old Debbie?'

Gina watched as Bella swung her head from side to side, searching for someone she knew wasn't there.

Digging deep, Gina replied. 'Yes, me *and* Jimmy have done well, but that's the reward for hard work and study I suppose. That's why we invested in this place. He redesigned it structurally and I took care of the interior. We make a great team. And mum lives in Leicester with her partner but was too poorly to make it.'

Debbie hadn't been invited but Bella would never know that. Already sick of the inquisition, Gina changed the subject. 'And what do you do these days and how come you're back in these parts? Don't your parents spend most of their time in Italy.'

'Yes, that's right, they followed the sun but I'm staying here at their place for a while. I'm in between homes so it's the perfect solution while I house hunt – which reminds me, Jimmy said you don't work. I suppose that makes you a stay-at-home mum... how sweet. Just like Debbie was.'

The sarcastic comparison was all it needed to rile Gina further and as much as she wanted to grab Bella by her blonde extensions and ram her face into the wall, Gina sucked in her rage and teetered on the edge of the moral high ground.

'What Jimmy meant is that I work from home and write for an interior design magazine. It suits us both for now, but I'll be back full-time once Mimi starts school so, if you'll excuse me, I need to circulate. Help yourself to food. There's a buffet in the conservatory and the waitresses will serve you from the hot-plates. Wouldn't want you setting yourself on fire, would we?' With that, Gina turned and walked away, unable to bear Bella's company a second longer.

If she thought that was the end of it, she was wrong and a fool because for the rest of the evening, each time she saw her husband, Bella was by his side. Standing far too close laughing loudly at his jokes, resting her hands on his arm as she did so.

For Gina the night was ruined the minute Bella stepped through the door, but it went from bad to worse once everyone had left.

'Why the hell did you let that bitch in? You should have told Guy to take her home...' Gina knew she was being ridiculous because she wouldn't have had the balls to turn someone away at the door. But she was raging and the hurt she'd bottled up forever bubbled over.

Jimmy dragged a hand through his hair. 'For Christ's sake, Gina. How the hell was I supposed to know who she was... you're being ridiculous, and you know it.'

Gina didn't care; she had to take it out on someone, and it was him. 'And then, to make it worse she was all over you, pawing at you, the bimbo-slag. I saw. You were lapping it up so don't even try to deny it and, you told her I was a housewife or what was it... Oh yes, "out of work".'

'I *did not* say that. She's twisted my words and *no*, I didn't like her, as you say, pawing me. And there's nothing wrong with you being out-of-work, or a full-time mum or whatever you want to call it. It's nobody's business so why don't you stop looking for a fight and ruining the night. You're being paranoid and acting like a bloody schoolgirl. Just listen to yourself.'

'*I'm* ruining the evening? And how dare you even say I'm out-of-work? You cheeky—'

'Mummy, why are you shouting at Daddy?'

Gina froze, her head snapped upwards. At the top of the stairs she saw Max holding on to the banister, eyes wide and tearful.

'Max, sweetheart, I'm not shouting at Daddy so don't worry.' She was already halfway up the stairs, her anger turning to shame then back to anger again as she swooped up her son and carried him back to bed.

As she covered him with the duvet and watched while he nodded off, fury consumed her. There was only one person to blame for all this, ruining her party and upsetting her son, let alone daring to touch her husband. And as God was her witness, Gina swore that Bella wouldn't spoil a second of her life, ever again.

It took a few days, but Gina and Jimmy made up, like they always did after a row. They made a pact that the B-name would never be mentioned again, and Jimmy promised to speak to Guy and make sure he did the same and knew what a bitch she was.

They got back into the Christmas spirit and then enjoyed New Year at Disneyland Paris, so eventually Gina banished Bella from her mind. Until the day Babs dropped her bombshell and told Gina she'd just driven past Jimmy, up by the Young Farm.

'Are you sure it was Jimmy?' Gina's heart raced and a river of dread swept through her body.

'Course it was him. Everyone knows your Jimmy drives a McLaren. I'd recognise it anywhere. Now, shall I start on the upstairs bathrooms? Then I'll do the kiddies' rooms. Back soon.'

In that moment, Gina's head resembled a melt-in-the-middle chocolate sponge, the hot centre oozing everywhere. Rendered immobile she remained on the sofa, trying to hold her dripping, dribbling mushed-up brain together. After a while one question somehow forced its way through the goo.

Why was Jimmy near the Young Farm when he'd told her he'd be in Chester all day, and having dinner with clients?

All it took was one quick text, asking if he'd arrived in Chester, telling him she missed him already.

The reply came six minutes and eleven seconds later.

He said he was at the conference centre; the traffic into the city had been a nightmare, and he was about to go into his meeting, and that he missed her too.

LIAR!

That's when it all began. The first lie; the text then the voice note; the nightmare; the return of Bella. Once suspicion took hold, Gina's imagination ran riot. Her paranoia knew no bounds and her latest meltdown began in earnest. It was all going wrong.

———

Gina checked her watch. Time to make her way home and then, as she stretched out, she had an idea. The Young Farm was only minutes away if she diverted from her usual route. What was the harm in taking a look? Seeing if Bella's car was there or maybe two, meaning she'd shacked up with someone and that was why the slapper hadn't been in touch with Jimmy.

It was worth a look, and she didn't even have to stop running, just skirt the perimeter of the farm, have a gander then head home. It was a no-brainer. She had to know and with her laces nice and tight and her mind made up, Gina reset her watch and began to run.

CHAPTER FIFTEEN

BABS

THE SOUND OF HER PHONE DISTRACTED BABS FROM THE laptop screen and Jess, the effervescent fitness instructor who was putting all the other online viewers through their paces. Babs ignored the phone and focused on the last few minutes of Disco-cise. This was her time, and nobody was allowed to interrupt.

Who would have thought that she'd enjoy working out? But she did and joining the online class was so much fun. Being part of a group with her far-away, puffed-out buddies who logged on each day. At first, she'd ached and some of the more intense sessions were a struggle, but a month in and she was feeling so much better, in herself and about herself.

She'd also joined a Facebook group where each morning they did steps and chatted via messages; and another for women going through the menopause. They shared their experiences, gave advice, and swapped healthy eating tips about superfoods and supplements. What Babs liked best was the encouragement and comfort. Knowing that others were going through it, felt less like she was going doolally, or alone.

Babs wished she'd done it before, had the guts to join an

online group but she'd been too shy and also, there never seemed to be enough hours in the day, until now. It was Gina who'd suggested it, ages ago when Babs had been there cleaning. She'd had a bit of a funny turn, a hot flush that sent her dizzy and Gina noticed.

It was the first time Babs had ever mentioned her symptoms. She'd felt daft... definitely embarrassed about discussing such a private matter but once she'd started, it was like she couldn't stop. Gina had listened and suggested Babs made an appointment at the doctors and also, had a gander at online support groups. It had meant a lot that she'd taken the time to listen.

Many of the women in the group were scared of what was happening in the world but at the same time, determined to make the best of a terrible situation, turning unexpected time at home into a positive, especially their hourly, outdoor exercise. Babs saved hers until after tea, where she left whoever was on the rota for washing-up to get on with it.

The house was at full capacity, so she relished her walk along the lanes around the estate, sometimes accompanied by Demi who'd reverted to being the daughter Babs remembered, the one that lurked beneath her teenage veneer. They'd chat about all sorts and nothing in particular and Babs suspected that being away from her peers was good for Demi. It gave her a break from the pressure of being a teenager and social media and it was nice, just the two of them.

Pete, despite being asked always declined as did Sasha. Fiona was superglued to Isaac who was superglued to the remote and never moved from in front of the telly. Anyway, she kept as far away from them as possible because they'd been out there, into the world and the thought of catching anything scared her half to death.

Refocus – that's what Babs had done in order to take her

mind off the news. It made her worry. She'd considered sleeping on the sofa because let's face it, she wouldn't miss anything, or be missed in the bedroom, not these days.

She'd also developed her own beauty regime after ordering some face and skin products and vitamins online. She was determined to have summer-ready feet, and had started painting her toenails; and now she wasn't cleaning so much her fingernails looked much nicer, too. She was halfway to being glamorous. And now she'd lost a few pounds and summer had arrived, she intended treating herself to some new clothes as well, thanks to her mum's 'little windfall,' as Bridie called it.

It had occurred the day after lockdown and the actual amount of the EuroMillions lottery win remained undisclosed – her mum loved to be mysterious. It was enough for her to transfer £250 into Babs' bank account with the strict instructions that it was for her and NOT for Pete. The three kids had been given an envelope with a £20 note inside. Pete got bugger-all. Poor Pete.

Her mother had always tolerated Pete and shown him respect for the simple reason he was the father of her grandchildren, but there was little love lost. In the early days Babs sought to defend Pete, wanting her mum to like him, and – if she was honest – for the truth not to sting so much.

'He's selfish and lazy, and yes, I know he gets up early for work on the bins but he's home and sat on his fat arse by two and that's it for the day. Your dad put in a full shift on the tools at the waterboard, started at seven, digging holes and laying pipes in all weathers. But he still found the energy to do overtime, do our house up, take you and Tom swimming or to the park, even when he was shattered. Pete's a bone-idle shirker who finds time and money for golf and football, but not for his wife and kids.'

Babs ignored the memory of Bridie's dulcet tones, pecking

her head and ringing in her ears, and instead, followed Jess's warming-down exercises. Once she'd waved goodbye, Babs disconnected from the feed and then checked her phone to see who'd been calling and speak of the devil, it was her mum. Jabbing the call-back icon, Babs waited for Bridie to pick up.

'There you are. What were you doing? I let it ring for ages.' Bridie always cut to the chase.

'I was doing my workout, Mum. You know the one I was telling you about on Facebook. Are you okay?'

'Yes, love, I'm fine. I need one of you to go and collect something from Argos for me. I've bought me and Mavis a marquee each.'

'A what?'

'A marquee, so we can sit outside on the front whatever the weather and have a natter and say hello to people when they pass. Then we're not breaking the law and we can do the clapping on Thursdays. I can't be doing with sitting inside. I got us camping chairs too, with cup holders and a little side table so we can have snacks and stuff. Oh yes, and nice blankets for our legs in case it gets a bit chilly on the willy.'

Babs giggled at one of her mum's favourite sayings, used on toddler Isaac when he ran round the house naked.

As always, Bridie was persistent and eager. 'So, when can you go? I'll send you the reference number and I'll need that fat lump Pete to put it up, unless you think one of my grandchildren are capable of following written instructions on a piece of paper.'

Bridie was convinced that the younger generation were physically and mentally incapacitated by overuse of the web, text messaging and emails and as a result couldn't spell or do anything practical and sat on their arses all day talking rubbish. Bridie, on the other hand was conveniently immune and embraced online shopping like it was a gift sent by God especially for her.

Still not sure what her mum had bought, Babs probed, worried also that Bridie's mystery windfall wasn't going to go far at this rate.

'Mum, I don't think a marquee will fit in your little front garden.'

'Bloody hell, Barbara.' She only called Babs by her full name when she was annoyed. 'I'm not simple. I checked the dimensions, but if it makes you happy I'll look on my app. Hold on...' some moments and a lot of tutting and deep sighs later, Bridie found what she was looking for. 'Right, it's a white PVC gazebo with detachable windows, aluminium frame and measures...'

'Mum, that's fine. I get it now. A gazebo is a bit different to a marquee and I think it's a great idea. It'll keep you dry and if it's too warm, out of the sun.'

Babs imagined her mum and Mavis on either side of their fence, camped under their gazebos, keeping an eye on the neighbours and taking part in the new tradition – clapping for the NHS workers on a Thursday night. Bridie had worked as a nurse at their local hospital for over thirty years and was really strict with all the family, ringing up to make sure they all went outside to say thank you.

'Thanks, love. I'll send you the details now and I'd be grateful if we could get them put up soon as. The forecast is lovely for the next week, so I want to get organised.'

'Leave it with me, Mum. I'll pick everything up and bring the girls to help. I'm sure between the three of us we can manage without the men. You'll have to stay inside till it's done though, and no interfering. I'll see you in a bit, okay.'

After her mum said goodbye, Babs had an idea and opened up the Argos app on her phone and began to search, clicking 'Buy Now' when she found what she was looking for. Smiling, she pictured her mum and Mavis sitting outside at dusk underneath their gazebos, all lit up with solar fairy lights.

Two hours later, after being supervised by her bossy mother who barked orders through the window, Babs and the girls had satisfactorily completed their task. Bridie and Mavis were sitting in their respective tented areas and loving life, while Sasha took photos from the other side of the gate. Blankets were draped over their camping chairs for later; two mugs of tea stood in the holders and both slipper-clad women were happily ensconced under their matching white gazebos.

'With a bit of luck, the solar panels will charge up by tonight but if not they'll work tomorrow.'

'Thanks, love, that was very kind of you. I didn't think about lights, but they'll look lovely. I'll pop the money in your account later on.' Bridie gave Babs a look that said *no arguments*. The prize pot was shrinking further.

'Righty-ho. We'll get off then. Ring if you need anything, and remember, don't let anyone get too close...' Another withering look told Babs to be quiet and minutes later, the three of them were heading home.

The grumbling started two minutes into the drive, led by Sasha. 'At least we got out of the house, and it was nice to see Gran. Better than another evening with Isaac and Fiona. I wish you'd said no to her moving in, Mum. It's too cramped and she spends hours in the bathroom doing Lord knows what. I can't wait for her to piss off home.'

'Well, I think she's okay.' Demi ignored Sasha's wobbly head and the ugly face she was pulling at the mention of Fiona. 'She's going to colour my hair. Vamp Pink it's called. We ordered one off Amazon last night, and she said she'll give me a trim, too.'

Babs had a question. 'Er, excuse me, Demi. I don't think

you're allowed to go to school with pink hair, and your dad will have a fit.'

'Mum... don't be such a spoilsport, and if you hadn't noticed, school's shut. I'll rock Vamp Pink so pleeease, let me... if you loved me you would.' Demi winked and gave Babs a nudge while from the back seat came a loud tut.

She'd heard the line many times before and always fell for it, but Demi had been a star since lockdown started, not shirking her online lessons, and actually making an effort to spend time with Babs.

'Go on then. But if your dad tells you off I'm having nothing to do with it, okay. Blame it all on Fiona.' Babs was pulling into the cul-de-sac so being hugged by a giddy girl was a bit inconvenient, as was the sound of her phone ringing. By the time Babs fished it out of her bag, she saw a message from Tom.

> Hi sis, give me a call when you are free. Need
> to talk x

Babs heart plummeted. Something was wrong so not bothering to get out of the car, she waited till the girls had gone inside and rang him straight back.

CHAPTER SIXTEEN

It was sweltering inside Babs' car and even with the windows down, rivers of perspiration trickled where they really should not, and the back of her thighs stuck to the leather seat and made a squelchy sound when she moved. No matter how uncomfortable she was, Tom came before being cool and she didn't want the girls to get the gist of what was going on, if there was actually a problem.

When he finally picked up after two tries, she braced herself for bad news. 'Hi, sis, how's it going over there? All good here, keeping safe and sanitised... there's not a bit of me that Cris hasn't rubbed down with an antiseptic wet wipe... or is that too much information?'

He sounded upbeat but that was Tom's way, always on a natural high, seeing the best in every situation and person, often at his own cost.

'Yes, it bloody well is too much info, and we're all okay. In fact I've just been to see Mum... wait till the girls post the photos on Fam-Chat, she's a hoot.' Babs was mildly relieved but not out of the woods, knowing he could be stalling, serving her a shit sandwich as he called them.

It was Tom's tried and trusted way of delivering unsavoury news to their parents when he was growing up. It was his special formula, disguising bad stuff in between something good.

'I got a Saturday job at the dairy, which will easily pay for the dent I made in Mum's bumper, and my mate said he'd fix it on the cheap.'

'Well, it's Mum I'm ringing about actually. Mad Bridie keeps asking me if I'm okay for money and if I need some, all I have to do is ask. I think she's stressing because we've had to close the bar and thinks we'll starve to death, but I told her we're okay. So how much did she win? Because she's acting like she's loaded.'

Babs smiled, knowing that her mum just wanted to look after her youngest chick even if he was over a thousand miles away. 'I have no idea but I'm letting her enjoy keeping us guessing until it runs out. She's obviously not that flush because she only gave the kids twenty quid and Pete got nothing, unlike Cris. My husband is the spawn of the devil as far as she's concerned.'

It was true, and Babs didn't begrudge Cris the £10 Amazon voucher her mum had sent him because he was a lovely guy and her whole family adored him. Well, perhaps not Pete who didn't go for all that man-love and hugging, and quite frankly the only people he adored were his annoying friends from work, oh, and himself.

'Are you really okay, though? Not just putting on a brave face for me and Mum? Closing the bar and café must have been a blow, especially so close to the holiday season.'

Babs was so proud of Tom whose beachfront eatery was really popular. He'd built himself a whole new life when he and Cris ran off to Spain. Well away from that nasty old bigot, Edmund.

'Yes, I swear, so stop worrying. Me and Cris are using the opportunity to revamp the interior and exterior, even the menu. When we do reopen, I want you to come over again as soon as you can and tell me what you think. You're my biggest critic but I respect your opinions, you know that.'

Babs' heart lifted immediately, imagining another long weekend with her brother and Cris. She made the trip once a year with Demi and Sasha, last time just Demi. It was such an adventure, jetting off from Manchester Airport, having a cheeky drink in the lounge and another cheekier one on the plane but it was always over too soon.

Pete didn't want to go and moaned about the cost and her missing work, so she'd fibbed and said Bridie gave her the money.

She adored Alicante, La Almadraba Beach, the bars and shops, the bustle of tourists looking for a great time – the time she'd imagined before her dream of working abroad was shattered. Babs loved to sit in Tom's place, watching the diners and soaking up the atmosphere and was so proud of her little brother. It always went too quickly though, her time with him.

'Of course I'll come over, in fact, I'm going to put the money Mum gave me aside for the flight; then it'll give me something to look forward to.' Babs could make do with the clothes she had. Seeing Tom was more important.

'And while I'm on, Cris is really worried about his mum, you know, being stuck in that creepy vicarage all day long with Satan's disciple.' This was Tom's name for Edmund. The man who'd said vile things to Cris and, by proxy, about Tom and the gay community in general.

'I know, poor love. I can give her a ring if you want, check in and have a natter. See how Willow is doing, too. The poor lamb has some good days and that always lifts Robin's spirits, gives her hope I think.'

Babs' heart broke for the young woman who she'd watched grow, served through the hatch at the school canteen and as she didn't pray, she wished hard that one day Willow would get better.

'Would you? That would be great. Cris Facetimed her last night and said he could hear the strain in her voice, and she looked tired, too. Then when he spoke to Willow she barely reacted, and it's really got to him. I know it's the drugs and her state of mind but being so far away makes her feel even more unreachable and he can't even help Robin with her care.'

Babs sighed, remembering with a heavy heart 'the trouble', when Tom and Cris's affair had been discovered. After trying his darndest to split them up, shame them, revile them and talk Cris into some freaky conversion therapy, Edmund snapped. He threw his son out and banned him from the house. Ever since, contact between Cris and Robin had been virtually. They had been so close, Cris and his mum, and what Edmund did was downright cruel. Man of God, pah!

'I'll give her a ring and ask her to meet me at the churchyard wall one evening. I can take my walk in that direction, and we can have a natter. That's not breaking any rules I don't think, as long as we stay apart and that way she might open up about how she's doing. What do you think?'

'That would be ace, thanks, Babs. Robin tries to put a front on for Cris, but he knows her so well and could see through it last night. He's got it into his head that she's too isolated, now she's turned her back on Edmund and is focused on Willow. And he wants to know if Nate is doing his bit, and not leaving it all to Robin, which I also suspect is the case.'

Babs knew only too well what was going on at the vicarage and how Edmund ruled the roost but didn't comment and listened instead.

'And now you can't even go round there, and you're probably one of the few true friends she's got.'

Babs' mind was made up. 'Don't worry, love, leave it with me. I have an idea how to get her talking and cheer her up at the same time.'

'Cheers, Babs. I knew I could rely on you. Now, tell me what you lot have been up to, and what's going on with Mum? You mentioned some photos.'

Tom sounded much chirpier, so Babs shuffled, wincing at the sound and feel of her skin as it pulled away from the car seat, like Sellotape. Once she was comfier she regaled her brother with details of Finch family life and the never-ending saga of the always empty fridge.

Later that evening, Babs was power-walking her way towards the village, Demi's school rucksack on her back. Inside was a bottle of cold-ish white wine and two plastic picnic glasses. She'd taken the wine from the fridge and in its place left a Post-it note saying – *Hi F, borrowed your wine. Will replace it ASAP. Needed it for an emergency. Love B x*

It had amused Babs no end, as she left the house with her haul, knowing the hoo-hah that the missing wine would cause. But last week, someone had eaten her Friday night treat bag of Maltesers, so tough!

Glad to be away from home, Babs was looking forward to meeting Robin who, sounding thrilled when she'd rang earlier, had eagerly agreed to meet at the corner of the churchyard. Both of them were convinced they wouldn't be breaking any rules.

They'd agreed on 7pm, by which time Nate would be home and Robin could relax a bit, knowing that he could keep an eye on Willow. It was such a sorry state of affairs, and it wasn't as though she was under lock and key twenty-four-seven, but due to her unpredictable nature, her manic ups and terrible downs, Robin more than anyone had to be vigilant.

She'd really had so much to cope with, had poor Robin, and it still flummoxed Babs how behind closed vicarage doors a family could be so riddled with problems when to the outside world, they appeared to be so perfect. That's what she'd always thought they were.

Lovely Robin who worked so hard in the community, the glue that held all the committees together let alone her private life. Lovely Willow who could be a little eccentric now and then but was kind and gentle. Shy sweet Crispin, who played the guitar and wanted to be a musician and was never any bother at all.

Edmund was just a bastard.

Babs was disgusted with the things he'd said about their Tom, that he was a sinner and all that God-bothering-nonsense, and that he'd groomed Cris and perverted him. Really!

What a hypocrite when half the village knew about him and Gina's mum and what they got up to in the one of the lanes by the dairy farm. There were rumours he had a mistress over in Macclesfield too. Nothing would surprise Babs about Edmund.

At least Robin had never found out, or Gina, because the shame would probably kill them both. Babs had longed to expose the pious prick when he slagged off Tom. She wasn't cruel though, and no good would've come of it.

It wouldn't have helped Cris, who had simply fallen in love with a man ten years older and was so terrified of his own dad, had been hiding his sexuality for years. Fortunately Cris had gathered the courage to finally stand up to his father otherwise he'd have been bundled off to some retreat and brainwashed into being straight.

The thought of it made her shudder. How dare Edmund be judge and jury on another human being's life or, take the moral and religious high ground when he was a sinner himself and had betrayed his wife and God all in one go?

No wonder after Cris left uni and ran away with Tom, Robin's world started to fall apart. And then there was what happened to Willow and how Edmund reacted. Robin had confided in Babs that she was punishing the vicar in her own way and as a consequence, the atmosphere in the vicarage was rock bottom.

Babs made sure she did her cleaning when Satan was out, whereas when she cleaned the church he was often around, skulking and giving her scathing looks. Babs suspected that the only reason he didn't sack her was because he didn't want any more scandal. After all, the whole bloody village knew what had gone on.

Edmund thought he was so clever, with his secretly controlling ways, but Babs was a worthy adversary and rather than resign in a huff at the names he'd called Tom, she stayed on. It was like rubbing his nose in it.

Each time he saw Babs, he'd be reminded of the day he came home early from a conference and caught Cris and Tom 'in flagrante'. That's how Edmund had put it when he rang Babs to tell tales on her twenty-nine-year-old brother. The bloody idiot. It had given them all a proper laugh, 'in flagrante' but she was grateful he didn't say bang-at-it, because that was just too much information even for her!

Despite 'the trouble' Tom found his true love, and even though Cris never completed his classics degree, he'd achieved his true dream of being a musician in his band, playing at venues all over Almeria during the summer.

And their mutual loss of a brother and a son, plus their loathing of Edmund, had further united Babs and Robin in friendship and against the enemy. They'd been gone for years now, and while she had been over to see Tom, Robin had never made the trip.

And because the man of God Edmund was actually

incapable of humility or basic kindness, Robin had borne so much alone. It broke Babs' heart, which was why she would always stand by her friend and if tonight's meeting went well they could do it again.

As she rounded the bend, Babs smiled when she spotted Robin, her red hair blowing in the breeze, her slender arm waving a welcome. Babs waved back and picked up speed, making the pale-faced woman who leant against the church wall a silent promise.

'Don't you worry, love, I'm here now and I've got your back. I'll make sure you're okay. No matter what, we'll get through this, and I'll never, ever let you down.'

CHAPTER SEVENTEEN

ROBIN

ROBIN WATCHED AS HER FRIEND DISAPPEARED FROM SIGHT, giving one last wave as she rounded the bend. It had done her heart good to see Babs again and the warm white wine they'd shared had certainly hit the spot. There was something about Babs that lifted Robin up. It was the way she managed to make light of things and never let stuff get her down, like her overcrowded house and her over-pampered family. Robin knew it was just Babs' way, to grumble about them with a roll of the eyes and a quip, finishing her mini-rant with, *'but I love them all really'*.

Oh, how Robin envied her friend with her haphazard yet happy family life, but not for a second did she begrudge Babs a second of it, or the sweaty socks she'd found rolled up down the side of Pete's armchair, or the brown stain that Sasha's fake tan left in the shower.

It was nice, though, to hear about a normal family who lived, laughed, and quibbled. Unlike hers that had crumbled, rotting at the foundations, bent and twisted like the ancient gravestones she passed on her way back to the vicarage.

If only Edmund had become all the things she'd hoped he

would. She'd convinced herself that given time, she'd mould him, soften the obtuse edges of his austere personality, rub out the thick black lines that guarded his heart and show him another way. Opposite to his upbringing.

To have that mission had seen her through those early years of marriage and what she knew were terrible mistakes: marrying Edmund and rejecting Arty. Instead of doing what she knew in her heart was very wrong but oh-so right, she'd sacrificed her happiness rather than let her parents down.

What was worse, unforgivable, was sacrificing the heart of another. Hurting Arty was like hurting herself. And in doing so, she'd set a course for disaster because that's what she and Edmund were, an utter debacle, a marriage built on lies, infidelity, misguided faith and now hate. Because she did hate Edmund, she really did.

Don't think about him now. You've had such a lovely time, Robin chided. *And it'll be such a waste of Babs walking all that way, and the Pinot Grigio. So buck up, like she does when she thinks of Isaac still living at home when he's fifty.*

Robin managed a chuckle and was about to say bye to Martha when her phone rang. Seeing the name on the screen she smiled and sat in her usual place, facing the headstone, her back resting against the wall. Swiping the screen, she was still smiling when she heard his voice.

'Hello, you. What are you up to?'

'I'm with Martha, and I've just had an illicit rendezvous with Babs. We shared a bottle of white. It was so good to see her and have a natter. She looks marvellous too, all tanned cheeks and joie de vivre. Her exercise regime is doing her the world of good.'

Robin could tell Arty anything, even about her chats with a long dead woman she'd never even met. He knew everything about her via their emails back and forth where she filled him in with the goings on in the village.

'And are you managing to get out?' Arty was also very direct.

'Not really, no. Apart from being in the garden with Willow. She's had a few good days. I persuaded her to keep me company while I did some weeding and I've been reading her angel books out loud. Oh, and we ordered some craft stuff off Amazon, jewellery making and a paint-by-numbers. I thought I could entice her to have a go.'

Robin took every day at a time but was just glad to report that Willow was out of the house getting some fresh air because sometimes the vicarage felt like a prison.

'I wish you'd get out more, Robin. Why don't you hook up with Babs, join her on one of her walks. Surely if you kept apart it'd be okay, and nobody will see you out there. I hate the thought of you being so isolated.' The worry in his voice echoed down the line.

Robin decided on mirth to fend off Arty's concerns. 'Says you, Mr Living-in-the-French-Wilderness. I bet you haven't seen a soul for weeks, unless your drinking buddies have been sneaking in, which wouldn't surprise me.'

Arty didn't deny her accusation which made her smile. He was always the rebel. The next few minutes were taken up swapping lockdown news from their respective dots on the map, the toilet roll epidemic appeared to be global like the virus, until the conversation reverted to them, via Cris's concerns for his mum.

'I spoke to my nephew yesterday and he's worried about you. He thinks you're struggling with Willow and obviously, having to put up with my brother. I'm sure Edmund is missing his pulpit and inflicting his special brand of misery on the congregation, so I imagine he'll be like a bear with a sore head.'

Robin sighed. 'You got it in one. Nate has set him up with a Zoom account so he can do a weekly sermon but most of his flock haven't a clue how to use it and neither has he, to be honest. He's resorted to calling them on the phone and the air was blue the other day when he had to say the Lord's Prayer about thirty-five times. Oh, how I giggled.'

She heard the loud tut that anything to do with Edmund or religion elicited so swiftly moved on. 'I know Cris is concerned; Babs told me, but I try to reassure him best I can and I don't go into detail about Willow if I can help it. I'm stuck in the middle, protecting them both. And Edmund is never going to change so I simply avoid talking about him. And let's be honest, being a recluse suits me fine and lockdown hasn't changed my day-to-day life. Apart from having the nice man from Sainsbury's bring my shopping which I have to say is a revelation and something I could get used to. So I'll be fine, I promise.'

'Well I bloody won't. I wish I'd got over there before we locked down. I'm still kicking myself over that. I don't know how I'm going to manage not seeing you every month or so. It was torture enough as it was, before all this. Maybe I should just find a way. Sod the virus and take a chance.'

'Please don't do that, Arty. I'd never forgive myself... I couldn't bear it if something happened to you...' She swallowed down the lump in her throat and forced her voice to remain steady. 'Just stay there, my love. Be safe, that's all I ask.'

After she made him promise, and knowing her well, Arty turned the conversation and made her laugh with school stories and the strange sights he'd see during online lessons with his students. Like the mother of Joelline, who didn't realise the camera was on so his class watched in fascination as she paraded through the kitchen in her very skimpy bra and knickers. He was about to tell her another story when the sound of a doorbell cut into the conversation.

'Bugger, that will be Gerard with my shopping. It was his turn to go so I'll have to get it from his car... Are you in a rush because I can call you back. I won't be long.'

Not wanting to return to the vicarage just yet, she said she'd wait and keep Martha company. After a swift goodbye, came the all too familiar disconnected tone.

Alone with her thoughts, Robin admitted that part of her had wanted to say, *Yes, get a flight, row across the Channel, anything so I can have you close by.* Their secret rendezvous were something she lived for, a chink of light in the murky grey. She missed him badly, and Cris, too.

Robin loved her shy son so much. For all the obvious reasons and also because he'd been responsible for reuniting her and Arty and for that she would always be grateful.

Robin never thought she'd see Arty again, not after he disappeared on her wedding day, but at the time she'd been glad he was gone. It had made it easier.

On the eve of her wedding, Robin had gone through a gamut of emotions. She'd even dared to pray for a miracle, that time could be rewound, back to the garden on the day she was introduced to Edmund. Here, she would have made pleasantries then left him to sip his Pimm's while she helped her mother in the kitchen or feigned a migraine. Anything other than become embroiled in a relationship with him.

As she lay in her bed, dear Francesca by her side, more than likely dreaming dreams of meeting Prince Charming at the reception, Robin also waited for the sound of stones being thrown against her window. For Arty to be in the garden below and beg her one more time to elope with him.

Quite ridiculous really because she wouldn't have had the guts to go. Maybe she would. Robin would never know.

She'd managed to march through the day, because that's what it was, a regimented order of service, then the reception and the part she dreaded most, the wedding night.

From the second she saw Arty, waiting by the altar with Edmund, the scowl on his face, the way he averted his eyes and the set of his jaw and shoulders told her that he wouldn't forgive her for what she was about to do. The real Arty was back.

It was torture and Robin accepted it as her punishment for all those glorious lunch times spent with her lover. How bizarre, that on what was supposed to be the happiest day of her life she acknowledged her sin and bore the brunt of Arty's anger like a horsehair shirt.

When he skilfully avoided congratulating her, made the shortest, best man speech in the history of wedding breakfasts, and managed to add a note of sarcasm that only she heard, when he toasted the happy couple. She took it all on the chin.

He disappeared immediately after the meal, not that Edmund noticed because he was far too busy doing the social rounds, chatting to the dullest bunch of wedding guests ever.

What a revelation the day was, like those halcyon hours with Arty in his room, consumed with lust, and what she now knew to be the real thing, a love that made you weep, cry out in ecstasy, crave, and covet so badly that even thinking of it sent a swell of heat through one's body. Even that was part of her divine act of penitence, thoroughly deserved, willingly taken. But if Robin thought the day was bad, God hadn't quite finished with her yet.

The next morning, as they left the city centre vicarage that she would now call home, the tears that stung her eyes were borne from so many things and nothing to do with her new mascara.

Memories of her wedding night clung to her skin, a taste of what was to come searing her brain. A fumble in the dark, her nighty raised just enough to ease the task, a minute or so of one-way pleasure. Then the broderie anglaise was tugged neatly into place followed by a peck on the forehead and the sight of his pyjamaed back as he turned on his side, facing the wall.

Tears fell freely, for her parents who she missed already and her bedroom with the candy-striped wallpaper and Teddy, the battered bear she'd had since birth who she'd left behind and would be wondering where she was.

Robin didn't cry for Arty though. Because he was gone, checked out of his hotel or so Edmund told her when he rang to ask him where the ruddy hell he'd disappeared to. The slight was discussed on the train journey to Wales. Reiterating that she'd no idea why he'd done a flit, agreeing with Edmund that it was very bad form but not unexpected, she took each crack of the whip. Self-flagellation by proxy.

According to Edmund as he droned on – and Robin tried to focus on the beauty of south Wales from the train window – it was a foregone conclusion that Arty would blot his copy book. Edmund had got used to his brother's flighty, inconsiderate ways and was mildly surprised he'd even agreed to be best man, seeing as he clearly wasn't. Especially as Arty had made Edmund feel most uncomfortable as they waited in the church because it was quite clear he still despised everything the place stood for and in turn, his own brother.

'Well just you wait until I speak to him. He can't hide in Japan forever and I will take him to task over his rudeness to you and your parents. It was most embarrassing, everyone asking after him, never mind his lacklustre speech and frankly indulgent fondness for the whisky.'

It turned out that Edmund was wrong. Because Arty could, and did, hide in Japan for what seemed like forever. Robin knew full well he engineered and exacerbated the row when Edmund finally got hold of him. Why, when Willow was born, he refused to be her godfather and to return for the christening to meet his only niece. Same when Cris was born, and, according to Edmund, he had the audacity to ridicule their son's name.

'Why the hell would you saddle a child with a name like that, after our father, an utterly bigoted man who lacked anything remotely worth honouring? And stop trying to foist your beliefs and ridiculous rituals on me because you're wasting your time, Edmund. As I told you before, I will not be returning any time soon. I cannot be saved, by you or anyone and nor do I want to be. Now please, let me get on with my life and you get on with yours. I wish you and your family well so let's just leave it there. Take care, Edmund.'

Robin had been hovering in the hallway, and made her presence known as Arty ended the call, leaving Edmund staring at the receiver, his face puce as he turned to her in astonishment. 'That's it. My brother and I are finished. How dare he speak to me like that?'

It wasn't often Robin resorted to sarcasm but on that occasion she simply couldn't resist. 'Whatever happened to forgiveness, Edmund? Surely you can find it in your heart or at least rustle up a parable that will guide you.'

The sound of the receiver being slammed into the cradle told her otherwise as she watched him stomp off, speaking to his back as he grabbed his coat and hat. 'But no matter, we'll carry on as planned and have a lovely christening for Cris, just like Willow's.'

Turning with a smile, Robin heaved a sigh of relief, knowing that Arty would stay away and as a consequence she would be spared the trauma of seeing his face again.

After that, Robin's best foot kept moving forward, making the most of a very bad job by throwing the love she didn't have for Edmund, into loving her children; and being the best vicar's wife in the county, making amends the only way she knew how and all the time, hoping that him upstairs would eventually forgive her sin.

For years Robin trundled on, for the most part content. Happiness came via the children who she swore would not be joined by more siblings, and the kinship she found in the parishioners. Life was bearable if she focused on the good things in her world, like living in a beautiful part of the countryside, and conversely, having a husband who was disinterested in the conjugal side of their marriage. Had it been the opposite, Robin would've accepted that God had a wicked side and was far more annoyed with her than she'd previously imagined.

And then Cris, out of the blue, decided to contact his long-lost uncle. Robin had no idea that her shy and sensitive son had tracked Arty down, or that they'd been secretly corresponding for months. Maybe his inquiring mind had created a family mystery he thought he should solve; or in an attempt to garner praise from his hard-to-please father, had the misguided desire to heal a rift and reunite warring brothers.

When he found her in the garden, knee deep in crocus bulbs, she knew in a heartbeat Cris was nervous; it was written on his face.

'Mum, can I have a chat? I've been waiting for Dad to go out, so we won't be disturbed.' Cris hovered, looking sheepish.

'Of course, darling. Now, is this a serious sit-at-the-table kind of chat or will here do, on the grass with your muddy mum?' Robin hoped it was the latter. Not like when Cris told her he didn't want to go to Scouts anymore, or Sunday school either. That was a biggie and the fallout had lasted for quite some time.

'No, here is good.' He sat cross-legged and began fiddling with the pokey-out bits of wicker on Robin's trug and in his clumsy, teenage way he made a hash of his little speech. 'The thing is, I have a confession and a bit of a surprise for you too. He told me I had to tell you because it wasn't right, keeping secrets.'

Robin's heart plummeted and she strained to hold a neutral expression as horror stories of online grooming flashed before her eyes. 'Who– who told you... what secrets?' She watched as he took a deep breath and tension zinged through her core, tightening every muscle in her body.

'Uncle Arty. I tracked him down. He lives in France, in a village just outside Lourdes and we've been emailing for a while now. Anyway, he's coming home, here, to see us all and said I should tell you, so you can be prepared. I think he meant get him a room ready or something, but he's going to ring Dad. Build some bridges, he said.'

All that Robin could think, as she listened to Cris and forced a smile to her lips was that she was ever so glad that she was sitting down, because she knew for certain that her legs would not have held her up.

Days passed in a blur and in all her years, Robin couldn't remember experiencing such all-consuming fear and nerve-jangling excitement rolled into one, each time she thought of Arty's imminent return. Fear, that he'd had some kind of epiphany, maybe a breakdown because she'd seen how fragile his temperament could be. She wouldn't be surprised if he still hated her, and now that Cris had opened the door, Arty was coming back to cause trouble for the hell of it. To tell Edmund and the children what a wicked woman she was, lay her life to waste, because why else would the prodigal return?

There'd been no cards, letters, or phone calls to Edmund, just a gift token each year for Willow and Cris, because what could he buy children he'd never met and knew nothing about? He couldn't possibly have missed them, so she doubted he longed to be an uncle, fill some void in his bachelor life. The lure was unlikely to be Edmund. Hence, she didn't trust him, not after all this time.

He was a stranger. The essence of the beautiful man she'd lain with had faded with time and she'd been able to lock it all away in a box labelled, 'My moment of madness,' been strict with herself, forbidding even just a peep inside. It had been a necessity, to enable her to get on with it, and now he was going to ruin all the progress she'd made.

Resistance was futile, though. The thrill inside her chest and the swirl deep down in her gut could not be ignored. No matter how many times she summoned the image in her head, pressing down hard with the plumpest pillow she could find to smother the notion that to see him again was all she'd ever wanted.

Madness, that's what it was. Like the day, all those years ago when he'd invited her for lunch. Asked her to come to his room. It was happening again, and Robin could sense him getting closer, the miles between her and the village he lived in France closing by the hour.

The potent promise of forbidden fruit, the challenge that awaited her, the battle between abstinence and temptation, a duel in which she would fight for her family if he sought to bring it down, was sending Robin quietly insane.

CHAPTER EIGHTEEN

THE STAGE WAS SET. EDMUND HAD LITTLE OPTION OTHER than to play the part of a benevolent man of God, to lead by example and accept the olive branch offered by his recalcitrant brother.

Maybe he was curious too, but Robin suspected Edmund wanted to show off, brag about his growing closeness to the bishop and the church hierarchy, still oblivious and arrogant enough to believe that Arty would even care. Edmund would be eager to parade his wife and children to demonstrate how being an adult should be done and what Arty could've had, if he'd been a better man.

The irony of her suspicions wasn't lost on Robin and as she'd polished the dining table and arranged the flowers in the hall she'd heard herself laugh out loud, followed by a snort of derision. There he'd be, preening himself at a job well done when in truth, Edmund's house was built on false foundations and a bed of lies, a shameful secret shared.

How Arty would enjoy it.

This judgement of her brother-in-law was based merely on the snippets Cris had passed on while they ate dinner, prior to Arty's eagerly awaited return. A second-hand and possibly tame version of his uncle's life told via their correspondence.

Never married, Arty had split with his partner of six years quite recently, no big drama because 'it was on the fizzle anyway'. He'd never had children but had taught thousands of the little buggers all over the world before settling in France where he taught languages at a local school.

Arty had sent photos that made her internal organs and other bits and bobs do strange things because apart from the obvious telling of time, he hadn't changed a bit. Still the same rakish smile, that look in his eye.

Willow was excited too. And had quizzed Robin while she pored over her parents' wedding photos, gazing dreamily at the tall handsome man scowling from the back row.

'So why did he stay away so long; and why did he and Dad fall out?' Looking down at the photos she squinted. 'They're nothing alike, are they? Poor dad, he definitely missed out on the cute gene.' Willow, being her usual forthright self, had stated the obvious.

Arty was clearly the most handsome of the brothers by a mile, and that was before you added charisma and all the other stuff that was coming back to haunt Robin by the hour.

'It wasn't a falling out so much... more a conflict of opinions because your uncle,' it was still impossible to say his name because it made it all too close and personal, 'well, him and God have never got on. He's a confirmed atheist and when he sets his mind to it, can be very belligerent and knows how to wind your father up.'

Then the million-dollar questions. 'Does he not wind you up, too? I don't mind if people have different beliefs, I like it in fact. We should just live and let live, but I can imagine Dad can't cope with any resistance or insubordination. But when *you* talk about Uncle Arty, you sound more forgiving. Did you like him when you met him?'

What to say? The truth in its barest form seemed best. 'Not the first time, no. I thought he was obnoxious and opinionated, and I was offended by his views and couldn't wait to see the back of him; but then the second time, he'd mellowed, and I saw a different side. Although I suspect he was just toeing the line before the wedding and then, after he'd done his duty, he was off.'

Willow was enthralled. 'So what happened next?'

'Your father pushed his luck, wanted him to be your godfather. He said he couldn't get back which was fair enough because Japan isn't exactly round the corner, but when it came to Cris's, I think it was the final straw for both of them. Your uncle point-blank refused.'

'Hmm, I can imagine.' Then the killer question. 'Are you looking forward to seeing him again?'

The heat that spread upwards from her chest to her neck and cheeks was hidden from view thanks to Robin's vigorous and industrious cleaning of the hob. Her answer was concocted during a moment of panic and yet as much as she wanted to deny Arty, she couldn't, so to her surprise her words spoke the truth. 'Yes, actually, I think I am. But I'm also a bit nervous so I hope he's going to behave because otherwise he'll spoil it for Cris, and that will make me cross.'

Willow nodded and flipped another page of the album. 'Well, I'm going to take him on face value and give him a chance. I really want to get to know him and all about Lourdes. I've always wanted to go... fancy a devout atheist living there!'

Robin allowed herself a chuckle because the same thought had crossed her mind the second Cris mentioned it. However, Willow was on a roll, so Robin tuned back into the Arty Show.

'... and not just that, rellies in this family are a bit thin on the ground and as far as Cris is concerned he's already on Team Arty. Honestly have you heard him? "Uncle Arty canoed down the Nile and he's been to the Antarctic, and to Peru to see the Inca treasure, and worked on a sheep farm in Oz and met the Queen." I think Cris has been looking for a hero and he's found one in Uncle Arty, bless him.'

Willow's words made Robin's heart sink, the notion that her son had looked elsewhere for a role model pained her greatly. Sadness consumed her and then anger that Edmund had fallen short, again.

A terrible husband *and* father whose focus was on the church and himself, the spotlight always dimmed where his family were concerned. He was a man of God first, maker of rules and regulations second, father third, lover... unplaced.

Willow, oblivious to Robin's inner turmoil, rattled on. 'So, that only leaves Dad. Do you think they'll get on okay?' Willow looked up from the wedding album and scrutinised her mother's face.

'The fact that they've been in touch via email and Dad's invited him for lunch tells me it'll be fine, although I wasn't surprised Arty has booked into a hotel. Vicarages aren't his thing.'

Willow laughed. 'What, like he's the anti-Christ?'

'Yes, something on those lines and anyway, we don't have a spare room so it's best all round.'

Willow persisted. 'Do you think it will be awkward? I mean, there's a *huuuge* gap to fill in, isn't there. I hope it's not going to be cringe while you pass the trifle and Dad avoids his favourite subject... and what about me? Do you think he'll think I'm a God-botherer? I bet he'll think I'm a real nerd. I know, I could wear my fancy dress nun's outfit for a laugh. I bet that will be a conversation starter.' At this Willow convulsed into giggles, highly amused by her own self-deprecation and Robin was reminded of how Arty had made her feel the first time they met.

What a state of affairs. Willow was obviously feeling a little self-conscious, Cris was eager to meet his long-lost uncle who was some kind of legend, and as for Edmund, he'd play the game and wait for Arty to mess up and revel in his brother's inferiority.

As for her, she floated between giddy Sandra Dee mode, albeit an older less naïve version, and wishing he'd change his mind regardless of how disappointed Cris would be. Then on top of that, it really irked her that one man could affect all of them in such a way.

Days before his arrival, she'd scrutinised her appearance in the bedroom mirror, peering closer to count the crow's feet under her eyes, wondering who the prodigal brother was expecting when he rolled up. The twenty-year-old bride he'd last seen on her wedding day, or the thirty-eight-year-old mother of two, wrinkles and all.

So she *didn't* go to the fancy salon in Chester for her roots done because of Arty, and as for the new dresses – they were in the sale, and she loved a bargain. The reason she couldn't sleep the night before was because she had so much to think about and do, like prepare the vegetables, cook the roast. Edmund would want it to be perfect, hence her jitters, nothing else.

By the time Cris shouted from the landing, 'He's here,' and raced down the stairs to open the door first and greet the uncle who he'd begun to hero worship, Robin had to hide her trembling hands by taking hold of Willow's.

The moment he walked through the door Robin knew. She fell hard, flat on her face and right back in love with Arty. Who, in his pale blue shirt rolled up to his elbows, faded denim jeans and tan suede boots must have co-ordinated his casual clothing to match his casual air.

Like he'd only seen them last week, Arty handed out hugs to Cris and Willow. 'Hey, what a sight you two are, even more grown up in the flesh.' Then a firm handshake and a smile to Edmund. 'Good to see you, Ed, you're looking well,' and finally his eyes rested on Robin.

'And here she is, the beautiful Robin, not changed a bit, just as I remember.' He stepped forward, arms outstretched and as he wrapped her in a hug, whispered in her ear, 'In all of my dreams.'

In that moment Arty reclaimed what had always been his.

Over the following week, Arty entranced Cris and thoroughly beguiled Willow. They soaked up his tales of derring-do and his views on the world, society, whatever subject arose, regardless of how out-there and opposed they were to Edmund's.

It was like a breath of fresh air blew through their home each time he turned up, often when Edmund was out. And in between discussing the Middle East conflict and the Premier League, Robin felt Arty's eyes on her whenever nobody was looking. She knew he was waiting, so was she; and when it happened Robin was ready.

Readier than she'd ever been in her life, for anything, ever.

They were in the garden, like garden proposals were their thing. The sun was about to set on a June day and even though she'd taken up a relaxed pose on the deckchair, every sinew in her body was taut.

Cris was practising his scales in the dining room; Willow was out with Gina; and Edmund was somewhere on the planet and thankfully not in Robin's orbit. She and Arty were drinking gin and tonic, she gulped hers down, glad of the extra slug she'd added in the kitchen. After dispensing with the usual banalities they adhered to in company, Robin decided it was time she asked him the question. Not daring to look sideways she focused on the bluebells that jiggled in the evening breeze.

'Why did you really come back? I need to know.'

Arty didn't miss a beat. 'For you. It was time.'

Panic and euphoria swept through Robin, another gulp, another question, she couldn't stop now.

'What do you mean? I'm still married, or have you conveniently forgotten that – like you forgot I existed for eighteen years?'

'I've never forgotten you, Robin. Not for a year, a day; sometimes a minute but I had to let you go. It was wrong of me to ask you to elope, stupid. It finally dawned on me over the years that it was too much to expect from someone as wonderful as you.'

Robin kept her eyes on the bluebells as he continued.

'But I still saw you in my dreams, and in my imagination. You were being a good wife and mother, not letting your parents down or bringing shame to their door and I didn't begrudge you that for a minute because that's what love is. Doing what's best for someone even if it kills you inside. And it did, almost kill me, leaving you behind but I had to go. I simply couldn't stay and watch you with him.'

Tears rolled down Robin's cheeks and she didn't swipe them away because they were a testament to how she felt in that moment, how his words had affected her. She wanted him to know that she felt the same. When Robin managed to speak, her voice betrayed her, anyway.

'You were right, about all of it and if it's any consolation for the mess we got ourselves into, I thought of you so much, even though I tried desperately not to.' She sucked in a breath to steady herself. 'But you still haven't told me, why now. Why you think it's time.'

He made a sound that was half-laugh, half-sigh before

answering. 'Coming from me, he of little faith in anything, this will sound hypocritical but when I got the email from Cris I saw it as a sign.'

He paused, turned to look, and she met his gaze and smiled before raising her eyebrows at his revelation.

'And then, slowly, by reading between the lines I began to form a picture of your life, how it had turned out and as much as Cris is very sweet and loyal, he is somewhat naïve. And being a teacher for so long means I'm fluent in the language of teenagers.'

Robin's tears continued to trickle, and when Arty lifted his hand as if to wipe them away her heart flipped but he faltered and for that she was glad, wary of being seen. Instead, he laid his hand on the arm of his chair, a millimetre from hers as she fought the urge to hook her little finger through his.

Instead she wondered out loud what Cris had said, 'What on earth has my son been saying in those emails?' She braved a longer glance at Arty who stroked her arm then removed his hand quickly before answering. His touch had burned a mark in her skin.

'Nothing bad, especially not about you, which would be totally impossible. Cris adores you and so he should. He merely confirmed my fears about Edmund, that he had become the husband I expected, a carbon copy of our own father with a dollop of God on top. It made me sad. So, I came to rescue you.'

Robin held him in her glare. 'And how exactly will you do that, considering also I haven't actually sent out a flare or requested an intervention. And there's still the matter of my wedding vows, and being a mother to my children, and I am not running off and abandoning them, now or ever.'

'Oh, don't you worry about any of that. Mere details and nothing we can't fathom as we go along and anyway, I have most of it worked out.'

Robin gasped because there it was, that irresistible confidence mingled with a sprinkling of arrogance, accompanied by a look of such mischief that it made you want to be part of the game. She stared, dumbfounded, and partly petrified of asking what he meant so Arty filled in the details for her.

'I respect your limits, Robin. I admire you for every bit of who you are. So I will never ever ask you to leave Edmund, or your wonderful children or the life and village you seem to love. I will simply wait until you are ready, and even if you aren't, ever, then I will take any snippets I can get, whatever morsel you can spare, whenever you can fit me in.'

Robin's heart pounded. 'That's impossible. I couldn't expect that of you; it's cruel and unfair.'

Arty shook his head. 'I disagree. I've done without you in my life for too long. My period of mourning is over, and Edmund has had his chance and blown it. So now it's my turn, our chance to find a little bit of happiness in this bloody awful world.'

Robin bit her lip, forbidding the sob to escape because what Arty said was true. Edmund had his chance to love her like she needed to be loved. She'd been a good vicar's wife, endured whatever the job title and marriage had thrown at her. She'd paid her penitence and if God didn't think being married to a cold, dispassionate narcissist was enough then tough. He could send her to hell. She was probably going anyway so why not make it worth her while.

'And what exactly are you suggesting, seeing as you live in France? Love letters straight from the heart. Do you think that will sustain us?'

'I most certainly do not! I propose something far more thrilling and clandestine because if we're going to do this, let's do it properly and set the world, our hearts, and the bed on fire... like the last time.'

When Arty swivelled in his seat to look at her, into her, at all of her, Robin saw a mirror image of how she felt. Longing, and a love like she'd never known before and in that tiny capsule of time, only the two of them existed, counted.

'What are you suggesting...'

With a wicked look in his eye he recited words from a scene in her parents' garden, many moons before. 'Well, you must get a lunch hour. What say I pick you up tomorrow? Would that suit? And they say it's going to be a bit of a scorcher so maybe after we've eaten, we could head to my room. I'll order us a bottle of something cold and fizzy and we can sit on the balcony and chat, or whatever you want. How does that sound?'

Robin heard the catch in her throat but managed to answer, remembering her young self, Sandra Dee, standing in the forecourt of his hotel. And even if she didn't sound bold then, this time, she did. 'I think that would be lovely.'

Robin's bottom was numb from sitting chatting to Arty who'd called her back the second he'd collected his shopping. She really needed to get inside and make supper so as much as it pained her, brought the conversation to a close.

'Listen, you. I need to get off. Willow might be hungry, and I've been gone a while, so I'll call you tomorrow and check you're behaving.'

'I will have you know I always behave unless I'm with you and I'm getting thoroughly peeved because being good is utter torture.'

This made Robin smile, knowing exactly what it was like, yet it also reaffirmed their feelings for one another. 'Yes, my love, it is. But it will soon be over, and I expect you on the first flight out the minute they say it's safe.'

'I promise I will be at the front of the queue for a ticket but before you go, how is Willow? You didn't say.'

Arty had grown to adore Willow, becoming the best uncle, present and correct at all her milestones. He was her ardent supporter who, despite his thoughts on the church, was furious with Edmund for swaying her from her vocation. And through all of what followed, 'the trouble' with Cris and the carnage of tragedy, not once had he begrudged his niece and nephew for the hold they had on Robin.

There had been the briefest of opportunities once they'd flown the nest but she was a mother first and foremost, and then a grandmother who wanted to be hands on, not far away. And now she was Willow's carer, determined and devoted, going nowhere fast.

'We've had a few good days actually. I ordered more angel books, as she calls them. She still pores over the photo album and sometimes she sleeps with... Robin couldn't bear to say it so moved on. But at least she's not had one of her episodes for a while.'

Willow rode the waves of her depression and when she was up, had discovered the power of angels and believed every word in the books she bought online.

'That's good... and when I come over I'll bring her some knick-knacks from the shrine. A girl can never have enough holy water and rosary beads.' Arty loved to tease Willow and she'd always taken it in good part, countering his quips by darting over and making the sign of the cross on his head and demanding in the most dramatic voice that Satan left his body. How Robin yearned for her child to be like that once more.

'Yes, she will, now, bugger off and sleep well. I really do have to go.'

Once they said their goodbyes, Robin stood, wincing at her bruised bottom and creaky knees and after dusting off her skirt, headed down the uneven path to the vicarage. As she passed the door of the church she paused and laid her hand on the door, closed her eyes, and made a silent prayer.

'Hello, it's me. The fallen one. Just dropping by to say I'm sorry, again, for being a big disappointment and to remind you that even though I'm in your bad books, not to take it out on Willow and if you can, amongst all the other stuff you've got going on, do you think you might give her a break, because she's a good girl, the best. That's it. And don't forget, let's keep this between us. Don't want anyone knowing I still care. I always will.'

CHAPTER NINETEEN

GINA

THE SOLAR LIGHTS DOTTED AROUND THE PERIMETER OF the garden gently lit the rockery and alpines that nestled between Gina's tasteful water features, and the not so tasteful colourful gnomes the children insisted on.

Above, in the blackened skies that shrouded the village in darkness, stars pinged into life, diamonds poking through a swathe of velvet. By her side lay Jimmy, arms behind his head, eyes closed and a smile on his face and when she looked at him, the only thought Gina had was, *He's beautiful*.

Behind them, Max and Mimi were sleeping in the tent, an online purchase that had thrilled them, and her other big kid, too. The excitement when the sleeping bags and camping stove arrived was off the scale and the second the four-man tent was erected, Max and Mimi took up residence. When Babs related the story about Bridie's gazebos it had given Gina the idea to create a makeshift campsite in her own back garden.

They'd had umpteen nights under the stars and the only thing that prevented them from bending to their children's iron-will and living the outdoor life permanently was Jimmy's bad back and his 'husbandly requirements' that weren't being met inside his sleeping bag.

Gina had given him a gentle slap for that, but his comment made her so damn happy because he still wanted her. Any niggles that popped into her head about being a stop-gap, or him making do were barred entry.

Not that she would tell a soul, for fear of sounding crass and uncaring but the Morgan family lockdown had been idyllic, an escape from the horrors of the world. If she had to use one word, Gina would choose *cemented*, because that's how she felt her marriage was in that moment in time.

They'd found their groove, a routine that wasn't the norm but had become it, a way of existing together as a family in harmony against the odds. Staying safe, staying sane, staying together.

And in his usual ingenious way, Jimmy had added a string to Gina's bow when he suggested she expand her online consultancy by setting up a Facebook page with ideas for upcycling bits and bobs around the home.

People were bored out of their heads and looking for something to do and it was her thing, saving the planet. Her special cupboard for recycled plastic was Jimmy's favourite tease because Gina *hated* waste of any kind so not only was she the 'Leftover Queen' she was also his 'Takeaway Carton Princess.'

Her reluctance to waste food came from a childhood of doing without and making damn sure you scraped your plate when a meal was put in front of you, just in case. The rest was borne from watching telly with Willow, where David Attenborough scared the crap out of anyone who cared about the world and all the species that inhabited it.

Gina had mulled Jimmy's suggestion over for a day or two. Lack of confidence was mostly to blame for her initial dallying, and then an attack of paranoia and too much reading between the lines.

Was he hinting that she was lazy, or perhaps getting on his nerves? Because while he was still busy working from home, once she'd done the housework, basically all the stuff Babs used to do, and put in a few hours on her column for the magazine, Gina was semi-redundant.

Jimmy, however, was loving home-schooling Max while she entertained Mimi who to be fair, pretty much toddled about in her own world of toys, and as long as she was fed regularly, got her daily dose of CBeebies, and had an afternoon nap, was a dream child.

I bet he's wondering what I do all day... I'm a lazy cow having a cleaner... I bet he sacks poor Babs... the sooner I get back to full-time work the better, then she can stay. Have I been hiding behind the stay-at-home-mum job description... am I kidding myself that I'm a homemaker... is it even a thing? What if being a kept woman isn't such a good look... makes me seem boring... I am boring... oh God... I need to do something, right now!

Once she got stuck in, Gina was on a roll. The editor at the magazine loved the idea and offered her a weekly slot on their Facebook page and blog where readers were encouraged to show off their own upcycling while Gina's job was to inspire.

She began by sorting out the neatly stacked pile of stuff at the back of the garage – tidiness was also Gina's thing after living in Dirty Debbie's hovel, and the stuff destined for the recycling section was pimped and jazzed up.

The wooden gift box that once held a bottle of fancy wine was sanded, painted, and transformed into a window ledge herb garden. The pretty but mismatched china plates found in the kitchen of Swallow's Nest, became cake stands. Soon, readers were posting photos of their hidden gems that'd been given a new lease of life and Jimmy's spark of an idea soon became Gina's little triumph.

The only cloud, the one thing that she had no control over was her inability to see Willow and even though Gina spoke to Robin every few days, it wasn't the same as seeing her best friend in the flesh. It had become part of her weekly routine, spending time at the vicarage, a place as familiar as her own home.

On the days when Mimi went to playgroup, Gina would drive straight over to keep Willow company and give Robin a break, especially when she went away for a few days, visiting her old friend Francesca.

It'd become a regular thing, that and the odd spa weekend or country retreat here and there. Robin accepted that Edmund had no interest in the type of holidays she wanted to go on, so they'd drifted further apart and took breaks separately. Even though Gina thought it was sad, that Robin travelled alone, she assured everyone of her modern woman status, that she was capable of taking a train and would enjoy a few days of tranquillity.

Gina could tell it did Robin good and she always came back looking so much happier and who could blame her? Living with Edmund couldn't be much fun. You didn't have to be a marriage guidance counsellor to know that Robin and Edmund barely communicated and were putting on a front for Willow.

Knowing what she did about him, Gina sometimes wished Robin would up and leave the dirty old git. Surely there was someone out there who could make her happy. Still, Edmund's affair with her Dirty Debbie remained a secret, and Gina hadn't even told Jimmy mainly because she was too ashamed.

It was something she'd thought about a lot, marriage. Holding one together and how Robin's life would pan out. For

Willow, and her husband, Nate, because now Willow was sick, what would become of their relationship?

They already slept in separate rooms. Nate was a lovely guy, handsome and funny, kind, and clever and even though he'd lost so much, still put one foot in front of the other, taught at the college and remained loyal to his wife, sharing the load with Robin as they cared for Willow round the clock.

But how long would that last? Would his patience run out, would his basic instincts, needs and dreams slowly erode the love he had for Willow? Would he leave her, lost in a world of angels and torment and at the same time, leave Robin in the lurch? It was too awful to contemplate but these things kept Gina awake at night, turning them all over in her head.

And throughout lockdown, that stretched on and on, the newsfeeds hard to watch, it struck Gina that if someone or something chooses to pull the proverbial rug from under you, it will. And the irony was that lockdown, a period in her life that had struck fear into the hearts of millions, was coming to an end, and this prospect terrified Gina.

This meant getting back to a new kind of normal where Jimmy would be free to roam, unguarded, and that thought was killing her. And then she found the key.

A couple of Jimmy's suits needed cleaning so as she patted them down, ready to give to the laundry service when they called, Gina felt something in the inside pocket of his pin stripe. A Yale key. Attached was a tag and on the reverse a word – *alarm* – and underneath a number. She knew immediately where it was for.

The discovery had floored her, but she picked herself up, hid the key, then carried on with pretending. It had, however, affirmed her resolve that going forward, nothing could be left to chance and the best things in life should be grabbed and held on to so tightly your knuckles went white.

And that was exactly why for weeks, Gina had been keeping a close eye on the Young Farm, running past every single day, not taking any chances that *she* had snuck back into the country.

Gina prayed they'd never open the borders again, or that the farm would burn down so there'd be absolutely no reason whatsoever for any of the family to come back, least of all *her*.

In fact, in Gina's very unhinged moments, usually after she and Jimmy had made love and he'd slipped into sleep, she'd lie there, wondering if he had sex with Bella, if it was on the cards, and if they had, how she measured up. Sometimes Gina imagined what it'd be like to set *her* and the farm on fire, watch the glow as flames lit up the sky.

She'd planned it all, down to the finest detail. How and when.

She told herself that thinking about murdering someone wasn't a sin; only doing it was.

And sometimes as Jimmy snored the night away and the gloom of the wee small hours wrapped around her, dialling anxiety up, lighting the gas on her carefully concealed rage, she hated Bella Young so much she might actually be able to do it. Kill her, then everything would be okay.

Turning her gaze from the stars up above, she looked at Jimmy, watching his chest rise and fall, breathing in, breathing out, knowing underneath his T-shirt beat a heart she once thought pure. Maybe it still was. Which was why she had to protect their bubble. Nothing could be allowed to pop it. And once again Gina asked herself the question and dared herself to answer.

'Would you really kill for him?'

CHAPTER TWENTY

Of course she would. She was sure of it. She would smother that bitch in her sleep with her bare hands, then set her house on fire and destroy the evidence. It would be for the greater good, for her children so they'd never know the heartache of a broken home.

Nothing was too good for them, no act out of bounds. Max and Mimi were her life, her reason for being the best she could be, the antithesis of Debbie. And Gina was nothing like Don either, who didn't fight for his wife and child and instead just walked away. He should've forgiven Debbie for the sake of his daughter; put her before himself; been a better man, then Debbie wouldn't have cheated. He should have stayed.

That was why Gina was better than both of them because she would do all of those things for her children, anything at all. Even if Jimmy had cheated or continued to do so, she would put up with it, and fight to get him back with everything in her arsenal. She would never give in.

Everyone thought she was weak, but she wasn't. Gina knew how to take control, and proving her point, she never let her food-thing go so far it'd be a detriment to the children. See, that took strength.

The hidden stash of laxatives waiting silently in the spare room were her equivalent of diazepam. Just having them there, resisting their allure, was a feat in itself. Gina allowed herself only one dose to purge her body of every last ounce of poisonous food from her system, the process cleansing her mind, allowing it to focus on banishing the hunger pains.

Control and strength also came in the form of resistance. Fighting the urge to call her mother and build bridges. See if she'd changed, let her back in her life, see if Debbie wanted Gina in hers. But Gina had erected solid boundaries around her heart and was confident that giving even an inch would herald disaster. So instead of giving in to such urges, the sentimentality that had crippled her during the baby-blues, she overcame them. That was how tough Gina could be.

And then another thought surfaced. What if the end of lockdown was a turning point, the perfect time to change, act. Like the crest on her school blazer had reminded them every morning – *Carpe Diem*, seize the day.

Not just for Gina, either. For everyone. People like Robin, too. What if it was time to set her free. Tell her the truth, rip off the plaster, then open the doors of her cage and let her fly away. But where would she go, and who to?

Robin had made her life in Little Buddington so who was Gina to take a hammer and smash another woman's world to pieces. Robin was devoted to Willow and would never leave her. And to her marriage vows that she wouldn't break no matter how vile Eddie was.

He'd been responsible for so many down points in Robin's life. The way he'd shunned Tom and Cris and forbidden Willow to follow her vocation and then the things he said when she tried to... Gina couldn't think about all that, what happened. It made her so sad.

Focusing her attention back to Robin, Gina thought back to one Saturday morning, when she and Willow were helping dress the pews for a wedding. She and Willow had playacted walking down the aisle and even though they were having fun, two silly girls getting giddy, Robin had stopped what she was doing and ruined the moment. It was so out of character that it stuck in Gina's mind.

She stopped sweeping the stray buds and leaves from the aisle, a hint of melancholy in her voice. 'It's all well and good joking, but when it's your time to walk down the aisle, think very carefully about the words you're about to say before God, because if you don't believe in them one hundred per cent, or that you'll be able to keep them, don't even step through the church door. If you do... well, you'll have to live with the consequences in more ways than one.'

At the time, Gina and Willow just looked at each other, both a bit disconcerted by the sombre turn of events and while Willow rolled her eyes, Gina was glad when they were interrupted by the arrival of Mrs Hopper.

Gina always thought Robin meant they should take the day seriously, that it wasn't just an excuse to wear a beautiful white dress and have a party. But in the light of recent events with Bella and further back, Eddie and her mum, even Cris and Tom, she wasn't so sure.

Was Robin thinking out loud? Even though she'd made her solemn promise, what if it bound her to Edmund and deep down, she wished she could escape? Gina resolved to do a bit of digging the next time she saw Robin, see if she gave away any clues. Or she could ask Babs but without giving anything away.

The last thing Gina needed was Babs having ammunition to shoot dirty Eddie with. No, it had to be subtle. Babs didn't do subtle, not really. At least she was one person Gina didn't have to worry about because Babs was fine, thriving in fact. Still moaning about her lot but that was her way because she loved them all to bits.

Babs really was the perfect mother, everyone's rock, even Gina's. A role model if ever there was one.

———

Gina's ponderings were interrupted when she was brought back to the present by Jimmy who'd given her a quick nudge. 'Penny for them. You were miles away and you look cross... so come on, what have I done this time?'

She turned on her side to face him and he followed suit, their voices lowered so as not to wake the sleeping monsters inside the tent. 'You've not done anything, not yet, well, as far as I know.'

That little nugget escaped Gina's brain via her lips and seeing Jimmy's raised eyebrow she hurriedly explained. 'I was thinking about the past, Robin and Willow and that business with Cris and Tom, and how horrid Edmund is, and why Robin never left him. If you're really unhappy with someone you'd just go, wouldn't you? Like Don did when he caught Debbie. And surely, you'd be able to tell if your husband or wife fancied someone else. I don't know how I'd cope if I was in their shoes.'

Once the words were out she couldn't take them back or ignore the bemused look on Jimmy's face.

'Flipping heck, and there's me watching for shooting stars so I could make a wish and you're raking up bad history. Why *do* you do that Gina? Worry about the past, stuff that won't happen or happening to someone else. And I wish you'd stop letting the past drag you down. You have to believe in yourself instead of striving to be the opposite of your mum. You're not her and never will be. You can do or be anything you want. An independent, successful, confident woman if only you'd give yourself a chance.'

It was the last line that had Gina's hackles rising and the whiff of suspicion swirled around the garden like early morning mist. Why had Jimmy changed his tune? Weeks before he'd been happy with her domestic goddess status. So why was he pushing her to be independent? What had altered? Was he preparing her for the future, one where she'd have to manage without him?

It made perfect sense. The little ventures he concocted for her, having faith in her abilities when actually, he was laying the ground so she wouldn't be a burden. A gin-soaked social security scrounger with bad nerves. He didn't want to be forking out shedloads of money to his clingy ex-wife.

Gina's mind was on a roll, like one of those big cheeses they chucked down a hill and her insecurity was running like the clappers behind it. She was angry now but losing her temper wouldn't get to the truth. Resisting the urge to stomp inside, Gina forced a passive reply, while aggression pulsed through her core.

'I'm sorry, love. It's my default setting and you know what I'm like when things change and, let's face it, everything's going to alter next week. Max is back at school, you'll be out more, the world around us will start turning again. I've got used to it, being the four of us.'

'But surely you've missed seeing people, like Babs and your mum's-world friends, and Willow. Now the rules are relaxing you'll get to see other faces, not just this rather handsome and totally irresistible one...' He gave her one of his cheeky winks and stroked her arm as he spoke. 'So please don't have a wobble, Gina, because that'll spoil all the fun we've had and how happy you've been. Nothing major is going to change. I'll still work from home, but I also need to get back on site when building starts again.'

'And what about me?'

'What about you?' Jimmy looked confused and that irritated Gina. Everyone, including him was about to get things moving, picking up where they left off and that's what pissed her off the most. Who he might be picking things up with.

She couldn't show her hand though, so bluffed, kind of. 'Because I'm stuck in a groove, and I don't know how to get out. Whether to do the right thing for us, the kids, me. Will anyone be hiring right now? Boris wants everyone to work from home if they can... and the LAST thing I want is to catch the virus; and what about you? We've all stayed safe and now you'll be off gallivanting all over the show...'

'Gina. STOP!'

He paused, gave her the look he used when she worked herself into a tizzy about poo stains on the carpet or squashed, disgusting things down the back of the sofa and with the monsters, there'd been plenty over the years.

'I'm going to be extra careful. I'll be meeting clients outdoors, on site. I won't socialise. No taking clients for drinks or anything like that. It'll be baby steps and until everyone has learned to navigate through whatever post-lockdown looks like. You should stay here, where you feel safe and comfortable and then, when you're ready you can make the big decisions, or not. It's your call, okay? Now promise me you'll stop worrying.'

Gina watched as he pulled her to him, kissing her hands as he did so then wrapping her in his arms. With the warmth of his body against hers, his breath on her hair, for a moment, everything was all right. 'Okay, I promise. I'm sorry for... you know, being a stress-head.'

He pulled her closer. 'And no more apologies. Let's just lie here and enjoy this, watching the stars, the monsters sleeping, the simple things. Tomorrow can take care of itself.'

Gina nodded and snuggled closer, closing her eyes, and reassuring the crazy woman within. *'You're wrong. You're mad, too. You have to trust him. Believe in the Jimmy you love. Nobody could fake this, his words, holding me close, stroking my hair, making me feel good and safe. There is no Bella. There is no them. Just us, me, him, Max, and Mimi. Stop with this stupid paranoia and bloody daft plots. I mean, as if you'd actually kill someone. This isn't a book or a film. You're not a vengeful psycho. You're Mrs Gina Morgan who got into a tizzy so relax, remember to breathe in, breathe out... nobody is going to die... breathe in, breathe out... cos she's not coming back... breathe in, breathe out... it's all going to be fine.'*

CHAPTER TWENTY-ONE

BABS

Make hay in May for you may never know what June is coming with and you may never know what July will present! When you see May, make hay! – Ernest Yeboah.

Babs read the meme on her timeline and muttered to an empty kitchen, 'Talk about stating the bloody obvious!' Memes got on Babs' nerves. Especially those silently making a point, telling someone who'd pissed you off, that they had pissed you off, via a deep and meaningful passive-aggressive meme.

Attention seeking, that's what it was. Like poorly posts. They really did Babs head in because NO she did not want to see the pus oozing out of someone's in-grown toenail or know how many Lemsips they'd taken that day.

But what sent her over the edge were the pity posts. With the sole purpose of whingeing about something so trivial and banal and utterly, flagrantly desperate, that on many occasions she'd had to stop herself from bashing out a comment saying so. And then, the nosey buggers who couldn't resist the lure of gossip and wrote, *You okay hun? Inbox me.*

People needed to pull themselves together, focus on important things like... she looked around the kitchen at the morning mess, the Kellogg's box that some imbecile had ripped open and now the flap didn't close properly. And Pete, the general, all-round knobhead, had filled his mug to the brim and left a trail of coffee splatters from the kettle to the table. He did it all the time. The marmalade and Lurpak were still on the side. This would be Isaac, and yep, she knew it as soon as she looked inside, toast crumbs in the melted butter.

And what boiled her blood was that because they'd actually managed to wash their own dishes... big round of applause for the Finch family... the rest of the kitchen would somehow, as if by magic... clean itself.

Well not today, José!

Grabbing her keys, she called up the stairs to Demi who'd just come out of the shower and was therefore absolved of sin.

'Demi, do you fancy going out for breakfast?' Babs listened, a door opened and footsteps preceded a reply.

'Where can we get breakfast? Nothing's open yet.' Demi peered over the banister.

Babs loved it when she was in-the-know. 'Ah, well, that's where you're wrong because Costa drive-through has reopened so we can go there.'

'But, Mum, there isn't a Costa round here.' Demi moved to sit on the top stair, pulling on her socks as she spoke.

Babs smiled and raised her eyebrows. 'There is in Rhyl.'

'Rhyl! You want to go all the way to Wales to get a coffee and a toasted sandwich?'

'I most definitely do. And fish and chips later on, once we've had a wander along the beach and worked up an appetite. I'm going back to work soon, and I fancy a day out. Let's make the most of the new rules and freedom, not to mention some nice nosh. There was an article online all about how takeaways had thrived during lockdown and there's a list of places that are open and a photo of a chippy on the seafront at Rhyl. So come on, chop-chop.'

Demi laughed. 'Okay then, let's go to the seaside... shall I wake Sasha up?'

'NO! She's got online interviews this afternoon with an agency so she can stay here and bag herself a job. I'm not giving her any excuse.'

Babs was about to fetch her bag when a voice shouted, 'I heard that,' to which Babs replied, 'Good. So, get out of bed, lazy arse, and make yourself look employable even if it's from the waist up.'

Demi was grimacing, even though everyone knew it was true. Sasha was bone idle, like her dad. So without further ado Babs grabbed her bag, gave a jerk of the head in the direction of the door, and smiled as Demi's footsteps thundered down the stairs.

It'd been a spur of the moment idea to go out, but Babs was looking forward to a day by the sea with Demi. It would be a nice change, especially as she was dreading going back to work, out there again, in the land of cobwebs and loo brushes and germs that could be lurking anywhere. But she wouldn't dwell. Today was going to be a good day, hers, and Demi's. Then, before she closed the front door, Babs remembered something and popped her head back inside, yelling in her jolly-Mum voice.

'Oh, and Sasha, be a sweetheart and give the kitchen a once-over. Your father and brother left it in a right state. Ta-ra, love. Best of British with the interviews.' And on that note she slammed the door.

Babs sipped her coffee and thought about the meme she'd read a couple of hours earlier. If this wasn't making hay, she didn't know what was.

By her side on the sea wall, Demi chewed on her toastie, a photo of which had been posted on Snapchat, along with numerous shots of her vanilla latte and the sea that was currently so far out it looked like a pencil line on the horizon.

The pale yellow sand was dotted with walkers, yappy dogs, blobs of seaweed and a couple of brave souls taking an early morning dip. It was just gone 10am and already the sun was warming her face and as she closed her eyes, Babs breathed in the sea air and listened to the obligatory sounds of seagulls overhead. Today was going to be a good day.

'Do you want your muffin?' Demi gave Babs a nudge and was holding out the paper bag containing their breakfast feast.

Dipping her hand inside she pulled out the blueberry delight as Demi did the same and for the next few minutes they ate and people, dog and bird-watched in amiable silence until Demi asked a question.

'When are you starting work again?'

Babs puffed her cheeks and sighed, the whooshing sound as air left her lungs surprised even herself, like an audible clue to how she really felt at the prospect. 'I've got two clients booked in. Some haven't got back to me yet. They're probably a bit torn between having a potential germ-spreader in their home and wanting their house clean and germ-free. Imagine the dilemma.'

Demi raised her eyebrows, picking up on her mum's sarcasm. 'So, I take it you're not looking forward to going back to work, then.'

'Not really, love. But I reckon there's lots of people feel the same way, but I need to earn a living. Simple as that.'

'I'm really going to miss you being at home, and our walks

and exercise routine. It's been fun.' Demi continued to eat, her legs crossed, her eyes focused on the horizon.

Touched by Demi's words, Babs could feel a lump forming in her throat. For the past few months she'd thought Demi was just humouring her or joining the online classes out of boredom.

'Well, I have to say that's made my day, and so has this muffin.'

Demi laughed, then became serious. 'Why aren't you looking forward to it? You love your job and you've never complained and, let's face it, you can moan about everything lately, especially Dad.'

This observation took the wind out of Babs' sails. Was she turning into the grumpiest Mum in the world? Choosing to gloss over the 'Dad' comment Babs focused on work.

'I *used* to like it. Some clients more than others but over the years I've wheedled the annoying ones out so now I've got nice houses and nice people to clean for. I can't say it's my dream job though, or something I thought I'd end up doing. I suppose I just get on with it for a quiet life.' Babs put the last of the muffin in her mouth and chewed it and her words.

'So why don't you change your job then?'

Demi had turned to face Babs. She was being scrutinised which made her nervous and also, a bit ashamed by the truth of the matter.

'But what would I do? I've been a mum all my life and the qualifications I have just about got me into college to train as a nursery nurse. I only went there one day a week. The other four days were spent wiping bums and toddlers tears so not exactly a scintillating CV. Unless you add being a dinner lady, which I bloody loved by the way, and my current career.'

'So why did you stop being a dinner lady if you loved it?' Demi brushed her hair from her eyes and focused them on her mum.

Babs sighed. 'Money. Simple as that. It didn't pay enough, and we wanted to move house, so I got a job with a cleaning agency. Then the owner moved away and left her workers and clients in the lurch, so me and a couple of the other girls went solo. It fitted in with home-life and at first, I enjoyed being my own boss. Told myself I was running my own little empire.'

'You are. But what now?'

Babs chuckled at her own delusions of grandeur then shuffled, her bum was aching a bit, and she wondered how honest she should be with her daughter. Demi didn't need to hear how fed up she was. Then again...

'I hate it.' There, she'd said it, and before she lost the courage or the audience who for once, was actually listening, expanded on life in the World of Babs.

'I can't put my finger on what it is, who or what to blame for how I feel inside. But it's like all the things I accepted as part of my lot, aren't acceptable anymore which, as you just pointed out, makes me complain all the time. My age, the flaming menopause to be precise, isn't helping my mood swings which are worse than the pirate ship at the fair. The one Sasha was sick on, remember?'

The atmosphere lifted when they both convulsed into laughter, the carnage caused when a hot dog and a stick of giant candy floss made a reappearance all over the heads of anyone sat afore Sasha on the good ship Vomit. Never had Babs felt so ashamed when all the people got off, picking carrots out of their hair.

But as soon as it arrived, the mirth quickly vanished as Babs admitted how she felt. 'I just get so angry, Demi. About everything. I even get angry with myself for being angry. I hate the sound of my voice when I moan about three pairs of trainers being dumped in the hall and then I shout at myself for making a song and dance over nothing.' There was a lapse, while Babs calmed herself and held in the scream that would scare the birds and everyone on the beach if it escaped.

Her calming app advised that in these situations, she should breathe in for three, out for six, and one more time for good luck.

'I'm sorry, love, for the moaning and if you think I'm grumpy with you and your dad. So I'll try to keep a lid on it.'

'Mum, there's no need to apologise. It gets on my nerves how everyone takes you for granted especially Sasha who is a lazy cow, and our Isaac is just an embarrassment. I mean seriously, he'd rather live in a box room, with his girlfriend than get a place of his own! It's a joke.'

'And it gets on my nerves how Dad just expects. I mean I love him to bits I really do but he's got it so cushy. It's like the whole house revolves around him and he's got you train–' She stopped, her voice trailing off as one does when they put their foot in it.

'Go on, he's got me what? Trained.'

Babs felt the sting of tears and shame and wished it was colder so she could blame her watery eyes on the weather. Feeling the urge to walk, Babs stood and picked up the paper bag then set off along the beach trying to squash down the ball of hurt in her chest.

In fact, she had the incredible urge to run, and run and run and not stop. To switch off thoughts and sounds, even Demi who was behind, trying to catch up, calling out her name. And this time, instead of heeding her maternal instinct, the one she'd obeyed for years and years and years, Babs kept on walking.

CHAPTER TWENTY-TWO

When Demi eventually caught up, she pulled Babs to a halt. 'Mum, MUM!'

Babs turned, reminding herself of a surly child so not adding another fault to the growing list, tilted her head upwards to meet Demi's eyes.

'Mum, I'm so sorry. I swear I didn't mean it in a nasty way, or an insult to you because I think you're perfect, I really do. Please don't be angry.'

Babs shook her head. 'I'm not angry at you, love. I'm annoyed with me.'

'Oh God, I've made everything worse now. Okay, what I should have said is that Dad has got us *all* trained, with his chair that nobody is allowed to sit on, like he's the king on his throne. And the little things bug me, like we can't have cheesy pasta because the smell makes him sick and if we dare, you go round spraying air freshener like something's died and rotted under the table.

'He's in total charge of the remote and basically watches shite, I mean total mind-numbing crap. About mad old men persuading madder old men to part with junk they've had in their garages for 700 years! He sends us to buy you your presents because he "doesn't know what you like" when actually it's because his life revolves round football and pool and his mates. And it should revolve round you, Mum. You're his wife; you should come first, always.'

Ouch! That was all Babs could think and as she reeled from a verbal slap and the bitter taste of home truths, she took both of Demi's hands, and grappled with how to react to an accurate analysis of home-life.

'What on earth brought this on? It's not like you to be so... critical. I hope *I've* not been making you fed up, banging on because it's all part of married life, and after a while you just get on with it.'

Demi vehemently shook her head. 'But, Mum, that's not right. I didn't really notice or let it get to me so much before lockdown, until we were all stuck inside together. I suppose, it's because I'm at school, then get on with my homework wherever I can find some peace and quiet, and spend most of my time with earplugs in, mostly to drown out the sound of Sasha. Or I'm out with my friends. I come and go. We all do but the person who's always there is you. I've had time on my hands to think about it all and compare. See how not to end up. And I don't mean you, either I mean be like Sasha and Isaac.'

Babs was hurting because Demi was, too. But perhaps there was a positive in all of this. Demi was taking stock, learning from mistakes and at least in a warped way it'd make Babs' cock-ups worthwhile. Then something occurred. 'What do you mean, *compare?*'

Demi had the grace to look a bit uncomfortable and then explained. 'I compared you to my friends' mums. Lots of them have jobs, but they also do things, you know, by themselves, or just for them but you do everything for us and put yourself at the back of the queue.'

At this Babs relaxed a notch. 'For a minute I thought you might be ashamed of me...'

Demi didn't give Babs chance to continue. 'NO! I've never been ashamed of you ever, so don't think that for a second. I tell everyone what you do, all my friends know and I'm proud of you for earning your own money and running your business. I swear I am. And I'd rather have you any day, over anyone, and that's God's honest truth. You're my rock and I love you.'

Babs gave Demi a squeeze and held tight for a while, smiling when she released her.

'Well I'm glad to hear it. So basically, me being a pushover is starting to get on your nerves, is that it?' She received a nod, and reassured Demi with a nudge and wink. 'Well, here's the thing, I get on my nerves too, and you're right, it's got to stop, and it will. I promise.'

'Seriously? When, and how?' Demi didn't look convinced.

Babs wrapped her arm around Demi's shoulders as they resumed their walk.

'I haven't got a bloody clue, love. It's a work in progress. But I'm going to start by telling your dad that I'm definitely one hundred per cent not going on holiday with "the gang". They can sod off. He can go, and you can too. But no way am I sitting on a plane surrounded by God knows who or what, to endure another holiday with that lot.'

Demi stopped, then stared at her mum open mouthed. 'I thought you liked them!'

'I do not. They get on my wick. I asked your dad if we could go somewhere on our own, the three of us, and you'd have thought I'd suggested going to a nudist colony or something. Apparently it'd be "boring" with just us... me. That's what he meant deep down. It's me he doesn't really want to be with.'

Saying it, out loud to Demi and the seagulls actually hurt

Babs more than she'd expected it to, and that surprised her, that she cared.

Demi responded with a loud tut before falling silent as they continued along the beach, stepping over shallow pools, eventually breaking the silence. 'That was mean of Dad, and just so you know, if you don't go, neither will I. The "gang" do my head in too. They're just a bunch of posers.'

Babs giggled at Demi's analysis but before she could protest and insist Demi had a holiday, she was hit with a big question.

'Mum... do you love Dad?'

Demi kept on walking while Babs kept on thinking and then stalled for time. 'Bloody Nora, you're not holding back on the deep and meaningful today, are you?'

Demi didn't respond, and Babs knew she wanted an answer and it had to be the truth. Now was the time.

'Okay, do I love your dad? Truthfully, yes I do, but in the way you love a friend, someone you've known for a very long time. We're a part of each other's lives, bound together by you three, a house, a mortgage and a heap of bills and history. We plod along, we get by, we make it work. But it's not like it used to be and hasn't been for a long, long time. And that's sad, and I'm really sorry, because it's not how I wanted it to be.'

'Is that what you meant earlier, when you said you were fed up with your life... did you mean Dad, too?' Demi kept her eyes fixed on her trainers that were speckled with wet sand.

'Yes, I think I did mean that, but like everything else I've resigned myself to getting on with it because I never want to hurt him. No matter how unhappy I am. He might do my head in, but he's not a bad person. I don't even think he realises, even though I drop enough hints and as you say, grumble a lot. It's like he's tuned me out and I'm just background noise.

'He might even be putting up with me like I put up with him. So we need to work it out somehow, me and your dad, find our way back. It's as simple as that so there's no need for you to worry. It's just a blip that lots of couples go through, okay.'

They'd reached some wooden sea defences in the sand and ahead she could see the steps leading into town. Babs suddenly felt weary, maybe from walking but more from talking. And guilt, that she'd shared her innermost thoughts and feelings with her child. That was wrong. Demi didn't deserve that.

The urge to sit suddenly overwhelmed her so Babs unhooked her arm and instead of continuing up the beach, plonked herself on the wooden groyne. Demi followed suit.

'Anyway, enough about me. Today was supposed to be fun, not a therapy session, so we should buck up! Let's talk about something else, now.'

Nothing, so Babs soldiered on. 'Tell me, how do you feel about your exams, or should we say the lack of them. I hope you're not worried about school estimating your grades. You're the Finch family clever clogs, so I know you'll smash it.' Babs hoped her voice sounded confident and full of the joys of May and that her optimism would rub off on Demi when she replied.

When she did, Babs admitted defeat because her words were flat, flatter than a cartoon character being squashed by a steamroller. 'No, I'm not worried. I've worked hard over the last two years and my predicted grades are all elevens and twelves. Still, I'd have liked the opportunity to show what I can do in exams but it's not going to happen, so what's the point in moaning about it? I'm focusing on September now and going to college. I'll get my chance to prove myself when I do my A levels. So, it's all good.'

Babs was confused because Demi had it all figured out yet still sounded downbeat. She had to enthuse some excitement into her, and the day, otherwise they could have stayed at home and been depressed by Sasha, and her non-existent job prospects.

'And then in a couple of years you'll be off to uni. How exciting will that be? That's when the fun will really begin, and you'll be proper grown up. My last little bird to fly the Finch nest.'

As soon as she said it, Babs knew what Demi was going to say, just by the way she sat up straighter, and her shoulders stiffened as though preparing for battle. Demi turned her head, a steely look in her eyes, the question that came out of her mouth no surprise.

'And then what will you do, Mum? When I start my big adventure, what will happen to you? That's what I want to know and what you need to start thinking about. Because you can't go on like this; it's not fair, and it'll make me sad leaving you behind if I know you're unhappy.'

Babs was dumbfounded, just for a second or two, but shook away Demi's rather forthright words and miraculously found her own. 'So... what do you want me to do?'

A sigh, long and loud and probably borne from sheer exasperation, preceded Demi's reply. 'I want you to think about *your* future, Mum, not mine. I've made my plan. And I'm sure as hell going to stick to it and not end up like Isaac the mardarse-saddo or Sasha the professional layabout.

'I want you to be happy, in any way that makes you smile and feel fulfilled and to do it for yourself, not us and *certainly* not Dad because he will always look after himself first and foremost.'

Demi took her mum's hands in hers and held them tightly. 'The thing is, I've had time to think about everything. Not just you and me. About how our lives changed over the last few months. We lost control. Were forced to stay home and do what Boris told us to. It made me realise how quickly life can be taken away, and how plans got trashed, and everything we took for granted became something we missed and craved.

PATRICIA DIXON

Simple stuff like seeing our friends and family. Can you believe that?

'I watched you. Saw how you started to change. You kind of glowed, like you were free to be you and jiggle about the front room in your pink pants and that bloody rainbow headband.

'You made rules and actually got our lot to do their bit. You made new friends online and it's like my mum found her confidence again. I don't want you to lose all that now you're going back to work, back to being the "before Babs". Does that make sense?

'So after all this lockdown madness has faded away and we get back to normal, I want you to promise you won't fade away or lose momentum. And talk to me, about anything. Will you, Mum? For me, for us both.'

Babs nodded and sucked in a breath, begging the tears not to flow but they did because Demi was right, and also, because she'd never loved her girl more than in that moment. Pulling herself together she nodded. 'Okay, I promise. In fact, I'm going to ring the doctor and get an appointment because my mood swings are dreadful, and I've tried vitamins and herbal tea, but they aren't working. I have to be proactive if only about my health and bloody sanity! And best of all I have an ally,' Babs clung onto Demi's hands.

'It'll make me stronger, having someone to talk to when I have a wobble, and by that I'm not talking about my bum.'

This made Demi smile, at last.

'But it's not right, is it? I'm your mum and I shouldn't burden my child. I feel so bad for bothering you. I'm sorry, Demi, I really am.'

Demi whipped her hands away and rested them on Babs' shoulders, giving her a stern look as she spoke. 'Stop that right now! I mean it. You've been there my whole life and now it's my turn to be there for you and, I'm *almost* an adult, so I'm allowed to give you advice and support. And even though I don't want to share *my* innermost secrets with my mother, we can still be friends, you know.'

Babs merely nodded.

Demi gave her a wink. 'Good, so it's a deal. We go into the future together and one way or another whatever is in store we'll work it out, fight the good fight and all that.'

'Deal.' Babs leant forward and hugged her wonderful daughter, not caring who walked by and saw them.

Demi broke away first and stood, holding out her hand to her mum. 'Right, Ma Finch, I think that's enough soul-searching for one day so let's walk up to the harbour and look at the boats and ooh, what about the miniature railway... Remember, we used to go on the trains when we were kids. Let's go see if it's open.'

Babs did remember, like it was yesterday.

Standing, she rubbed her achy knees and then brushed down her jeans while Demi took photos of a seagull resting on the rocks, ignorant to the fact he would soon be a Snapchat star.

The ping of her own phone told Babs she had a message so pulling it from her bag she checked the screen. Perhaps it would be Sasha saying she'd bagged the job as head of the BBC. Anything that would make three years at uni, debt, and a media degree worthwhile. Instead, she saw Gina's name appear and read the words underneath.

> Hi, just checking in. Do you know what day it is? It's the anniversary. Should we do something? Go see Robin and Willow. Let me know later on. We can call this evening if you want. No pressure. G x

She'd forgotten and Babs immediately felt dreadful. Reading the words again, and despite the seriousness of her conversation with Demi, thinking of Robin and Willow and how they would be feeling brought her situation into sharp perspective so without hesitation, she sent a message straight back.

> If Robin says it's okay I'll come with you. In Rhyl at the moment. Will be back early evening. Let me know what time. Babs x

Shaking off the cold hand of sorrow that had settled on her shoulder, Babs grabbed the warm hand of her daughter and as they stepped over the groynes and headed up the beach, gave thanks for all she had, and for the future Demi had before her. Babs then painted on a smile and put the visit to Robin's on hold.

The next few hours were for her and her own little girl, making special memories they could keep forever.

CHAPTER TWENTY-THREE

ROBIN

Robin watched from the bedroom window as a trickle of parents and children walked past St Mary's, heading into the village towards school. It was such a shame, though, that so many others were missing out on their education, a proper one, instead of being taught remotely at home.

It was driving Nate mad because the college where he worked was like a ghost town and he missed teaching real students in the classroom. It was the same for Arty in France and even he was missing 'the little buggers.' Maybe soon all the children could go back. Robin hoped so.

She wondered what was going on in the heads of the adults who held the hands of their children. She managed a smile for those who might be glad to have their little darlings back in the classroom. And then her heart constricted, the familiar sense of loss when grief reminded her of all the things they'd miss out on. Like holding hands in the rain, wellies splashing in puddles as they raced to school, trying to beat the bell.

May 12th. Today was a turning point in so many lives as lockdown began to ease yet Robin had already faced up to the stark reality that for her, life would stay the same. She came to this conclusion at 6.08am when she heard the hum of the milk float, and then a whistle as Bobby trudged up the path, the bottles clinking as he deposited them on the step. She'd closed her eyes, not wanting to face the next twenty-four hours, or see the date on the calendar that was pinned to the kitchen wall.

Today was Maya's anniversary.

Moving away from the window, Robin let her gaze fall on her sleeping daughter, and she felt grateful for her current state of oblivion. She'd brought her a cup of tea, as she did each morning, knowing it would go cold and she'd make another later, but routine gave Robin comfort. It saw her through the day.

Before she left the room, Robin paused by the dresser and rested her palm on the little white box, then moved silently away.

As she closed the door behind her and made her way downstairs to the empty kitchen, she wondered if there would ever be a turning point in Willow's life. A turning point that would confound all of them so they could laugh in the face of fate, who'd been so cruel, callous in the extreme.

Sometimes Robin couldn't bear to think of that day and then other times, she found herself going over it, reliving each moment for no other purpose than to see it clearly. Accept that as much as she wished it, there was no going back. Instead, they had to live and cope with the consequences. That and caring for Willow. It was her job as a mother and one of the things you do for love.

In the quiet of the kitchen, only the sound of a ticking clock, out of love and respect to her granddaughter, Robin remembered.

It happened in the centre of Macclesfield. Robin and Willow had taken Maya into town for a spot of shopping and some lunch. It was a mild day in May. Cloudy overhead with a hint of sun. Maya was four months old, and they took turns pushing the pram, a trendy thing, light and easy to manoeuvre. They'd had such a lovely time and were on their way back to the car park when Robin remembered she needed some bread. After spotting a bakery she left Willow and Maya on the main street and nipped inside.

She heard the sirens approaching as she waited in the queue, there were two people in front of her. The clock on the wall told her it was 2.58pm and as she glanced at the pastries inside the glass cabinet, decided to buy some for Edmund and Nate.

One more person in front, the sirens were getting closer, so she craned her head to look for Willow, but she was out of sight somewhere further along the street window shopping.

By the time the sirens were on top of them, the wailing piercing ears and brains, Robin had reached the front of the queue and was about to be served when it happened. The dreadful screech of tyres, the sound of metal hitting metal, screams and the thud of something ploughing into brick, the shattering of glass and then more screams.

She could still hear them, every time she thought back to that day. At some point as she rushed onto the pavement, terror gripping every part of her body, Robin's screams merged with those of the onlookers and pedestrians who'd managed to dive out of the path of the speeding car.

The car that had skidded out of control during a police chase, the spaced-out teenage driver careering through the metal fence by the crossing, then into anyone who was standing on the other side. It came to a halt in front of the newsagents.

Robin knew. Knew instantly when she saw the crumpled

lump of metal impaled into the smashed shop window, saw the bricks and glass scattered everywhere.

Because what she couldn't see was Willow's face in the crowd or hear her voice calling out, telling Robin she was okay. Her legs ran, into the road and around the scene of carnage to the other side. Even though she knew she screamed their names, all she heard was a pounding in her ears so fierce that it drowned everything else out.

Then she saw it, Maya's upturned pram pushed against the crumbling shop wall, and then a flash, the horrific image of it flying through the air before it came to land.

From that moment, everything happened in slow motion, as Robin dragged her eyes towards Willow's legs protruding from a coat, a huddle of strangers kneeling by her side, two women sobbing into their hands, the yellow and black of police officers rushing, pushing, shouting to the crowd and into their phones.

The sight that met Robin when she reached her daughter's side was lost in a black hole. It swallowed her whole and in some ways spared her from the true horrors of that scene.

But Willow hadn't forgot. And neither could she forgive herself for surviving, for not taking the impact and saving her baby, for standing where she did and not getting out of the way in time.

Robin knew, because Willow had told her, many times in the hours when she held her daughter tight, during the longest days and nights. That Willow wished she'd died too.

Unlike Edmund and Nate, Robin understood. Because there'd been moments since, during what felt like a hundred years had crawled by, when she wanted the same. And, had the devil approached her first, before he took his prize, Robin would've willingly offered herself in Maya's place.

Hell held no fear, not when you'd watched your child suffer the way Willow had, still did.

Robin was also no stranger to guilt, regret, deep remorse, and such immense frustration. The shopping trip was her idea. Had she not gone for bread, had the man in front not wanted his ham slicing thinly then hummed and hawed about pickle or salad cream, had that stupid woman not counted her change onto the counter like there was all the time in the world...

Each time she trod the path of memories that brought them to this point in their lives, seeing it in snapshots, turning each one over in her head, the guilt and the outcome remained the same.

Willow wasn't physically damaged; she escaped with cuts and bruises from flying debris, but her mind, that was a different matter. She never recovered.

A trigger was pulled, a bullet loaded with pain had exploded inside her head and the blast shattered her psyche into a million pieces. Fragments of happy memories floating beside the most sordid images. The remnants of her life broken beyond repair. Haphazard thoughts colliding with confusion. Deep sorrow bouncing off atoms of despair. Shards of anger slicing through the darkness. Blinding flashes of hate, then an explosion followed by the boom of loss.

That's how Robin imagined the turmoil in Willow's head. A burning star cascading across the universe, screeching through the atmosphere before plummeting to earth.

And she'd vowed to catch Willow whenever she fell, and she had, a few times.

Standing, Robin wearily took her cup to the sink and began to wash it, her eyes focused on the bubbles, her mind lost in the past.

Nate had done his best, to help Willow amidst his own grief. Then as weeks turned to months it became clear that whatever had lurked within Willow for so long, had her firmly in its grip. Nate was struggling to cope with her night terrors and the rages where she would attack him or try to hurt herself, pulling at her hair and scratching her skin.

Most of the time, she was silent and wouldn't eat or speak, let alone wash. Robin had done her best, gone round every day. Encouraging, praying, silently raging inside.

And then in the early hours of a Tuesday morning, Robin took the call from Nate. He was panicking because Willow had disappeared. He'd woken to find her gone, the duvet pushed back and when he ran downstairs the front door was open, the car missing from the drive.

They'd found her eventually, or the police did, sitting on the motorway bridge ready to jump. It took over an hour to talk her down. When the marvellous, kind young officer finally managed to coax her into taking his hand, then into the back of the ambulance, Willow's fate was sealed.

CHAPTER TWENTY-FOUR

Willow spent six weeks in hospital. The longest of Robin's life. Imagining her child with strangers, disorientated, frightened. Her little girl alone without her mum, the person she had relied on since birth. It felt like she'd lost Willow, as well as Maya.

Shuddering at the memory she grabbed the tea towel and began to dry the pots on the draining board, remembering the day they were allowed to visit. She and Nate had gone alone. Edmund was appalled that Willow would even consider taking her own life, which he saw as a sin.

Robin could still hear his words that night, as the ambulance sped into the distance. Each syllable burned into her brain, repeated as an excuse when he refused to visit her at the hospital.

'I can't bear to see her right now. What she was about to do, it goes against everything I believe in. Everything I've taught her. She knows that life is a divine gift, to value and respect. No human has the right to take his own life or the life of another. I am so thoroughly disgusted and disappointed with her.'

During the first visit, Robin and Nate may as well have been invisible, ghosts chatting to another ghost, a faded grey image of the Willow they knew, who didn't even acknowledge their existence. Instead she stared out of the window, silently mouthing the words of a conversation nobody else was privy to.

Slowly, though, they made progress and little by little Willow had come back to them. She smiled occasionally, ate food of her own accord, remembered how to wash and dress, it was progress. And even though Willow was not whole, not Robin's technicolour, vivid child, she was a child who was present, who Robin could touch and hold and comfort. She hadn't lost her.

They still weren't out of the woods, not by a long chalk. Willow was diagnosed with persistent depressive disorder, or dysthymia, a continuous long-term chronic form of depression.

While Robin had sat there stunned, the consultant explained Willow's condition succinctly and as he spoke it was as though her young life was laid before them, but a different version than the one Robin remembered. Like she was seeing it all again through new eyes, acknowledging and ticking off the symptoms one by one.

'The patient loses all interest in normal daily activities, feels hopeless, lacks productivity, has low self-esteem and an overall feeling of inadequacy.'

That was an accurate description of Willow since Maya's death, followed by a sobering warning.

'These feelings can last for years. This is a major depressive disorder also known as clinical depression, and it affects how one feels, thinks, and behaves and can lead to a variety of emotional and physical problems. She may have trouble doing normal day-to-day activities, and sometimes may feel as if life isn't worth living.'

A flashback to seeing her sitting on the motorway bridge had chilled Robin's blood, and she silently vowed to never let Willow out of her sight again.

From what you've all told me, I suspect that Willow's depression began in her teens and early twenties, but it could have struck at any age. From the notes provided by her GP and those from the university practice, my team have been able to piece together how her condition may have gone undetected or certainly diagnosed incorrectly, for years. However, the medications she has taken intermittently over the years strongly suggests she's been struggling for a while. This has been corroborated by the therapist she saw at Cambridge who was most helpful, while adhering to patient confidentiality.

The slap in the face stung. Flat palm, full force, on target.

Robin had no idea, and neither did Nate who sobbed in his chair, inconsolable in his own shock and grief and whatever else he was feeling at that moment. Robin asked herself one question: why didn't she notice?

It was so obvious, all the things she'd put down to teenage angst or premenstrual mood swings, being highly strung, overly sensitive. It was always there.

The consultant then reinforced his theory with facts Robin knew to be true.

However, factors that seem to increase the risk of developing or triggering depression include certain personality traits, such as low self-esteem and being too dependent, self-critical, or pessimistic, and more recently a traumatic or stressful event and the death of a loved one.

Oh yes, Willow was dependant all right. On everything Edmund had forced down her throat since she was old enough to understand his rules, his ethics. The most critical man on earth, who expected everyone to meet his high standards. Robin and the children included. Willow had strived to impress him, seeking his praise and when she failed it was as though she'd failed in a world that was too dark for her, too hard.

An example sprang to mind of how Edmund's behaviour hadn't helped their daughter's hidden low esteem and over-critical nature. Willow studied theology and the philosophy of religion at Cambridge, coming out with a very decent 2:1 even though Edmund had grumbled that with her background it should have been a first. Robin was astounded and wanted to throttle him, then push him in an empty grave that had been dug for a funeral.

When, after her graduation, Willow announced that instead of teaching she'd set her sights and heart on becoming a priest Robin rejoiced. Although her dreams had been denied, the door to the priesthood was now open to women and Willow had the chance.

Oh, the irony. Of having a daughter so devoted to the church, her beliefs, and her parents only to be lumbered with a father who couldn't see past his own bigoted ways and ambition; was totally incapable of supporting or allowing Willow to follow her vocation. And hell hath no fury like a vicar scorned.

Edmund was and remained firmly against the ordainment of women into the priesthood, as was the bishop and his cronies. Therefore, Willow's intention would have placed Edmund in a wholly disagreeable position. How could she do this to him?

Robin had taken Willow's side, told Edmund to back off. But Willow wasn't strong enough to stand up to him, to reap the rewards of her hard work and devotion, to follow her vocation.

And Robin had been weak too; should have done more, but what?

In all of it her greatest regret was not realising how fragile Willow actually was. Not until the consultant had laid the past bare, and shown Robin every single sign she'd missed.

And then, what could be worse than the trauma of losing your baby, right there, in front of your eyes?

Erasing that image, Robin decided she needed something to do, to keep her mind and hands busy until Willow woke, so chose ironing, fetching the basket of laundry where on top lay one of Nate's work shirts.

When Willow was discharged, she and Nate had moved into the vicarage. It was the best solution. Away from Maya's bedroom where Willow would sit for hours in a trance, holding the little casket of ashes in her arms, or sobbing until her eyes were so swollen she could barely see.

Robin couldn't bear it. Where had her happy little girl gone? Who embraced each day like the start of a great adventure. She loved the snow, thunderstorms, the seaside, singing hymns, swinging higher and higher at the park. She loved school, her teachers, Gina, all God's creatures.

Why had Robin not seen the shadows? Because to believe in God, should one not accept that the devil exists. That he lurks in those dark recesses of our souls, in our subconscious, waiting for his chance to strike, to creep in unnoticed and take a prize. And what a prize, a child of God, a wannabe bride of Christ. The devoted, the pure of heart, the daughter of a vicar.

The shadows must have crept in when Robin wasn't looking, at first, perhaps manifesting themselves in sorrow. When she was eleven, Willow found a dead sparrow in the garden and couldn't understand the cruelty of the cat who'd mauled it, or the mummy bird who'd thrown it out of the nest, and why God or Jesus hadn't saved it.

Robin had tried to explain the circle of life, that it was nature's way but for days Willow sunk into herself, barely eating, staying in her room and being, as her teacher Mrs Turnock said, rather belligerent.

Then Willow emerged, a little sunbeam, as though nothing

had happened so Robin moved on, until the next time and the next.

It had been easy to put her mood swings down to growing up. Her intense reaction to a flood in Pakistan or an earthquake in Turkey would render her speechless, sucking it all in then spewing horror at the unfairness of it all.

Willow dealt with her confusion and disappointment in God's inaction by balancing it with action. Rallying Gina, making cakes, raiding their toys and books to sell on the village green, then donating the money to charity.

She always forgave God though, because of Edmund. Whenever Willow wobbled, Edmund via the power invested in him, would set her straight and because she was fragile, and needed strength, she grasped onto those words and assurances like a life raft. She became dependant on her father's every word and sought his approval and counsel above others.

While she waited for the iron to warm up, Robin experienced a similar warmth, the heat of her anger towards him reaching boiling point and had she a handy button to press, steam would be released from every pore of her body.

The steam, real not imagined, billowed around the ironing board as Robin set about the pile of laundry, imagining Edmund's face each time she pressed down really hard on Nate's shirt. Even he had succumbed to the legacy of tragedy.

He was pulling away from his marriage, closing down his feelings for Willow, and Robin understood why. The wife he knew was no longer there. Then other times she was so angry with him, for giving up because he had. Robin saw it in his eyes. It was so sad. The loss of love, hope, a future, their child.

Wiping her brow, Robin could feel herself descending.

Focus on good things... for pity's sake.

Okay. She was blessed to have some good friends, people she could rely on. Like Francesca who'd drifted out of their social circle many years ago but had, in her way remained useful as an alibi for when Robin met Arty.

Edmund always thought Francesca trite, and probably never gave her a thought, which was good. Sandra Dee's sidekick now lived on a residential caravan site in Tenby with her third husband who grew marijuana and did a bit of this and that. At least Francesca was happy, and high, by all accounts. They kept in touch by texts and the odd phone call but hadn't seen each other in the flesh for many years.

Then there was Gina, who used to visit Willow often. Reading to her, or they'd watch television, an old *Friends* box set was their favourite. Sometimes they'd go for a drive and a walk around the park if Willow was up to it. Robin adored Gina.

And Babs. An absolute diamond, her chatter and positivity lifted Robin up. Her little whirlwind, whooshing in, full of gossip and funny family dramas. Robin envied Babs, with easy-going Pete and her feisty brood who she adored and cared for like a clucky hen. And her big summer holiday with her group of friends where they drank and ate too much and lay by the pool doing bugger-all. It sounded like bliss.

But Robin also had things to be grateful for. A roof over her head, food in the cupboard, her health, because all of those, placed her well, allowed her to dedicate what was left of her life to Willow.

And that was where she was. While everyone else was getting to grips with the new way of the world, she would simply nurse her child. Forever. And that word, was like a punch in the gut.

Did forever also mean her and Edmund? Fighting the good fight. Her against him. Separate. No longer a team. The only reason she slept next to him was because all the bedrooms were occupied, and she needed to hear Willow if she called out.

Robin eyed the pile of ironing and realised that she didn't

just miss Babs' incessant chatter; she missed her housekeeping skills, too. And she realised how mind-blowingly sick she was of the vicarage, and Edmund, and that she missed Arty so much, too much.

She needed company, not just a chat and a glass of wine at the graveyard wall with Babs, surrounded by bones and headstones.

And Facetime with Cris wasn't enough, either, because she wanted her son there, not a thousand miles away because his father was a pious arsehole.

She needed... something, anything to break the monotony of being her. A glimmer of hope for Willow. To see Arty's face and be able to touch it, touch all of him. Was it too much to ask? Maybe for a bit of help, even a miracle.

When her phone began to vibrate, a text message pinged onto the screen. Squinting her eyes she read the name. It was Babs, being Babs, lifting a wing, offering a place of safety to nestle on the hardest of days. A friendly ear and a hand to hold if she needed one. They would be round later, her and Gina, if that was okay. If she wanted company.

As tears blurred her eyes, Robin typed a message back, one simple word.

Yes.

AFTER

14 months later
July 2021

CHAPTER TWENTY-FIVE

GINA

The sound of Henry the Hoover being dragged along the landing should have made Gina smile, but it didn't. Neither did the sight of the tea tray, laid out with the biscuits she got in especially for Babs.

She'd thought having her guardian angel-cum housekeeper back would be a source of comfort; the familiarity of Babs' presence and their easy routine had always been so.

Instead, it had heralded another era. A new order in their lives where most of the restrictions had been lifted and they'd been told to get on with their lives – and Jimmy had. Out the door like a rocket and eager to get back on track. And she could understand why he and much of society were embracing their re-found freedoms after the most dismal of times.

Parts of the country had been put into bands, forced back into isolation and when that didn't work, everyone endured a stripped-back Christmas and two more lockdowns. Who could blame anyone for wanting normal? Even she did, would, if it hadn't been for her discovery.

Her dogged determination to seek the truth and obsessive desire to prevent a catastrophe went hand-in-hand. You couldn't have one without the other and she wished she could've turned a blind eye, feigned ignorance, and carried on regardless of what her gut was telling her.

It started just after Jimmy began venturing out, the odd trip into the city for a socially distanced meeting, more frequent site trips in the open air. But for the main, he kept his word and worked from home and Gina was able to breathe, believe that it was going to be okay.

She'd monitored the news channels for the whole of the previous year, rejoicing when travel corridors were closed and most of Europe swapped and changed lists, green to red, amber to green. Gina would've been glad if all of the world had been painted red, and a barrier of barbed wire erected around the coast of the UK to keep everyone out, especially anyone returning from Italy.

And she'd got her wish, the big man upstairs had been listening but now, thanks to vaccinations and PCR tests, the populous was on the move and inevitably, one in particular headed in her direction.

Gina had been vigilant on all fronts. Making the home a happy loving place from which no man would wish to wander; the bedroom, where she put a concerted effort into ensuring all of Jimmy's needs and desires were met.

In between ring-fencing her life, Gina ventured out every day to patrol the perimeter of it, running along the lanes, circumnavigating the Young Farm, checking for signs of life.

The day she saw the car on the drive Gina thought her legs were going to give way. She steadied herself on the stone wall, sucking in air, trying to still her booming heart. Bella was back and even though common sense told her it could be anyone, a neighbour checking the house, a relative staying over, Gina knew. It was on the fourth day she saw her with her own eyes, for sure, no doubts at all, as Bella came out of the front door, tanned and looking radiant as she unlocked her car then zoomed up the drive.

Gina had panicked, thrusting herself into the undergrowth and crouching behind a tree, feeling foolish as she scrunched her eyes like a seven-year-old playing hide and seek. But it wasn't a childish game and as she stood, brushing dandelion fluff from her legs, and ignoring the sting of nettles on her hands, she was overcome by a sense of foreboding, ignoring the voice of reason that told her she was overreacting.

NO, I'M NOT!

The threat was back and so were every single one of Gina's demons.

That had been two weeks and five days ago. The text came three days after she'd seen Bella at the farm. A simple missive but enough to trigger what Gina imagined a cardiac arrest to be like.

She'd been checking Jimmy's phone and emails ever since she'd been alerted to the threat, and because he trusted her far more than she trusted him, she had access to his laptop and phone. Gina was nothing if not rigorous and methodical in her snooping which she carried out when Jimmy was in the bath. He loved a good soak did Jimmy.

So, while he and Alexa whiled away an hour, Gina snooped and like every stupid person gone before, was ridiculously unprepared for the moment they actually found something earth shatteringly, chest crushingly, incriminating.

> Hi, I'm back and tentatively wondering if you want to pick up where we left off. Still up for it if you are. No pressure. I'm back in Blighty for the foreseeable. You know where I am. Ciao for now ;)

> Hi, I was wondering if I'd hear from you. Welcome back and yes, I'll come over as soon as I can get away. Sooner the better. I'll be in touch soon. J

And there it was. Proof she hadn't imagined it. Proof that he'd been biding his time for over a year. Proof that Gina had been nothing more than a convenient stop-gap and source of sex and entertainment while he waited for his lover to return.

What a mug she'd been. *The sooner the better.* Christ, he was gagging for it and yes, her husband knew where Bella was all right... two point seven miles up the road. Ready and willing to show him what he'd been missing.

As she'd sat there on the swivel stool, staring at the phone which lay on the kitchen island, Gina swooned. The floor flipped, the edges of the room blurred, and invisible hands gripped her throat preventing her from breathing. Cold dread engulfed her body and in the midst of pseudo heart failure, all she could hear was Jimmy singing in the bath.

By the time he wandered back into the kitchen, having learnt how to live with the fear and knowing how to mask the stain it left behind, Gina faced his deceit head on, the only way she knew how. With more of her own.

Slipping his phone into her pocket, out of sight until she could stuff it back down the side of the sofa cushion where she'd found it, Gina sucked in air and steadied her trembling body.

'You okay? You look like you've seen a ghost. You haven't, have you?' Jimmy pulled his robe tighter around his body and feigned a terrified look, then made his way to the fridge.

'No, course not. I think I'm getting a migraine and came over a bit queasy, in fact my period's due, so it'll be that. I think I'll have an early night.' Gina slid off the stool and tested her legs. Yes, they still held her up.

Jimmy prattled on. 'So, you won't fancy a beer... shall I make you a brew?'

'No, no it's fine.' Gina spoke to his back as he grabbed a mug, and flicked on the kettle, her voice trailing off as she threw his phone onto the couch then made her way towards the stairs, not wanting to look at his face or hear his voice for a moment longer than necessary.

'You go to bed, love and I'll bring one up, and some toast to settle your stomach... take a paracetamol, there's some in the cabinet in the bathroom.'

She heard the fridge door open and the sounds of rummaging as he raided the shelves for his obligatory pre-bed snack. He was totally oblivious to his wife's true state of distress as she wearily climbed the stairs.

That night Gina didn't look in on Max and Mimi or remove her make-up and brush her teeth. Instead she dragged off her jeans and climbed straight into bed not caring if her bra was uncomfortable and her T-shirt would make her hot. She just wanted to sleep. Close her eyes and then maybe in the morning it would all be...

Don't be so ridiculous. It's not a dream and it won't all be better after a big sleep. You're not a child so face facts. It's all going wrong, and you know what? It's going to get a whole lot worse.

CHAPTER TWENTY-SIX

THE STOMPING OF BABS IN HER SLIPPER-CLAD FEET AS they made their way back down the stairs forced Gina out of her maudlin state. She plastered another fake smile on her face, however, she'd forgotten that today's masterclass in 'let's pretend' wasn't for her distracted, randy husband's sake. She had a rapt audience and, as always, Babs didn't miss a trick.

As she wiggled onto the spinney-stools, as she called them, and rested her *very weary feet*, Babs gave Gina one of her looks and wasted no time in explaining it.

'So, what's up with my Skinny Minny? I can tell something's bothering you and if I'm not mistaken you've been crying...' Babs then cast her eyes downwards as if giving Gina time to think, taking the pressure off while she busied herself with the wallpaper and fabric swatches scattered across the island.

Gina scrabbled for something to say, anything but the truth.

'Ooh I like this one, it's got sparkles. What's it for?' Babs held up a square of wallpaper, flock embossed with gold.

Glad of the momentary diversion, Gina explained. 'I've been asked to prepare a mood board for my magazine editor.

She has a friend in London who wants her whole house redecorating and she put my name forward, but I'm not sure if I want the commission, even if I get it.'

A half-truth would have to do because Gina had already decided she wouldn't take the job. Would not be going to London on the train and staying overnight or meeting the client for dinner. In fact, the whole lot was going straight in the bin as soon as Babs went home. She hadn't even told Jimmy about it because he'd be mega enthusiastic and shuffle her out the door like a shot so he could have a night with shag-bag Bella. She wasn't stupid. Well, she was, but not a total pushover.

Babs helped herself to a chocolate covered marshmallow and began to unwrap the foil, then gave Gina a bemused look. 'Why on earth not, love? It'd be lovely to get out and about, especially a trip down to London. And I thought you were looking for a bit of part-time work when Mimi starts nursery. This might be perfect for you.'

Gina sucked in a deep breath and forced down the swell of panic that the mere thought of leaving the house, the village, Jimmy, the kids, brought on. However, in a rare moment of clarity, or perhaps for want of a better excuse, she made a confession to the only person who she thought would understand.

'Yes I was... but I don't think I'm ready, you know to get a job and face people and I'd worry about germs and being around strangers, so I think I'm going to email her and tell her to find someone else...

'... and anyway, why do I have to go to work? Jimmy said I don't. Not yet, so there's no rush, and these are just a bloody waste of time...' And before she could stop her hands from scraping together the swatches, or the tears and the sob that escaped as she strode over to the bin and stamped on the pedal, she'd stuffed them all inside. Seconds later she was back at her spinney-stool.

Silence descended as she accepted the tea towel Babs offered, and while she wiped her eyes, wished she could stop bloody crying and erase the mess in her head by telling someone about her Jimmy. But once those words were spoken out loud they would sound the death knell on their marriage, of that Gina was convinced.

'Gina, love. Hey...' Babs reached forward and took Gina's free hand. 'I get it, I really do. I was absolutely blooming terrified of going back to work in case I got the dreaded virus. And if it hadn't been for the fact I'd have looked like a bloody Teletubby, I'd have bought some paper overalls. But I'm getting used to it now and if you're sensible...'

Gina cut in, shaking her head as she spoke. 'It's not just that, though, Babs. It's me, how I feel inside. About leaving the security of home and being away from the kids. I don't have the confidence to go out there to meet new people. I can't do it. I know I can't.'

Babs let go of Gina's hand and paused for a moment before asking a question. 'Do you think you've got claustrophobia?'

For a second Gina was non-plussed, then realised. 'You mean agoraphobia... I don't think so because I can go to the shops and out for a run... but sometimes I have to force myself out of the door so who knows. I *might* be getting it.'

It then occurred to Gina that it would actually be a solution, to be afflicted by the same condition her bone-idle mother pretended to have. But never, ever, did she want to be likened to that waste of space no matter how desperate she became.

'I don't think so, love. It sounds to me like you're suffering from lack of confidence, and I reckon lots of people will be feeling the same right now.'

Gina nodded whereas Babs was on a roll and settling into counselling mode.

'Okay, then. Tell me what you *want* to do. What your plan for the future would be if you could concoct one.'

I'd want my husband to not be having an affair. To love me like he used to do and for Bella Young to fuck off back to Italy and never come back. Or die. Yes, actually I would want her to die.

Instead, she looked straight at Babs and said, 'I'd want to be just like you.'

'Me!' Babs' hand flew straight to her chest, a look of utter surprise transforming her previously worried face. 'Why on earth would anyone want to be like me?'

With the attention on Babs, Gina was able to relax slightly and leant forward, resting her elbows as she fiddled with the soggy tea towel. 'Because you're the best. The best mum and wife, and friend. I've known you almost all my life and to me, you're like a shining example of what a proper mum should be. You've always put your family first and worked around them and they love you for it. So if I could be someone, I'd be you.'

'Aw, love, that's such a nice thing to say, I've come over all of a do-da now.' Babs fanned her cheeks as she spoke, 'But, love, I'm not perfect or a shining example, that I can promise you.'

Gina shook her head. 'To me you are. You know, when I was growing up I used to pray, I mean really pray, that you'd adopt me, and then I could live at your house because I loved going there. It was a proper home, my idea of family life and I was always so happy when for whatever pathetic reason she gave, Mum asked you to babysit. I remember feeling light as a feather when we headed to yours for tea, and like a lump of lead when it was time to go home.'

'Oh, love, I never knew that. You poor bugger. But there's always room for one more round my table especially if it's you... and not one of our Isaac's bloody annoying girlfriends.' Babs winked and then grabbed the tea towel to dab her leaky eyes, her remark somewhat lightening the mood and jollying things along.

Just like good mums do, Gina thought.

'But you can't waste your degree and all that hard work, staying here for the rest of your life. And you're so talented, Gina.'

Babs turned and waved her hand around the kitchen. 'Just look how beautiful you've made this house and I've seen your lovely sketches and mood board thingies on your laptop, and what you can do with a tatty old cupboard is amazing so please, don't give up. Give it some time and some thought. Maybe once Mimi is in nursery you'll get fed up with just having me for company and be climbing the walls, desperate to get out. And please, don't end up like yours truly, a grumpy old nag, Mrs Frustrated Finch who's left it all too late.'

The best Gina could manage was a weak smile, and then something occurred. 'What do you mean, *frustrated*? And what have you left too late? I thought you were happy running your little cleaning empire around the Finch family. You've never said otherwise... I mean yes, I know you do grumble about them *a lot*, but you're only joking because you love them really... and you always seem so fulfilled. Busy but happy.'

Babs regarded Gina for a moment and looked deep in thought, as though she was pondering how honest to be but when she rallied, it was to give support and a bit of a confession.

'Yes, I am busy, but I can't say I'm fulfilled and that's my point. I did what I did for my family, my babies, and my husband. I made a home they'd want to come back to, food they liked to eat. And I'm proud of all that, and being self-employed, and knowing that my clients need me as much as my family do. I work hard and don't have a bad life, but lately I've had a bit of a wobble of my own and thinking a lot about the past and where it might have gone wrong. Things I could have done differently and funnily enough, how I can change the future. You know, perhaps do a few things just for me.'

This revelation had taken Gina by surprise and hadn't turned out to be the security blanket or get out of jail card she'd been expecting. 'I didn't know you felt like that, Babs... so what would you like to do, you know, if you could? Because maybe I can help.'

'Oh, love, you've done enough already, especially pointing me in the direction of all those online classes and groups and this job, because you pay me above and beyond what the others do. And all the little treats you sneak in over the year. Like those gorgeous candles that make this place smell like paradise, and the bits and bobs you reckon you ordered by mistake and can't be bothered to send back, that always seem to fit me just right, or that lovely posh bedding that you weren't keen on when it arrived.'

Gina just smiled, knowing she was busted.

'You look after me the way a daughter would and do it in a way that's kind and sensitive, and that means such a lot to me, it really does.'

Sometimes, it was best not to say anything, and Gina knew they were in one of those moments so let Babs continue. At the same time, she calmed the swell of love that threatened to burst its banks and leak from her eyes.

'I've made a bit of progress, even during lockdown which is a miracle, because I'm fitter, healthier and a bit happier too. I've made lots of new virtual friends who I chat to all the time. I'm in book groups, cookery groups, menopause groups, exercise groups, cute pet owners groups, you name it there's a group for it and I don't feel so alone now. But I don't want you or either of my girls feeling like I have, so we need a plan, and you need to speak up more about what's going on in your head, and then I can help you, okay?'

'Okay.' Then a question pinged into her head. 'Babs, why are you in a cute pet owners group? You don't even have a pet?'

Babs chuckled. 'Oh, that's just a technicality, love. All you needed to join was your pets name, so I made one up and boom, I was in. Then I found a lovely kitten photo on Google and bunged that on the comments. Everyone loves Poppet, that's her name and I love looking at all the lovely animals and their funny stories.'

'You're potty, you know that don't you.'

'Yep, and an imaginary pet kitten called Poppet is loads easier to look after than a real one!' Babs winked and shuffled off the stool then made her way to Gina, wrapping an arm around her shoulder, pulling her close. 'There, at last, I got a smile out of you. So now, my little bag of bones, can we make a pact?'

Gina relaxed against Babs shoulder, enjoying the warmth of her body and the embrace. 'Oh, oh. Should I be worried?'

'No, love, it's nothing bad. I just want you to put any ideas about going back to work on the back burner for a bit because you're clearly not ready. But you do need to talk to your Jimmy and tell him how you're feeling and... I think this is going to be the toughest one of all, we need to get to the bottom of why you're so thin because I was shocked when I saw you.'

Oh, the shame. That's what Gina felt in that moment, about it all: her life; her failure to keep her husband, to be a good enough wife and lover, to conquer the demon that was eating away at her flesh; and causing Babs distress.

To the request, Gina could only nod. Signing a pact in silence.

'Right then. Now, I'm going to hoover the lounge while you, my love, are going to make us a nice butty for lunch and while we eat, we can have a good old natter and see if we can't cheer ourselves up. How does that sound?'

'It sounds like a great idea. I'll get cracking and rustle up something nice. I'll surprise you.' For this she received a peck on the forehead before Babs bustled off, humming something unintelligible and tuneless, yet surprisingly upbeat.

Babs' pep talk still hadn't lifted Gina's spirits and neither would a sandwich that she'd have to force down and dispose of later. A natter, the diversion of picking apart Babs' unfulfilled life wouldn't solve her problems either.

Gina knew what was happening. Her life was unravelling and so was she. She had to find a way to stop it. And it had to be soon.

CHAPTER TWENTY-SEVEN

BABS

Seeing as she'd only had Gina's house to clean that day, and in a determined effort to stick to her healthy living regime, Babs had decided to walk there and back. September had brought with it an Indian Summer and as a consequence of the chat she'd just had, Babs was glad of mild weather and the time alone to think things through – not just the pickle that Gina appeared to be in, but the predicament she was wallowing in, too.

As she walked, Babs unwrapped a Mars bar. It was important to keep her energy levels up after a vigorous morning of cleaning and a long walk home.

While she ate, Babs' thoughts returned to Gina who'd definitely benefit from a Mars bar, in fact a multipack because from the look of it, she was struggling with her eating disorder again. It was such a shame, that every now and then it surfaced and for the life of her Babs couldn't understand why.

Even though they'd known each other so long, and Gina was more like family than a friend, there were just some things she felt were out of bounds and that was one of them.

Babs tried to think back to the last time she'd seen Gina so thin, and it must have been before she was married. Yes, that was it. During her pregnancies she'd been a picture of health and really did blossom, but that was because she put her babies before herself. The poor lamb did fall prey to the baby-blues but after that she'd seemed fine.

For some reason, every time Gina should have been happy, for instance before her wedding, something caused her to self-destruct and ruin what should be a happy time. It had been a lovely day especially because Demi had been a bridesmaid with Willow, the chief. And thankfully, they'd not had to endure Edmund officiating because that would have made Babs sick, seeing that hypocrite join Gina and Jimmy in holy matrimony.

Babs had been worried that having him do the honours would be a curse, yet Gina had unwittingly saved the day by insisting he came as a guest and asked her old university chaplain to do the honours. She was a lovely lady, who made everyone smile all though the service and many of the parishioners, who sat near the back, were heard to comment what a breath of fresh air it had been. No bloody wonder!

Sometimes Babs was really pissed off with God, who she didn't actually believe in, because he needed to get his finger out and do nice things for the nice people.

Realising she was wandering off subject, Babs refocused. It was the image of Gina nibbling at her sandwich that set more alarm bells off, and Babs had wondered whether Gina had kept it down once she left.

Might it be worth ringing Jimmy and having a discreet word with him. Surely he'd noticed how frail she looked. He was such a lovely man and devoted to his wife and kids so Babs couldn't fathom why he'd not acted because anyone could see Gina looked ill. Then it dawned on her.

Oh no. It couldn't be that, could it? That Gina was proper poorly, with something terrible and that's why she'd been crying and couldn't tell Babs because it would upset her, or they hadn't had the results yet. All that about not wanting to go back to work was a smokescreen to avoid the truth. It was obvious now she thought about it.

Please let me be wrong, please let it be anything but that. You're putting two and two together, so stop it. It's not that, it's her eating disorder and you're blowing everything out of proportion as usual.

But what to do? That was the biggie. She needed to speak to Jimmy, it was as simple as that. One way or another she had to say something and if it meant poking her nose in or hearing something dreadful, then so be it. She would ring him later, once she'd got home and sorted out whatever needed doing there. Feeling relieved she'd made some kind of plan, Babs scrunched up the Mars bar wrapper and popped it in her bag, then pulled out a bottle of water and took a gulp to steady her nerves. Fortified, Babs picked up the pace and strode on as her thoughts turned to home and her current dilemma.

It had been a huge shock when their Sasha actually managed to find a full-time job, working at an online call centre. The only problem was that the call centre was situated in her front room, or the kitchen, or Sasha and Demi's bedroom, wherever it was quiet. Hence, Babs' dream of having an empty nest, even for a few hours a day wasn't going to happen anytime soon.

Then there was the 'Fiona' problem because even though it was July and there was no real reason why she couldn't go back home to her parents, there was no sign of her budging.

To be fair, having Fiona live with them had been a revelation because over the past few months she'd shown herself to be a lovely person. Devoted to Isaac, and willing to do her bit around the house, a hard worker, too. She'd been putting in extra shifts and from what Babs had gleaned, was saving the extra she earned for a deposit on a flat.

Sometimes, Babs had guilty thoughts that Fiona could do better than Isaac and for a mother to think that of her son must surely be some kind of sin, if you believed in all that malarkey. It was true, though, because she'd had time to observe her work-shy, self-obsessed ungrateful son. Unfortunately, in Fiona, Isaac had found another willing servant, albeit thirty years younger and a lot more attractive than the one he'd trained up since birth!

That's what really irritated Babs. Not that she'd been replaced, in fact she was relieved yet at the same time, she'd begun to feel protective over Fiona. She didn't even mind her calling Isaac 'Zac' anymore. In Fiona, Babs saw an eager young woman trying ever so hard to be the perfect girlfriend, potential spouse, good daughter-in-law; and it made her feel so bloody sad.

Or was she just projecting her own insecurities and frustrations onto someone who was happy being them? After all it was Fiona's life and Babs had no right to interfere or judge. But she couldn't help herself otherwise Fiona would end up with a Pete-clone for a husband, and Babs wouldn't wish that on anyone.

Pete. Now there was where the true, deep-rooted problem lay and as she passed St Mary's, glanced across in the hope she might spot Robin. Babs had to wrestle with a choice – to think about her husband and their marriage or stuff it into the recesses of her handbag with the Mars bar wrapper and the spare Twix she carried for emergencies.

It was too late, the niggle had been set free and was determined not to be ignored so with a sigh, Babs gave in.

They were at the end of the road, her and Pete. There was nothing there. They may as well have been brother and sister.

Siblings who annoyed the hell out of each other but would come to the rescue out of familial duty and love. The kind of love you have for a friend, not what you should have for your spouse.

Did she feel sad? Yes.

Did she think it could be salvaged? Maybe.

Did she want to try? No.

And that was the shocking crux of the matter. That over the past months, in the weirdest of circumstances Babs had begun to find herself. She used to think that saying was cringey, but it wasn't, because she and many other people did get lost.

Lost in their lives, their jobs, buried under paperwork and piles of ironing, dirty nappies, and potato peelings. Beneath the duvet they wanted to stay wrapped in all day, hiding from the black cloud that hovered over their heads because they'd simply lost sight of themselves and a way-out sign.

Babs was desperate to find the exit.

Pete wasn't a bad person; he was just selfish and ignorant. He loved his kids as long as they looked after themselves and didn't expect anything from him apart from a Christmas and birthday present. Pete wanted to live life his way and was happy to let you live yours as long as it didn't interfere with his.

In his head he was an easy-going, good bloke who provided and therefore deserved. On paper and to his mates, down the pub, at pool and football, he passed the test; whereas if anyone asked Babs, she'd say he'd failed miserably.

And lately he'd become a bit mean. Babs was the catalyst, she accepted that. But how she was, how she felt, was not of her own making. It was the consequence of a chemical imbalance going on inside her body, something she had no control over. It hurt like mad that he didn't understand that. He hadn't even tried to.

Babs saw the menopause as nature's cruel joke. When you're little more than a child, menstruation hits – and in her case it really did feel like a curse having to endure painful periods for years. So your body is preparing, becoming a useful vessel to procreate. Good job, well done.

And then suddenly, your body and the universe no longer needs that magical part of you and all those hormones that kept you useful for half your life start to leave your body.

With no regard, or respect, you begin to dry up like an old crinkly leaf, not just your skin on the outside, but on the inside too. Your bones shrink and crumble, and just for a laugh, a cheeky encore in case you're not already truly pissed off with life, nature sends you half mental, too.

Not that she'd said all that to Pete, but she *had* tried to explain to him how she felt, that she was struggling with her mood swings. That it wasn't her fault if she disturbed him in the night after a hot flush, then had to get up and have a shower and change her nighty in the middle of winter.

Or that sex was really painful and made her sore for days after, and it wasn't that she was going off him either. She wouldn't want to make love to anyone, not even George sodding Clooney! He'd taken the huff over that, not the sex bit, the fact he never knew she fancied a man she was never likely to meet, ever. Let alone drag him under her second-hand duvet set.

His answer to her problem was simple – go to the doctor and get some pills. Apparently he'd heard about them on the radio, while he was driving. There was stuff for women like her and it worked wonders. Thank you, Dr Pete, for that kindly given advice.

Babs power-walked along, the anger at remembering the conversation fuelling each stride. Well, unbeknown to dear well-informed Pete, Babs had finally seen the doctor, a very nice young man with a kind face and manner that she'd actually burst into tears in his surgery, such was her relief at his understanding and sympathetic nature.

And yes, Pete, she had in fact got something for women like her and gradually they'd made her feel so much better, inside, and out. Not that she had any intention of telling him that because there would be no more bunk ups, not with Pete and if she was honest, not with anyone. Hanky-panky was the last thing on her mind. What took precedence over everything was what to do next, about her life, the future and Pete.

CHAPTER TWENTY-EIGHT

THEY WERE IN THE KITCHEN. SHE WAS SEATED AT THE table while Pete made himself a pre-tea ham sandwich and Babs feigned interest in what he was saying. She was more interested in not smudging her nails and admiring the cherry blossom pink varnish that Fiona had bought her. Currently Babs had very nice nails and she was determined to keep them that way. She'd bought extra thick Marigolds for that very purpose.

'So I said to Calvin, "Calvin mate, we need to get this holiday thing sorted whether Barry and Sheryl want to go or not. Just because he's too scared to go I don't see why we should be penalised."'

Pete looked at Babs who stared back in belligerent silence but still he ploughed on, ignoring her lack of input.

'Anyway, Calvin said he agreed with me and after what we've all been through lately, especially the likes of us key workers, we deserve a bloody good holiday in the sun and he's right. So he's going to have a word with Barry and see if he can persuade him and if not, ring the travel company and see if he can alter the booking... Babs, are you listening?'

After replacing the brush inside the varnish bottle, she

began turning the lid, screwing it on tightly as she looked up and replied. 'Yes, I heard you, but you obviously didn't hear me the hundred times I told you that I'm not going on holiday with them ever again so, could you tell Calvin I want a refund too. And one for our Demi.'

The slam of the knife as it hit the worktop cut through the silence that followed her statement that was met with a look of horror from Pete.

'Why do you insist on being awkward? I thought you were just having one of your narky days when you said you didn't want to go. What the hell is wrong with you? We need a holiday, Babs. Surely you can see that. It'll be good for us.'

A minuscule glimmer of something ignited in Babs heart because it was the first time Pete had alluded to there being the need for anything in their marriage, that he might want to sort things out even if she didn't. Or could she still be persuaded?

'Okay, then tell me why it will be good for *us* and why you think we need a holiday, then I'll consider it.' Babs blew on her nail polish while she waited, knowing that Pete was under stress, desperate to pitch his jolly-bob dream and win her over.

'Because... because it might cheer you up and now you've lost a bit of weight you'll enjoy a dip in the pool with the others rather than sitting by the edge and not joining in. I know you don't like wearing a bikini, but you could get a new cossie.'

He was putting the butter back in the fridge so couldn't see the look of thunder on Babs' face, the fool.

'And you don't have to cook either, and you're always complaining about making tea...' he was floundering and as far as Babs was concerned had more or less drowned and still, in his last breath there'd been no mention of how it would be good for *them*.

She could sense him racking his brains when they heard the

front door open, followed by the appearance of Isaac and Fiona, abruptly ending the conversation and saving Pete's skin.

Ignoring his stupid flustered face that she wanted to slap and resisting the urge to ram the ham sandwich down his throat, Babs walked out of the kitchen and into the hall where Fiona and Isaac were slipping off their shoes.

'Hi, Mum, where's Dad? Dad, can you come into the lounge...' As Pete appeared holding his sandwich and as always, no plate, Isaac then shouted up the stairs, 'Sasha, Demi, come down here will you, me and Fiona want to tell you something.'

Seconds later the Finch family were all gathered in the lounge while two thoughts ran through Babs' mind. One of them was good. The other, she wasn't sure about. Holding her breath, she sat next to Sasha and opposite sat Demi on the armchair that didn't face the telly while King Pete was firmly ensconced in the one that did.

Holding court in front of the fireplace was Isaac, who was holding hands with Fiona, both wearing stupid grins on their faces.

'Right, fam. We have something really exciting we want to tell you all...' Isaac left a dramatic pause which was filled by Sasha.

'You're moving out, at last, hurray, now can I go back upstairs?'

Isaac scowled. 'No, it's not that...'

Bugger, thought Babs. So, it had to be the diamond ring option but before that little gem had time to settle, Isaac blurted out his news.

'We're having a baby!'

They were once again settled back on their respective perches, with Demi being downgraded to the pouffe when Pete told her to let Fiona sit down. Not for one nanosecond did Babs expect him to offer up his smelly old chair. He was now looking decidedly peeved because he was missing *Deal or No Deal*, and even mouthed, 'When will tea be ready,' out of sight of the happy couple, obvs.

He'd seemed genuinely chuffed at first and had hugged Fiona and shook Isaac's hand. Babs had joined in with the whole family as they'd clapped and whooped and shown their happiness. Yes, of course she was pleased for the two of them and Fiona, bless her, looked radiant and nervous all at once during the announcement.

And it was always lovely having a new baby in a family but there were so many questions buzzing around in her head which resulted in what the kids called her 'mithered face' and Demi had noticed.

Leaning forward she whispered over the hubbub of Sasha oohing and ahhing at a grainy image of a blob. 'Mum, are you okay? Try and smile a bit or they'll notice.'

Babs immediately tensed and felt guilty so took Demi's advice and made the effort.

'So, you'll have to get organised now you've a little one on the way and for a start, I don't think three of you will fit into that box room. Unless you get bunk beds!' She thought that sounded okay, jolly but with a hint of sensible, until she noticed a quick exchange between Fiona and Isaac, then wasn't so sure.

'Flipping heck, Mum, talk about dropping a hint! We will be out of your hair eventually so don't worry, but we were hoping we could stay on here while we get organised and find somewhere suitable.'

Isaac was perched on the arm of the chair and slipped his arm around Fiona protectively, the word 'eventually' causing alarm bells to ring, and she was about to say so when she saw Fiona give him a nudge and a nod. In the direction of Babs. *Oh, Oh.*

'Anyway, we have been making plans and thinking through our options before we told you the news, especially for when the baby arrives. Fiona wants to go back to work as soon as possible because we'll need two wages coming in to have a decent standard of living so...'

Two sets of eyes were firmly locked onto Babs whose feeling of dread was far worse than anything she'd experienced during the menopause.

'We were wondering, seeing as private childcare is so expensive, if you would look after the baby during the week and instead of paying a nursery, we'd pay you.'

They were both still locked on, expectant faces waiting for Babs to burst into tears of joy at being given this unexpected honour. So when she remained silent, the awkward void was filled by Pete, who'd suddenly turned into Granddad of the century.

'Well, I think that's a brilliant idea, don't you, Babs? I mean as long as it's equivalent to what you earn now the advantages are obvious. You'd not have to clean other people's houses anymore, thank God, and you'd be here all day and get to put your feet up a bit. Sounds like a plan to me.' He looked rather pleased with his erudite appraisal of the situation, and so did Fiona and Isaac until Babs opened her mouth to speak.

'And what's wrong with cleaning people's houses?' She glared at Pete but didn't give him the chance to answer. 'And what's all this "thank God," malarkey? As far as I remember you've not done bad out of my job that you're suddenly looking down on. The job that's took us on holiday for the last umpteen years, and Christmas and birthdays and other little luxuries that your wage alone doesn't run to. So before you go making me redundant, I'd like a bit of respect and a say in the matter, thank you very much.'

A beat of dumbfounded silence was followed by Pete blustering his way through what was never going to be an apology, it wasn't his style. 'Bloody hell, Babs... I didn't mean... there's no need to take the huff...'

It was Isaac that helped him out, as usual. 'I don't think Dad was putting you down, Mum. He was trying to say you'd get to spend quality time with your grandchild and get paid for doing it and he's right, in a way, it would be a nice rest from cleaning...'

'STOP.' Babs held up her hand like she was a lollipop lady halting traffic. 'Have you listened to yourself, Isaac? You're talking utter rubbish *and* I also object to you or your father taking it upon yourselves to plan my life and tell me what would be *nice* for me.'

The wide-eyed look and the O-shape of Isaac's mouth told her he hadn't, but for once they were all listening to her.

'Yes, it will be lovely to have a baby in the family and I'm very pleased for you both, but you seem to be missing the point. That it's YOUR baby, not mine so no, I don't want to look after it five days a week, to put my life on hold, or change it, just because you two want easy-option childcare on tap. And as for your ridiculous comment that it'll be a nice rest, you two have a bloody big shock coming if you think for one millisecond that looking after a baby is restful.'

Babs' cheeks were on fire, set alight by the rage burning inside that had whooshed up from nowhere, like a pilot light heating every radiator in the house. So, I'm sorry, Isaac, Fiona, but I've done my childcare shift, got the badge and the T-shirt and I have no objection to the odd night of babysitting, but no way am I looking after a baby full-time. So you're going to have to rethink your plans and just like everyone else who starts a family, take responsibility, work hard, save up, and get on with it.'

Fiona burst into tears at that point and Isaac stood, clearly annoyed or in shock, both sentiments reflected via the anger in his voice.

'Well thanks for that, Mum, for throwing cold water on what was a nice evening and ruining a happy memory because now you've upset Fi and basically told us you don't give a shit about your grandchild, or us for that matter. All we're asking for is a bit of help and support but that's clearly too much to expect...'

Babs had had enough. 'No, that's not what I said, and you know it, Isaac. But the thing is, I, we, have always supported you, and why you can afford your flash car and save up in your mystery bank account for a deposit that never materialises, oh, and live here for the bare minimum. So it's time to put your big boy Spiderman pants on and grow up!'

She chanced a glance a Pete who kept his lips firmly shut, no surprise there, so ploughed on. 'You're going to have to face facts, and your responsibilities and get on with being a partner and a dad. You can't stay at home forever so maybe you should flog your flash car and get a runabout, do extra shifts, cut your cloth, do without if need be. Just like me and your dad had to when we had you, but don't you dare say I'm not supporting you because this, what I'm saying now is support. It's a life lesson and it's been long overdue.'

'Bloody hell, Mum. Say it like it is, why don't you!' Sasha's folded arms and sulky face told Babs that her daughter had also taken on board some home truths.

Babs was in no mood for mard arses. 'Oh shut up, Sasha, otherwise it's your turn.'

Then she addressed Fiona, because she felt bad that she was upset so adopted a softer tone. 'And, Fiona, love. I think you'll be a fantastic mum and role model for your baby, and I do admire you for wanting to go back to work, I really do. But Isaac has got too used to living here, having everything done for him just like his dad and I'm just not prepared to do it anymore, so don't cry. One way or another you'll make it work and I am very happy for you. I really am.'

Fiona just sniffed and nodded in the uncomfortable silence, and Babs suddenly felt unwelcome in her own front room. Needing strength and support when it seemed like everyone around her thought she was selfishness personified, Babs looked over at Demi because she was losing her nerve. Tears threatened and everything, her whole life felt like it was about to blow up in her face.

Until Demi gave her a smile and a wink, and a silently worded message. 'Well done, Mum.'

Babs was in the garden keeping out of the way and intended staying there till they'd all gone to bed. It was still so warm, and she had her fluffy boots and her fleece to fend off the chill when night fell.

Opposite sat Demi, dunking her custard cream into a mug of tea, in between explaining the aftermath of Babs growing a pair. Just after Pete had asked what was for tea, to which he was told to piss off and fetch his own, and Babs had stormed out and zoomed off in her car, Isaac rang for a takeaway and treated them all to a Chinese.

'Well at least everyone got fed. Your gran made me a bacon butty.'

'Did you tell her what happened?' Demi wiped tea and biscuit crumbs from her chin.

'No, she thought I was just passing, and I didn't want to ruin things *again* for Isaac and Fiona. Is Fiona okay, by the way? I really didn't mean to upset her you know. I've actually got a bit of a soft spot for her. It was your dad and Isaac that riled me and I just saw red and lost it... and I could have said more but reined it in, somehow. I'm sorry though, for causing a scene and trashing their big moment.'

Demi stopped mid-dunk. 'Mum, don't you dare apologise. I was well proud of you for speaking out and our Isaac deserved it. And I think what you said hit a nerve with Sasha too.'

Babs watched as Demi continued to dunk, eat, sip, glad of her company and support. And it was true, because for a second, she'd been tempted to turn on Pete, tell him exactly what was going on in her head, but common sense prevailed and reminded her it wasn't the time. What she needed to say to him was private, between a man and a wife.

'Mum.' Demi nodded towards the mug of tea she'd made. 'Drink up, it's going to go cold.'

Babs did as she was told and picked up the mug, holding down the sigh that ballooned inside her chest, knowing that eventually she was going to have to go indoors and face them all, if not that evening, in the morning.

And there was something else she had to face up to. What the hell she was going to do about Pete, and when? Because if she was uncertain about many things in life, one thing she knew for sure that whatever it was, one way or another, it had to be soon.

Otherwise, she'd go down for murder!

CHAPTER TWENTY-NINE

ROBIN

WHEN SHE ENTERED THE KITCHEN, NATE WAS ALREADY there making coffee, looking smart in his habitual teacher garb, a freshly ironed blue shirt and black trousers with a razor-sharp crease down the front. And how nice, a jaunty yellow tie to bring a splash of jolly colour into a day, that for her was going to be anything but.

After a sleepless night she was mentally exhausted and physically drained, and surprised that her battery had just enough charge to generate anger and even a trace of sarcasm at the sight of him, acknowledging the intention of his attire. He had that 'new term' spring in his step and Robin was envious and irritated by his demeanour.

It had been a terrible night that leaked into the new day, where, for around four or five minutes that felt like hours, she, Edmund, and Nate had been trapped right there in the kitchen.

Willow had experienced a psychotic episode, heartbreaking to witness, painful to endure and once it was over, the struggle for power ensued. Not with Willow, but with Edmund who wanted to ring for an ambulance and the on-call team who cared for her. To him, having his daughter incarcerated was the answer to his problems.

Robin often imagined Edmunds of the past, watching from the step as their irritations were carted off in the back of a horse-drawn carriage to the lunatic asylum. Out of sight and mind.

Willow's episodes occurred rarely, mostly when the dose of drugs she took daily needed a tweak. Willow's mostly placid, locked-in state was replaced by mania and violent tendencies. Then, as with the previous evening, anything could happen.

Nate had come in late and had the shock of his life when Willow emerged from the shadowy hallway and tried to open the front door, saying that she was going to collect Maya from school, and she was late. When he prevented her from leaving she'd darted into the kitchen and tried to unbolt the back door. Nate had blocked her exit and without warning she erupted.

A screaming banshee was let loose, swiping everything off the work surfaces, dragging out drawers and upending them onto the floor and by the time Robin and Edmund arrived, alerted by the noise, Willow had found the cutlery.

That part Robin remembered in slow motion, as her screeching daughter grabbed a fish knife and began brandishing it at anyone who approached. If they attempted to get close she would press the tip against the vein on her inner arm, her meaning clear. Throughout Robin and Nate had remained calm. Edmund, lacking patience and irked at the inconvenience, could never relinquish the alpha male role, so took control.

Bellowing like he did when Willow was a child, as if she were one of Satan's demons, the look in his eyes betraying his inner anger, his voice pious and laced with threat, he pointed his finger.

This alone pinned his daughter to the spot while he commanded, 'Willow, desist.'

The word itself had made Willow gasp.

'You will stop this nonsense immediately, I mean it. Do not dare spill a drop of blood in your father's house, or so help me God you will be punished. Put down that knife, NOW!'

Robin gulped, her dry lips unable to form words, her legs and hands shook as she watched her daughter closely. Willow's glazed eyes were round with shock. Then a frown, a hint of confusion, and her lips moving as if conversing with someone unseen.

At the time Robin wished she'd grabbed a filleting knife so she could slice out Edmund's tongue and then the rest of his vital organs, until she realised that his words had actually registered with Willow who, miraculously did as she was told. The relief in the room was palpable when she dropped the knife like it was molten steel, looking at her hand in horror as though it was burnt and blistered.

Nate stepped forward, kicking it out of the way and as it skidded across the tiles, Willow sank to the floor in a heap, replete, covering her ears and began talking to her friends the angels.

'I'm sorry, please forgive me. Dear angel, hear my prayer. I'm sorry, forgive me. Dear angel, hear my prayer...' and so it went on, in a loop as Robin tentatively made her way towards Willow. There, she slid to the floor by her child's side, relief rushing through her body, legs grateful of respite, her heart rate returning to normal.

Maybe the notion that her actions would be punishable by God – Edmund's go-to method of parenting – had got through, somehow penetrated the ether and touched a nerve, reconnected a severed wire in Willow's brain. Willow had regressed, resembling an ageless, hunched and frail being, a little girl locked in a nightmare, totally lost. Robin wasn't sure where but ironically, she was glad of it when Edmund began issuing orders.

'Nate, ring for the ambulance, or whoever it is you need to call. She can't stay here like this. She's a danger to herself and us and, whether you like it or not, she needs professional care, not a nursemaid.'

Robin had heard it before, the derogatory tone in a comment directed at her but she was beyond hurt, by Edmund anyway, and stood her ground. Thankfully Nate sided with Robin who refused, and then forbade Edmund to call 999, reiterating that they'd weathered episodes such as these before.

Once exhausted Willow would sleep, sometimes for a day, maybe more, in which time her medication would be adjusted. Edmund, red-faced and knowing he was beaten had stomped off to bed, leaving Nate to clear the kitchen while Robin settled Willow in her own room.

Then throughout the night, a mother kept vigil over her daughter, fending off demons, especially the one known as Edmund.

As Nate buttered his toast, Robin sucked in her temper, resigned to facing the care team, the day ahead, her thoughts and anxieties alone. She was part irritated, part glad, but allowed the force with which she yanked the chair from under the table to express her mood. The ear-piercing scrape of the chair legs to speak her feelings.

'So, you're going into work then?'

Nate brought the coffee pot and his plate over to the table, then set them next to his bowl of cereal, taking a seat opposite. Evidently his appetite undampened by the predicament of his wife or mother-in-law. The look he gave Robin as he poured milk into his bowl was one of resignation.

'Robin, I can tell you're annoyed with me, but it's the start of the new term and an important time. Yes, I know that sounds terrible because Willow is important too but,' his shoulders sagged and he looked into his bowl as though it were a pit of doom, 'but I can't help her anymore. I wish I could but I'm sorry, I just can't. But I can help the kids I teach at college. Do you understand what I'm trying to say?'

Nate picked up his slice of toast then put it back on the plate, his shoulders slumped as he waited for her reply.

It was so hard, seeing it from everyone's point of view, exhausting. And Robin did see, especially when it came to Nate so softening her tone, she let him off the hook.

'Yes, yes I do understand, Nate, and I'm sorry for being snappy but I didn't sleep a wink. There's no need for you to be here today other than to give me a break but I might ask Gina if she can come over for a few hours, after the nurse has been. She'll sit with Willow, I'm sure, so don't worry.'

At this Nate brightened, like a kid who'd been told he could go to the party after all. 'I'll come straight home after classes and do any paperwork I have here. But we have student induction and I'm on the rota for some late-night courses so going forward...'

He halted when Robin raised her hand, not having the patience to hear more excuses. 'Nate, it's okay, just eat your breakfast. I'll cope.'

Silence descended, not exactly companionable but it gave Robin time to pour herself a coffee and a few moments to think before the peace was once more interrupted by Nate.

'What will you tell them when they ring?'

Robin bridled, sipped, then answered. 'The truth.'

'Even about the knife?'

She crossed her ankles because he could see all her fingers. 'Yes, of course. Otherwise, they won't get the whole picture and her medication needs to be right. I'm not stupid, Nate. And anyway, she didn't actually harm herself, did she? It was the heat of the moment and she's not done anything like this for a while, so there's no cause for alarm.'

Her mind replayed a scene she'd tried hard to erase, one where Willow had torn at her clothes and hair, banging her head so hard against the wall her face was covered in bruises, her skin left scratched and sore.

'Yes, yes you're right.' Nate then spooned in cereal, his brow furrowed and deep in thought as he avoided Robin's eyes.

While she drank her coffee she wondered what was really going on in his head and his life. So, when he swallowed and raised his head, she was somewhat taken aback to be given a rare glimpse. It set her hackles rising and warning bells went off in her head.

'Do you think, though, we might need to consider the future and what's best for Willow and you, all of us really?'

Nate's expression told Robin he was nervous yet there was something about the forthright way he'd delivered the question suggested he'd been wanting to ask it for a while, rehearsed it even.

Not missing a beat Robin retaliated. 'And what does that mean, exactly? What's best for all of us might not necessarily be best for Willow, so do expand. Get whatever you really want to say off your chest because I'm all ears.'

As he gathered his breakfast dishes and mug, then stood, Nate answered, hunched over the sink, hiding behind industry and the sudden need to wash the pots, quickly. While his hands scrubbed, he explained and with each word, Robin threw another dagger into his back.

'I mean that eventually, we'll need to make proper arrangements for Willow because you can't be expected to care for her long-term. It's unfair and it's putting a strain on your marriage and life, and if she's not going to get better...'

'She might. There are new drugs and therapies emerging all the time and she's only been like this for...'

'Too long.' Nate turned and appeared to have remembered he had a spine, which was now erect, his expression determined.

'I think we need, the two of us, to make an appointment with the consultant and have a proper face-to-face discussion about Willow's treatment and prognosis. This past year we've managed with Zoom meetings and phone calls and rare visits from the nurse, and it's not enough. We need to know if this is how it's always going to be, if there is actually another route we can take, trials, or even permanent residential care where Willow will get one-to-one...'

'NO!' Robin shouted the word, causing both of them to jump at its ferocity. 'No, I mean it, Nate, I will never allow Willow to go back into one of those hospitals. I couldn't bear it; it's cruel taking her away from home and putting her amongst strangers. Why do you think I literally dedicate my days to her? To prevent just that.'

When she noticed that his expression hadn't softened at her words, his shoulders remained stiff, his lips set in a line, Robin felt a trickle of fear down her spine. A firm voice in her head urged her to tread softly, with care.

'Look, I know you're worried and so am I. And I'm sorry for shouting but you have a lot on, with the new term and all the responsibilities that come with it so just leave Willow to me. I promise I don't resent you or Willow one bit. I'm glad to take the burden off so please, Nate, please hold off on making any decisions. We're okay as we are for now.'

A sigh, then he pushed away from the sink and grabbed his jacket from the back of the chair. His silence gave Robin hope, and a sense of relief that the conversation was almost at a close. She just had to bide her time and he'd be gone. Off to college and free from the responsibilities that having a poorly wife entailed, unshackled for a few hours from the chains of married life. All she needed now was his answer, then she could breathe.

'Okay, we'll leave it for now but one more episode like last night and we'll have to look at alternatives. For Willow's sake, if nobody else.' He picked up his bag from beside the table and was about to leave when he turned. 'I'm sorry if I've upset you, Robin. That wasn't my intention and please try to get some sleep today. I'll give you a call at lunchtime and see if you've had any joy from the care team.'

And with that he gave her the briefest smile and turned, leaving Robin alone with her cold coffee and a head full of thoughts; but if she'd hoped for a few moments to put them in order, she was sorely disappointed. As one problem left the building, another greater one entered the room. Edmund.

CHAPTER THIRTY

AFTER BRIEF MORNING PLEASANTRIES WERE EXCHANGED with Nate, Edmund strode purposefully into the kitchen and flicked on the kettle, occupying a minute or two with the gathering of pots and cutlery, setting them on the worktop next to the drainer. His silence didn't perturb Robin. It was nothing out of the ordinary in fact it was their ordinary, the way things were, and she was glad of it.

Had she not been tired and unsettled she might, as she'd done many times before, allow herself a smile at the ridiculousness of the scene. Acting like student flatmates who'd had a tiff the day before over something trivial, like not cleaning the communal bathroom, or taking the last of the other person's milk.

The problem, if it could be called that because actually, it was more of a status quo, was far from trivial. It was their lives and despite her stubborn determination not to budge an inch, Robin still had the common sense to see how sad it was, how futile and unnecessary being them had become.

Today, however, she had a feeling Edmund would have things to say because he couldn't bear being overruled and the events of the previous evening were about to be aired. When he'd finished making his cup of tea he turned and took the seat recently vacated by Nate. Not wishing to be lectured to, and wanting the upper hand, Robin pre-empted his opening line.

'I don't have all day and I need to check on Willow; then I have calls to make. So let's get it over with, I know you're dying to tell me where I'm going wrong and how it's going to be.'

The cafetiere was almost empty and its contents probably lukewarm. Robin was in dire need of more fresh, hot caffeine, but that would entail spending longer in the kitchen so instead she opted for the dregs. Robin poured, Edmund sighed, and then she listened.

'Willow is sleeping. I went in to pray with her and she was out for the count the whole time. Didn't even stir when I left, so we have time to talk.'

Hackles rising, the mere thought of him spouting his useless rhetoric ignited the desire for flight. Robin pushed back her chair, halted only by the first two words of Edmund's next comment.

'Nate's right, you know. We can't go on like this indefinitely and now we're getting back to normal it's time to think about where we go from here, with Willow. Last night was dreadful and it's clear she needs professional help around the clock.'

The coffee dried on Robin's lips as another wave of anger surged. 'Ah, so you've taken to eavesdropping. Typical.'

'I overheard as I came out of my study, and anyway, nothing he said surprised me because we've already discussed it at length, prior to last night's events. As I said. I agree with Nate and whether you like it or not, he's her next of kin, her husband and if push comes to shove, his wishes will take precedence over yours.'

With that, Edmund sat back in his chair and sipped his tea, eyeing Robin like she was prey, a hint of a smile on his lips.

His words had wounded Robin; how could they not? He and Nate were conspiring and that scared her.

I hate you so much. That was all she could muster, a thought so pure and true that each word stuck in her head, swam in front of her eyes, poisoned her blood. And still he continued.

'The thing is, Robin, this isn't about you, and your indomitable belief that you alone can care for Willow. It's about this family and whether you like it or not the situation is taking over all our lives and Nate for one, deserves a chance to live his, even if you've given up on yours.' His eyes fixed Robin to the spot while he waited, seemingly satisfied thus far with his analysis.

The word, when it burst from her lips came unbidden and possibly as an antidote to the fear that was infecting her heart.

'FAMILY!' She laughed out loud, then, and shook her head. 'What do you care about family when you've destroyed ours? You shamed Cris, then pushed him away once you knew you couldn't control him and as for Willow, she's been your pet project since she was a child, moulding her in an image you found suitable until once again, someone dared to go their own way.'

Her body visibly trembled as she spat her hate across the table.

'That was the cruellest thing you ever did, Edmund, using her love of *you*, her faith and loyalty and… and purity of soul against her. Taking away her dream of becoming a priest, a vocation that would've brought her great joy and maybe saved her from all of this…' She waved her hands around the room to signify where they were, their situation, and then she pointed directly at him. 'And saved her from YOU.'

Anger consumed Robin. Edmund merely rolled his eyes and then stood, made his way in silence to the worktop and began removing slices of bread from the bag then placing it into the toaster. The casual way he went about his task infuriated her as did his next words.

'Not that old chestnut again, Robin. I am beyond bored of hearing it and have no intention of raking over old ground when there are far more urgent matters to consider.' Then he turned, held up a piece of bread and asked, 'Toast?'

Robin scowled and even though her instinct wanted to storm from the room, it was also telling her she should stay. Discover what he and Nate had discussed.

Edmund tutted and shrugged. He pushed the lever down on the toaster. 'You'd rather wither away like a martyr to the cause than do something sensible like eat and stay healthy, or perform your parish duties, honour your vows and the promises you made to me when we were married. You're ridiculous. As is your desire to be Willow's saviour and out of selfish spite, your quest to punish me.'

Next stop was the fridge to retrieve the butter which he brought to the table. Robin watched and silently steeled herself for whatever came next.

'You don't see it, do you? How Nate is suffering. Because it happened to him too, you know, or have you forgotten that? He also lost his child, and as a consequence his wife,' he held up his palm, 'and before you put the same old record back on, it was not my fault that some drugged-up car thief ploughed through that barrier and killed Maya. So don't even think about laying that at my door, or anyone else's for that matter, apart from the scum who was driving.

'Since that day we've all grieved but we can't hold Nate prisoner here, waiting for Willow to get better when she won't. She's never going to be the woman Nate married, the daughter we knew, and you need to face up to that. Willow needs professional care, and we need to get on with our lives.'

When she stood, it was with such force that her chair

toppled over and when her palms slammed onto the surface of the table, the cutlery and china rattled, as did the whole of Robin's body. Rattling and shaking as tremors borne of sheer hate splintered through her body.

'And THERE we have it! This isn't about Nate, so don't you dare pretend it is. You're pathetic. This is about you wanting control and *your* life back to how it was, so you listen to me, Edmund, and listen well. If Nate is so unhappy and frustrated or whatever the hell it is that's bubbling under the surface, he knows where the door is. I don't need his help and neither does Willow. I'll manage just fine by myself and, for the record, if you think for one second that by shuffling Willow off to some institution, that I will just slot back into my role as devoted vicar's wife then you have a big shock coming... Do you hear me?'

She'd studied Edmund's face throughout and with each word his skin had moved through the colour chart from rose pink to puce and now, back down the scale to a funny white-grey.

Good. He was annoyed. Her speech had hit a nerve and boy did it feel good, so she carried on. Fatigue had left her without a filter, an unnecessary reserve that left the way clear for a green light and a chance to get it all off her chest.

'So, where does that leave you, us? I'll tell you, shall I. Those marriage vows you spoke of earlier go both ways and despite what you think, I do take my promises seriously, more so because I made them before God. The funny thing is, nowadays I just *love* that they serve a most wonderful purpose.'

She saw his eyebrow twitch, noticed the set of his lips drawn in a tight line, his jaw, his whole body tensed.

'You see, Edmund dearest. Those rules you live your life by, the ones in the Bible that you've turned into an instrument of control, to keep your wife and children at heel, will be your downfall because as you know, I would never divorce you. And even if you had the balls to divorce me, you won't, will you?'

It was her turn to smirk.

'For a start, what grounds would you have? Your wife neglects you, in order to care for her grieving, mentally ill child. She refuses to carry out her duties, in all areas, because she is exhausted, drained, traumatised, yet selflessly devotes herself to the care of her daughter. Won't you look like a good egg!'

And then she went for his Achilles heel.

'I mean, how disappointed would the bishop be? All that arse-kissing gone to waste. Years of yes, bishop, no bishop. And I'm sure your parishioners would be shocked and unsympathetic towards the man of God who even considered divorcing his poor, bereaved wife. Are you getting the picture, Edmund?'

At this point he rallied and stood to face her and even from the opposite side of the table, the wooden barrier between them, the salt and pepper pots standing guard, flanked by a pot of jam and two mugs, he still seemed to tower above her.

Edmund didn't need a pulpit to look down on anyone, a place from where to preach, it all came naturally.

'Where has all this come from? I *have* been patient. Allowed you to grieve and never once tried to force you back to work, expected anything more than you're prepared to give but enough is enough, Robin. Whether you like it or not we cannot continue as we are. You are my wife first, a mother second, and the vicar's wife third and I expect you to start behaving as such.'

When Robin threw her head back and laughed, the sound wasn't one of mirth, more like a loud crack that cut through the air like a fork of lightning.

'Expect. You expect. Well hear this, Edmund. When I married you I expected love, tenderness, kindness, passion, unity, hope even. But all I got from you was a sense of duty, and we all know who comes first on that list. You were the biggest disappointment, Edmund, but I got on with it. I tried and hoped that as time went by you'd learn how to love me properly, the children too, but I might as well have wished on a star because praying didn't work, and I prayed so hard for us, I really did.

'But it's no use. So somehow we need to get on with it, this life, our marriage, and in my case, looking after my child because I might have given up on you, but I will never give up on her. So, this is how it's going to be...'

Robin then turned and picked up the chair and set it straight before pushing it under the table, resting her hands in the cool wood of the frame, because what she had to say next, she had to get just right. When she looked up, Edmund was waiting.

'Remember that this is my home, too, even if it's owned by the church. And this is where I will stay, caring for Willow where she feels safe. If Nate wants to be released from his purgatory, then fine, the sooner the better then I can move into his room. Then the days of us chastely lying side by side can come to an end.

'You give me no warmth or comfort, and I have no intention of offering any to you. We can live adequately but separately. I won't cause you any embarrassment and from the outside, the parishioners, the villagers, whoever, will believe the illusion that we've created.'

Robin turned side on, a signal that the conversation was ending. 'It's your call, Edmund. See it as some kind of test from God, your very own version of a long walk into the desert only for you, it will last more than forty days and nights. It will last for as long as you can bear it.

'And every time you see me, whenever we cross paths on the landing, each time you sit by Willow's bed and pray, I hope it reminds you of what you've lost and what you could have had.'

She could feel her voice about to crack, such was the depth of feeling, the truth in her departing line.

'And I hope the devil whispers in your ear and tells you that he's won because in your devotion to God, you lost the most precious gift of all, your family.'

And with that, not giving him time to respond, Robin turned and left the room.

CHAPTER THIRTY-ONE

GINA

GINA LAY BY WILLOW'S SIDE, SQUISHED TOGETHER ON THE bed like they'd done so many times over the years, the three-quarter divan still wide enough for two skinny-minnies. They often spent hours that way, when Gina called, holding hands, staring at the ceiling tracing cracks that had appeared over time. Like lines on the palm of their hand or face, marking time and life.

Sometimes, depending on Willow's mood and lucidity she would talk, not always making sense, not always for long but Gina loved hearing her voice because for much of the time her friend was locked in a silent room inside her mind.

In those instances, when silence descended, Gina would fill the gap, hoping that her words would seep through the drug-induced fog of Willow's mind. She'd ramble on about nothing in particular, a soap on telly, the inconsiderate moles that were digging up their garden and the bane of Jimmy and the gardener's life. Other times, sharing memories of their glory days and funny stories that she swore made Willow smile, just a hint on her lips, a teeny crinkle of the eye.

Mostly, Willow just listened or slept, and sometimes Gina

wasn't sure if her beautiful best friend was even there or knew she was, either. It didn't matter, though, because no matter what state Gina found Willow in, they were still best friends forever, steadfast, and true.

A month had passed since the last episode, when Gina had called for her weekly chat and Robin, looking drained, had explained in hushed tones about what happened in the kitchen.

And it seemed to Gina that ever since, despite Willow's medication being altered and calm prevailing, Robin was the opposite, agitated, nervy and often wearing a miles-away expression on her face.

Gina always asked if she was okay, reminding Robin that she was there for her as well as Willow, and was happy to share a problem. But the answer was always the same.

I'm fine, just tired, don't worry.

And even though Gina didn't quite believe Robin, who was she to judge? Wasn't that exactly what she said to Babs when she asked how things were, why she wasn't eating her carrot cake.

'I'm fine, just not hungry, don't worry.'

Whatever was bothering Robin remained a mystery but Gina suspected it was something to do with the worrying nugget of information Babs had passed on.

Perhaps later would be a good time to broach it because they must; the rumours couldn't be ignored. Gina, Robin, and Babs were having a girls' get-together. A bite to eat and a catch-up, a good time to tentatively raise the subject. She and Babs had decided, after much rumination that they needed to tell Robin what they knew; then she could decide what to do for the best.

There was another thing on Gina's mind, stuff she was desperate to share yet still the words wouldn't come. She could always tell Willow what she'd found at home by eavesdropping on a phone call. She'd regretted it, then didn't because it proved that Jimmy's affair was gathering pace and told her that she needed to act.

Turning her head, Gina smiled at her peaceful friend whose eyelids barely fluttered, while a soft whistling-wind escaped from her rose-bud lips as Willow's chest rose then fell. Her cheeks were flushed pink, reminding Gina of a fair-haired Snow White, waiting for her prince to come. This thought made Gina feel incredibly sad because Nate was no prince; he wasn't even a good husband. And neither, it seemed, was Jimmy.

By her side Willow roused, shifted position slightly then continued her slumbers but it had jolted Gina from her meanderings and back to the tired bedroom with the fixtures and furnishings that hadn't changed for years and years. It was weird, how one's perceptions changed in adulthood, and you began to see places and people through new eyes. Like the vicarage, that to little Gina had seemed huge and posh, with three bedrooms and four rooms downstairs and a giant tiled hallway that was cool in summer and draughty in winter.

Back then, to her wide eyes it was a colourful labyrinth of rooms, the lounge painted in deep purply hues with patterned throws that might have come from Peru; the sunny yellow kitchen with jars of spices on the shelves, something delicious baking in the oven and crayon drawings, notes and reminders stuck to the fridge under magnets said, 'a family lives here'; the posh dining room with the polished mahogany table, walls stencilled with leaves and flowers weaving around the room, like the forest had crept indoors.

Gina often attributed her love of interiors to the inspiration provided by Robin, who they'd often find wearing paint-splattered jeans, a roller in one hand, a dripping tin of something colourful in the other. Through grown-up eyes Gina saw a 'family' held together by a magnet – Robin, who'd hid behind smoke and mirrors, preventing those on the outside, seeing in. Now she'd seen the sadness behind Cris's eyes, the fragility inside Willow and the true face of the vicar. And now the colours had faded, on the crayon drawings and the yellow kitchen chimney breast. The butterfly wallpaper along the stairway was dull and tatty and there was never anything baking in the oven. The whole house felt cold, empty, soulless.

Looking around the room, Gina spied the pile of 'angel books' as Willow called them, written by Lorna Byrne, whose words she took as gospel. Gina believed too, and sometimes recited a paragraph or two that described their technicolour robes and gave their angel names.

Willow had always believed in angels; said they spoke to her in her dreams and listened when she asked for help. And it was one of these angels that told Willow to let all the birds out of the cage at the pet shop in town. What a day that had been!

Gina nudged Willow. 'Do you remember when you talked me into liberating the budgies in Mr Murphy's pet shop? You said an angel told you they should all be free, and it was cruel to keep birds locked in a cage. I was so scared and prayed that my angel would tell your angel it was a bad idea.'

For a moment Willow didn't react, then, joy of joys, Gina saw a smile appear on her lips and her eyelids opened. When she turned, her wide, olive-green eyes shone with that mischief of long ago.

'I remember. Bird poo everywhere. Flapping and tweeting and lots and lots of poo.' Willow rolled onto her side, and Gina mimicked the action so their faces met, nose almost touching nose.

Willow's barely used voice was raspy. 'And Mr Murphy shouting at us, with a big blob on his head, saying he was ringing our parents.'

Gina could feel her eyes awash with tears but didn't swipe them away. She was holding on tight to Willow's hand, not wanting to break the rare moment of connection. 'Do you remember how fast we ran out of the shop and through town, and for days we thought we'd be in the paper, or on wanted posters in the library, and on *Crimewatch*. We watched it on telly that week, waiting for our faces to appear on the screen.'

'I think that's the naughtiest thing I've ever done but it was fun...' Willow's expression changed. Lines appeared on her forehead and merriment transformed to concern.

Please don't go, thought Gina, *please stay a while, talk to me, come back to us, Willow.* And like a miracle, a prayer answered, she did.

CHAPTER THIRTY-TWO

'WHY ARE YOU CRYING?' WILLOW KEPT HOLD OF GINA'S hand and with her free one, wiped away the tears.

'Because I miss you so much and I need you to come back to us. We love you, Willow. You know that, don't you? Please don't forget.' Gina held in the sob, forbade her voice to betray the pain and the desire to scream and beg Willow to hold on to the moment, not to retreat to wherever it was she went when she closed her eyes or stared into nothingness.

'Of course, I know. Do *you* know that I love you, too? Because I do, always and forever.' Willow stroked Gina's face, her touch gentle.

Gina nodded. 'I do, always and forever.' Compelled by some inner voice, Gina planted seeds that might grow while Willow slept, because she would, eventually. 'And your mum loves you so much. She's your angel here on earth and never leaves you. She misses you too. We all do.'

And then Willow's hand became still, her eyes held Gina with a look of such honesty, that when her words came so pure and to the point, the message in them was clear to read and hear. 'I love Mum. Will you tell her I know when she's here, sitting in the chair, reading to me, or singing. Always close... but... I miss Maya. And that's why I don't want to be here anymore. I want to be with my Maya. I need to go to her. She's waiting for me, so will you help me...?'

At first Gina wasn't sure what she meant so asked. 'Help you, how can I help you?'

When she replied, Willow's voice was barely audible, and they could have been thirteen again, making secret plans for the future. 'Help me decide, if it's okay to go because Dad says it's a sin, that I'm wicked for trying to go before. But God will understand why I want to go to him, because that's where Maya is, with him in the arms of Jesus, isn't she?'

The blood in Gina's veins cooled, her stomach clenched, and the firm hand of dread gripped Gina's heart, but she had to answer, keep the lines open now that Willow had reached out. 'Of course, that's where she is. And our mate Jesus will be keeping her safe because he loves the little children, and the birds and all the animals. Remember, we used to read all about it, and it says so in the words of our favourite song, so please don't worry...'

'No, I need to know that it's true. That she's okay, so I have to go too, to be with Maya. Don't you see? But Dad won't let me go. He says it's evil, and so am I if I break a commandment because only God can decide when I go to him. That's not fair, is it? She's my little girl and I miss her, and I should decide when I go.' A frown had creased Willow's forehead, then it smoothed as her eyes widened with what looked like fear.

'I'm scared, though. Scared of going to hell because that's where Dad says I'll end up, that I'll burn, and the maggots will eat me, and then I won't see Maya ever again.'

Willow's voice had raised, her chest rose and fell, her breathing was laboured, and Gina imagined her poor broken heart going like the clappers. Her grip on Gina's hand was so tight it hurt, her eyes boring holes, the olive irises now deep pools of emerald, agitation seeping into every word.

'I've asked the angels over and over what I should do, but they won't help, they won't even answer. They look away and whisper amongst themselves and I can't hear what they are saying. So you have to tell me, tell me what to do, how to get to Maya without going to hell because my head is a jumble sale, and I can't sort it out.'

Gina swallowed, panic racing around in her brain desperately trying to find an answer, but what? Then it came, 'Willow, listen to me.'

Willow stared, her lips silenced yet pursed, her hand-hold remained firm.

'I don't know how to find Maya, but I *will* do my best to help you, okay? I promise, cross my heart.' Gina did just that, tracing two lines onto her chest while in response, Willow gave a tiny nod.

'And maybe the angels don't know, either. Perhaps when they're whispering they're trying to find the answer so don't give up on them just yet. We have to give them a chance.'

And even though she was making it up as she went along, stalling for time, Gina wanted it to be true. Her glimmer of hope was then tempered by deep sadness at Willow's plea, washed away on a river of hate for the vicar, a two-faced hypocrite. The mere thought of his words tormenting Willow while she was asleep, wandering, or awake, was abhorrent and cruel.

Gina was convinced that the God they'd worshipped at Sunday school, to whom they'd made Brownie-Guide promises and wedding day vows wouldn't want this tragic lost soul to be scared. He was there for comfort in the darkest days, a light that shone and led you home, so she had to erase from Willow's mind any thoughts planted by Eddie the Fake before she drifted off again.

Taking both Willow's hands in hers, Gina held them close to her chest while she spoke softly, her words simple yet firm. 'I want you to promise me something,' Gina waited a beat, then realised that nobody could do that until they've heard the conditions so laid them out.

'Try to remember what I'm saying, Willow, please, it's really important. From now on you mustn't take any notice of what your dad says. Because it's not true. You are *not* evil, and you will *not* be going to hell. Your dad is wrong, okay?'

Willow didn't respond yet appeared to be hanging on Gina's every word.

'We always believed that Jesus was one of the nice guys and God was good. They're our heroes, so trust in them *not* your dad. You are beautiful and good – inside and out – so don't let him scare you or make you sad. Promise me, Willow, promise me you won't listen to him anymore.'

Willow scrunched her eyes and nodded, her voice cracking as she answered, 'I promise.' Then pushing her face into Gina's chest she repeated, 'Don't let him scare me, I'm not evil, I promise not to listen,' and as the tears began to fall, her frail body was racked by each sob.

Taking Willow in her arms, trying hard to be brave, Gina stroked Willow's hair, soothing her with hushes, promises to be there, to find the answer... and then a glimmer of inspiration.

'I think we should be patient, and if we trust and believe in our heroes and the angels, they'll come through for us. I know they will.'

Maybe it was wrong, to give Willow false hope but it was better than the alternative, a nagging gnawing thought that was crawling its way to the front of her brain, remembering another little nugget passed on by Babs.

Was the vicar purposely trying to antagonise Willow? It wouldn't surprise Gina because he was a sly one, she knew that for a fact. And according to Babs, who'd recently overheard a conversation as she silently polished the banister in the hall, so was Nate.

Nate and the vicar were in the study, the door slightly ajar, sharing their concerns about Willow, and Robin's unhealthy attachment to her. They'd agreed that Willow should be cared for professionally. This thought had chilled Gina to the bone.

When finally, the tears subsided, Willow's limbs and head became heavy, lolling into Gina's shoulder as she drifted gently into sleep. And in the silence of the room relief made its presence known. They'd ridden out a moment that could have easily whipped up a storm.

A wave of sorrow washed over Gina, not knowing if or when Willow would be back. As it ebbed, the sadness was replaced by something useful. Knowledge.

Never before had Willow shared her desire to be with Maya, but in doing so she had given Gina a window into her mind and some idea of what she saw through misty eyes. A clue to what she might be saying to the invisible angels, her lips mouthing words only they could hear.

And then came a revelation, and that word alone sent shivers down Gina's spine, tingles along her arms, her mind racing all over the place to put her thoughts in order. A passage from the Bible had pinged into her head. Not word for word, more a vague imprint on her subconscious.

The end of the New Testament, in the Book of Revelation. God sent down his angel to tell the disciple John what will come to pass, and Willow believed in angels. Was it a sign? And then something else... what was it?

Goosebumps covered her body when she remembered that Satan is the deceiver of the whole world, and this was apt because as far as Gina was concerned the vicar could be one of his covert disciples. A father, masquerading as a man of God, using holy words to keep his daughter under control. Or, as he would argue, God's law in order to keep her safe. That was the greatest deceit of all, and Gina saw through it. Twisting the rules, the commandments, breaking them, bending people to his will. That was the vicar's trademark and if they resisted, like Cris had done, then they were cast out.

How she despised the Reverend Edmund Hilyard, one of the greatest narcissists of all, hiding in plain sight. In that instant she knew she had to tell Robin what he was up to, and together they could protect Willow, shield her from his influence. It wouldn't take much for her to spiral. They couldn't let that happen again and give the vicar a reason to cast Willow out.

It would not come to pass and with or without the help of the angels, Gina swore a silent oath that while she had breath in her body, Satan wouldn't win.

CHAPTER THIRTY-THREE

BABS

THE OCTOBER EVENINGS WERE DRAWING IN BUT CHECKING her watch, Babs still had plenty of time before dusk when the country road became a bit too creepy to walk alone. With each step she took the two bottles of Prosecco clinked against each other in her rucksack, that also contained a giant bag of Doritos and a Mexican Dip selection. She'd decided to leave her car behind so she could have a glass or two and relax, then Gina was going to drop her off home, to save walking back in the dark.

She was a good girl, was Gina and since their little chat seemed to have perked up because there'd been no more mention of job-anxiety, although, what if she was just putting on a brave face? Babs decided she'd wait for an opportunity to ask later.

Babs was really looking forward to the get-together with Robin and Gina. The atmosphere at home was rock-bottom ever since she'd earned the title 'worst expectant-gran in the world, ever'.

The only person on her side was Demi who was also sick to the back teeth of being squashed into the noisiest three-bed semi in The Willows. She too was praying that Isaac and Fiona would bugger off, so she'd finally have her own space. Poor kid. All she wanted was a quiet place to study and not listen to Sasha yakking on in her 'customer service phone voice' while she booked appointments.

Living arrangements and frosty vibes aside, as she marched towards the vicarage, Babs focused on a more pressing matter – the worrying bit of info about Nate. At first, when Demi mentioned it, Babs erred towards overactive imaginations and girly gossip, but now she wasn't sure, and neither was Gina.

Thinking back, she went over the conversation with Demi, so she'd get her facts right because messengers always got shot but it'd been decided that at their girls' lunch, Babs was going to put her life, or less dramatically, her friendship, on the line.

Nate probably had no idea who Demi was, or just hadn't recognised her. But why would he, amongst the thousands of new students who'd enrolled at the college? However, she knew him and was adamant she hadn't misread what she'd seen.

Babs and Demi had been enjoying a bit of them-time and as always after a hard day's slog, one in lectures, the other with a loo brush in hand, they sat at the kitchen table with a brew and biscuits and shared notes on their day.

On this occasion, Demi had more than notes, it was an exposé. 'Mum, I'm *not* imagining it. I saw him as I walked through the car park to the bus stop. He was in his car. I've seen it parked at the vicarage when I've come to meet you after work, and one of the English lecturers was in the passenger seat. I've seen her around. She's got long dark hair that was tied in a ponytail, and he reached over and was fondling it.'

'Fondling! What do you mean, "fondling"?' Babs was in the 'shocked and incredulous zone' but wanted to be sure and know more, obviously.

Demi tutted. 'You know, like stroking it and twisting his fingers in her hair. It was well cringe. They were laughing about something, but you could just tell they're at it... I mean you don't fiddle with someone's hair, do you? Not when you work with them. That's just weird so they must be having an affair.'

Babs was horrified. A million thoughts zinging through her head but the one that made her feel sad, was the thought of poor Willow. Hence, her knee-jerk reaction was to pour cold water on Demi's assumption, because it couldn't be true, it was just too awful.

'Well, we shouldn't jump to conclusions. There could be a totally reasonable and innocent explanation for it,' – not that Babs could think of one – 'so best not go repeating all that and spreading gossip, okay, love.'

At this Demi had rolled her eyes. 'Whatever you say. But you might live in La-La-Land, however I know what I saw, especially when the woman got out of the car and they did this cringy holding hands thing.'

Babs had gone cold and placed her hand on her chest. 'Oh my Lord, what do you mean?'

Demi laughed and reached out, her fingers wiggling. 'You know, when you don't let go of the other persons hand for ages, their fingertips were just touching and then when they broke apart they both wiggled their fingers to say goodbye. So gross, but it was funny too. Me and Hannah stood behind a van and watched. I wish we'd recorded it now, as proof but we will next time, if we spot them. The dirty gets.'

Babs was in shock as she pictured the scene and while Demi rummaged in the biscuit tin and slurped her tea, the ramifications of such incriminating evidence were hard to ignore.

Gina had felt the same after Babs had re-enacted the whole thing during a break from cleaning the patio windows and while they tucked into a slice of carrot cake. Well, Babs did. Gina mostly chopped it up and moved it round her plate until they'd both come to the same conclusion. Men were all dirty bastards, and they'd have to tell Robin about Nate.

And today was the day because neither of them could sit around Robin's table and not mention it and seeing as she'd heard it first, Babs was going to bring it up.

She was lost in rehearsing her lines and didn't respond to the first honk of the horn, but when Pete's car pulled alongside her, Babs was startled and for a second worried as she waited while he lowered the passenger side window.

'What're you doing here? Is something wrong?' Babs expected him to be settled in his favourite spot in front of the telly, remote in hand.

Pete leant over and pulled open the door. 'I was hoping to have a word, while there's nobody at home but when I got in the house was empty and when I saw your car on the drive, presumed you'd be out for a walk.'

'So nothing's wrong. Bloody hell, Pete, you gave me a right scare then and anyway, what do you want to talk about? I told you I was spending the afternoon with Gina and Robin, so can it wait?' Babs was annoyed because once again he hadn't listened; but still, she was a bit curious why he'd made the effort to find her.

'Look, can you get in, Babs, so we can talk. It's important and lately it feels like we never get chance to have a proper chat because you're in bed so early–'

'That's because I'm tired and you want to stay up till stupid o'clock watching shite and the house is so full we get no peace. Yes, Pete, I know. Which is why I was pissed off with you when you didn't back me up with our Isaac. So don't blame me for living in a mad house.'

In response to the accusation, Pete held his hands up. 'Okay, okay. I get it and I'm sorry, but please will you get in before someone comes round the bend and whacks the car up the jacksy. I can pull over in the lay-by further on, then I'll drop you off at Robin's.'

Babs huffed. He'd ruined it now. Her peaceful walk *and* preparing how she'd tell Robin. She'd have to wing it, but curiosity won out and after a tut, just to let him know how much he'd bugged her, she got inside.

It was very awkward, being sat beside your husband, in a lay-by, like lovers sneaking off for a quickie. But instead of a moment of passion, you find yourself lost for words and minus the inclination to get your knickers off. That ship sailed many moons ago.

He'd turned off the engine so ruling out anything slightly romantic, Babs figured the only other option was her imminent murder so he could claim on the insurance. He'd made no move towards either and she was fast losing her patience. 'Pete, what exactly do you want to talk about because I'm going to be late?' She rested her hands on the rucksack, which was perched on her knees, the Prosecco inside getting warmer by the second, which was also very annoying.

'Me and you, because things aren't right between us, and we can't go on like this. We don't communicate at all, and I don't want it to get worse.'

Pete, not known for shows of emotion or come to think of it, deep thought, had taken Babs by surprise. That he'd even realised they were in the shit gave her a smidgen of hope and a flutter of happiness because maybe he did care. That was why her reply was softer and not like the huffy mare everyone was used to.

'I know, and you're right... and I'm glad you've noticed because it's a starting point, isn't it? Acceptance.' She had turned slightly and watched Pete in profile as he nodded his agreement. 'So, what do you think we should do about it?'

She wished he'd turn to face her and not just stare out of the windscreen but reminded herself that having a heart-to-heart would be hard for him, against his instincts and out of his comfort zone, so she quelled her irritation and waited.

'I honestly don't know. What if we made a list of our faults and tried to work on those, so we don't get on each other's nerves as much.' He turned then, his eyes wide, a look of hope on his face, not realising he'd come up with the worst and most annoying idea ever. And Babs told him so.

'Oh, so I get on your nerves, do I? Thanks for that, Pete. And making a list has to be the most stupid idea because picking each other's faults apart is a sure-fire way to start a row. So let's move on.'

In her heart she'd already signed Pete's big gesture off as a waste of time but decided to give it one more go; it was the least she could do. 'What if we said how we feel, instead. Let's focus on that. Then how we can make our lives happier.'

'Okay. Mine was a daft idea because I already know I annoy you loads more than you annoy me.'

The loud huffing that came from Babs was meant as a hint to get on with it, which he took. 'So, who goes first?' Pete looked at his hands and fiddled with the cuff of his sweatshirt.

'You go first. I'm interested to hear how you feel seeing as you never talk about it.' Babs waited, not expecting much.

'Okay... well... I feel lonely if you must know. Like I've lost my best friend because I bug her so much she can't be bothered with me anymore.' He paused.

Babs didn't interrupt which was a miracle and it took immense willpower to remain silent while he forged ahead.

'Sometimes, even before you started on this menopause thingy, I used to feel left out because you focused on the kids so much. If it wasn't them you were out at work or fussing round your mum, and I always came last. I kept telling myself that it was normal, that you were doing your best to be a housewife and mum, and I couldn't complain because you worked, too. But now, it's like you don't even care that much about the kids, and we all irritate the life out of you and as for me, I sometimes think you don't know I'm there, or wish I wasn't.'

A waggon approached on the opposite side of the road, distracting Babs, giving her time to calm her temper. In its windscreen, resting on the dash next to a teddy and a Leeds FC flag, was a number plate that said TINA.

Babs wondered if that was the driver's wife, who he loved so much he'd had a sign made, one that went everywhere with him, keeping her close until he got home, where Tina would be waiting for the love of her life. Kev. That's what Babs decided the waggon driver was called and in that instant Babs envied Tina and Kev. Their love and perfect imaginary world that wasn't hers.

'BABS! Did you hear me? Look, you're doing it again. Shutting me out, making me feel like I don't matter and that my feelings don't count.'

She turned. 'Is that how I really make you feel?'

Pete nodded. 'Yes, Babs, it is.'

CHAPTER THIRTY-FOUR

Stunned. And stung. That's how Babs felt and even though her mouth opened, no words came out which was wise. Keeping her gob shut while she processed his words and her feelings.

Up ahead, at the end of the lay-by and over a wire fence was a field full of cows so she watched them while she waited for the pain and anger to subside. Babs loved cows, their doleful eyes, their nonchalance. But nobody knew whether they had bad days, bad thoughts, sad thoughts, like the many bitter, confused ones that passed through her head on a regular basis.

Perhaps they did. Got fed up of being rained on while they guarded their patch of dry grass, boring green stuff they were sick of chewing day in, day out. And trudging across the fields to the milking sheds, accepting without question their monotonous fate so some human could have milk on their cornflakes.

Come to think of it, she could be a right nasty cow who was also endowed with an ample rump, so there was a mighty good chance that her spirit animal did in fact, have horns and hooves. And going by what the heifer on the other side of the fence was doing, extremely empty bowels.

'Babs… say something for God's sake.' Pete gave her a nudge.

Ping. Babs was back in the car, and after rearranging her rump, she turned to Pete and tried to explain, make it better.

'That's hurt me, hearing how I've made you feel and I'm sorry, I really am, because I don't like to think of you being lonely or left out. That was never my intention. But I'm also angry because I was doing what I thought was best. So the idea I was getting it wrong has really pissed me off. What a sodding waste of time that was! It's like we've been living a lie, or you have. And I feel stupid. Like I've failed in some way.'

'No, it's not like that at all. Maybe I've not said it right. I didn't mean for you to feel like this. Look, Babs, family life is a struggle, making ends meet and bringing up kids and we both knew it wasn't going to be easy at the start. We were young and had nothing… but we got on with it and made a life for ourselves and I'm proud of what we did.'

'Well, that's one thing we agree on then. We got something right.'

'Of course we did. I just thought once we'd got through all that, when they were more independent, we could enjoy what we've achieved. Our time to have some fun. Maybe that's what you're feeling too. Our Isaac's announcement made me take stock and reminded me where we started from. And your reaction to their idea, about being a full-time babysitter was spot on. It's time he stood on his own two feet.'

'Hallee-bloody-looyah! At last. But it would've been nice if you'd backed me up a bit instead of siding with him like you do all the time. Instead you made me look like the baddie and that hurt, and now they've taken the huff and I feel awful. But that's another issue and before I move on, you might as well know I won't be backing down no matter how much Isaac sulks. So you can all get used to it.'

'It's fine, and I promise I'll have a word with him and

explain that he really does need to find somewhere else to live...
okay?' Pete reached out and placed his hand over hers, a gesture
that was as welcome as it was alien.

*When was the last time he'd comforted her? And why
couldn't she remember?*

Batting that unhelpful thought away, but not Pete's hand, it
was Babs' turn to say how she felt so, wary of bombarding him
with the inner workings of her mind and battered soul, she trod
carefully. 'Before we can go into fun mode, you need to
understand what it's like for me, being me I suppose. And
seeing as you mentioned "the menopause thingy," I'll start
there.'

Clasping her hands together, she spun her wedding ring
around her finger as she spoke, the rhythmic movement a habit
that died hard.

'It's crap, totally and utterly crap and there's been times
where I've felt lonely too, completely lost in a pit of worry,
consumed by anxiety and dread, swamped by uncontrollable
anger and untameable emotions so bad that I thought I was
going mad.

'And added to this, the pounds were piling on and
settling on all the bits of me that I already hated the most.
Then the hot flushes arrived, trying to drown me in my bed,
or in the middle of the supermarket while I was chatting to
the lady on the check-out. Imagine what it's like, Pete, being
a human kettle. Boiling on the inside. The heat escaping like
steam and running down your body, your forehead, being
soaked up by your hair as you pack away the weekly shop. I
used to go in looking half-decent and come out like I'd been
in the sauna.'

Pete gave her hand a gentle squeeze. 'It must be bloody
awful... but why didn't you say something, tell me what was
happening to you and how it felt? And as for putting on a few

pounds well, I don't mind about that. It just means there's more to grab hold of.'

Seriously, Pete. For once read your audience.

The cheeky wink didn't cut it this time and resulted in a withering look from Babs which silenced him immediately. Gritting her teeth and abandoning ring spinning, Babs forged on, determined to make him understand.

'I hated them, the hot flushes, and I hated me, and that self-loathing started to spread out like roots that took over every part of my life and soon I hated every part of it and no, I didn't tell you because I was messed up enough, and I couldn't bear the thought of you saying or doing something stupid and making it worse. You know, like one of your un-funny jokes.'

'Well thanks for that. Nice to know you have zero faith in your husband and clearly think he's a prat.'

On hearing this Babs turned away from him, leant her head back and closed her eyes as she spoke. 'Irony really is lost on you, isn't it, Pete?'

When he didn't answer, Babs resisted the urge to laugh and instead, enlightened him some more on the secret world of his wife.

'You know what the weird thing is, that lockdown, as hideous as it was, probably did me a favour because for the first time in I don't know how long I had something very precious. I had time. Time to focus on me. Sleep when I was exhausted, at any time of day. And not worry myself daft if I woke up at 3am because I was due to get up at six thirty.

'I put on face packs, painted my toes, joined groups and exercise classes. I walked and sucked in fresh air and slowly I found a bit of me again. I started to feel better about myself, but no matter how far I walked or what colour nail varnish I chose it didn't stop the hormones leaking out of my body and I swear I could feel them leaving.'

Pete just stared. Babs just carried on.

'With every symptom came a reminder that my body was changing inside and out. The old me waved a hanky and said au revoir. That's when it hit me, that I needed help. I booked an online consultation with a doctor who looks not much older than Isaac... I'll spare you the gory details about what bits of me are drying up, aching, falling out or springing up in the most unwelcome of places, but in the end he wrote me a prescription for HRT. And it's actually starting to work because I do feel so much better.'

When she turned her head, she was slightly perplexed by the wide mouthed, annoyed expression on Pete's face.

'So for all this time you've been taking pills and not even told your own husband. I had no idea it was as bad as that, or you'd spoken to a doctor so I'm sorry, Babs, you can't blame me if I didn't know. How can I help if you won't explain.'

Why was it always about him?

Barbara sucked in her annoyance and soldiered on. 'I'm not taking pills. I have gel that I rub into my skin at night, and I didn't tell you because I was struggling coming to terms with such a huge change and feeling dreadful on top of it all. So please forgive me if I didn't feel like sharing or risking you not understanding because to be honest, Pete, that would have been the last straw.'

'And what do you mean by that?' Pete's tone was narky, which narked Babs.

'I mean that when you're walking a mental and physical tightrope day in, day out the last thing you need is to hear an insensitive comment. It's the tiniest things that can tip me over the edge, like a flippant remark or a smirk, especially shoulder shrugs. They make me want to scream.'

In fact, Babs realised that she was getting to that point now and that this heart-to-heart was going nowhere fast and she really needed a bloody drink.

'Look, Pete. I've explained as best I can. So shall we focus on what we do next because as much as I appreciate the effort you made hunting me down we're not much further on, are we? So, instead of niggling, let's think of a way we can rescue our marriage.'

The thing was, even though she was giving him a chance Babs had a dreadful feeling this was a battle neither of them were going to win. She'd been over and over the rules of engagement many times, as she lay by his side listening to the sound of obliviousness.

And as for Pete, he was confused, she could tell by the look on his face, and she also wished she'd put a fiver both ways on his next words being a flippant retort. It would have been five pounds well spent.

'Well at least you didn't suggest counselling because all that shrink malarkey isn't my thing, holding a tennis ball while the other one yaks on. Having some stranger listen to personal stuff. Nah, not on your nelly. But I think there is a way we could take the pressure off, let our hair down and get away from the family for a bit.'

Babs heart dropped because in that second, when he mentioned getting away, she realised there was something more to his sudden desire to chat. A hidden Pete agenda.

I should've known.

Babs sighed deeply. 'Go on, then, enlighten me.' And as she listened, preparing for the worst, she unclipped her rucksack, flipped open the top and began to peel the foil from one of the bottles of Prosecco.

'Are you going to drink that now! In the car?' Pete sounded like she was about to snort a line of cocaine.

Babs ignored him and as she twisted the wire undone,

wished she could do the same with the tension that was winding its way around every nerve and sinew in her body.

Then a thought, so she asked. 'Since when did you know so much about therapy and tennis balls? Or did you see it on telly?'

She was genuinely curious about this, as she irreverently chucked the wire casing over her shoulder and into the footwell behind. Pete gave a little gasp. He liked a tidy car did Pete, and a berry crush air freshener.

'From Calvin. Him and Penny went a while back. They were having a few marriage problems, you know, in the bedroom department, so they got help. He was telling me all about it yesterday.'

As she twisted the cork, her fingers squeezing, her grip firm, Babs imagined it was Pete's neck, or his nether regions. '*So*, you were talking to Calvin about what exactly... to end up talking about his sex life?'

'Well, we weren't actually talking about that to start off with. We were discussing holidays and going away for New Year. He's found a brilliant place in Lanzarote and wanted to know if we'd be up for it so I said you weren't keen on group holidays, and we'd been having a few difficulties... that's when he told me about him and Penny.'

And after the blissful release of the cork that made Pete jump, relishing the pop and fizz of pressure escaping in a whoosh of bubbles, Babs yanked the bottle from the sack and glugged down the cool liquid, eyes closed.

Then she asked, 'What about him and Penny?'

Pete must have thought she cared, when in fact she was actually storing up evidence for her defence when she committed murder and seriously, who would blame her? The only sound after that was Pete, unburdening himself while his wife swigged from the bottle.

'Well it seems she's on the menopause thingy too and turned

into a right dragon. Calvin wasn't getting any action – those were his words not mine, by the way – so he decided to book them into therapy for the sake of their marriage.'

Yeah, right, thought Babs. 'And did it work?'

'I don't know, because he'd just got to the bit about the tennis ball when his phone rang, so I didn't hear the end, but ever since I've been thinking about the Lanzarote idea, and I reckon it's the perfect solution.'

Babs glanced in his direction and raised an eyebrow. 'How so?'

'Well, you're always run off your feet at Christmas so after all that madness, you can have break from the kids and a nice rest in a swanky five-star hotel. No cooking and cleaning and it might take your mind off your mental problems and put a smile on your face at the same time. You know, having some fun in the sun.'

Mental problems. He seriously just said that?

Babs twiddled the cork in her hand and said nothing because she was waiting for the burp to arrive and when it did, she let it out loud and proud. It was a cracker. One that went on for ages and ages, much to the disgust of Pete who grimaced beside her.

It made Babs laugh, not just the burp, which was the perfect response to his stupid idea, but his disgusted expression, and once she started laughing, at him and everything, she couldn't stop and soon tears were rolling down her cheeks as her body jiggled in the seat.

And as always, Pete read the room wrong. 'See, I knew it'd cheer you up! It's what we both need, a bloody good holiday away from the kids. So, shall I tell Calvo we're in? He's going to book it tonight and he needs to know, and then I'll send the deposit over.'

Babs wiped her eyes, and as suddenly as the giggles had

arrived, they departed, like guests who'd turned up at the wrong party wearing fancy dress, realising it was actually a wake. Turning to face him, in a surprisingly calm voice, Babs asked Pete a question of her own.

'Do you honestly think that's all it will take to fix us, or me for that matter? That a holiday will cure my "mental problems," as you so kindly put it.' He opened his mouth but shut it when Babs raised her hand to silence him.

'Do you really think that going away with four of the most obnoxious people I have ever met will glue you and me back together? Will stop you from feeling the way you described, will ease any of the troubles I've just poured out to you. That a suntan and all-you-can-eat buffet will be the miracle that women like me all over the world are waiting for?' She took another swig.

Pete opened his mouth, then shut it. Babs wondered if he needed to phone a friend. Or go 50/50. She'd have loved him to ask the audience. Instead, spurred on by the demon unleashed inside her, who absolutely loved Prosecco, Babs got her bitch on.

'Oh, *I know*,' she heard the sarcasm in her voice, 'maybe getting me drunk on cocktails will loosen up all the bits that don't work anymore. A couple of glasses of sex on the beach will do the trick, I reckon. Actually make that three or four because Lord knows that's what it'd take to get me into bed with you ever again.'

His head nearly spun off his shoulders, and using his right arm to steady himself in what was clearly a moment of revelation Pete asked, 'Don't you fancy me anymore, is that what you're saying? That you'd have to be drunk to... you know... have sex.'

Babs exploded, unable to contain her frustration any longer. 'Yes, Pete, I would. I told you last time we did it, that I had to grin and bear it and thought of England the whole way through.

It's painful, no matter what I squirt up there to make it easier. It's shite, totally, completely, abysmally shite and it gets worse, when I can't have a wee the next day without grimacing! I told you all this, Pete, but you clearly didn't listen or care enough to talk about it, with me, your wife not fucking Calvo the stupid knobhead!'

'Babs, I'm sorry, just calm down, okay.'

Oh, my God, he said it. That's how stupid he is. He actually told me to calm down.

Babs was on the verge of hysteria and her high pitch reflected that, along with her hot cheeks and watery eyes.

'So you reckon it'll work, do you? A holiday. Then let's go. What have we got to sodding lose? In fact, fuck it. Let's go right now. Come on. We can nip home, grab the passports and my envelope of cash, leave a note for the kids, and go straight to the airport... come on, smart arse... let's do it... follow the holy grail to happiness and a NICE BIG SHAG FOR PETE!'

Pete's eyes were like moons. His voice laced with disgust and a thinly veiled hint of anger. 'You're drunk.'

'And you're an arsehole.'

'Jesus, Babs.' Pete did his wobbly head and raised palms thing. Looking bemused was his go to expression.

But Babs had no intention of answering, she'd had enough. Of being stuck in the car with Pete, stuck in a marriage with Pete, in fact she was sick of just being stuck so reaching for the door handle she yanked and pushed, then grabbed her rucksack and still holding tight to the bottle, got out of the car.

Pete was flummoxed. 'Babs, what the hell have I said now?'

As she hooked the straps over her shoulders, shouted, 'You know what, Pete. You might be a boring, self-centred pillock but you never cease to amaze me with your ignorance so if you don't know, it means you haven't listened to anything I've just said so what's the bloody point in being here... In fact, what's the point in any of it anymore?'

Babs saw Pete shuffle round in a panicky flap as he grappled with the door and tried to get out of the car. She couldn't be bothered to wait or listen to what he had to say when he managed to squeeze his beer belly from between the steering wheel and his seat. Instead she marched off to the strains of his voice, issuing orders and asking questions.

'Babs, get back here right now! You're not walking around on your own pissed as a fart.'

Ah, maybe he does care, bless.

'You're showing me up!'

No he doesn't, you fool.

'Babs, Babs, what time will you be home? What will I tell the kids about their tea?'

Babs kept on walking and called back. 'Never... and tell them what you like. Tell them to make a jam butty, and that I've run away with the vicar, to Mexico, and I'm having his love child.'

'Babs, you're being ridiculous. Making a bloody show of yourself, you know that don't you.'

To that remark Pete received a reverse, one finger salute, and then Babs marched on. No going back. Well, not until she'd drank the other bottle, anyway.

CHAPTER THIRTY-FIVE

ROBIN

Robin poured crisps into the bowl and as she listened to Arty tell her all about the hoo-hah that was rumbling on his village. It seemed that someone had taken the liberty of painting the front of their house in pale pink which, according to commune rules was akin to sacrilege.

The *maire*, by all accounts was up in arms and threatening action. The village was split in two. The old guard were all for getting the stocks out of the church cellar, baying for the blood of those who wanted the freedom to express themselves with a tin of paint and a roller.

'So, which side are you on? Let me guess...' Robin smiled, knowing exactly where Arty's allegiances would lie.

'Put it this way, I'm toying with the idea of a nice candy pink once spring arrives... and maybe, you could come and help me. You're a dab hand with a paintbrush if I remember rightly. I fancy some stencilling. That'd send the maire right over the edge I reckon.'

There was a smile and a hint in his suggestion, and it wasn't the first time he'd given her a gentle nudge lately and it made her sad and unsettled. Regrets and what-ifs were far more active than they'd ever been before. Perhaps he was feeling it too, the sense of time running out.

Robin carried the bowl to the table and set it amongst the assortment of sandwiches and finger food that she'd ordered from a little catering firm in town, spreading the post-lockdown love by helping a small business and saving herself a job at the same time.

'Did I tell you I'm having a bit of a do? Gina's upstairs with Willow and Babs will be here soon. We're having a girly night in.' What she didn't say was that after the row with Edmund, she'd needed comfort, to feel love and friendship and solidarity, which was why, when Babs had suggested it, Robin had readily agreed.

The taking in of a deep breath was audible, as Arty acknowledged the changing of subject. 'So, what's the occasion? I hope there are no handsome chaps in attendance that might turn your head or I shall have to come over there and punch their lights out.'

At this, Robin laughed and explained it was just a spur of the moment thing, an idea that quickly morphed into firm arrangements and a date being set. It seemed to do the trick and soon he was telling her all about one of the 'little buggers' at school who'd been caught selling vapes to the other pupils, apparently turning over a tidy little profit. Robin was relieved the subject of her going there had changed.

Avoidance was her speciality lately and her stand-off with Edmund had been proof of that because ever since, and as much as she hated it, he'd forced her to take off her rose-coloured specs and look at Willow's situation more clearly.

It had scared the hell out of her when she realised what a gap her daughter would leave in her life if she was gone, and wondered how she would fill it. There'd be no more excuses, no more turning her back on what Edmund regarded as her 'duties'. Also, Arty might go back on his promise and ask her to leave her marriage for good.

'So, how's Willow doing? I'll be going into Lourdes next week, so I'll pick her up some trinkets and send them over. Oh, and while I think on, I know it's only October, but am I invited for Christmas? I do love the excuse for a legitimate visit.'

Robin's stomach flipped, at the thought of seeing him, of the terrible shame she often felt at what they were doing, followed by a wave of love and desire so strong and yet pure that it washed away any trace of sin.

Having him sitting opposite at their table, two actors playing a part, smothering their feelings for one another, waiting for a moment alone in the kitchen when they moved the dishes. Hoping that her contrived excuse for a day or two away from Willow would be believed. Praying that dear hippy Francesca would always provide an alibi and live in her caravan forever. Marvelling as she lit the Christmas pudding that nobody had guessed about her and Arty; and that Edmund couldn't see the lies reflected in the flames. Was she that duplicitous? And from nowhere came another thunderbolt question. Had she made a terrible, terrible mistake?

Before she had time to process it the words were out. As though some hidden force had come from behind, given her a firm push, thrusting her through an open doorway and now she was staggering onto a stage, blinking, shocked and in the glare of an expectant audience of one.

'Arty, can I ask you something? And I want you to be honest, not kind or jollying me along.'

'Of, course, always, ask away.'

'Do you think it's all been a terrible mistake, the years we've wasted, that you've wasted on me? Do you ever regret it?'

Arty replied, stuttering, unsure, 'Wha... why, what do you mean, Robin, a waste? I don't regret one minute of us, not even a second. What on earth makes you ask that now?'

Her voice cracked. 'Because I can feel it, Arty. Everything's changing and I don't like it... it's in the air, outside, now the world is getting back to normal and moving on and I liked it, being here, with Willow. Taking care of her... not having to think about the future just the now and getting her through each day...'

'Robin, has something happened? Has Edmund upset you?'

'No, it's not him, I can deal with him. It's us, Willow, me. Suddenly, when I thought it was all so simple it isn't any more and I'm questioning myself and I don't like what I see when I look in the mirror.'

Arty attempted a response, but she ignored him and forged on, the words desperate to escape, be said and heard. 'Have I been selfish? I think I have because I could've made a move, a bid for freedom when Cris went to university, that was the carpe diem moment, when I should have seized the day and come to you but instead I was a coward and hid behind my faith, telling myself I couldn't break my vows when I already had, committing a sin. Yet I managed to convince myself I was being righteous and that makes me a huge pathetic hypocrite, doesn't it?'

Again Arty tried to speak but she rushed on. 'No, don't, Arty, because I couldn't bear you to disagree because that's not who you are so don't let me down. Not now when I need you to be true, like always. I've been selfish, wanting it all my own way.

'Like when Willow married Nate. I could have called it a day with Edmund. She was married and starting a new life and didn't need me, but I wanted to be near her, for when the babies came, so I wouldn't be a faraway granny.'

This time Arty got a word in, barging into the conversation.

'But you know I'd have come back for you, relocated. All you had to do was ask and yes, I always hoped you would, of course I did. But I understood, kept my side of the bargain, and never pressured you one way or another.

'And as for all those things you said about yourself I don't believe it's true at all, because they're not faults. They are you being you, the wonderful, beautiful woman I love and admire. For all the reasons and excuses you came up with. They were the best intentions, just you, never putting herself first. It's as simple as that.'

'So you don't despise me, for the years we've been apart and had to make do with snatched moments here and there? For choosing here over being with you.'

'Oh, Robin. How could I ever despise you but yes, I have been frustrated, some days I'm consumed by the desire to march over land and swim across sea to make you mine and then it subsides. I know you love me and nothing, not your bloody God or your bloody husband or hundreds of bloody miles, will change that.'

And then the words she had to say, her truth, that was gnawing at her brain.

'I should have set you free, not been selfish. I've always been selfish and scared. Taking the easy option, avoiding fuss and scandal and shame yet that's what I feel most, if I'm honest. Shame. I've messed up. Messed people about. Lied, cheated, dangled you on a string and that's wrong, very, very wrong and I need to find a way out of it. This cycle I'm in.'

'Robin, stop this. Right now. Otherwise I'm going to get on a plane and come over because I can tell something isn't right and I'm worried... this isn't like you at all.'

'No, please, don't come over. I'm just being silly... getting muddled in my head. I've not been sleeping, that's what it is.

And it's hearing your voice. It always makes me silly, and now I've rattled you and I feel bad. I'm sorry, Arty.'

'I'm not convinced; this is so unlike you.' He sounded wary and knowing he could be impulsive and intuitive, too, Robin sought to allay his worries.

'I promise I'm fine, and this evening will cheer me up and do me good, especially now you've set me straight and said lovely things about me... my head has definitely swelled a few sizes, that's for sure.' Robin thought that sounded okay but the bluff hung in the air, and she held her breath, waiting for Arty to speak.

'Okay, but you'd better ring me tomorrow, first thing. I mean it, Robin. I want to know you're all right, and you can tell me about your wild girls' night in. Is that a deal?'

'Deal.'

'And no matter what, I'm coming over. I'll wangle some leave and join you lot in burning effigies on bonfires and all that lunacy.'

Arty was doing a great job at being jovial and Robin wondered if his little speech was also a bluff.

'I'd love that. Now, I have to get off and remove lots of cling film and open some wine otherwise Babs will have my guts for garters.'

Arty laughed, and again she imagined him smiling even if perhaps all those miles away, he wasn't.

'Ha-ha, good old Babs. Bloody Nora, best not tell her I said that! Give her my regards will you and tell her I spoke to Tom just last week and he's doing great. He and Cris have some exciting plans for next year. But I'll tell you all about that tomorrow so until then, remember this. I love you, Robin, that's all you need to know and the rest, we'll make up as we go along, okay.'

Robin heard footsteps on the landing above, Gina was on her way downstairs, so they needed to end the call. 'Okay. And I love you too, Arty, so much it hurts. Now, go and mark some exercise books or look at paint charts, and I'll call you tomorrow.'

'Till tomorrow, my love.' And then he was gone.

After deleting Arty's name from the call list, a well-practised precaution of an adulterer, Robin placed her phone on the side and set about uncovering the food until movement in the hall caught her eye. Heading towards the kitchen was Gina, wiping her eyes and immediately Robin went into panic mode, her heart dropping and her hands ceasing their task.

'What's wrong? Is it Willow?' Robin rushed over and placed a comforting arm around Gina's shoulders, yet her legs were preparing to dash upstairs.

'No, no, she's fine, dozing when I left her. It's just that...' Gina's lip wobbled as Robin pulled out a chair and guided her into it.

'It's okay, take your time.' Robin crouched by Gina's side and held her hand and waited. Not as patiently as her calming voice and outward expression might suggest.

When Gina finally looked up, there was a second of hesitation and then she explained. 'It was something that Willow said, and it's broken my heart because she's never ever... never once said it out loud and that time on the bridge, I thought it was a one off, grief and exhaustion talking but now, well now I'm not so sure.'

Cold. Robin was cold despite the warmth of Gina's hand in hers. Robin's body had frozen, even the air around her seemed to have chilled. She swallowed, imagining her lips blue, barely able to speak. 'Tell me what she said. It's okay, I'm her mum, I need to know.'

As tears rolled down Gina's face, her eyes sad and scared, she repeated word for word what Willow had said, about the angels, and wanting to be with Maya, and how Edmund was twisting God's words. Robin listened in silence, and just when she thought Gina was finished, there was more, a revelation, and one that came as no shock.

'And there's something else you should know and please don't think we've been talking behind your back in a bad way, but neither of us knew what to do so we were going to tell you together, tonight.'

Gina paused. Robin's silence was her permission to continue. 'It's Nate. We think he's having an affair with someone at college. I'm so sorry Robin, for Willow and for you. It's all too cruel and wrong.'

Patting Gina's hand, Robin sighed and then stood, before pulling Gina towards her while she cried into her apron, rubbing her back in magic circles as she spoke. 'Shush now, love. I understand it's hard, sharing something like that, but if I'm honest, I suspected he was up to something but just didn't want to admit it. But thank you for telling me. You did the right thing.'

At this Gina pulled away and looked up. 'Really, you're not mad with us?'

No, just falling apart inside.

Somehow Robin forced her voice to sound calm. 'No, not at all. Now, you go and wash your face and pour yourself a drink while I go and check on Willow. Babs will be here soon and when she arrives the three of us can have a good old chat, talk this through and decide what's to be done, okay?'

Gina nodded and Robin released her from the embrace, almost giving in to the urge to run from the room, such was her desire to be with Willow. Instead, she watched for a second as Gina headed towards the kitchen sink before leaving the room.

Only when she reached the foot of the stairs did she flee, taking them two at a time, her daughter's name screaming in her head, panic taking control of her heart, fear guiding the way to Willow's bedroom door. Not caring about waking her, she yanked on the handle and burst into the room, terrified of what she would find there.

CHAPTER THIRTY-SIX

OF COURSE SHE WAS FINE. WHAT ON EARTH HAD SHE expected to see when she opened the door other than Willow, turned on her side, facing the window? No pills scattered on the floor, empty bottles strewn on the duvet, no blood splattering the wall or whatever dreadful gut-wrenching scenario Robin had tortured herself with as she raced along the landing.

She'd overreacted, that was all, and she needed to pull herself together before she approached Willow who was clutching one of Maya's teddies, stroking its head. She was still there, alive, it was okay.

Moving around the bed, Robin smiled when Willow looked up. 'Hello, sweetheart, I thought you were sleeping but wanted to check before Babs arrived. Did you have a nice chat with Gina?'

Willow nodded.

'I was wondering if you'd like to come down and have some food with us. You don't have to stay long but I'm sure Babs would love to see you and I've got some special treats downstairs.'

Willow turned away and focused on the window. She insisted on having the curtains open at all times, so she could watch the birds and the stars. She hated feeling caged, always had done since she was little.

'Okay. I like Babs. Is Gina still here?'

Robin's heart soared. For Willow to leave her room was a good sign, progress, and if Edmund or Nate saw her downstairs it would be a win, one she badly needed.

'Yes, she's waiting in the kitchen. Now, let me find your slippers... ah, here they are.'

Her heart was thumping, whether caused by happiness or tension Robin didn't care, only that she got Willow into the kitchen. She intended taking a photo of them together. Proof, that's what she had to gather, evidence for the care team that Willow did have good days and Robin wasn't pulling the wool over anyone's eyes. Least of all her own.

Holding out her hand to Willow, Robin waited.

'Come on, I'll brush your hair. Wait till you see the food, it's very fancy. Lots of sandwiches, there's a lovely assortment, egg and cress too, your favourite.'

Willow took Robin's hand, not responding to the lure of party food as she was pulled upwards and then guided towards the chair in front of the dresser. Still silent, she sat patiently while her hair was brushed, and Robin reminded herself to take things gently and resisted the urge to talk to Willow like she was an eight-year-old being readied for a birthday party.

Yet it was hard, because sometimes it felt like Willow regressed, to a time and a place where she was of indeterminate age and needed assistance to eat a few mouthfuls of food, to bathe and dress.

Each day was a challenge, cajoling Willow from her bed, jollying her along so she'd put on some clothes instead of pyjamas. Sometimes she co-operated, others she refused and pulled the duvet over her head and slept. Other days she just stared, at the ceiling, at one page in her precious photo album, at Maya's teddy, or out of the window.

But today, today Robin was determined would be a good one regardless of the news she'd just heard from Gina. Something positive had to come of the last few hours of a grey day, even if it meant Willow eating a damn sandwich and a fancy cake.

Robin brushed Willow's fair hair. It had grown so long, was ramrod straight and silky clean from the bath she'd taken earlier that morning. Then Gina's words poured like boiling water into her brain followed by alarm bells. She would never close the bathroom door on Willow again. She'd leave it ajar and sit outside in the hall just in case...

Looking up, she was about to ask Willow if she'd like her hair tied up when Robin saw she was being watched by eyes that changed colour with her mood. They were darker, greener, embellished by flecks of caramel, intense.

'Mum.' Willow's voice was firm, one not often heard. Robin proceeded with caution because every so often, anger showed its face.

Please not today.

'Yes, love.'

'I don't want Dad to come into my room anymore.' Willow held Robin's gaze.

Robin continued to brush, glad her shaking hands were occupied but she had to ask, even though she knew the answer. 'Why? Has he upset you, sweetheart?'

'Yes. I don't like him. He says things I don't want to hear. He scares me. Make him stay away, please.'

Willow appeared calm, sure, and Robin was determined she'd stay that way.

'Of course. I'll tell him, don't worry.' But how could she not ask... even at the risk of a flare, Robin wanted to hear it herself. 'Do you want to tell me what he's said? It's okay if you don't.'

In the silence, she reached over and took a bobble from the dresser and began to tie Willow's hair, the motion soothing the anxiety that riddled her. Again, when she glanced upwards, serious eyes met hers. Watching, waiting.

There was something different about Willow, Robin felt and saw it. It had happened before. Moments of lucidity, as though she'd emerged from her locked room refreshed, batteries charged. It never lasted long though.

Days or hours, never the weeks and months and forever Robin yearned for. She clung on though, making the most of each minute, talking, talking, talking, like she'd stored up a zillion words that she had to share with her child. It was like having her back, eating toast, watching television, the simplest things that brought Robin the greatest pleasure. Then Willow would turn away, fade, then lock the door. And Robin had to wait on the outside without a key.

When she finally spoke, Willow's voice was low. 'If you are bad, you go to hell. It's horrible there. Worms crawl over your skin, demons pull your hair and scratch your eyes, and you never sleep because they keep you awake and remind you of all the bad things you've done. He says that's where I'm going to go because I don't pray, anymore. God is very angry with me for thinking bad thoughts. I'm scared because I don't want to go to hell, Mum. I want to be with Maya in heaven.'

Robin was horrified. How could a father do this to his child? Why was he pushing a fragile woman to the edge, saying all the things that he knew would terrify her? Gina was right. He couldn't be trusted.

Knowing that Willow would pick up on any hint of panic, the merest trace of doubt, Robin gently put down the brush then knelt at the side of Willow, pulling her skinny legs so her body twisted and faced her. Taking her pale hands in hers, Robin sought to soothe her wide-eyed girl.

'Now, you listen to me, Willow. The only person who is bad, is your father for telling you such nonsense and I promise, he will never ever say these things to you again. You, my darling girl, are the most beautiful, the most kind, with a good soul and God would never turn you away because he forgives us our sins, doesn't he?

'Remember, we used to say the prayer in Sunday school and look at the pictures in the books, of your friend Jesus. He's one of the good guys, isn't he? And he wouldn't lie so please, believe me, and believe in him. Will you promise me that, Willow? And in return I'll promise to keep Dad away.'

Willow nodded. Her hands tightening as she spoke. 'I promise.'

Robin pulled her best *it'll be okay* smile from the bag and then leant forward, kissing Willow on the forehead. Leaning back, Robin intended to stand, however, Willow's grip intensified, as if holding her in place with her hands and a stare. A chill ran through Robin.

'I want to be with Maya. In heaven. The angels know the way but when I ask them they won't tell me how to get there. I asked Gina. She's going to help. Will you help me, too. Please, Mum. Please help me.'

Unable to look agony in the face a second longer, Robin wrapped Willow in her arms and held her tight, pulling her as close as she could and whispered into her daughter's ear.

'Of course, of course I'll help you. We will pray, together, ask the angels and the good guy. See if he can get a message up to the boss and somehow we will find the answers and one day, you will see Maya again. I know it. Just hold on, Willow. Hold on to me. Please don't let go just yet. Please don't leave me.'

Clinging on, to her child and the hope that her words had

got through, Robin forbade herself to give in to tears. Willow needed to see her mother strong and sure. Able to fend of that despicable man they called father and husband.

So, when she felt Willow's arms move, gentle hands resting on her back, reciprocating, Robin held her breath and scrunched her eyes, relishing the moment. They stayed like this, locked in embrace, until the ringing of the doorbell broke the mood, the precious moment was lost and as they pulled apart, Robin realised one thing. Willow hadn't answered, she'd held on, but she hadn't promised she wouldn't leave.

'I think someone's at the door.' Willow turned towards the sound, a wary expression on her face.

'It'll be Babs. I wish I'd not invited them now. I'd rather spend the evening with you.'

And as much as it sounded ungrateful and mean, it was true. Robin had lost heart and interest in her girly night in, because in light of the recent revelations it seemed trite and inappropriate and her mind was racing, trying to think of an excuse to send them home.

Until Willow spoke. 'But we're having sandwiches and cake. I want to see Babs and Gina, just for a bit.' Averting her gaze from the door she turned it on Robin. 'Can you get my slippers, please. My feet are cold.'

Robin, fearful that Willow might fade, acted on instinct, following the signals, not wanting to miss her chance to score a point over Edmund and Nate and at the same time, lift the mood and make Babs and Gina happy. Grabbing Willow's slippers from beside the bed she pushed them onto her feet before forcing creaky knees to stand. Without being bidden, Willow copied and wordlessly headed for the door.

'Do you want something warmer? The fire's on in the kitchen, but perhaps a jumper?' Robin was fussing but couldn't help it.

Willow shook her head, then glanced at the bed, then the door, as if her courage and energy were waning. From behind, in her yellow sweatshirt and black leggings, her precious child looked so small and frail, her little chick, her very own will-o'-the-wisp.

Willow was searching for the impossible. Asking a question nobody had the answer to. Trying to reach somewhere uncharted, as mythical as Brigadoon, the end of the rainbow, nirvana. Heaven and Maya.

It was with a bittersweet combination of melancholy and determination that Robin led Willow along the landing and down the stairs, her voice soothing, telling her pale-faced child how pleased they'd be to see her, hoping that Babs and Gina would hear and be suitably excited when they entered the kitchen.

At the same time Robin vowed that somehow, she would find a way to help Willow. Keep her away from Edmund's mind games for a start, and then focus on keeping her daughter safe from harm, because the message earlier was clear.

Willow was stuck, just like Robin, but that was her own fault, a situation of her own making that she could have changed any time she'd wanted. But as she'd said to Arty, she'd been weak. A coward, bound by faith and duty. Hiding behind motherly love and she'd got it wrong. No matter what Arty said, she was to blame for so much.

Her daughter's predicament was infinitely worse. Not only was her husband cheating on her, he wanted to unburden himself. Willow was trapped there on earth by her mind, a slave to clinical depression, at the mercy of a cocktail of drugs that sometimes failed her. And she was tortured by the images of that fateful hideous day, and those of the beautiful baby she longed to see again; and, thanks to Edmund, by images of terrifying demons, and the fear of going to hell.

It couldn't go on. There had to be a solution and if it was the very last thing Robin did, she would find it.

CHAPTER THIRTY-SEVEN

GINA

BABS HAD HAD ONE TOO MANY ALREADY AND BY HER OWN admission needed to sober up so, while she nipped to the loo, Gina scooped a very large spoonful of coffee into a mug and waited for the kettle to boil.

She was less stressed than an hour or so before, when Robin surprised them all with, 'Ta-da, look whose joining us for tea.'

Gina had been recovering from her confessional with Robin when the arrival of Babs wiped out the lingering sense of gloom. Rosy cheeked from her power-walking, tipsy and in a foul mood, Babs had slammed an almost empty bottle of Prosecco onto the side. Then, as she yanked a full one from her rucksack, began to tell Gina what a raving pillock her Pete was.

The arrival of Robin and Willow stemmed the flow and in a heartbeat the conversation flipped from ripe language to welcoming words. As hugs were given, and chairs pulled from under the table Gina could feel the crackle of tension, like a spell that could be broken at any second. And judging by the wary glance Babs gave her, no doubt her friend could feel it too.

Nervousness was written on Robin's face, but gradually the telltale lines eased, her shoulders relaxed. With the innate powers of sensory perception cultivated by womenfolk across the land, signals were read, leads were followed and eventually, they all relaxed.

Willow sat by Gina, who'd pulled her chair a bit closer, their hands linked, the gentle stroke of a thumb for reassurance, while Babs fussed, clearly thrilled to see her. Willow had nodded here and there, nibbled on this and that, smiled occasionally and drank half a glass of her favourite raspberry pop. Even though her concentration wandered and her energy waned, the time she'd sat with them was a gift, and the photos Robin insisted on taking, precious mementos.

By the time Willow asked to go back to her room, Gina could see that she'd almost left them anyway, retreating further into silence. Still, it was progress, Gina was sure of it. So rather than feel sad it had ended she told herself to look forward to the next time.

Footsteps on linoleum signalled the return of Babs who plonked herself on a chair while Gina passed her a mug of coffee.

'Thanks, love. I need this. Got a bit carried away with the plonk.' She took a tentative sip then placed it on the table. 'Wasn't it lovely to see our Willow. She looks well doesn't she, a bit on the pale side but I suppose she doesn't get out much. It made Robin's day that she joined in, I could tell.'

Gina nodded her agreement and took a place at the table, wanting to speak quickly before they were interrupted. 'Listen. I told Robin about Nate. It came out in the middle of another conversation, but it felt like the right time.'

'Oh bloody hell. No wonder she looked a bit mithered when she came down and while I think of it, missy, you looked a bit tearful when I arrived. Is something going on?' Babs had leant forward, her arms crossed on the table, a frown relaying her concern.

'Yes, but I don't want to mention it unless Robin does... just the vicar being his usual self.'

A noise overhead caused them both to look upwards and Gina changed the subject.

'This spread is lovely, isn't it. Have you tried one of these?' she held up a tiny savoury and put it on her plate.

'Yes, I had three, but you do know that you're supposed to eat them not just look at them!' Babs gave Gina the pursed lips, raised eyebrow look that she'd perfected to a tee.

The arrival of Robin saved Gina from a telling off and grateful for the distraction, she turned the focus of the conversation to Willow. 'Is she okay?'

Robin flopped into a chair at the head of the table, nodding as she poured herself a glass of red wine. 'Yes, out for the count. She's had her night-time meds and will probably sleep straight through now. She's exhausted.'

Gina and Babs watched as she took a glug of wine before replacing the glass on the table. 'I *so* needed that! Are you two not joining me?'

'No, I'm driving, and I promised Babs a lift later. I'm fine with tea. I'll make myself one.'

Robin waved Gina in the direction of the kettle, while Babs gave a little chuckle and picked up her mug. 'I'll have this coffee and then join you for another. Sod it. I've been looking forward to tonight so I'm not going teetotal, but I will pace myself. And I'll have another one of these sandwiches, they're bloody lovely.'

After a lull in conversation, while Gina made a mug of herbal tea, Robin drained a glass of wine and refilled it. Babs munched away and no sooner had Gina plonked her bottom, than Robin made a surprise statement.

'Men are total, utter bastards.' A more genteel sip, followed by a less forthright comment directed at Babs.

'Gina's told me about Nate and frankly, I'm not in the least bit surprised. In fact, I've had my suspicions for a while. I suppose I convinced myself that he wouldn't do that to Willow, but he has and now I can deal with it so thank you for being honest.'

Babs reached over and gave Robin's hand a squeeze, the gesture reciprocated. 'So what are you going to do?'

'No idea yet. I'll give it some thought but I know one thing. If he's carrying on with some woman, he's not living under my roof any longer. He can bugger off. I can't imagine what Edmund will say when he finds out. Another sinner living under his roof... no doubt we'll have a fire-and-brimstone lecture, and he'll see it as some personal attack on his impeccable reputation.'

She took another sip, a breath, then rolled her eyes. 'I mean, as if having a gay son wasn't bad enough, then a daughter, a mere woman, wanted to take holy orders and then in the midst of despair tried to take her own life. And then there's having me for a wife. Poor old Edmund, it'll be worse than the ten plagues of Egypt all over again.'

Robin took a glug of wine this time, while Gina shifted uncomfortably in her chair, knowing full well that dirty Eddie's reputation was far from impeccable. God, she bloody hated secrets.

Babs looked outraged. 'Well he can't say a single bad thing about you, Robin, because as far as I'm concerned you're perfect and he's bloody lucky to have you. We all are, isn't that right, Gina?'

Gina nodded.

Babs was on a roll. 'And not all men are bad. Our Gina's Jimmy is a good lad, so we can't lump him in the bastard category with the vicar and my Pete who's bloody useless as far as I'm concerned.'

Babs was looking to Gina for affirmation and met by silence.

A big lump of something was stuck in her throat, and in her head, all her worries, fears and confusion were pushing their way to the front like a great big ball of fire, burning a hole in her brain, making her eyes sting.

Babs had noticed and still holding on to Robin's hand, spread her arm sideways and took Gina's hand in hers. 'Love, what's the matter? You've gone a funny colour. I've not upset you, have I?'

Gina gripped the handle of her mug, and Babs' hand and before she even had time to think about the words she'd kept trapped inside for so long, blurted them out. She couldn't bear to keep them in a second longer.

'No, you've not, but Jimmy has.'

Babs looked from Gina to Robin then back to Gina. 'Why, what has he done?'

'Well, for a start he's not the "good lad" you think he is. He's having an affair too!'

Two gasps filled the room and beating Babs to it, Robin spoke first. 'Oh, Gina. Surely not. What on earth makes you think that?'

Gina was losing control. All the months of evidence gathering. The nights she'd spent talking herself in and out of her suspicions were swelling up inside her and about to burst forth from her throat.

The anger and humiliation, the disappointment and bewilderment needed to get out and be heard because otherwise she would go mad. When the tears came, they were followed by the scraping of chairs and arms around her shoulder.

Then once she'd been patted and shushed, had drank a full glass of water and used three sheets of kitchen roll, Gina was finally able to explain about Jimmy.

CHAPTER THIRTY-EIGHT

BABS

BABS WAS LOST FOR WORDS AND THAT WAS A RARITY. NEVER would she have thought that Jimmy would be up to no good, it was inconceivable. But with that Bella Young. Well that had knocked the wind right out of her. He'd lost the plot, he must have. Jeopardising his marriage and family for that stuck-up floozy. Bella had always been a horrible child who'd grown into a horrible woman.

And no matter how much they'd dissembled all the evidence that Gina laid before them, as much as Babs didn't want to admit it, it looked like Jimmy had joined The Bastard Squad. He'd be in good company with Edmund, Nate, and Pete.

It had been awkward enough earlier; hearing Robin describe Edmund as having an impeccable reputation. It'd made her cringe but how could she expose him without shaming Gina? The last thing the poor love needed was to hear that her own mum had been at it with the vicar all those years ago. And Robin needed it even less.

Babs bloody hated secrets but for the sake of her two dearest friends she would keep the one about Edmund, for the time being. She quite liked having that little nugget in her pocket, just in case. The matter most urgent was what to do about Jimmy.

'I think you need to confront him, Gina. And I know you're scared that if it comes out in the open he'll leave, but you can't go on like this. It's clearly making you ill and there still could be a reasonable explanation. So I think it's worth giving him a chance.'

Babs poured herself a glass of Prosecco, telling herself she needed it and didn't care how merry it made her. The evening was going rapidly downhill, and she'd not even got round to telling them that she was going to leave Pete! That could wait.

Robin leant forward, her fingers spinning the base of the half-full wine glass. 'I agree with Babs. This is clearly making you ill and you have to think of your own health, as well as protecting the children. I do understand though, what you're doing. I'm guilty of the same and I'm sure Babs is too.'

Gina looked up, her eyes swollen and her gaunt face blotchy and red. 'What do you mean?'

A sigh, then Robin explained. 'Keeping the peace. That's what I mean, maintaining the status quo so that the children don't get upset. And because you think the situation you're in is better than any you can imagine alone. I've made all the excuses, told myself I was doing it so Willow and Cris could live in a childhood bubble of bliss. I made sure arguments were kept from little ears. That they never heard me cry and thought the smile I painted on at breakfast was real. I know you're scared of what the future holds if the balloon goes up, but is living a half-life fair on you or, ultimately Max and Mimi?'

Robin turned to Babs who took the baton. 'She's right. I've done it for years with my lot. I've plodded on, kept the peace, agreed to things I shouldn't have, put my three first, like it was my goal in life. And if I'm honest, put Pete after them but when it comes down to it. I always came last.'

Gina sounded shocked. 'But that's what mums do! We put our kids first and that's what I'm doing now. I want to keep the family together for them, so they don't live the life I had. I'll never be like Debbie because she was the most selfish woman on this earth. I just can't accept it, let him go. I have to find a way to keep him, for them.'

Babs' heart was hurting for her friend, because while she was trying to get it right, she was getting it so wrong. It was hard to explain. Then she had an idea. 'Look, Gina. I've known you since you were a little girl and love you like family which is why I can be honest. I know all about your mum, and how you strive to be the total opposite of her in every way, but you have to stop because it's blurring your judgement and affecting how you live your life.'

Gina's hand went to her chest, her expression one of confusion. 'What do you mean?'

'You know when I slag Pete off and complain about the kids, and I do, a lot. You brush it aside. It's just Babs going on with herself. The thing is, my family, my life, my marriage might not be something you should aspire to. I'm certainly not perfect and recently I've had to face up to the mistakes I've made and one of them, you're making right now.'

'Like what?'

'Like settling for second best. Putting my dreams and wants aside. The kids first. To some extent that's okay when they are little, toddlers who can't fend for themselves, or seven-year-olds who think their dad's the bees' knees, teenagers who need stability, but when does it stop? When is it ever the right time to say, *yoo-hoo, look at me. I deserve to be happy, too.* One day you wake up and realise life is passing you by and it's a horrible feeling.'

'Is that how you feel? Seriously, that life has passed you by.'

Babs gave a nod. 'Yes, love. I do.'

Then Robin. 'And I'm sure thousands, millions of women have turned a blind eye to an affair, thinking it will blow over and it's a phase, a mid-life crisis, whatever. It probably always ends in tears.'

For a heartbeat there was silence followed by a question from Gina. 'So what would you two do? If you found out Pete and the vicar were having affairs? Would you leave them?'

Babs answered immediately. 'Too bloody right. He'd be bin-bagged and out the door in a flash. To be honest I've often wished it, that he'd run off with someone from the office and then I could play the injured party and have a cast-iron reason to call it a day.'

Gina was aghast. 'Oh my God. Are you really that fed up, with Pete? Would you really leave him and the kids.'

And there it was. The million-pound question and now it'd been asked, Babs was suddenly desperate to voice her intentions, ones that right up until that moment had seemed like an out-of-reach fantasy. 'Yes, I am that fed up. And there's a strong possibility that I am going to leave, once I've worked out how to do it.'

Even Robin sounded shocked. 'Would you really leave Demi? I mean, Isaac and Sasha are adults now but surely Demi needs you. She's only just started college. I honestly can't believe you'd even consider it. And that's not a judgement by the way. It just sounds so un-Babs-like. To abandon her family.'

Babs puffed out her cheeks. 'But I'm not abandoning them. Two of them are adults and need to stand on their own feet and I don't think they ever will while I'm around. And as for our Demi, she's got her head screwed on and she'll be leaving for university in a year or so, and what'll happen to me, then?'

She looked from one to the other, then answered her own

question, 'I'll still be there. Stuck in my life and another year wasted in coasting. I'm not doing it anymore.'

'But what about Pete? Don't you love him anymore? Has he been horrible to you or something, and you've kept it quiet?' This was from Gina.

Babs reached for Gina's hand and gave it a jiggle. 'No, love. He's not been horrible, not in the way you mean. He's just been Pete and that's probably my fault. I have to take some responsibility for how it's all turned out because I should've stood up for myself more, made the effort to get him to understand how I felt. And been firmer with the kids, so many things.

'I can't change the past, but I can bloody well change my future. And as for whether I love Pete, yes I do, but like an old friend I've known for all my adult life. I don't wish him any ill, but I have to make a choice. Do I plod on? Or, do I take a chance?'

Gina nodded. 'Only you can decide that, but I'm curious. Have you actually explained all this to Pete and given him the chance to change... or do you not want him to?'

Babs sat back in her chair, weary from her exchange with Pete and opening her heart to her friends but there was no point in telling half a story and if it meant helping Gina in any way at all, it'd be worth it.

'I did want him to change, and I've tried to make him understand but today, just before I came here, it dawned on me I was wasting my breath. Gina love, pass me that bottle. I'll have a top-up then I'll tell you about our lay-by rendezvous... and then you'll see why I was half-cut when I got here!'

By the time she'd given them chapter and verse, Babs could tell that Gina and Robin were on the same page and it was a relief, to have got it all off her chest. It had been stupid, keeping it all bottled up and she wished she'd confided in one of them beforehand. It might have eased the burden.

Turning to Gina, she asked her a question. 'So now, do you understand what I was trying to say? I know you love the bones of Max and Mimi and want to protect their lovely world for as long as you can, but please, love, don't sacrifice yourself in the process. In the end you'll be more miserable than you are now, and they deserve a happy mum. With or without their dad, who, for the record, deserves a chance to prove you wrong.'

Babs was relieved to see Gina nod, yet not surprised by her answer.

'I'll give it all some thought, proper thought. The kids are going for a sleepover at Jimmy's parents' this weekend. He's dropping them off on Friday, so I'll have time and space to approach him. I just need to get it straight in my head and pluck up courage.'

Robin spoke next. 'Well I'm glad to hear it, and both of you, please, please promise you'll ring me, or each other from now. I can't believe you've both being going through the mill and kept it to yourselves. Let's promise to be here for each other, day or night. That's what friends are for, and I am so glad to have you two in my life.'

Instinctively, all three of them stretched their hands towards a space on the table and formed a pile, one hand on top of the other in solidarity. It was a special moment, and it meant a lot to Babs, and she hoped to the others, too.

Then something pinged into her head. 'So, that's me and Gina all unburdened, so now I think it's your turn, Robin. We still haven't discussed Nate and what to do about him. We need to get our heads together.'

With a release of hands, they all reclined in their chairs and Babs could see that Robin was deep in thought, her brow furrowed, and then a light in her eyes. 'Yes, we do, but before that we need something very important.'

Babs was intrigued. 'Ooh, what's that?'

Standing, Robin headed to the fridge, smiling as she went, a mischievous look in her eye. 'It's obvious,' she pulled open the door and reached inside before showing them what she meant. 'We need... chocolate cake!'

CHAPTER THIRTY-NINE

ROBIN

IT HAD BEEN A BLUFF, STALLING FOR TIME BUT THE chocolate cake had done the trick and even Gina had accepted a thin slice which seemed to please Babs no end. Robin had taken a portion but had zero appetite for food whereas the rest of the bottle of red was sorely tempting. She'd have to abstain, though.

A couple of glasses was her limit in order to remain alert in case Willow needed her. And in the light of Gina's information, Robin would have to be doubly on the ball now she knew Edmund was playing mind games.

The reason for her stalling tactics wasn't actually down to avoiding a conversation about Nate; it was because Babs' heart-to-heart and the baring of her soul had deeply touched Robin. It also rattled her cage because some of what she'd said had been uncomfortable listening.

It was no secret to Babs or Gina that her marriage to Edmund had more or less broken down. The parishioners most likely believed she'd had some kind of breakdown to match that of Willow, or she was grieving. Robin didn't give a toss what they thought.

She and Edmund were never seen together outside the

vicarage. She never attended services, and even if Gina or Babs were unfortunate enough to be there when Edmund was around, you could cut the air with a knife.

Robin had even mentioned in passing to Babs that she wished there was space in Willow's room for a small single bed, or that they had four bedrooms; anything to not share a room with Edmund. The desire to draw a line between them, even down their mattress, was immense and secretly, she knew Arty hated the thought of her lying in the marital bed. The whole thing reeked of shame and embarrassment.

At least after the news about Nate, that little problem had been solved and at last, there would be room at the inn, the second she gave him his marching orders. For the time being she would endure it.

What she couldn't shake was Babs' mention of dedication, to her children and how she wished she'd acted sooner, compared to Gina's intention to put them above herself. Robin had done both and hated seeing a reflection of herself up close and personal.

If Babs did leave Pete and the family, would Robin admire her, or despise her? Not for the act, but because it would make Babs seem strong and that made Robin feel weak.

She'd missed her chances, but at the same time had she not stayed with Edmund, Willow would be alone, or would she? Would Robin's affair with Arty have profoundly changed all of their lives, many courses of events? Would she have moved to France and if so, they'd never have gone to town that day because the shopping trip had been Robin's idea.

Oh God, help me.

Someone tapping the table saved Robin from her mental torture.

'Earth to Robin.'

Robin looked at Babs who gave her a quizzical look. 'Are you okay, love? You've gone a bit pale.'

'Yes, yes, I'm fine... this is my autumn shade of unhealthy. I need a daily dose of sunshine to keep my fair skin and freckles looking perky and this dreary October grey isn't helping. Do either of you want more drinks?' Robin attempted a jovial tone, but it hadn't managed to reach her heart that was wallowing in the past and wary of the future.

It seemed Babs was determined to sort everything out. 'So, do you know how you're going to approach it with Nate? I don't envy you that conversation.'

Robin sighed. 'No idea. He's away for a couple of days and won't be back until Thursday. He's taken a field trip to the Lakes, or so he says. Let's face it, he could be with his lover for all I know.'

'I could get our Demi to find out, you know, ask about at college and see if there are any field trips at the moment. I know her name though if that's any help. Then you can hit him with all the info, so he can't wiggle out of it.'

Did she want to know? Then spend all night trying to put an imaginary face to a name. 'What's she called?'

'Josie Bilton. She teaches English. I can find her on Facebook if you like. Or would you prefer not to see?'

Of course she wanted to see, now she had the name, she wanted a face to hate and blame for stealing Nate away from Willow. And then, in the time it took to Babs rummage in her rucksack, find her phone then jab and scroll the screen, Robin had realised what a big fat hypocrite she was being. Where was her understanding and humility?

Had she forgotten that Nate had suffered too. Had lost not only Maya but his wife and marriage as he knew it. And from somewhere, he'd found the strength to get up each morning and go to work, forge ahead, forge a life that didn't contain the two people he'd once loved the most and perhaps still did. But they were gone. Maya for sure. Willow, indefinitely.

Josie Bilton's smile lit up the screen. She was pretty, a brunette, and petite. Who could blame him? How could she look Nate in the eye and say she didn't understand why he wanted to be with someone who made him happy, lightened his load, made him look forward to the day and leave at home the sadness he carried around with him.

After she'd looked at the screen, she asked Babs and Gina the same question.

Gina answered first. 'Because he's married. He should stick at it and not just throw in the towel the first chance he gets. He has responsibilities, a duty of care to his wife and the memory of their baby. Surely he can see that. And it's so easy, isn't it, because he has you here, twenty-four-seven, leaving him free to do what he wants.'

Babs had her say next. 'I see it from both sides. I don't think there's a right or wrong. Nate's had to cope with so much, too, and who knows how loss affects people in different ways. The only person who seems to be totally absolved of any feeling or responsibility is the vicar. Unless he just doesn't show it.'

'Okay,' said Gina. 'So we have to take into consideration Nate's feelings and maybe I'm projecting my anger and confusion at the "Jimmy situation" but I'm so let down. That's my overall feeling. That people always let us down, don't they. And as for the vicar. I'm sorry, Robin, but I can't imagine what goes on in his head and I don't think I want to.' Gina's shoulder's sagged as she began tearing up a serviette, leaving shreds of paper on the tablecloth.

'I know what you mean, Gina. That's how I feel. Very let down. I'm not angry at Nate and in some ways I'm sorry for him. The man he used to be wouldn't find deceit easy and I hope that his betrayal of Willow, and of my trust in him, weighs heavy. That would be some punishment, I suppose. I'm not condoning what he's done but I can't castigate him for it either.'

'Well I think that's very generous of you, Robin. I don't think I'd be so, what's that word that begins with m...?'

Gina helped out. 'Magnanimous.'

'Yes, that's it.' Babs paused, then had another question. 'Are you going to tell Edmund?'

'I suppose I'll have to. But I can't bear the thought of listening to another one of his pompous rants and no matter what he's done, I wouldn't wish the wrath of Edmund on Nate. I'll deal with it when he comes back but he'll have to leave. He can't stay here, not now I know.'

'I think you're right, love. Nobody needs a big drama and shouting match so maybe if you just have a sit down, adult conversation with him you can come to some arrangement. He could still come and visit Willow, couldn't he? And she probably won't even realise he's gone.' Babs gave Robin a reassuring smile and her words had made a lot of sense.

Gina didn't sound so convinced. 'But we'd have to lie to her, and I don't think I could do that. Pretending Nate is still here seems even more cruel than her knowing the truth.'

Robin focused her attention on Gina who looked on the verge of tears. 'Gina, you know as well as I do that for much of the time Willow doesn't even know what day it is, let alone who's in the house. She has no concept of time and hours, and weeks can go by. What would be the point in trying to explain to her that Nate has left? I also think if she grasped it, it might cause a reaction that none of us want to see or deal with.'

Gina nodded but didn't reply, instead she wiped away her tears.

Babs leant across and gave Gina's hand a gentle pat, before turning to face Robin.

'Can I ask you a question? It's something I've wanted to

broach for a while but there never seemed to be the right time but seeing as we're having a proper heart-to-heart, I hope you don't mind. It's a bit personal.'

Robin could only stare, curious and a tad nervous about what the soul-searching question might be. A slight nod gave Babs permission to ask away.

'What about you? Are you happy? And forgive me, I don't mean with Edmund because you've made it perfectly clear over the past few years how you feel about him... I mean with your life in general.'

Robin couldn't speak, simply because she didn't know, and that shocked her. To have no true concept or opinion of her own state of happiness. Where she was on the smiley scale. Her silence only encouraged Babs to embellish.

'The thing is, Robin, you dedicate yourself to Willow, day in, day out and I know you have your little jollies to see your friend Francesca now and then, but if Nate goes, that leaves you as sole carer and from where I'm sitting, it could mean putting the rest of your life on hold. Are you content with that? Living here with Edmund in limbo?'

Defence, that was the word that first sprang to mind, and Robin came out fighting. 'Willow could improve, one day she could live as a fully functioning adult. It's early days and there are so many new drugs in trial and therapies too, that we haven't even tried yet so don't write her off, Babs. That's what Edmund has done and from the looks of things, Nate, too.'

'Love, I know this, and I hope with all my heart that the doctors will get her better and she comes back to us. Our Willow is in there somewhere and tonight I saw a glimmer of what could be. I'm just worried that in the meantime you're going to burn yourself out and have nothing left for you.'

The anger had abated somewhat, and Robin reminded

herself that Babs meant well, her question was fair so sought to reassure rather than take offence.

'Perhaps Nate going is a watershed and it'll force me to take a look at our situation differently. Maybe I can search for some alternative therapies and ask the team if she can go on one of the drugs trials. But as for my dedication to her, that's non-negotiable and I'll put her before myself always. It's my duty as a mother and whether it's right or wrong, that's how it will be.'

Robin watched as Babs nodded her understanding, but there was one more thing she had to say.

'I get what you are saying, Babs, and I know it comes from a good place because like you said earlier, you put your three children first but now, it's not enough. The good thing is you really are free to go and if you do, I want you to be happy.

'And I understand why Gina wants to stay for Max and Mimi and would sacrifice her happiness for them, even if it means turning a blind eye to what Jimmy may or may not be up to.'

She gave Gina a smile that she hoped conveyed many things, most of all solidarity.

'I used to imagine that I might catch Edmund having an affair with someone, anyone would do, preferably the bishop because that would have made me so bloody happy for the most perverse reasons.'

This was followed by titters and lifted the mood slightly.

'But if I was ever going to leave my unhappy marriage then it had to be on my terms, for my reasons and not as a result of Edmund's fall from grace. Like you, Babs, I stayed, got on with it. I know I missed my windows of opportunity, and I cannot tell you how I regret that for so many reasons...'

It was there again, that dreadful thought, like a portent, that whispered '*It's your fault. Cris would have been much happier away from his bigoted father. You'd never have gone into town...*'

'But I can't change the past, or the one thing that also held me back.'

'What was that?' Babs asked.

'My faith.'

Gina's head flicked up. 'What do you mean?'

'I mean that in the most perverse way, the thing that made me who I am, was at the core of my whole life and filled me with great joy and peace, has trapped me. My faith, in a way, has kept me prisoner here.'

Gina frowned. 'I don't understand, how?'

It was so hard to put into words that wouldn't sound like an excuse. Even though it probably was. 'No matter how unhappy I was, I couldn't condone breaking my marriage vows because divorce was, is, just something I wouldn't contemplate especially when my parents were alive. It would've horrified them, my father in particular and you know what,' she looked from one to the other, 'I think I was hiding behind it. Making an excuse because I hadn't the gumption to leave. And that makes me so angry with myself.'

'So why don't you change things, then?' This was from Gina.

Robin sat back, tired, her spine aching from sitting upright and she had the greatest desire to lie down for a very long time. To give her body and her brain a much-needed rest, and with her next words, squashed any chance of that.

'Because I simply cannot abandon Willow. The thought makes me shudder because Edmund has already hinted that she needs better care than I can give her and with Nate gone, I'm her only hope.'

Gina's face suddenly showed signs of comprehension, most likely at the mention of Edmund. 'Ah, I see. And I agree, she needs you to protect her from the warped mind of our dear reverend and her philandering good-for-nothing husband.'

The bitter sarcasm in Gina's words wasn't lost on Robin and neither was another fact that she chose to keep to herself – that just as she had been trapped by faith and duty, Willow was in a similar situation. Her beliefs and the fear of breaking a commandment was holding Willow prisoner inside her head and there on earth.

Edmund hadn't helped. Robin would do whatever it took to prevent Willow from harming herself but unlike Edmund, could *never* stoop to mental cruelty. Willow was tormented enough and to use her faith as a tool was warped especially when it, and her own father should be bringing comfort.

The clink of glass connecting with a side plate saved Robin from her plagued mind as Babs took the bottle from the table, sighing as she poured.

'I don't know, the things we do for our children boggle my mind. We never stop being mothers, do we? Even when they're grown up we still love them and want the best for them and that makes it harder, to make decisions for ourselves.'

'Unless you get lumbered with a mother like mine who had no trouble whatsoever doing exactly what she wanted. The person she cares about most is herself.' Gina was scraping her pile of shredded serviette into a neat pile. 'As far as I'm concerned you two are perfect, and you've always looked after me like I was one of your own and for that I'm so grateful.'

Babs placed a hand to her chest. 'Oh, that's a lovely thing to say, Gina, in fact I remember you once told me that me and Robin reminded you of a mummy bird, who'd put the little baby bird under her wing. Stayed with me for days that did. But I'm not perfect, but I reckon our Robin here is...'

Robin halted Babs mid-sentence. 'Whoa. No way am I perfect I can assure you of that!'

To this, both Gina and Babs rolled their eyes which made

Robin laugh, and as she did, in an unguarded moment allowed her innermost secret to escape.

'Ha! Well, what if I told you I'd been having a mad passionate affair for the past fifteen years and instead of going to visit Francesca, I actually meet my secret lover whenever he can slip away. We have rendezvous all over the place and make love for hours and hours.' Robin's eyes swept around the table, suspecting hers were as shocked as the ones staring straight at her, open mouths adding to the looks of horror, until...

'What are you like, Robin! You're a bloody nutter sometimes. I don't know, I'd more likely believe that our Pete was having it away with Mrs Boland down at the library. You daft bugger. Right, shall we clear this lot away then we'll be getting of your hair. Secret lover...'

Babs stood, chuckling, and shaking her head, and accompanied by Gina who also thought the idea was hilarious, they began moving plates over to the sink.

Robin remained seated, watching them as they fussed and tidied. She was glad the night had ended on a merrier note after their soul-searching and revelations but still, one thing, one person was weighing heavy on her heart and mind.

She couldn't help thinking of him, them, and how they'd ended up so far apart, yet so deeply in love. Before she stood to help Babs and Gina, Robin spoke to the man she'd put last. And in many ways, had trapped, just because he loved her so much.

I'm sorry, Arty, my love, I truly am. And somehow I'm going to put it right, I promise.

CHAPTER FORTY

GINA

It was a sunny, dry Thursday and as she walked back home that morning, the picturesque village of Little Buddington was carpeted in golden-russet leaves. It had been two days since their very heavy, yet illuminating girls' night in. And between the school and nursery run rigmarole, and life in general, Gina had thought of nothing else. The advice she'd been given played on a loop in her head.

Just reminding herself of what she *should* do made her stomach turn and had it not been for the parcel that had arrived that very morning, she might have convinced herself again that it was a silly mistake. If only she had the courage to talk to Jimmy about it, the whole thing would be cleared up in a roll of the eyes and a 'What are you like' jokey moment. Or perhaps not.

Gina *never* opened Jimmy's parcels when they arrived and vice versa. It was a rule they both adhered to simply because she'd once ruined a Valentine's Day gift that arrived much earlier than Jimmy expected. However, now it was spooky season and that didn't warrant a cheeky pressie. Her birthday wasn't until next April, with their anniversary shortly afterwards.

Therefore the box she accepted from the courier was unlikely to be for her. And that was why she opened it.

Two new mobile phones. Identical apart from the cases. One was gold, the other silver. Cheat phones. What other explanation could there be? Gina had sat and stared at them for... possibly hours, she couldn't remember. It was only when she realised that he'd know they'd arrived from the tracking advice, that she panicked. Not because she'd broken their rule, but because their presence was forcing her hand, goading her into asking him who they were for.

Minutes later, they were back in the nondescript jiffy bag that she'd laid face up on Jimmy's desk in the hope he wouldn't notice she'd opened it and if he did, she was going to bluff it out and blame Mimi. Mimi owed her one anyway, for the time she'd put one of Jimmy's favourite limited edition trainers down the toilet. The bowl hadn't been empty, either and it took ages to get rid of the stains.

From the arrival of the parcel, the day had crawled torturously on and when Jimmy came home from a meeting, later than expected but in a particularly upbeat and attentive mood... or was he nervous? He seemed agitated for sure.

Gina put it down to one thing. Guilt.

He hadn't even gone into his office when she told him a parcel had arrived and she'd left it on his desk. He didn't rush to open it but of course he wouldn't, would he. He'd then insisted on making dinner; and made quite a point of telling her all about his meeting and how tedious it was.

He was currently giving her a running commentary of the conversation he'd had with his mum on the drive home.

'She's planning all sorts of Halloween activities for the kids this weekend. Literally can't wait to see them tomorrow. Dad's excited too. He's such a big kid at heart. Do you want a brew? I'm going to have one.'

'No thanks, I'm good.' Gina continued to stare at the television, unable to meet his lying eyes.

Over-compensating, that's what he was doing because her paranoia whispered that he'd really been with Bella. The thought made Gina want to throw up. In fact she couldn't bear being in the room with him a second longer and for a terrifying moment almost screamed out that he should shut the fuck up and stop lying and being a fake and that she knew he was a cheat.

It was only the thought of Max and Mimi upstairs that helped her swallow down the words and the howl of despair lodged in her throat.

'I'm going for a soak. My back's aching and I've got period pains.' She wasn't even on her period and the quizzical look Jimmy gave her hinted that he thought the same, but she ignored him *and* his offer to run a bath for her. Instead she made her way upstairs, feeling his eyes watching her take each step. She knew he knew she knew. Gina could sense it.

Closing the door behind her, she turned on the taps and sat on the side of the bath, watching as it filled, and as she did, a thought occurred. The sleepover had been planned for a couple of weeks, and in all that time, knowing they'd have a full kid-free weekend, Jimmy hadn't suggested they do something fun and make the most of the time.

And it was half-term the following week and nothing had been mentioned about days out with Max and Mimi, or even a little getaway like he usually did. In fairness, she hadn't mentioned it either but that was because her head was a mess and anyway she didn't feel like being fair. He didn't deserve it.

Bath bomb. Gina opened the cabinet and searched for one and remembered they were downstairs, in the utility room where she left them when they arrived. She wanted to see the fizz and watch the colours explode and for the scent to tickle her nose. Christ, she needed cheering up and if a bath bomb was all it took... so rather than spoil her soak, she turned off the taps and opened the door, intending to make a quick dash downstairs to grab the box and avoid Jimmy.

She'd reached the bottom step when she heard his voice, he was in the lounge, the door shut, and he was speaking quietly. Seconds later her ear was pushed against the wood, listening.

'She seemed okay when I got in, a bit quiet I suppose... no, no, she didn't ask where I'd been.'

Gina's gut churned.

'I feel awful though, like it's prolonging the agony and I should just tell her now...' Someone had interrupted him, he was silent then continued. 'Yeah, you're right. One more night won't hurt, and like you say, we don't know how she's going to react when I tell her, so it's best the kids aren't around, just in case.'

Gina's hand flew to her mouth, her eyes scrunched shut, as if smothering sight and sound would also block out the truth. There was a period of quiet while the person at the other end of the call, and Gina knew exactly who that was, spoke.

And then Jimmy. 'School's shut tomorrow, something to do with the boiler being repaired so Max is off and I'm taking the kids to my mum's after breakfast and then when I get back, I'll tell her. All being well we can leave straight after so should be on the road by midday.'

Oh dear God, no. He was leaving her. He was really going to end it.

Gina could barely stand but she had to listen to it all. Hear as much of her fate as she could and then just like him, she could prepare.

'No, don't worry, I'll mention that, too. It needs saying and she's going to have to face up to it... No, I won't let her persuade me... yes, I promise I'll make her understand.'

Gina was in actual physical pain. Her chest was so tight she could hardly breathe and every bone and sinew in her body was rigid as Jimmy hammered the last nail into their marriage.

'I'll let you know how it goes as soon as I can, so try not to worry, okay. Look, I need to go...'

By the time Jimmy had ended his call, and Gina heard the lounge door open and close, followed by tuneless humming and the click of the kettle, she had collapsed in a heap at the top of the stairs.

From there she somehow managed to stand and on legs like jelly she staggered to their bedroom. After peeling off her clothes, down to her bra and knickers she dragged back the duvet and folded her trembling body into bed. Eyes staring at the window, out beyond the glass, seeing nothing, hearing nothing, feeling nothing.

There was only one thought inside her head, that repeated over and over and over, stating the obvious and demanding an answer.

This is my last night with Jimmy. He's going to leave me. How can I stop him?

And there she lay. Time running out. Only hours until Jimmy said goodbye.

While the bedside clock marked the longest minutes ever. As later, she felt Jimmy slide into bed and lie silently in the dark so close, yet a million miles away, Gina wondered what was going through his mind.

The urge to slide her hand across the sheets was immense. The desperation that consumed her, the need to connect with him one last time in any way he desired, was nowhere near as powerful as her pride that forbade it. Pride told her to get up and sleep in the spare room. Weakness made her stay.

Soon his breathing relaxed into the pattern of sleep, and while she listened, Gina marvelled at his ability to leave tomorrow in the hands of his conscience. She despised him for it too. For everything. For what he was about to do to their family. For whom he was going to leave them for.

Gina wasn't sure which of these killed her the most because that's what he was doing, second by agonising second. Death, right at that moment seemed the easiest of options because checking out would save her so much pain. No fallout to deal with. That was what she dreaded the most. The after. Once he'd said the words.

It was all going wrong. Again.

And it was so unfair. All of it. To feel such despair that she'd even consider leaving behind her children. No. NO. That was so wrong. Sick, appalling. She wasn't the one that should die, be taken from their equation.

And then slowly, from the darkest recesses of her mind, crawled forth a solution. A mad idea, a thought borne from anger during one of her runs when she'd stopped by the Young Farm. She'd imagined it burning to the ground with Bella in it. And the seed of crazy, quickly grew shoots of possibility, and as the roots of a plan began to form in her head Gina's despair was replaced by drive. A chink of light had lit the gloom of a blackened room. She had hours to think it through, work it all out, get everything straight in her head.

Then in the morning, she would change the course of her life, and Max and Mimi's, forever.

CHAPTER FORTY-ONE

MORNING HAS BROKEN. I LOVE THAT SONG EVEN THOUGH I could never sing it in church without sounding like I was actually murdering the blackbird. Nobody could apart from the choir.

The bedroom is still dark, but I can see a sliver of light where Jimmy didn't draw the curtains properly when he came to bed. I can hear the dawn chorus outside and even though my heart and body are like lead, their chatter lifts me because I'm glad for them. The little birds that are free from human troubles.

Oh to be a bird right now. To be able to put my head under my wing and hide from the day that I know, once it has begun will alter my life and that of my children's forever.

It's been the longest night and I am exhausted from taking apart my plan, walking through it every step of the way and weighing up the consequences.

All I have to do is slide gently from this bed for it to begin.

I won't wake Jimmy because he can sleep through a storm and Mimi having a night terror. And he's used to me, and my early morning runs so won't think anything of it.

I'll dress quickly in my running gear then head into Jimmy's study and take the key for the Young Farm. Next, I'll go down to the kitchen and take my trainers from the utility room. And from the store cupboard above the washing machine I'll take the two small disposable barbeques, a pack of firelighters, and matches. I will slip them into my backpack then creep out of the back door.

Nobody will take any notice. The neighbours, if they're up, will have seen me many times before and anyone I pass on the route, commuters, dog walkers, won't take a bit of notice. Why would they? Joggers jog at stupid o'clock.

But remember. Bad things still happened in the nicest of places and nutters still roamed free, even in Little Buddington. One of them might be on their way to burn down a house and kill its occupant. Or maybe light two barbeques in the bedroom of the woman who wants to steal their husband.

Carbon monoxide poisoning is painless so she should be grateful for that. However, there's a margin of error because I won't decide until I get there which method I'll use. I'd like to make it look like a suicide, but what if Bella wakes when she smells the fumes? I might have to restrain her or knock her out, but logic tells me that's too risky.

These CSI chaps are very clever. Which is why I might just start a fire and burn the witch until there's no trace of a hammer blow, or a pillow stuffed into her smug, botoxed face. Lord, I might pop her trout-pout lip fillers in the process. Never mind. Once she's toasted to a crisp, nobody will care.

It will all be so magnificent, my moment of triumph, watching from the top field as the orange and yellow flames flicker in the windows and out there, far from the road it'll be a while before anyone notices the smoke. They might even think it's the chimney. Who cares? All I care about is getting rid of

Bella because once she's gone, I'll put my marriage back together. Simple.

Nobody will suspect me. Babs and Robin especially. They'd never believe I was capable. Jimmy doesn't know I know. It will just be a terrible tragedy and afterwards, if he's sad, I'll be there to comfort him. Me and the children will save him.

It's kept me going through the night, this plan and all I have to do is push back the duvet and place my feet on the floor and then it can start. The new day.

I turn my head and look at him, the love of my life. One of the three reasons I get up each morning. I want to lean across and kiss him, but I resist. There'll be time for that later. Instead I slowly crawl from under the duvet. Sit. Swing my legs to the side and place my feet on the floor.

As I leave the room I don't dare look back and silently, close the door behind me.

CHAPTER FORTY-TWO

BABS

<small>Happy Friday. What are your plans for today?</small>

Babs read the Facebook post and scrolled through some of the comments before clicking off the app. She had zero interest in the wonderful or mundane things people were filling their Friday with. Not when hers was going to go exactly the same as all the others she'd scrubbed and dusted and hoovered through.

She looked up at the house she was due to clean, knowing that the occupants would've left to catch the commuter train into the city, leaving her alone to tidy up their mess. It was 9.30am and as much as she tried to summon the energy, knowing she had three more homes to get to before the end of the day, try as she might, Babs couldn't muster enough enthusiasm to get out of the car.

Maybe she'd fried her brain so badly that it couldn't be bothered to send messages to her limbs in which case, she'd be stuck on Mrs Glynn's drive for the foreseeable future. Her bidet would not be getting bleached any time soon. Hilary, as she preferred to be called, liked her three bathrooms to have the Domestos treatment once a week and the thought didn't fill Babs with pleasure.

Babs blamed her bout of malaise on over-worked grey matter being at the end of its tether. Ever since Robin's, she'd taken apart their conversations in the hope it would make things clearer for herself. It hadn't and if anything she was even more bemused than before.

In a way, once she'd sobered up the next day, Babs was left feeling like the bad apple because she was the only one thinking of bucking the trend and doing the unthinkable – leaving.

One good thing was they'd all got a lot off their chests and in Gina's case, Babs hoped that her and Jimmy could sort things out. But she'd said all she could on that matter and now, would have to wait and see.

Her thoughts then turned to Robin who really did have it tough. It'd been incredibly uncomfortable when she'd brought up the vicar having an affair and Babs had been so flipping glad she'd never outed him.

She'd so admired Robin in that moment, saying that if she was going to go then it would be on her own terms not because the vicar had forced her hand by being caught with his cassock up.

Robin might not believe it, but Babs thought she was a tough cookie and really did need to stop beating herself up about mistakes she might have made. As far as Babs was concerned, Robin was a saint and she'd challenge anyone to prove her otherwise.

But none of this solved Babs' problems. That was what she had to focus on because the atmosphere at home was truly shite and she couldn't stand being there a moment longer.

What the hell are you doing, Babs? Sitting here like a wet Wednesday, getting nothing done.

Babs sighed and went to take the key from the ignition, knowing that Mrs Glynn's woodwork wouldn't polish itself. Wasting time. That's exactly what she was doing.

Wasting bloody time and if there was one thing she was sure of in that very second, was that her road didn't stretch out like Route 66. It was getting shorter with each day. She wasn't eighteen anymore with a whole life ahead, so far out of sight that anything had been possible but now, the end of the road might be just around the bend. So if she wanted to reach the rainbow, she needed to get her finger out.

Remembering her promise to Robin, that they would stop bottling things up, Babs had the overwhelming desire to talk to the one person she should've confided in. Someone guaranteed to call a spade a spade and put her straight. Her mum.

Without a ping of hesitation, Babs turned on the engine and put her car in reverse, shooting backwards down the drive and onto the main road where she did a very nifty one-handed spin of the wheel, straightened up then zoomed off.

Sorry about your bidet, Hilary, but you're going to need to buy some Marigolds!

Bridie's back door was never locked during the day. It was open house for family and neighbours alike, where you knew to stick the kettle on, get the mugs out and start making a brew.

On this occasion when Babs pushed the door and entered the kitchen, it smelt of burnt things. The usual suspect was toast or crumpets, Bridie's staple breakfast diet.

'It's only me, Mum.' She could hear her mum chatting on the phone so as law dictated, Babs began making tea, and knowing Bridie only drank from her own fancy china mug she bought in Tesco, her favourite daytime haunt, Babs nipped into the living room to hunt it down.

Seeing her daughter, Bridie waved and related her arrival to whoever was on the end of the phone, his identity soon becoming clear.

'Tom, love. I'm going to go 'cos our Babs is here. I'll sort that transfer out in a bit, yes, yes, I know there's no rush at your end but you're not eighty-seven. Who knows if I'll make it to bedtime, so it'll be with you soon.' Bridie paused, listening to whatever Tom was saying as Babs swiped the special mug from the arm of the chair and returned to the kitchen.

'Yes, I'll explain to Babs, but you can tell her the nitty-gritty. I'll only get it all mixed up. Right, ta-ra for now. Give my love to Cris. Love you too, son.'

As Babs stirred two sugars into Bridie's cup, her curiosity was piqued but knowing her mum, it would only be a matter of minutes before she spilled the beans. After whipping off her coat and hanging it over the back of a chair, Babs carried the drinks through to the front room, eager to find out what was going on.

'A boat! Our Tom's actually bought a boat. Well, I didn't expect that.' Babs sipped her tea while Bridie explained all.

'I know. It's very exciting. You know like Cris has his band that tours round the resorts in the holiday season, well, they're going to do music cruises. The idea is holidaymakers will take a moonlit trip around the coast, and they'll serve food and drink. Maybe even pick up some wedding customers too. I think it's a marvellous idea, don't you?'

Babs could only agree and admire her brother and Cris for their entrepreneurial skills. 'I think it's absolutely brilliant, Mum. He's done so well, hasn't he? Really got his life sorted...'

And it was those words, and perhaps being sat in her old family home, with her lovely but slightly bonkers mum, that caused her lip to wobble and a great big whoosh of despair rise up. Even if she'd tried, Babs wouldn't have been able to hold it in.

'Are you okay, love?' Bridie put down her mug and sat forward. 'Come on, you can tell your old mum what's wrong.'

And that was it. All it took. Soft words and kindness broke the barrier and the floodgates opened.

'Oh, Mum, I'm in such a mess and I'm so bloody fed up...' Babs covered her face with trembling hands and within seconds Bridie was by her side on the sofa, hugging her close and telling her it was going to be okay.

'That's right, love... you get it all out, have a good cry then we'll sort it out. I'm here, Babs, I'm here, love.'

An hour later, Babs had vented, explained, cried some more and been round the houses telling Bridie everything. That she was unhappy and unfulfilled, and feeling that life was passing her by. She didn't expect her mum to have all the answers, however, just getting it off her chest felt like progress of sorts. It kind of made her decision to leave Pete a thing, not a fanciful whim.

'I knew things weren't right. I've suspected it for a long time but whenever I've hinted and hoped you'd say something you clammed up. But I'm glad you've told me the truth now because it means I can help you sort it out.'

Bridie stood, picking up their mugs then made towards the kitchen. 'Come on, let's go and make another brew; this one's gone cold, and our Demi will be here soon. She always calls on Friday when her lectures have finished. I don't know. These bloody students have more time off than soft mick. I'll text her and tell her to bring you something from the bakers. We can all have a nice chat and some dinner together.'

Babs followed her mum, buoyed by her assurances and breezy nature. Bridie had the ability to switch from cuddly to practical Mum in a flash, as though she could read the room and knew what was needed to jolly everyone along and get things done. It was comforting and made Babs smile as she pulled out a chair at the battered Formica table that had been there for donkeys' years. It was where her grandkids had poster-painted, play-doh'ed, argued, and eaten special Grandma Bridie teas.

Bridie filled the kettle and once it was switched on, she sent a text to Demi then turned, sighed, and asked Babs a question. 'So, madam, what's the plan?'

CHAPTER FORTY-THREE

Babs shook her head. 'Apart from I don't want to be with Pete anymore, I haven't a clue what's next or how to go about it. That's what scares me. The unknown. And how I'm going to get from where I am to something else. A future I can't even see or imagine. I just know it's out there.'

'That's understandable. And it's a big thing, serious stuff, leaving your husband and family, but they're not little kids anymore, Babs. And I can tell from what you said before that you've been agonising over it for a while. One thing I am pleased about is that you've decided to leave and not do what some women do and kick their husbands out.'

'Oh no, I couldn't do that. It's my choice to end things so I have to be the one to go. I wouldn't be able to live with myself and anyway, where would he go? I want us to part amicably for everyone's sakes. He's not a bad bloke and it may sound two-faced, but I do want him to be happy.'

Bridie nodded, then made an offer. 'You're more than welcome here, that's a given. There's two spare rooms up there so you won't be homeless.'

At this, Babs' whole body relaxed. 'Thanks, Mum. Are you sure you wouldn't mind? I know you like your independence.'

'I am independent whether you live here or not and this will always be your home and there will always be a welcome under its roof. Just say the word and I'll air your old room out, okay.'

Babs welled; a nod of acceptance was all she could manage.

'But before we become roomeys or whatever they call it, I think you need a holiday and I know just the place to go.' Bridie gave Babs a wink.

'Tom's?'

Bridie smiled. 'Yes. You should go and stay with our Tom and Cris. It's still lovely over there this time of year and it'll do you good, seeing them. And he'll spoil you rotten which is what you need right now. You'll be able to put some space between you and Pete once you've told him how you feel.'

A bloom of happiness swelled inside Babs at the thought of going to Tom's and yes, putting a thousand miles between her and everything. Time to think and work out some kind of plan.

'Okay. Tom's it is. Which reminds me. Where do you come into this boat thing, because from what I heard earlier, you're involved, too?'

Bridie gave Babs a knowing smile. 'Oh I am. But only in that I've given them some money towards doing it up and getting it ship-shape for next year. See what I did there, ship-shape.' Bridie chuckled at her own pun while Babs rolled her eyes.

'They want to do a full refit of the interior and that won't be cheap so I'm helping out. We all know there's no pockets in shrouds and I'd rather him have some of his inheritance now when it's useful. You'll both have to wait till I pop my clogs to get half each of this place which is worth a bob or two, I reckon.'

'Mum! I wish you wouldn't keep saying that. I'd rather you live forever than get a share of your house. God you can be so morbid sometimes and I have to say, this lottery win seems to be going a very long way. How much did you actually win? I know it's your closely guarded state secret, but I'm curious, and so is Tom.'

Bridie chuckled. 'Well our Tom knows now, 'cos I've just told him, and he made me promise I'd tell you, too.'

Babs waited.

Bridie had a glint in her eye that said she was going to enjoy her moment. 'I won eight hundred and forty-nine thousand pounds and seventy-two pence precisely!'

'Oh my dear God!' Babs was stunned. Her hands automatically covered her open mouth.

'And before you ask, the reason I never told you at the time, is because there was bugger-all any of you could do with it. We were in lockdown and if I'm honest, in your case, my reasoning was entirely spiteful and selfish.' Bridie was known for being forthright and her honesty came as no shock, yet her motive left Babs slightly hurt.

'Why, what have I done to upset you?'

Bridie tutted. 'Nowt, love, so don't look so crestfallen. It's that great gormless lummox of a husband of yours that I'm peeved with, and I'll be jiggered if I'm giving him any of my winnings. Thing is, seeing as you're wed, owt I give you will be half his. And he doesn't deserve it. He thinks he's a hero if he changes a bloody plug!'

Babs was speechless. She couldn't even find the words to defend Pete or be hurt that her mum regarded Cris as more worthy. It didn't even seem unfair because when it came down to it, it was her mum's money to do with as she wished.

Bridie elaborated. 'Don't get me wrong, I was dying to tell you all and have a big party to celebrate. I don't know how many times I almost rang you, but something told me not to. Call it a gut feeling. I thought loads about how the money could help you all, making lists of who'd get what but at the time, when the world was going to pot it actually felt wrong, and also a bit redundant.' Bridie stood, never one for being still, and set about fetching plates and plopping teabags into mugs as she spoke.

'Nobody could go anywhere. And the more I thought about it, people losing their lives and loved ones, I didn't want it to be wasted on something trivial like a holiday to Disneyland or a fancy car... stuff like that. Life had suddenly become very precious, so I decided that once we came out the other side I'd make sure it was put to good use. I made a new will, so it was all written down just in case that horrible germ got me, and then I bided my time.'

'Oh, Mum. I know it was a nice thing to happen, but it makes me feel a bit upset, thinking of you keeping it to yourself and worrying about it all. If you'd told me I'd have understood.'

Bridie opened the cutlery drawer and brought knives and forks to the table. 'I know you would but at the same time you'd have been keeping a secret from your husband and that's not right. To put you in that predicament.

'And as I said before, he's legally entitled to half of anything you have, I know, I checked with my solicitor. I'm sorry, Babs, because I know it sounds mean but he's not getting the very large lump of money I will be giving to you once you've sorted yourself out. Do you understand?'

Babs nodded.

'The kids will be all right, too, but they'll have to wait for theirs – especially Isaac who, in my opinion, is taking the bloody piss now, especially as he's going to be a dad.'

Babs could only agree so let Bridie forge ahead.

'I'm going to wait until he actually stands on his own two feet, and if he does, I'll help him and Fiona out with the money for a deposit. Our Sasha has surprised us all by getting a job so same with her. I'll help with her student loan and as for our Demi, our golden girl, she won't have to worry about her university fees. Out of the three of them she's got her head screwed on right and I'm beyond proud of that girl.'

Had it not been a bit weird and inappropriate, Babs would have stood and given her mum a standing ovation.

'And as for Pete. He'll be okay. He has a roof over his head and a good job and all the luxuries he's become accustomed to. Your mortgage must be almost paid up so he won't starve and can afford to pay his bills and that's all I'm saying on the matter. It's up to you to decide what you do about the house and all that. Just know that financially, you'll be okay. No more worrying.'

Pushing back her chair, Babs rushed around the table and flung her arms around her mum, squeezing her tight. 'Thank you. I love you, Mum. I'll make you proud, I promise.' When Bridie pulled away and placed two firm hands on Babs' arms, the mother-daughter look was stern, her words a touch softer.

'Proud. I already am proud of you and don't you ever bloody forget it. Never once have I thought any different and that's a fact. Yes, I was upset when you fell pregnant so young; but I was oh-so very impressed by the young woman who put her best foot forward and became a wonderful mum.

'I watched you juggle it all. Like I did with you and Tom. It wasn't easy working shifts at the hospital and bringing up a family. I have so much respect for you, Babs, running your own business, a home that you've helped pay for, not to mention three good, very polite – if not slightly spoilt – kids.

'So from this moment onwards I want you to promise me you'll hold your head up high and be proud of who you are and what you've achieved. You don't have to make me proud, Babs, because I am already. What I want you to be, is happy, okay.'

It was Bridie's turn to be the hugger and they were midway through sniffling and smiling when Demi burst through the back door holding up a carrier bag, her face saying, '*Oh, oh, what's going on?*' Her next words proved it.

'Oh, oh. What's going on? Gran said to bring an extra pie for mum cos she's a bit fed up... but this looks serious. Like I should have got cakes, too.'

Babs unfurled herself from Bridie's embrace and faced Demi, smiling reassurance, and beckoning her inside. 'Honestly, love. It's nothing bad, but I do need to have a word about something, so come on, sit down and I'll explain. I promise, we don't need cake.'

So far as Babs could see, Demi appeared to have taken the news quite well. There hadn't been any recriminations or tears and she'd listened in silence as Babs explained it all.

'Is there anything you want to ask me, or say? I'd rather you be honest, love.'

Demi shook her head. 'No, honestly I get it. And after our beach conversation at Rhyl, I'm truly not surprised especially after the baby news. So, you're going to stay with Uncle Tom?'

'That's the plan but I need to ring him and book a flight.'

At this, Demi's eyes widened. 'What? You're going to go like, right away?'

Babs nodded. 'I think I should. Now I've decided, before I chicken out. I need to speak to your dad first, and the others but I have to know you'll be okay. I don't want my actions to derail your studies by upsetting you.'

The eye roll said it all. 'Mum, I'm seventeen. I'll be fine and anyway I'm out most of the time, either at college or the garden centre and they've promised me more shifts now the flipping Christmas trees are all over the place. I'll either be working or studying, if I get the chance, or here with Gran. Just go and do what you have to. I swear I'll be fine.'

Babs had a huge lump in her throat and was unable to tell Demi how bloody wonderful she was, and most definitely the most golden of her children. Fortunately, she had no need because when Demi's eyes widened and her mouth made an O-shape, Babs braced herself for whatever was coming next.

'OMG!'

Babs and Bridie exchanged wary glances then focused on Demi with Babs asking the obvious. 'OMG what?'

A huge smile lit up Demi's face as she clapped her hands together, a sure sign she was excited. 'I've just had *the* best idea, *ever.*'

CHAPTER FORTY-FOUR

GINA

SHE CHECKED HER WATCH AGAIN. JIMMY WOULD BE BACK any minute so she made the most of each second going over and over how she would react when he walked back through the door.

After kissing Max and Mimi goodbye and waving them off, she'd raced upstairs to take a shower, determined to look her best when Jimmy delivered her sentence. If she was going to be a single, divorced parent then so be it, but his memory of her on the day he confessed wouldn't be of a haggard snivelling wreck. Which was why she'd done her hair and make-up and chosen a dress that he used to say she looked gorgeous in.

And so she waited.

Gina had chosen to receive the news in the lounge because it was a room she used the least with the children and so she minded less if it became tainted with unhappy memories. It was bad enough that the utility room would always be the place she broke down in a pitiful heap when she realised how absolutely ridiculous her pathetic plan was.

As if she had the guts to kill someone, to smother them in their sleep or gas them to death, let alone start a house fire.

Two hours. That was how long she'd sat on the floor, slumped against the tumble dryer feeling even more foolish than she had for a very long time.

Those two hours had, however, been used much more wisely than those where she'd lain awake planning to murder Bella. The questions came fast and furious as did the answers. Where had her dignity gone? Down the toilet with her dinner and almost every other meal she'd eaten that week.

She needed to be more like her friends. Robin conducted herself with an abundance of dignity: holding her head high in the face of village whisperers, staring eyes, and tragedy; refusing to turn her back on Willow; surviving grief; standing up to the vicar who'd slowly and surely eroded a whole family.

Robin was made of strong stuff. Be like Robin.

And then Babs who was about to change the course of her future forever. The days of sacrificing her dreams were gone. And as much as she loved her children, always would, she was convinced that being a good mother didn't mean making yourself miserable for them. Max and Mimi had Gina, had each other. She had a talent and a future. And if she was brave, that would be enough.

Babs was brave. Be like Babs.

Jimmy was going to leave. In which case Gina had two options. Let him go and retain her dignity and, no matter how terrifying it might seem, forge a new life for herself. Or she could scream and rage and beg, then when he'd slammed the door, grab a bottle of gin, curl up on the sofa and turn into her mother.

Debbie was weak and selfish. Don't be like Debbie.

And then there was Willow. Her beautiful lost friend dealt the cruellest of hands, who had the kindest soul and saw good in everyone, who hoped to change the world and earn a Blue Peter badge. But the little girl who'd set the caged birds free had ended up trapped inside her own head, forsaken by the man who'd promised to be there in sickness and in health.

Willow was powerless and at the mercy of her husband's whim. Don't be like Willow.

Looking in on the lives of others had brought clarity to Gina's own, a kind of revelation. By the time she'd heard her little monsters stomping about above, and their voices on the stairs her bum was numb, but her tears had dried. And Bella Young wasn't dead.

She was still a dirty marriage-wrecking slag who Gina hoped would ruin Jimmy's life but that was by the by. She had dippy eggs and soldiers to prepare and a husband to say goodbye to.

The sound of Jimmy's McLaren pulling onto the drive made Gina swoon but not in the way she used to. And when she heard the key in the lock and the creak of a door, she thought she might faint.

Her fingers gripped the arm of the chair as she waited for him to spot her, having left the door open wide. Footsteps from behind, and then his voice. 'Oh, there you are. Just give me a sec, I need to grab something from upstairs...' His feet pounded on the glass panels, his voice trailing, '...the kids were a bit giddy in the car... Mum and Dad will have their hands full this weekend I can tell you...' More footsteps returning and then he was in the room.

He'd been to his office. Gina knew every sound their house made, pinpoint footstep accuracy. The manilla envelope in his hand confirmed it, and more.

Jesus... divorce papers, he's going to give them to me right now.

Jimmy was nervous, she could tell by the pinched expression so when he came and sat by her side on the sofa, far too close for comfort and laid the envelope on the coffee table, she almost flinched, not sure how to react. When he took her hand in his it only added to her confusion.

'You and I need to talk, don't we?'

She couldn't speak so stared instead, not wanting his hand in hers but too stunned to pull it away.

'I wanted to speak to you last night, but I wasn't sure... I didn't want a massive row in front of the kids, but I felt terrible knowing you're upset with me, and I really needed to explain. I almost did about ten times. When you went to bed early it kind of made it easier, but now the kids are...'

'What do you mean, you know I'm upset with you?'

He sighed. 'Babs rang me last night, just after I spoke to Mum. That's why I was late because I had to pull over while she gave me a right royal rollicking.'

'Babs rang you...' Gina wasn't sure whether to be relieved or cross. 'What did she say?'

'She said a LOT of things because that one's got the gift of the sodding gab, but in a nutshell she told me you think I'm up to no good with Bella bloody Young of all people. Which I'm certainly not.'

'You're not?' Joy, pure unadulterated joy, and relief had begun to flow through Gina's body, starting in her heart. And then she tensed. How could she be sure?

Jimmy shook his head and answered Gina's question before she could ask.

'I have no idea how you've come to this conclusion, but Babs said you'd discovered a key, some texts, and bizarrely, two sex phones.' His lips quivered slightly, and his eyes crinkled at the corners, but he managed to quell an inappropriate giggle and carried on.

'And she felt really guilty because it was her – and I quote – "big gob" that started it all off when she saw me going to the Young place.'

Gina allowed the flow of happiness to continue and relaxed slightly. He was being far too glib and unconcerned for someone who was about to serve divorce papers.

It was time she had her say.

'Yes, all that's true. I saw the texts just before lockdown and I did give you plenty of opportunities to tell me you'd been up there, but you didn't, which made me suspicious. I found the key later, in your suit jacket pocket.

'And then, all through lockdown you seemed happy, with me and the kids so I convinced myself it was a ridiculous mistake. Then, just when I'd convinced myself to move on I saw another text, asking you if you wanted to take up where you'd left off. When I found out she was back in the village and then the phones turned up...'

'You put everything together and decided I was having an affair with that bunny boiler – because she is. And when I explain it all, you'll feel sorry for me... what I've had to put up with, for us.' Jimmy dragged his hand through his hair, tension etched on his face.

'What do you mean?' Gina was on the border of being deliriously happy, yet still wary.

When Jimmy slumped into the sofa, looking more drained than she'd felt for a very long time, she braced herself, imagining Bella throwing herself at him, luring him into the farm and all sorts happening. 'Just tell me. I need to know because I've been driving myself mad for so long.'

A deep sigh, then the answer. 'Okay, so it seemed like a great idea at the time and was meant to be a surprise, but that's gone tits up so just hear me out because after all this, there's half a chance you might not want to kill me. And neither will Babs, thank God.'

'It began a couple of days after our Christmas' party. I was mad busy when I took a call from a number I didn't recognise and seriously, I nearly fell off my chair when I realised it was Bella.' Jimmy reached over and took Gina's hand, holding on tight as he explained it all.

Despite her flannel about being in between jobs, it seemed Bella was actually in the country to start packing up her parents' belongings and then put the farm on the market. Old Mr and Mrs Young had no intention of coming back to Blighty, so had decided to sell up.

She'd called on the off-chance Jimmy had any contacts that might be interested in buying it privately, a quick sale would save on estate agent fees.

'I fobbed her off by saying I'd have a think, then rang Guy and gave him a roasting for passing on my private number without asking. Once Guy had apologised, he told me something interesting.'

Bella was lying. She was also in a lot of debt. Her sunbed shops were in receivership and in desperation she'd asked her parents for help otherwise the bailiffs would take everything. After they got over the shock, they'd agreed to bail her out, via the sale of the farm and in lieu of her inheritance. Bella was relying on the sale to clear her debts and start over and would no doubt sell to the first bidder.

The day Babs saw Jimmy, he was on his way over to check out the farm and seeing as Bella was actually in court, trying to buy some time with a judge, she'd left the key so Jimmy could have a mooch about.

'I immediately saw huge potential in the house, outbuildings and masses of land and knew it was a great business opportunity. I also knew you would hate the idea so decided to keep it to myself until I'd done the sums and had something concrete in place. The plan was to sit you down, tentatively mention the B-word and if you didn't go ballistic, I prayed you'd get onboard with what I had in mind.

'A price had been agreed via both parties then out of the blue, Bella's dad fell seriously ill, and she flew to his bedside, the day before Italy went into lockdown. Mr Young had Covid. Nothing could be signed because he was in a coma, and everything stalled.

'Then the UK went into lockdown, too. It wasn't until the flight corridors opened again and Mr Young recovered that the deal could go ahead, with Bella returning to tie up the sale. Then, once her debts were cleared, she intended to start again in Italy.

'So you see, love. There was never any affair, just a business opportunity that I hoped would change our lives forever.'

CHAPTER FORTY-FIVE

THE WHOLE TIME JIMMY SPOKE, HE HADN'T TAKEN HIS eyes off Gina. She knew, because she'd been doing the same. With each word, her world came back into focus. Yet she still had so many questions, not to mention apologies for not trusting the man she should have known better.

'I've been a complete idiot, haven't I? And I feel so ridiculous. I let my imagination and terror at the thought of losing you cloud everything. Then lockdown happened and I had you all to myself and it was perfect. Just us in our bubble with the kids and even though the doubts remained, I hoped it was a phase or a mistake. Bella had gone and it was over.'

Jimmy dragged his hand across his face and sighed. 'Gina, you are such a bloody nightmare! Why didn't you just confront me, then you wouldn't have gone through hell for all this time? Come here, you infuriating woman.'

He pulled Gina into his arms where she buried her face in his chest, happy tears wetting his shirt as she tried to explain.

'I was scared. Right up to telling Babs and Robin, who, for the record, didn't believe a word of it. They made me see I had to say something, and I intended to this weekend, but maybe

Babs knows me better than I know myself and suspected I'd chicken out. She was probably right because in my head, the minute I said the words to you that would be it. No more pretending it would be okay. No more silent prayers that you wouldn't leave me.'

Jimmy held her close, gently stroking her arm as he spoke. He sounded sad. 'So, you'd have carried on, thinking I was having an affair, worrying day in, day out?'

Gina nodded. 'Yes... I think I would because I didn't want you to leave us. I couldn't bear the thought of Max and Mimi... telling them you had left.' She flicked a tear from her right eye. She was making Jimmy's shirt very soggy.

Jimmy gently pushed her away and sat up straight, turning his body so he could see her face. 'That's probably the saddest thing I've ever heard and it's killing me inside, knowing you've been like this. But please, Gina, from now on promise me you'll never bottle stuff up again.'

She sniffed and sat up straight, too, her body lighter than it had felt in a long time. 'I promise. And there's so much I want to tell you, explain, because I feel incredibly sly and just horrible really, snooping on you and thinking terrible thoughts.'

'There's plenty of time for that. Don't worry. The main thing is you know the truth.'

It was true, she had plenty of time to tell her shameful side of the story but there was something more pressing she wanted to talk about.

'Okay, I'll tell you later but I'm curious about this plan of yours and yes, I am a bit shocked that you've been communicating with Bella, but under the circumstances you're forgiven... I think.'

'Ah, my grand plan for world domination, yes, I need to explain and then I have another surprise for you.' Jimmy winked and brushed a stray hair from Gina's face and tucked it behind her ear.

'So, if you're sitting comfortably, my little worry bean, I will begin.'

It had been the seed of an idea for a while, to branch out on his own but the sensible side of Jimmy kept reminding him he had responsibilities, and it wasn't the time. Until the Young Farm came up for grabs and he saw it as a sign, an opportunity that couldn't be missed. He could still work for his firm and the farm could be a sideline, a long-term project.

He did a bit of research and found that the land was classed as brown belt, which meant there was the possibility of developing it. Through his previous contracts and gift for networking, he was well-connected at the local council. His dad's building firm was a ready-made source of labour and expertise, so all he had to do was join the dots – and acquire the farm, of course.

Lockdown made everything a million times more longwinded and complicated. Jimmy expected the deal would fall through so put his ideas on the backburner, quite glad of an excuse not to have to fend off Bella's tiresome, flirtatious innuendos each time they spoke. Instead, he settled into life at home which he loved. And this led to another epiphany.

'I wanted working from home to be the norm. I also saw you were battling some preconceived notion that women have to go out to work once their kids went to school. I could tell you were putting undue pressure on yourself when you were already lacking confidence and there was no need.

'No matter how much I reassured you, it was like you were bowing to the unseen face of society and far too conscious of how being a stay-at-home mum would be perceived. Bloody Bella Young and her catty remarks didn't help, either.'

He'd tried to point her in the right direction, to build her self-esteem by encouraging her to go running, to do the upcycling Facebook page, whatever made her happy. Then, once lockdown eased and Bella got in touch and it looked like the farm was back on the table, he had a magnificent idea.

Jimmy sat forward and let go of Gina's hand then clasped his together. Expectation written all over his face, he took a deep breath and blurted out his idea.

'I want us to work together. You and me. I'm going to leave the firm, and the two of us are going to start our own business. Morgan Architectural... something like that. You can decide, you're the arty one.'

Gina's jaw dropped. 'Are you serious?'

'Never been more serious in my whole life, apart from our wedding day. Don't you see, it's the perfect solution? We can create the ideal work-home life balance. I have my office and, if you want, we'll make you one of your own, spilt mine in two. Whatever, they're mere details.'

'But what can I do? I'm not an architect.'

'No, but you are a fabulous interior designer, and this is the best bit... I want to build one hundred per cent environmentally friendly homes, totally sustainable, zero carbon emissions. We can transform the farmhouse into our flagship property. That, my darling wife, is where you come in.'

Gina had been rendered speechless.

Jimmy not so. 'Well, what do you think? Are you in? Me and you. Partners in every sense of the word. It's going to be epic, Gina, I know it. Combining both our talents and you can ease back into designing at your pace, with me by your side. I swear I've never been so fired up about a project in my life.'

'You are totally batshit crazy, you know that don't you, but yes, I think it's a brilliant idea and yes, I'm in. One million per cent in. I bloody love you, Jimmy Morgan.' Gina took his face in her hands and kissed him like her life depended on it.

When they came up for air, Jimmy took her in his arms, pulling her close as he said the same. 'And I love you, Gina Morgan, you bloody lunatic.'

Another question pinged into her head, just one amongst the millions clamouring for attention in her head. 'Was that Babs on the phone last night? I overheard your conversation and presumed it was Bella and went into meltdown. I could only hear your side of the conversation and...'

'And you put two and two together, again. Honestly, Gina, I still can't get my head round why you... look there's no point in going on about it, but yes, it was Babs. Her battery had run out mid-roasting, so she called back later to make sure I'd got the message and wasn't going to let her down. As if. I'm scared to death of her!'

From the comfort of his embrace, so many things were making sense, like the saying about eavesdroppers for a start. Then a thought.

'So that's what the sex phones are for? Our new business venture. You do know I'll never be able to look at them and not think that.'

She could feel Jimmy laughing. 'Yes, they are for us. It was all part of my big surprise pitch that I'd prepared for this weekend, when I presented you with the paperwork for the farm and our his 'n' hers fancy work phones. I just need you to say yes and then the deal can go ahead. Which reminds me. We need to get going.'

Gina heaved herself upwards and faced Jimmy. 'Get going where?'

'To the Lake District. I've booked us a luxury cottage and a fancy restaurant. I thought it would be nice to get away for the weekend while the monsters wreck Mum and Dad's house. I was going to tell you about the plan when we got there in case you went ape shit. Don't want blood all over our very fancy wallpaper; and in the country nobody will hear you screaming at me. Are you pleased? Say something.'

Jimmy had both his thumbs raised and wore a grimace while he waited.

Oh how she loved this man.

'Of course I'm pleased and excited and happy all at once.'

'Well, Mrs, in that case you need to pack. We can talk all this through properly on the drive up.' And then he paused. 'But there's one more thing that I promised scary Babs I'd mention.'

Gina was about to stand and drag Jimmy upstairs, hoping they'd have time before they left for her to make amends, but instead, she waited.

'Now don't flip, because against the odds today is going well...' he paused but noting Gina's *get on with it* look, did just that.

'I think we need to have a serious talk about your weight, or more to the point your eating habits. Everyone's noticed you've lost pounds and I'll admit I've been scared to broach it, but Babs said I have to and if Babs says it, I does it!' Jimmy, as always, had chosen to lighten the mood.

Gina could tell her cheeks had flushed and for a second couldn't look at Jimmy so focused on her fingers that were twisted into a knot. But the day was turning into one about truths and she had to be Robin-brave and Babs-honest. Looking up she met his eyes that held nothing but concern.

'I do it when I feel like everything is going wrong and getting out of control. It's my safety mechanism because taking charge of at least one thing in my life makes me feel stronger. It helps me cope. That's the only way I can explain it. But at the same time it makes me feel ashamed and weak, and terrible because I know it isn't healthy and I am letting you all down. It never gets totally out of control because usually things buck up, like now. Do you understand?'

He took both of her knotted hands in his. 'I understand why you do it, yes. But I think it's time you got to the bottom of why you started acting this way because I have a feeling it's rooted in the past. I'm not going to ask you to make any promises today, but I am going to ask you to think about going to see someone just for a chat. Will you do that?'

And as much as she had the urge to yank her hands away and scream NO! Tell him she didn't need a shrink or counselling, a tiny part of her did. She was weary of fighting off the demon inside that fed on her memories then fed on her. Enough was enough.

'You're right and yes, I will go and see someone. I don't need to think about it, so I promise. I have to get it out of my system once and for all, whatever "it" is.'

His smile could always light up a room and Gina felt the warmth of Jimmy's like it was a sunny day, right there in their lounge.

'Oh thank God for that. I can now report back to Sergeant Major Babs that I have completed her mission and she won't need to beat me to a pulp. And for the record, I'm so proud of you, Gina, for saying those words out loud and if you want me to come with you, anything, I will.'

'All I want right now is to pack and get away for a few days and make up for lost time. So let's save talking for in the car, come on,' Gina stood and pulled him upwards. 'When do we have to leave?'

He checked his watch. 'In the next hour. I thought we'd stop on the way for a bite to eat...' He was interrupted by a finger to his lips.

'Good, we have time then... I want to show you how sorry I am for doubting you.'

Jimmy's eyes widened and without waiting to be asked twice, led Gina from the room. As they made their way upstairs he stopped and turned, a wicked smile preceded a question. 'Do you think we'll need the sex phones?'

To which he received a slap from Gina. 'NO, Jimmy. We do not need the bloody sex phones, now get up those stairs!'

And as they headed to their bedroom, happy tears clouded the way, but Gina didn't care. She was safe, with Jimmy. Holding her hand, staying by her side and for once, instead of it all going wrong, it was all so perfectly right.

CHAPTER FORTY-SIX

ROBIN

Leaves swirled around Robin's feet as she made her way to Martha's headstone. She was checking for signs that the village teenagers had been up to their shenanigans. It was the same every year around Halloween when they couldn't resist the lure of the graveyard and scaring themselves to death once it was dark.

She was alone on her quest, save for a chap and his little dog who were picking their way between the rows, his head bowed, oblivious to her presence. She'd seen him many times before but always left him to his thoughts and that day; she was oddly glad he had his canine friend for company. *Everyone needs someone,* she thought as she continued on her solitary way.

In past Halloween forays, Robin had found skeleton and werewolf masks on the angel statues, no doubt some kind of dare, and empty WKD bottles, no doubt for courage. She didn't begrudge them their spooky fun as long as they didn't damage anything, hence why she was checking Martha's resting place. Her unspoken duty of care to a woman she'd never met.

The other reason she'd nipped out was to avoid Nate who'd turned up unexpectedly. He'd been ominous by his absence all

342

week. Skulking in late at night and back out again first thing. Blanching at her death-ray stare, skipping breakfast in his haste to escape. Whether it was his guilty conscience or, he'd sensed a change in her attitude towards him she had no clue, but it had been enough to postpone the showdown.

She'd heard Nate rustling around in his room while she kept vigil in Willow's. Since she had found out about Edmund's mind games, Robin had kept her promise and prevented him from entering Willow's bedroom. There'd been no arguments, only a look of disdain before he turned, following her instruction to GET OUT.

It was unusual though, for Nate to be home during the day on a Saturday. He was usually at the gym, or so he said. However, seeing as he'd deigned to spend time with Willow, Robin took the opportunity to get fresh air and see Martha. As she wove her way through the leaves and graves, Robin wondered if when she returned, it would be an opportune time to grasp the nettle and have it out with him. She hated confrontation but she hated sleeping next to Edmund more.

Having reached the headstone she put Nate to the back of her mind and leant against the wall. It was far too soggy and damp to sit and she could feel a chill rising up through her wellington boots.

Digging her hands inside her overcoat that flapped in the wind, Robin said hello to Martha, speaking softly, lest her words be carried on the wind and heard by the chap tending his wife's grave.

Just like all those who came to pay their respects, or so she imagined, Robin told her eternally sleeping friend her news. About Nate, Babs and Pete and the text she'd received the day before from Gina.

'I'm so pleased for her. In my heart I was sure that Jimmy would never betray her, and I can't tell you how her words lifted me because there *are* some nice men left and if anyone deserves one, it's Gina. They're off to the Lakes for a few days and when she gets back, she's got lots of exciting news to tell me and Willow. Very mysterious I must say, but all's well and that's the main thing.

'Things aren't so good with Babs, though, and I haven't heard from her since Tuesday. I think she might have had a bit of a hangover after our get-together as she did give it some welly. I'll drop her a line later, check she's okay. It seems to me she's made up her mind about Pete and I do feel sad for him but at the same time, I can't imagine having that conversation, can you? Saying you're leaving and ending a relationship. I just wouldn't have the bottle. Yes, yes, I'm such a coward. You don't have to remind me of that.

'If only. How many times I've thought those words and now look at me. Mrs Cowardy Custard. Nate hasn't any such qualms and once I've had a word with him he'll be gone and you know what else I've realised, he won't even have to have the "goodbye I'm leaving you" conversation with Willow.

'For one I won't allow him to upset her, and two, she probably wouldn't take it in. I never know what she absorbs but this is one thing she certainly doesn't need to know.

'Oh, Martha. There's something else, worse than the Nate business. Gina told me something terrible the other day. Something I have never been able to say out loud or admit to anyone other than you, because the words are too cruel and cold and horrible.

'I already knew, though, deep down, that Willow wants to take her own life. She's tried it a few times. I think I've told you. Maybe not. She sees it as the way to Maya, or she would, had Edmund not reminded her what happens to people who take that path. I hate him so much, so badly that there aren't enough adjectives in the dictionary to adequately describe it.

'Does he not see that she's trapped and tormented? So desperate and sad. And okay, I do accept that his cruelty is actually keeping her safe, but at the expense of her sanity and well-being. And I know that man so well to also understand that anything he does or says is for his own ends.

'He simply couldn't bear the shame of having a child commit such an act. It would offend him deeply, his morals and beliefs so he takes control in order not to fail. In my opinion he failed as a father to Willow and Cris many years ago, but you know all about that. You've been here for me through thick and thin.

'How I wish you could talk to me, Martha. There are so many things I want to ask you. One thing in particular because despite my secret faith, where I still trust in God, to know the truth would be a blessed relief. It really would.

'Where are you now, dear friend? Are you happy? Walking on fields of green under a blue cloudless sky? Are you with your boy, and your husband?

'I always picture you holding hands and the three of you laughing in the sun. I hope that's where you are, where our dear sweet Maya is. In the care of my parents until we all meet again. I have to believe that. Otherwise all of those prayers, all that trust in someone I cannot see, only feel, will have been for nothing.

'One thing I do know, without a doubt, is that the pain you suffered in loss, all the hours you waited on that bench by the duck pond, the tears you cried in the dark, ended when you left this mortal world. Was it a blessed relief? I truly hope it was.

'So many questions. Not enough answers. All I can do is focus my energy on facts and one, the most important, is that my daughter needs me more than ever and I won't fail her. People think I am her rod and staff when in fact she is mine, my reason to get out of bed in the morning.

'And dear Arty, of course, who I keep at arm's length, so he leadeth me not into temptation on a regular basis. Who stands patiently in the wings, the understudy, waiting for a chance he may never get. I've often thought I should set him free, but that man is stubborn as a mule, and I fear if I tried to, he'd come storming over here and make a terrible scene. I hate scenes so try to avoid one.

'Anyway, we've come this far in our dysfunctional affair, hiding our feelings, living our separate lives, grabbing the most treasured moments so it would be silly, cruel, to stop now.

'He's given me space to be, to love and care for my children and never asked more from me than I'm prepared to give. That's why I adore him because he is my saint, my knight. His light and shade entrances me, thrills me and simply knowing he is there would actually be enough. I think of Arty as my fearless rebel yet in some ways he is my meek slave. A slave to our love. And for my sins I hold the key to his chains.'

The sound of the little dog barking at his owner rudely interrupted Robin and Martha's one-sided chat. Checking her watch she sighed. 2pm. She needed to get back in case Nate buggered off out again, now he'd done his bit. It was this thought and her irritation at his fickle fakery that made her decide.

It was high time she put a stop to such nonsense. She should follow Babs' lead and make a reverse-stand of sorts and give Nate his marching orders. Otherwise she'd be following Gina's path, turning a blind eye. Of course there was still a chance that Nate would astound them all and rubbish the rumours, be affronted at the accusation then pledge his undying dedication to Willow.

Resisting the urge to laugh or look for flying pigs and spotting the man and his dog approaching, she bade a silent farewell to Martha and pushed away from the wall then followed the well-worn path towards the church. Ducking her head against the wind she pointed herself in the direction of the vicarage.

Minutes later, seeing that Edmund's car was still on the drive next to Nate's she tutted, sighed, and gritted her teeth in irritation. Still determined, despite the full house and captive audience that awaited she sucked in a lungful of Cheshire air and strode purposefully on, sights set on the vicarage door; mind set on a showdown.

CHAPTER FORTY-SEVEN

Edmund and Nate were seated at the kitchen table, talking in low voices which silenced when she entered the room. Straightening her hair that was tangled from the wind, Robin ignored them both and headed for the kettle until Edmund halted her.

'There's tea in the pot if you'd like some.' He pointed to the table where lo and behold there stood the teapot wearing its knitted cosy and in her usual place, an empty mug.

Bridling at the imperious way he had of indicating where one should sit, Robin followed his direction, unease washing over her. Edmund's next comment added to it further.

'Nate and I would like a word.'

Pulling out her chair and sitting, Robin rested her arms on the table and folded her hands together, then waited, glancing at Nate who wore a sheepish expression.

Ha, he's been caught out. Good. Edmund thinks he's going to shock me with a sinful revelation but who cares. He can tell him to go. Save me a job.

Edmund, never one to hold back or miss an opportunity to be lead dog, launched straight in. 'It's about Willow.'

Robin's stomach lurched and mother bears claws came straight out. 'What about Willow?' she looked from one to the other trying to second guess what came next.

'Nate and I have been discussing her current state and it's clear that she's not making any progress. In fact, it's two steps forward three back.'

'I disagree...' But she wasn't given the chance to state her case because Edmund took over.

'Robin, you must listen to what we have to say because it's obvious to both of us that your judgement is severely clouded by your prevalent maternal instinct and quite frankly, we feel you're hindering her treatment and recovery.'

Her whole body began to tremble. 'How dare you! If it wasn't for me Willow would be left to the mercy of carers who popped in twice a day and what good would that do her?'

Nate remained mute. Edmund closed his eyes briefly as though irritated by an insolent child, then continued.

'She needs continuous and dedicated psychiatric care and evaluation and she's not getting that here. Willow requires supervision so she won't harm herself, and access to professionals who can monitor her and offer her therapy on a day-to-day basis. She's surviving on the occasional visit from the district nurses and the on-call team when she has one of her episodes.'

Oh dear God, NO! This cannot be happening.

Her mouth had gone dry and a thousand drums were beating in Robin's ears, so loud she almost couldn't hear what Nate was saying. Her head turned to face him while her eyes watched his Judas lips move.

'You're not being fair on her, Robin. I know you love her and want to do the best by her, but this isn't the way. There are so many new treatments and therapies on offer and she's missing out. Don't you see that?'

The eruption when it came made the teapot rattle as Robin banged her fist on the table, her words hot lava on her tongue. 'Liar! Hypocrite! That's what you are, Nate! Oh I see everything. I really do so don't you dare try and play me for a fool or place the blame on me when this is merely your way out of your marriage.'

Her hand trembled as she pointed a finger almost in his face. 'I know all about your affair, with that woman called Josie. That you've been carrying on with one of your colleagues so won't it be convenient if Willow is shuffled off to hospital then you can get on with your sordid little affair.'

Her head swivelled, her eyes burning with hate as she looked at Edmund, and for a second, relished having one over on him. 'So, how do you feel reverend dearest? Knowing your son-in-law has been unfaithful to your sick daughter and you're playing right into his grubby hands!'

Edmund sighed and shook his head. 'Nate has already confessed to me and whilst I do not condone his behaviour in any way, I see it as a separate issue to that of Willow's mental health. The facts remain the same. Our daughter requires specialist care, and we are going to see that she gets it.'

We?

Robin was rendered catatonic by rage and shock. He was giving her an ultimatum. They had decided, taking her out of the equation like she was surplus to requirements.

Speak, for God's sake. Say something, anything to stop this.

'And where the hell do you think you're taking her? To that dreadful place she was last time, at the general? You didn't even visit her, Edmund, but I did and it's... it's truly awful. Understaffed and run-down. So what makes you think the NHS are going to provide the care she needs when they're already on their last legs?' Robin was nauseous even thinking about the place where the staff did their best, but no better than her. She was sure of it.

Edmund made a clicking sound with his teeth, like a pin being pulled from a grenade and in a way his answer was just that, a bombshell. 'Willow won't be going there. They're short of beds and the waiting list is too long so I will be paying for her care. Nate and I have found a private clinic in Derbyshire that can take her almost immediately. It's been arranged. She's going on Monday.'

Robin had to grip the table and press her feet into the floor in an attempt to remain conscious, her voice when it escaped was a mere whisper. 'Monday... you're taking her away on Monday? But that's only two days...' and then from somewhere within, mother bear found her roar.

'NO! NO, NO, NO. I won't allow it. I'll fight you all the way... you won't take her. I mean it, you will not take my child.'

'ROBIN, STOP!' Edmund's voice boomed around the kitchen bouncing off the walls, making Robin wince.

'Nate is Willow's next of kin and he's signed the paperwork and if you put up a fight I will back him all the way. I'm quite sure the authorities will take the word of a respected teacher and a man of the cloth, husband and father who only have Willow's best interests at heart over that of an overprotective, exhausted emotionally frail mother who is putting her own wants before that of her child. You won't win, Robin. So give up now.'

She looked to Nate, but he had his head in his hands.

'Nate, look at me. You owe me that at least.' Robin watched as he slowly met her eyes. 'You do see what he's doing, don't you? Because the minute you admitted your affair you gave him the ammunition he needed to punish me for rejecting him. Can't you see that? This isn't about Willow, it's about *him* taking control.'

She glanced at Edmund and gave him a look, scathing and disgusted, like she'd tasted something repulsive.

Robin couldn't bear to look at him for one second longer so returned to Nate. 'He thinks by taking Willow out of the equation he's onto a winner... he can't lose. He's a sick, twisted narcissist who would sacrifice his daughter to make me come to heel and if I don't, he will happily watch me suffer. Dear God, Nate, don't you understand?'

Nate's eyes were wide, like he was actually seeing things her way. There was a glimmer of hope.

'I'm sorry, Robin. I truly am but regardless of what you suspect his motives are, I think Edmund is right. Willow needs proper help and... and... I can't go on living a half-life and you will hate me for that but it's true. I lost my baby, too. And now I've lost my wife and I grieve for them both more than you know but I deserve a chance of happiness.'

The glimmer had been extinguished and in its place, a void, deep black, like despair. Robin was astounded. *You deserve.* Nate, have you heard yourself? We've all suffered, and we've all grieved. I lost my beautiful granddaughter that day. I was there, I saw it all, remember... lived through every second and still do when I can't fight the memories, but do I complain? I've sworn to dedicate my life to Willow because it's *my* job, mine. And you can't take it from me. You have no right.'

'He has every right, Robin. And you've just demonstrated why you're not in the correct frame of mind to care for Willow because it's clear you're suffering from post-traumatic stress of some kind. You admitted it only seconds ago. You're transferring the trauma of the day and projecting it onto Willow, seeing it as your duty to care for her when in fact you're using her as a crutch.'

Robin stood, her body leaning in Edmund's direction as she screamed, 'And when did you become a fucking psychiatrist?'

Whether it was the high-pitched accusation or the profanity that caused Edmund to recoil and Nate to gasp, she didn't care and turned her attention to her disappointing son-in-law. Knowing she had to get a grip and not fuel Edmund's ridiculous hypothesis; Robin lowered her voice.

'Nate, please don't listen to a word he says because he's brainwashing you like he tried to with Willow and Cris. But you're not a child like they were, or a silly naïve young wife like I was, who didn't realise what she was getting herself into. Think for yourself, Nate, I beg you.'

Nate's eyes flicked to Edmund, but his lips remained closed. Robin tried again.

'Why didn't you come to me? We've always got along well, and I thought we had a good enough relationship. You could have talked to me about how you were feeling. If you'd been honest, told me you were unhappy we could have worked something out, we still can. If you want to walk away and start a new life then go but please, don't send Willow to a strange place... please, I beg you...'

She was about to break down, her voice cracked, and she was struggling to breathe let alone speak but forced out the words. 'Don't take my baby away from me.'

Twenty-seven minutes had passed since Robin had collapsed in a heap at the table, unable to speak, allowing the tears to flow while her body was racked with sobs so intense they made her ribcage hurt.

Nate had brought her tissues and a glass of water and through it all she was aware of Edmund to her left, still in his seat, the fingers of his right-hand drumming on the tabletop. When her tears ceased, she kept her face hidden in her arms that were folded beneath her, resting on the cool pine. She could hear the constant thrumming transmitted through the wood.

It was Edmund's way of showing impatience yet strangely, it had the opposite effect and soothed her, like a baby listening to its mother's heartbeat. It gave her time to think.

By the time she raised her head to face Nate, she had realised one thing and decided on another. They weren't going to change their mind, no matter how much she begged. And she would never look Edmund in the eye again.

All she could do was ask for time. Time with Willow before they took her away but before that gave it one more try.

'I'll ask you again. Please leave Willow with me and just walk away? It really is that simple, Nate.'

When he answered, he had the decency to look sincere, but the steel in his voice made his feelings clear. 'I'm sorry, Robin. I can't. You might think I'm doing this for purely selfish reasons, but I assure you that's not the case. You'll be able to visit her and it's a lovely place. Edmund and I were there this morning and once you see it I'm sure you'll agree. I'm so grateful to Edmund for offering to pay the fees because it's taken a weight off my mind.'

Well, that's okay then. As long as you're fine and dandy, we'll all just jog on like nothing's happened, shall we.

When she spoke, Robin couldn't hide her sarcasm. 'Yes, I'm sure Edmund couldn't wait to get his cheque book out and spend some of the fortune his mummy and daddy left him. It's a pity he's never fancied sharing it with charity, you know, doing good in the Lord's name for the poor and needy of the world but hey-ho, such is life living with a devout hypocrite.'

Nate bowed his head and Robin hoped shame had just kicked him in the gut.

'If you won't change your mind, will you allow me one wish. It's easy enough to grant seeing as you'll have other things to be getting on with.'

She received a nod of the head. 'Ask away.'

'Let me have the rest of weekend with Willow, alone, just the two of us. I don't want Edmund anywhere near her. I would also prefer it if you kept well out of my way and in the meantime, make alternative living arrangements. I don't want you here any longer than necessary. I take it you'll be going with Willow to the... whatever they call the place you're locking her up in.'

Robin couldn't bring herself to say the word 'home' because as far as she was concerned it was a prison. 'And don't think for one second that I'll take her. I'm not having her think I betrayed her, because she will. If you do this, you do it yourself.'

Surprisingly, Nate didn't even consult Edmund before he answered. 'That's fine. I'll make myself scarce, but would you pack her things? You'll know what she needs better than me.'

Then after he had the grace to blush at his request he confirmed arrangements. 'And yes. I'm going to take her. I won't come back afterwards. I think that's for the best. But if you change your mind and want to...'

Robin raised her palm. 'I won't.'

Nate nodded then his focus turned to Edmund. 'Edmund, please respect Robin's wishes for the next two days and give her space and time with Willow. The last thing we want is any more upset.'

She didn't see Edmund's response and in the absence of a verbal objection, presumed he'd agreed with a nod. Then without another word, Robin rose from her seat and left the room, her wellies slip slapping on the tiles. Like her, they were muted as they made their way up the stairs. Her only thought was Willow and being with her.

From that moment on the clock was ticking, counting down the hours minutes and seconds until they took her precious child away.

CHAPTER FORTY-EIGHT

BABS

THIS IS THE HARDEST THING I HAVE EVER DONE IN MY LIFE. Don't ever let anyone tell you leaving is easy because it isn't. It's agony.

This is my home. A place of safety that saw us all through the saddest and happiest times and its walls have wrapped themselves around me from the day we moved in. I know every stick of furniture, each knick-knack and plate, where I bought them and probably when, if I set my mind to it.

I built my nest here, and looked after my chicks one by one, imagining how they would grow and the people they would become once they fledged. And I have to laugh at the irony of that thought because they're all still here! My big daft chicks still haven't buggered off. Maybe once again mummy bird needs to show them the way, and I will.

I've been lying here on the sofa, listening to the dawn chorus outside as I went over it all one more time in my head. Planning what I'm going to say to Pete and the kids. I'm scared they'll cry or get angry. I've settled on angry because my lot aren't really criers, Pete especially, unless his team goes down a league and then it's a different matter.

I've tried to salve my conscience with the fact that I'm not deserting three babes in nappies, and that I've got them all to a stage in their lives where they have the tools and moral compass to navigate the road ahead.

That said, our Isaac might need a nudge from Fiona and I'm starting to think our Sasha is welded to her bed, her laptop and her earbuds but at least she's working. It's the perfect job, sitting down and talking all day, albeit to customers about car insurance.

All in all, I think they'll be fine. Demi especially. She's got her head screwed on and I truly think that her spirit and common sense have helped me these past few months, yesterday at Mum's, more than ever.

It's Pete that I worry about the most. He could go either way. Vegetate in front of the telly feeling sorry for himself and drive everyone nuts, or just be Pete, doing all the things Pete loves to do. You never know, he might even book that holiday with 'the gang' and have himself a holiday romance. How would I feel about that? I honestly don't know until it happens, but I do want him to be happy and for us to stay friends. It might be a big ask but we'll see.

Last night, while Pete was down the pub and the kids were watching *Gogglebox* downstairs, I felt so sly, gathering my toiletries and make-up, and hiding them in the drawer. Secretly putting my shoes in a carrier bag and folding my getaway clothes in a pile, ready to take from the wardrobe later. Then I did a big online shop, so they'll have everything they need for the week ahead. I got them loads of treats, and all their favourites. Comfort food, I suppose, seeing as I won't be here to give them any. It'll arrive later this afternoon.

You know what would've been easier? A bloody big row!

Like the other day in the car. I missed a trick there because I should've stormed home, dragged my suitcase from the loft and thrown in whatever came to hand. Then I'd have stomped off to Mum's, booked a flight and buggered off.

The anger would have fuelled me on, got me onto the plane at least, but I can feel myself wavering, overthinking things and that's not helpful. Being organised, giving the house a thorough going over while they all slept through the early hours. Preparing a text to my clients saying that for the foreseeable they're cleaner-less. Trying to do my best for them before I do my worst has kind of made it harder, but I can't go back now. I have to do this.

The other thing that's bugging me is what people will say when word gets round The Willows that I've left Pete. They'll all know down the Co-op, and at the church. That lot of God-botherers are a right bunch of gossips and will love this.

Now I know how Debbie, Gina's mum must have felt having the whole village talking about her and they did – me included. Karma is going to come and bite me on the bum for that, I reckon.

That's one of the reasons why I rang Jimmy because as much as I love the bones of Gina, she's a ditherer and something had to give. It's bad enough that everyone knows about the vicar and Debbie, and there were more rumours that he was a bit too touchy-feely with some of the WI ladies, the dirty dog. Who knows who he's been having a dabble with over the years and poor Robin never knew, and neither does Gina.

I didn't want her to be gossiped about behind her back. One way or another she had to be put out of her misery.

I didn't actually intend to spill the beans about Bella, just give Jimmy a hint and a nudge that Gina was struggling and getting herself into a state but he more or less ground me down for information. Then I blabbed. He was going to go home and have it out with her but when he said he'd booked a weekend away, I suggested he left it till the little ones were at their gran's.

I hate it when kiddies are upset and a few more hours wouldn't make much difference.

All's well that ends well though. They both texted me to say that they'd sorted it out and thanked me for my help. I have to say I sighed with relief when I read it, knowing neither of them were cross with me.

Not like Pete. He's not spoken to me since our row in the car. He said my behaviour was embarrassing and he thinks I'm unhinged so I told him to get stuffed, or words to that effect and I've slept on the sofa since.

Oh my. I can hear movement overhead. I've got terrible butterflies, but Demi promised to be with me when I tell everyone. I feel so guilty that my daughter is in some ways an accessory to my departure. I've told her not to take sides and be kind and supportive to her dad when I've gone. She's promised she will and I'm glad because I don't want their relationship affected. This is between me and Pete.

Here they come, baby elephants. Time to face the music. It's weird, because the minute my feet touch the floor, it will begin, the day I change my life, and that of my kids, and Pete forever. I can't put it off anymore. Duvet off, slippers on, big girl pants hitched up. I'm ready. It's now or never.

CHAPTER FORTY-NINE

PETE HAD GONE OUT IN A HUFF. THE PILLOCK. HE'D waited till Babs went into the shower then hot-footed it downstairs, telling Sasha he was going to Calvin's to help him take down his garden shed and would be gone all day. His absence had scuppered her well-rehearsed plan and he was ignoring her calls and texts that basically said come home now, we need to talk TODAY and it's urgent. That was almost two hours ago and still nothing.

Still it had given her time to put all her stuff in her wheelie case that was standing at the bottom of the stairs. She'd left it there on purpose, hoping the sight of it would be a conversation starter, rather than launching straight into – just wanted to let you know I'm leaving. Her passport and travel documents were in her bag and all she needed to do was tell Pete and the kids.

Easier thought than done.

Checking the clock on the mantelpiece Babs saw she was running out of time and patience. A tight band of anxiety began to pull at her chest and her breathing became more rapid. She had to do something otherwise she'd snap, the tension and expectation of hours of thinking was getting to her which was why she stood and marched into the hall.

Calling out, her voice making it quite clear she wasn't in the best of moods, she summoned her children from whichever room they were hiding, sleeping or Lord only knew what-ing in. 'Isaac, Fiona, Sasha, Demi, will you come down here right now. I need to speak to you all. And I mean NOW!'

They looked like the three wise monkeys lined up on the sofa. Sasha, Isaac, and Fiona who Babs had included in her summons because well, she was family too. Demi had taken one of the armchairs leaving Pete's free, in case he bothered to show up. None of them had commented on the shiny black case in the hall, so maybe they weren't so wise after all, or they just didn't care.

Babs was standing in front of the fireplace, her heart hammering but after an encouraging smile from Demi, followed by an almost imperceptible nod, she got on with it.

'I was hoping your dad would be here too, but he disappeared before I got chance to speak to him in private and he's ignoring my texts so, I'll tell you, instead.'

She swallowed, took a breath then got it over with. 'It probably won't come as a shock to you, but me and your dad haven't been getting on for a while now, so I've decided to go away for a while, put some space between us.'

Nobody spoke.

'I'm going to stay with Tom and Cris for a while and–'

Sasha piped up, 'Is that your case then, in the hall? I just presumed Demi was going somewhere.'

'No, it's me that's going and–'

'Why don't you take Dad? A holiday will be do you both good. You can sort out whatever's bugging the pair of you.' Like father like son. Isaac obviously thought that two weeks away was the cure-all.

Babs suddenly felt weary, so she perched on the edge of Pete's chair and tried to explain. 'Isaac, I don't think a holiday is going to fix me and your dad and that's the other thing I want to tell you. I'm not just going on holiday, I'm leaving. I'm leaving your dad.'

Isaac leant forward, arms resting on his knees. 'What?! You mean as in splitting up. But why? Does Dad know?'

'No, because he shot out this morning and like I said, I'd wanted to tell him alone and in private but if he can't be arsed coming back then... then I'll just go.'

'But what about us? That means you're leaving us as well! You can't just go, Mum, and another thing, how long have you been planning this?' Sasha's tone was accusatory.

Babs had expected questions like this. 'I haven't been planning it as such, but I've been very unhappy for a long while and over the last week lots of things have made me realise I can't do it any longer. But as for leaving you, I'll always be your mum, Sasha, no matter where I live and let's face it, you and Isaac are adults now and it's about time you both stood on your own two feet. You wouldn't think twice about moving out and leaving me if you met someone, would you?'

Sasha folded her arms in a huff. 'Oh, charming. Just turn it round on us, like we're at fault too, not just Dad.'

'No, I'm not saying anything of the sort. Look, you both have jobs. Isaac and Fiona are expecting a baby and maybe this will be a turning point for all of us.'

Isaac butted in. 'Well our Demi isn't an adult so what's your excuse there?'

Babs went to answer but Demi got there first. 'Demi is actually in the room and Demi is fine with Mum going. She deserves a chance to be happy however or wherever that is and I support her one hundred per cent just like I'll support Dad, too. But not actually from this house because I'm leaving, as well.'

There was a unified 'what' from Sasha and Isaac, the latter taking the lead. 'What do you mean? Are you going with Mum?'

Demi shook her head. 'Of course not. I've got college. I'm moving in with Gran for a while because this place is doing my flaming head in. It's too noisy and I never get any privacy or peace to study, and she's got two spare rooms. I've thought about it a few times but didn't want to suggest it in case it upset Mum but now she's going, I am too.'

Isaac huffed. 'Well I don't know what you were worried about *her* for when she's clearly not bothered about you *or* us.'

'Zac, don't talk to your mum like that!' Fiona had turned pink but looked furious.

'Right, that's it. I'm ringing Dad. This is getting ridiculous.' Isaac pulled his phone from his back pocket and jabbed the screen in temper.

Babs watched and sighed, not wanting to hear what her son said to his father so stood and left the room, heading for the kitchen. Demi stormed upstairs, shouting that if Isaac was going to be a knobhead she was moving out straight away and going to pack. Babs was followed by Fiona.

'Would you like me to make you a drink, Babs?'

Pulling out a chair, Babs declined. 'Thanks, love, but no, I'm okay.'

'I'm sorry about what Isaac said and for the record, I think it's really courageous what you're doing, and I hope you find happiness, I really do, even though I'll be sad to see you go. I know it's been a pain, me being here but even through lockdown I loved being part of your family and around you. I wish I'd said so before.'

Such an unexpected remark set Babs off and her lip wobbled as she sought composure. 'Oh, love. Thank you. And I wish I'd said that I think you're a lovely young lady and our

Isaac is lucky to have you.' She gave Fiona a warm smile and received one in return.

'And I promise I'll be a good grandma when the little one comes along. I want to be a big part of their life, I really do. Actually, I've wanted to have a chat with you for days, clear things up but I didn't think it was the right time seeing as you and Isaac were upset with me over the babysitting thing.'

She saw Fiona go to speak but halted her, desperate to put things right. 'I swear it was nothing personal, please believe that. It was more about what's been going on up here,' she tapped the side of her forehead, 'than anything.'

Fiona was leaning against the worktop. 'It's okay, I get it, I really do. It was wrong of us to presume. I see that now even if Isaac doesn't.'

Babs could tell Fiona meant it and suddenly wished she could turn the clock back and put a bit more effort into getting to know her properly. They'd wasted time and the fact she'd been under the same roof caused a rush of sadness, so Babs decided to make amends in a positive way.

'Fiona, I want to give you a bit of advice and whether you take it or not is up to you. I love Isaac dearly but you're going to need to be tough if you don't want to end up a carbon copy of me because him and his dad are peas in a pod. I've made lots of mistakes and with hindsight I'd have done things differently. I can try to help you, though, be a friend and a mother-in-law.'

Babs paused, Fiona said nothing, her eyes wide.

'I've realised there are many different ways to be a mother. And the bad ones aside because there are lots of those about, there's no easy answer to how we do things.'

She paused as Sasha left the lounge and headed upstairs, probably to talk Demi out of leaving. Isaac would be sulking. Picking up where she left off, she tried to put her heart into words.

'The bond between a mother and child is unique, but while we do our very best we can forget that so are we. So please, when baby comes along, in between being super mum, every once in a while step back and remember yourself.'

Fiona nodded.

'Make your own rule book. Use bad examples for good. Don't conform, or think you have to be like anyone else, or make everyone happy. Start with yourself. The best example, the best role model for your baby will be to see a content, fulfilled mum. And if you need any advice or just want a chat, ring me anytime. I might not have the answers but I'm a good listener and even though I've left it till now to say it, I love you to bits.'

The sound of the front door opening and slamming, then voices. Isaac and Pete muttering in the lounge, caused Babs to stand and within seconds, Fiona was by her side, giving her a rushed hug and a whispered message. 'And I think you're amazing and I love you to bits too.'

Their embrace was soon interrupted by Pete, ashen faced and short of breath. 'Babs, what the hell is going on? Isaac says you're leaving.'

Fiona scurried from the room and closed the door behind her.

This was it. The big reveal. Like on telly when you *finally* get to see what Alan's done with the garden, or the house looks like on *Grand Designs*, or what the celebrity has cobbled together on *MasterChef*, but this was more like – Pete, feast your eyes on this – the rest of your life minus me!

'Yes, that's right. I'm going to stay with Tom.'

'Well I must say that's charming, seeing as you point-blank refuse to go anywhere with me.' Pete was pacing, circumnavigating the table, until he reached Babs then he turned and went back the other way like he'd met a rabid dog on his journey.

Babs was fast losing grip on her temper and time was ticking. 'That's because, and this will sound harsh, but I don't know how to say it any other way, I don't want to go on holiday with you Pete, now or ever. Do you understand? I've had enough of us and I'm leaving and if and when I decide to come back I *won't* be coming back here.'

His mouth dropped open, then clamped shut, then opened again. 'But... but where will you stay... I don't get it... I thought this was just a tiff and we'd sort it out like we always do.'

'NO! Pete. It's not. And I'm sorry, I truly am, but it's over. I can't think of any other way to say it than that. If you want to talk, you can ring me, but I've been waiting for you all morning and I need to go.' There. She'd done it.

'What do mean *it's over*? Babs, what the hell is wrong with you? Is it your menopause sending you doo-bloody-lally because if it is you need to whack some more of that jelly on in fact, use the whole tube if it brings you to your senses.'

The moment of calm after she'd said the words, was replaced by a rush of anger but rather than react to it, she used it as rocket fuel, to eject her out of the building.

Marching down the hall, Pete hot on her heels, she went to grab her handbag from on top of her case, but he beat her to it and before she could react, he'd pulled out the wallet containing her passport and documents before turning and racing up the stairs. She'd never seen him move so fast.

As she screamed at him to give them back he screamed louder, telling her she was going nowhere. The last sound she heard was the bathroom door slamming. The last sound he heard was Babs doing the same with the front door.

Bridie was furious. Babs was in tears. Pete wasn't answering his phone to Bridie who was going to give him a piece of her mind.

Babs couldn't believe he'd taken her things. On the drive to her mum's, the wheelie case on the back seat jiggled about like a giddy child, asking 'are we there yet?' Babs told the case that thanks to knobhead Pete it looked like they weren't going anywhere fast. Her plan was ruined. The taxi from her mum's was booked and she needed to check in at the airport.

'Don't worry, love, he'll calm down and we can sort you another flight... in fact no. I'm going round there to give him what for and get your stuff back. Sod this for a game of soldiers.' Bridie marched into the hall to get her coat when the doorbell rang and when she opened it, Demi and Fiona were on the step.

In Demi's hands was Babs' folder. 'Is Mum okay? I talked some sense into Dad and Fiona drove me round.'

Babs appeared in the hall, wiping her eyes but the sight of Demi and Fiona set her off again.

Demi gave Babs a hug. 'Mum, stop this. It's all okay, here.' Demi passed the folder. 'But you need to get going or you'll miss your flight. Do you want Fiona to drive you to the airport?'

'No, no it's fine. The taxi is due soon and I want to do this next bit by myself and if you come I'll just get upset. I know I will.' That was how Babs had imagined it as she'd lain in bed the night before. The next stage in her journey had to be solo.

If she could do this she could do anything.

The wheelie case was in the boot of the taxi and the driver was raring to go.

Bridie smoothed Babs' hair from her face like she did when she was little then gave her a kiss on the cheek. 'Now, you be brave, young lady, and whatever comes next, we can sort it out step by step, okay. Just remember how proud I am of you, and that all I want is for you is to be happy.'

Fiona stepped forward. 'Have a safe trip, Babs. I'll text you all the time and I promise I won't forget your advice.' She planted a kiss on Babs, then made way for Demi.

'Right. No more tears, mardy pants. We'll be fine here so don't be worrying about a thing. Get a drink in the bar and on the plane in fact, get wasted and give Uncle Tom something to worry about when he picks you up.'

Demi wrapped her arms around Babs who could only nod into the embrace as she listened to a whispered message.

'I love you so much. You're the best Mum in the world forever, so please, go make memories and have fun. I'll see you soon. Now go!'

Babs did as she was told and was about to go when she remembered. Fishing out her car keys she passed them to Demi. 'Here, for you. Look after it while I'm away. Gran's going to sort you some driving lessons and as soon as you pass, you'll be able to use it.'

Demi bit her lip, took the keys, and nodded.

Without another word, Babs got into the cab and shut the door. As the driver pulled away she turned. Her heart was aching for those she was leaving behind while her head warned her not to chicken out. Before the car rounded a bend she blew one last kiss to three wonderful women, Bridie, Demi, and Fiona, still standing on the pavement, waving goodbye.

CHAPTER FIFTY

ROBIN

Oh, my beautiful girl. Look at her. Oblivious. Floating on a sea of nothingness. Caressed by the soft fuzz of chemicals that swim through her blood. I often watch her while she sleeps. It brings me comfort to see her this way. Selfish, I know. But when her eyes are closed I don't see the pain reflected in them. Her tears don't flow, and I don't have to mop them up.

The thing is, we both need respite and I tell myself, as I coax her into taking her medication that I'm no different to those mothers, like me, who thanked heaven for Calpol. If only it were as simple as a fever, a bad cold that two teaspoons of red liquid would soothe so we could all sleep.

How many hours I've sat in this chair, in her bedroom. The wallpaper is tatty, peeling here and there. The peonies that were once vibrant now faded. The paintwork is scuffed and yellowed while the oak wardrobe with the wobbly hinge and the chest of drawers with a missing knob, stand like centurions guarding their ward.

Willow was always scared of the tree outside her window whose branches tap on the glass in the wind, and no matter how often the gardener cut it away, eventually it grew back to haunt her.

How many times have I raced along the landing, burst into the room, and folded her in my arms, telling her it will be all right? I never thought that in adulthood I'd do the same, spend nights lying by her side.

Me and this chair and the battered cushion I lean against have seen her through the worst of times. Teething and tummy bugs, teenage tantrums and angst, break-ups, pre-exam, and pre-wedding nerves. Yes, these four walls have witnessed it all but *nothing* like what we've been through since we lost Maya.

Yet here, no matter what, the two of us are safe. We are able in the midst of storms of the mind, which strike often, to find peace. This room is our sanctuary, away from Edmund and Nate, where we fight the good fight, and most of the time the devils and demons are banished.

I wish you could have seen Willow before, when my darling girl was so full of life and fun and love. A delight. That's what she was. The best big sister to Cris, the best, best friend to Gina, the best daughter I could have wished for.

And now, the disease of the mind that eats away at my precious child is out of control, rampaging, cruel and irreverent. The devil is winning. I'm waging war on two fronts, with the Prince of Darkness and my husband, and I suppose Nate, too. And muddying the water further is the irrefutable fact that Edmund is to blame for where we are now, and he is the root cause, I truly believe this.

He changed the course of Willow's life, turned her away from the priesthood and towards teaching. She followed another path and met Nate. Then just when life seemed perfect, when Willow had found her truest vocation, motherhood, it was all snatched away. In the blink of an eye and the screech of tyres, the devil took his prize. But he won't take another.

He won't take her away from me. To that place where they say they'll care for her, but *nobody* can look after Willow better than me. She's my child not theirs. And who will be there when she cries out in the night and who will comfort her? She'll be confused, scared, and want me, her mum. And that is why I can't let the devil win.

And now, I have worked it all out. It's what Martha has been trying to tell me all along and why I was so drawn to her and her story. She's the clue.

I know what I need to do. I have to set Willow free. I can make my child happy. Let her be with Maya, guilt free. I will let Arty go, cheat the devil, and punish Edmund all at the same time.

It's been there, staring me in the face for so long and with my back against the wall I was able to see it clearly. The solution is so obvious.

Being a confirmed sinner made it easier. I gave in to lust and I broke a commandment when I committed adultery. I doubt that being a good girl where the others are concerned will save me, so what have I to lose? All I have to do is commit one final sin – wrath. And break one final commandment – thou shall not kill.

Edmund deserves to be punished and the best way to do that, is to take away control and beat him at the game he's been playing for years.

Arty has been my prisoner for too long and deserves a life without me in it. Not to be sat in life's waiting room, hoping I'll be on the next train.

Willow wants to be with Maya but is trapped in a hell on earth, too scared to find the exit by herself. So I will show her the way.

It will be the ultimate sacrifice. A gift of love and

understanding from a mother to her child. And best of all, I only have to sacrifice one thing.

Me.

CHAPTER FIFTY-ONE

THE CLINKING OF MILK BOTTLES WAS ACCOMPANIED BY Bobby's whistling as he made his delivery, followed by footsteps on the gravel and the familiar whirring of the electric engine on his cart as it faded into the distance.

Sunday morning had broken in all its autumnal glory and Robin mused that if one was going to go, it might as well be on a fine October day while the sun shone. The window was ajar allowing in a fresh breeze, the curtains open to give her a view of the sunrise.

She shifted slightly, pulled the blanket further up her body and readjusted the cushion behind her back that ached from sleeping in the armchair. Robin didn't mind, though. The pain was worth it to keep Edmund from Willow's room. Her sentry-like presence was a warning should he dare to disobey her wishes.

Perhaps the dull throb in her spine was also her penance, a precursor for what she might expect once she'd committed the greatest sin of all.

Still, she'd been through it all one more time, to make sure she was doing the right thing. Gone right back to the beginning taking great pleasure and experiencing intense pain remembering the most significant parts of her life, the insignificant ones too. They all made up the whole of what she hoped had been a worthwhile journey.

The high point was giving life to her two children and holding their hands for a while, as she guided them through the world. Even though she'd had to let go, the part she'd always dreaded, Robin hoped she still held a special place in their hearts. In fact, she was sure her children loved her and that was all the reward she ever needed, to be in receipt of a smile, a hug, their love.

Robin's eyes were drawn to Willow who'd slept soundly through the night, not waking when the owl outside hooted to its mate, or when the dawn chorus of little birds heralded a new day.

While Robin listened to the sounds of Little Buddington waking, and Joe zooming off on his motorbike regular as clockwork, she'd tried to identify each bird as it sang its song, remembering the poster on the wall at school. But the time for pleasant enterprise was over and she had things to do once Edmund left for church.

He would be gone all day, thank goodness. A christening first and then he was off to Macclesfield to take a service for one of his holidaying vicar friends. She had no idea who and cared not, only that he would be out of the way.

Just like Nate, who was going to see his parents in Manchester, no doubt to tell them his news and how once he'd shuffled his poorly wife off to the mental hospital he'd be shacking up with his fancy woman. Or more genteel words to that effect. Whatever, he wouldn't be back until late that night by which time it would be all over.

Once she moved from the armchair, that was it. It would

begin. Robin would solve everyone's problems once and for all. It was time.

Robin turned and looked around the kitchen. She'd brought in the milk, bread and juice that Bobby had delivered because she hated waste and the sight of them on the step may have alerted an observant passer-by. There could be no deviations or interruptions caused by visitors or kindly souls.

The flowers that Gina had brought on the day of their get-together were wilting but might last a day or so. They'd received a reprieve and remained on the windowsill. Her next thoughts were for her friends and their recent change in circumstance.

Robin was glad they were out of the way, and that she'd not had to face or speak to either of them prior to her decision. It had made it all a little easier. And she was so glad that before she went, she'd heard their news and had smiled, picturing them both.

Gina was with Jimmy, planning some new adventure; and Babs had texted from the airport lounge, two gins down and about to start a Spanish adventure of her own.

The goodbye letters were in Robin's handbag. One for Gina, larger than the rest because it contained those destined for Cris, Arty and Babs. Explanations for her actions, and apologies for not letting them say goodbye to Willow. Robin had entrusted Gina with her very last words. Letters of sorrow, thanks, absolution and eternal love to good friends, her son, and the man she was setting free.

Robin didn't trust Edmund and had said so in her very succinct message that would leave him in no doubt of her everlasting damnation of his soul. Her words to Nate were somewhat conciliatory and in a reserved way, she'd wished him well.

Not wanting to dwell or have time to wish for things that weren't meant to be, not for her anyway, Robin moved on.

She had charted the day meticulously and would work through it, grateful for the sensation of being wrapped in a daze, a blanket of warmth that cushioned her from the reality of her actions. It was somewhat like being in a dream albeit one where she could choose the outcome or wake. Robin opted for neither.

Opening the old larder door that was used nowadays as a utility cupboard, she moved the wicker trug and from behind, pulled out the ironically named bag-for-life that contained Willow's medications. Not wanting a repeat of the day she opened the lot onto her bed and began eating them like Smarties, Robin had made sure she'd never find them again. The two-month supply was everything they needed to sedate and calm a troubled mind and soul, the very thing that would send her and Willow into a peaceful and dreamless sleep.

Taking them back to the worktop beside the sink, Robin emptied the packets onto the marble. After fetching two glasses from the cupboard, straws from the drawer and the bottle of raspberry pop from the fridge, she set them next to the packets. Sliding the pestle and mortar towards her, Robin began.

Willow was sleeping when Robin entered the room and set the two glasses of fizzy pink onto the bedside table. Outside the bells of St Mary's rang as worshippers flocked to a longer than usual morning service where a christening would take place.

As Robin sat on the bed and waited for Willow to stir, the irony of the moment wasn't lost. While the Lord was welcoming a new soul into the arms of the church, she was going to send one up to heaven. A busy day for the big man and his angels.

The smile on her lips quickly faded as Robin forbade herself to think where she would end up, and even if the pearly gates were padlocked shut she was resigned to her fate. No going back.

As the thought left Robin's mind and the grip of fear eased a touch, a gust of wind from the open window caused the curtains to flutter slightly, a draught of cold whipping around the room. The tiny bell-chimes that hung from Willows lamp tinkled and her eyes opened a touch, then closed again.

Robin had no desire to alarm Willow, and as the distant strains of organ music reached her ears and the church service began with a hymn she knew so well, another sprang to mind. It was Willow's favourite as a child and one Robin often sang to her at night, before she went to sleep.

Stroking Willow's head as she'd done back then, Robin softly sang the words to her own little bird...

> Little bird, I have heard,
> What a merry song you sing
> Soaring high, to the sky
> On your tiny wing
> Jesus' little ones are we
> And he loves us you and me
> As we share in his care
> Happy we must be.

Willow woke just as Robin stopped singing.

'Good morning, sleepyhead.' She reached over and took Willow's hand in hers and watched as she yawned and stretched, rubbing tired eyes.

'I was having such a lovely dream. I didn't want to wake up.' Willow roused and pushed herself upwards, her pale face a picture of eagerness, unusual for early morning. Unusual for Willow full stop.

Robin leant across and took one of the drinks from the side, her movements steady, her body now on remote control.

'That's nice, darling, but here, drink this. It's special. From the health food shop. A mixture of vitamins and the nice lady said I could put it in your favourite drink. Look, I have one too.'

The time for worrying about lies was gone as Robin pointed, then passed Willow the glass. Sometimes she refused to eat or drink, and sometimes didn't have the energy or strength to hold a spoon but she took the fizzy mixture with ease. Holding the glass in two hands, Willow leant forward and rested it on her knees.

'Let me tell you about my dream... it was *so* vivid.' Willow stirred the drink with the straw, eyes wide and innocent as she waited for Robin to answer.

'Go on then, but drink your drink, it's good for you.'

Willow nodded and put the straw to her lips, but instead of sipping, lowered the glass and related the dream.

'I was in the most beautiful garden. Oh, Mum, you should've seen it. The grass was so green it was like emeralds, velvety and soft and I could feel it under my feet.'

With that, still holding the glass with one hand, Willow pulled back the covers with the other and checked her soles, rubbing them with her fingers, a bemused look on her face. 'It was so real. I swear I felt the grass and the dew.'

Robin pulled the covers back over Willow's legs, wanting to keep her warm while she chattered on, becoming more animated by the second.

'And the angels were there singing and dancing around me, holding my hands,' again Willow checked, looking at her palm this time, turning it over as if remembering a touch. 'And they were excited about something...' she looked up and around the room, searching for a memory and when it came her face lit up.

'I know. I know where we were.'

Robin had to ask, becoming swept along by one of Willow's rare moments of complete lucidity. 'Where?'

'Lourdes! We were in a garden in Lourdes and the church bells were ringing and the angels were singing because they were happy... and they were telling me something, too. One of them whispered in my ear.' Willow touched her lobe.

'I can feel it, just there, where her lips touched me, soft and gentle. I know I can. But I can't hear what she said.' Willow closed her eyes as if in meditation and with her free hand stirred her drink, then went to take a sip.

Robin watched as her own heart almost stopped, as the straw touched Willow's lips. But again something halted her. Willow looked like she was tuning in, listening to words on a radio that only she could hear.

'Love, drink your drink. There's a good girl.'

Willow had responded and took a sip then grimaced and spat into the sleeve of her pyjama top. 'Urgh, that's horrible...'

Lowering the glass her lips began moving again, her eyes misted over, then she spoke, softly, full of awe as she turned her gaze to Robin.

'Mum,' almost a whisper. 'I remember what she said...'

Robin had the strangest feeling. Her arms were prickled by goosebumps, and she felt odd. As though her resolve was being drained away while a question rushed from her lips unbidden 'Who? What did she say?'

Willow's olive eyes had turned the deepest pools of green. 'My angel. She said we have to go to Lourdes because... because that's where I'll find the answer.'

Robin held in a gasp, caught it in her chest as Willow continued.

'I knew they would help me... I knew they'd hear my prayers and find the answer. Oh, Mum, can you believe it, can you believe it?'

Robin couldn't. She also couldn't move, not at first because a wave of something ice cold washed through her veins but the second it was banished, it was replaced with heat. The most overwhelming rush of warmth, like her whole body was basking in the light of an indescribably beautiful moment.

Her hands trembled, as did her voice when she finally made her lips move.

'Yes, my love, I believe.' But as she said the words Willow lifted the glass and placed the straw to her lips and Robin panicked. Grabbing the drink resulted in a startled look from Willow who recovered and asked a question.

'Mum, can we go, to see Uncle Arty in Lourdes, can we, Mum? Please say yes. That's where the angels told me to go... it's where I'll find Maya. I can feel it right here.' Willow touched her chest. 'They said I'll be happy there so that must be what they mean...'

Without warning Willow pushed the covers back and leapt from the bed while with trembling hands Robin removed the other glass from the bedside table, watching as Willow grabbed the white box of ashes from her dresser and clutched it to her chest.

Willow didn't say a word, instead she waited, her stance firm, eyes boring holes into Robin. The room was warm, the sun shone brightly through the windows casting silver streaks onto Willow. Radiant, surrounded by a halo of light.

'Just give me a minute, sweetheart. I need to get rid of this nasty pop and while I'm gone, perhaps you could get dressed. I'll be back very soon. Go on, get your clothes out.' Robin saw Willow nod and a huge smile spread across her face.

Robin's legs were like jelly but she turned quickly and ran into the bathroom then tipped both drinks into the toilet and flushed the chain before racing downstairs. In the kitchen she dumped the glasses in the sink and went to her bag, hands shaking uncontrollably as she grabbed her phone and prodded the screen.

Please be there, please answer, hurry up, please be...

'Hello. Well, I must say this is a very nice surprise. And what can I do for my favourite person on this fine Sunday morni–'

'Arty, shut up and ask me.' Robin heard her voice crack as her heart pumped so hard she thought it might burst.

'Ask you what? Robin, what's wrong...? I don't understand. Has something happened?'

'Ask me the question you said you never would. Ask me now, Arty. You have to ask me, right now.'

The silence was deafening, apart from her short shallow breaths that she desperately needed in order to stay alive and upright.

Finally, Arty spoke, his voice deep, choked with emotion that she heard clearly, across the many miles that had separated them for so long.

'Robin, will you leave him? Will you come and live with me?'

'Yes, yes I will.'

She was crying, and when she heard his next words Robin suspected so was he.

'When, when will you leave?'

She smiled through her tears and wiped them away, laughing as she answered.

'Now, my love. Me and Willow are leaving right now.'

LOURDES, FRANCE.
TWO YEARS LATER

Today we are blessed with a cloudless sky and a flaming June sun. It warms my arms and face while I sit out of sight, watching Willow. It's something I do often because seeing her laughing, carefree and as she is now, playing barefoot on the grass of the convent reminds me of how lucky I am. And how close I came to making a terrible mistake.

It plagues me, you know, that day. I have recurring dreams about it. Even the moments right up to driving away from the vicarage, the car loaded with our possessions. We didn't have much really, just our clothes and treasures like photo albums and Willow's precious angel books.

In my dreams Edmund comes home as I am loading our cases and bin bags into the boot and stops us from leaving.

In reality, it went very smoothly although those final few yards, from the doorstep to the car, as I hurried Willow along almost shoving her in the front seat and racing around to mine, seemed to take an age not seconds.

I did stop though, for a second when we reached the road and looked up to the graveyard to where Martha is. I imagined her standing there on the hill, waving me off, her voice clear in my head.

'Off yer go, girl. Be 'appy, mate. We'll meet again, one day.'

I hope we do.

I drove to Dover. There we caught the next ferry to France. I should have been exhausted after hardly any sleep and a four-hour drive, but adrenalin and fear kept me going. I must have checked the rear mirror a thousand times expecting the devil to be on our tail.

I relaxed somewhat when we arrived in France, and we took our time driving south to Lourdes where Arty was waiting. He'd offered to come and get us, but it would've taken too long, and I wanted to be gone.

And you know what the strange thing is. That from the minute we arrived at his house – our house now – it felt like home. Like it had been waiting for us.

From then on, Arty took control, which was a relief. He phoned Nate to tell him where we were, and after the bomb went up and the dust settled we've been able to work things out. I swear there's not a useful person that Arty doesn't know either here or in the UK and the old school tie network has been invaluable.

The very slow cogs of law turned and now the authorities in England are eventually satisfied that Willow's legal affairs are in good hands, she and Nate can divorce. He got what he wanted in the end and so did I. My daughter.

Talking of which, Edmund kind of got what he deserved when the bishop decided, in his infinite wisdom, that it was time for a new broom at St Mary's and shuffled Edmund off to a dusty office at diocese headquarters. I like to think of it as dour and depressing, a place where he also shuffles paper, day in, day out.

By all accounts, and much to my glee, a female vicar and her young family are now in residence and have brought much-needed life back to St Mary's and the village.

I haven't spoken to Edmund since the day we argued at the kitchen table. I doubt I ever will. I don't know if he suspects Arty and me of being together, now or in the past, that his arrogance presumes his brother is merely providing safe haven. In truth, I really don't care what Edmund thinks anymore.

Cris, of course is deliriously happy that me and his sister are here, on the same continent as him and he's visited us many times. He knows the truth and hasn't batted an eyelid, in fact, he said he's always suspected Arty was in love with me and admitted that in another world, he'd have happily swapped dads. No surprise there.

Which brings me to Gina and Babs. Gina and Jimmy are well into developing the Young Farm and she's loving life, both professionally and personally with a new baby on the way, plus a host of new clients she fits between motherhood and mood boards. Gina forgave me instantly for whisking Willow away once she understood Nate's plans. She Facetimes us regularly, keeping her best-friends-forever promise like I knew she would.

And Granny Babs. Where should I begin? In a nutshell her family are fine and in between Easy Jetting back and forth whenever the fancy takes her, she works with Tom and Cris, running their cruise boat business. She's so very happy and lives in an apartment overlooking the beach, bought by money-bags Bridie, who had a big win on the lottery. Babs is a wonderful granny and adores her grandson Erling, named after a footballer, apparently! She's even been to visit her old schoolfriend, Lynda.

Demi is settling into university and goes to see her mum during the holidays, as do Sasha and Isaac who miraculously got over the shock of their mother leaving. Even Pete managed to survive and, according to Babs, is dating a woman he met at a pool match.

See, life really does go on, even when none of us could ever imagine changing the one we had. I'm proof of that.

And what about my Willow? Well, as I said, Arty arranged everything. Unlike Edmund who was prepared to use the bank of mum and dad to incarcerate her, Arty used his inheritance to do the opposite.

He found a wonderful doctor, Professor Barerra, who has taken her under his wing. They've made magnificent progress using a combination of new treatments, for example sending magnetic impulses to the brain. The change in her is remarkable and it's given us all hope for the future.

Willow leads a much more independent life now. Still living with us, but by day she is here at the convent. It's part of the hospital, where she works as a volunteer, helping the sisters, a nursing order of nuns. Willow helps in the garden, or in the kitchen and is a favourite with the little ones. That's what she's doing now, playing catch with the children from the ward, running barefoot on the grass just like she did in her dream.

She takes great comfort from being around the sisters. The nuns have infinite patience and seem to radiate something, signals of love, kindness, whatever. Willow receives them loud and clear.

She also loves to sit in church and listen to the incantations and prayers, finding great peace in her surroundings and amongst those she calls angels here on earth. Who am I to doubt that? She's thriving and that's all I care about. Perhaps she will convert and if she does I will support her because I've always known her place is beside the God she believes in. Imagine Edmund's face if he found out his child had become a Catholic!

And me?

I keep my faith deep inside. I'll always have my demons but

with Arty to fight them off, I think I'll be okay. Nobody, apart from him will ever know what I planned to do that day at the vicarage. I tore the letters up and threw them into the Channel as we crossed on the ferry but when we got here, I had to tell Arty the truth.

I couldn't start a new life with the man I love without him knowing who I was. It would have eaten me alive, keeping that secret and I would've understood if he'd been so appalled he turned against me, but he didn't.

Arty is adamant that it was a result of deep trauma. And it does make sense because ever since Maya died, I'd put Willow first and I'd not properly mourned her loss. I refused counselling. Put my grief to one side and bottled it up. I focused on Willow instead. And when faced with having another precious child taken away the shock and fear of losing Willow pushed me over the edge.

Caring for Willow had kept me going. That innate mother's love that places their child before them muffled the scream in my head when I remembered the day we lost Maya. When Edmund and Nate said they were taking Willow away, the void opened and I was once again bereft, before the event, after the event, and it was too much. The balance of my mind drove me to act that way, nothing else.

Yes, I was prepared to sacrifice my life to help Willow and pay the ultimate price a mother can for their child, an act borne from love, not malice and certainly not evil. And when I worry that God will punish me, for the thoughts I had that day, for the thing I almost did, I remember that the angels came just at the right time.

Perhaps they didn't just come to save Willow; maybe they came to save me, as well.

Did Willow simply wake from a vivid dream? Or was it her angel?

I suppose I will never know, or maybe, one day I will.

What I do know is this.

That the love a mother has for her child is infinite, and the sacrifices we make, the wrong turns and mistakes, the good days and the bad are all part of the things we do, for love.

There's no right or wrong way to be a mother. We learn on the job and that terrible day when I almost got it very wrong, it somehow turned out right.

My beautiful Willow was trapped inside her head, locked in a cage, no escape in sight but just look at her now, smiling in the sun, laughing. The days of torment are behind her. The future looks bright because in the end, and perhaps with the help of the angels, I found a way.

I set her free. My little bird.

THE END

ACKNOWLEDGEMENTS

Dear reader,

Thank you for choosing my book and I hope you enjoyed it. I loved writing it for you and the hours I spent with Gina, Babs and Robin were some of my happiest creative moments, so involved was I in their lives.

Oh Gina, she caused me such heartache while I wrote her part. Because Gina is loosely based on someone whose story hasn't always been happy or easy, but who was determined and hard-working, who held their head up and, against the odds, has made a success of their life. She brought love and pride into the lives of others, a beautiful woman who deserves only the best, to be happy. At the core of her story was a simple message. Don't let the past or the actions of others ruin your future or define who you are.

And being a woman of a certain age, I have also faced the same challenge as Babs. It's a tricky subject and, while it has a detrimental effect on the lives of so many women across the world, I tried to balance the serious nature of the menopause with a touch of humour. Sometimes it's the only thing that gets us through. Babs represents the ladies I know well, who have shared their troubles, and those who suffer in silence. I hope that Bab's story might encourage anyone who is struggling to reach out and find a hand to hold.

The subject of faith is a topic I've wanted to explore in my writing for a while. I feel lucky to be comforted by my spiritual beliefs, thankful too. Religion has always fascinated me and was one of my favourite lessons at school. Yet it can be such a contradiction. Something that brings great joy and contentment to many, can also be the cause of confusion, conflict, and pain. Hence Robin's story, and of course dear sweet Willow who had to have a happier ending and hope for the future. Thanks to her friends, the angels.

The common denominators that bound them, brought together their individual stories was friendship; and on a deeper level, a question that perhaps many people have asked themselves at some point in their lives, whether it's in relation to a child, a parent, a sibling, a friend, a lover, a spouse. What would you do for love?

Throughout the story, as always, I have left little treasures, memories of my parents, things they said, essences of my childhood. A kitchen table, special grandma teas, good dads, favourite hymns, and Blue Peter appeals. Hints and clues, thoughts and thumbprints, bits of my life, the dark and the light, my demons now vanquished. By writing these things down they remind me. I know they're not lost. They are too precious. Like words, life, family, love.

It's time to say thank you and I want to begin with the marvellous team at Bloodhound Books. Betsy and Fred, Tara and Abbie, Clare and Kate. I love working with you all.

To Lynda Checkley aka Cheeky Checkers who very kindly donated to the Bloodhound Books Ukrainian Refugee appeal by bidding on my prize bundle and won the dubious honour of being a character in a book. Lynda, I hope you're happy in your villa in Spain. At least I didn't kill you!

And finally to my own very special treasures, my family.

Brian. Owen and Jess. Amy, Mark and Harry. Albie and Elvis.

I love you.
It's as simple as that.
x

A NOTE FROM THE PUBLISHER

Thank you for reading this book. If you enjoyed it please do consider leaving a review on Amazon to help others find it too.

We hate typos. All of our books have been rigorously edited and proofread, but sometimes mistakes do slip through. If you have spotted a typo, please do let us know and we can get it amended within hours.

info@bloodhoundbooks.com

Printed in Great Britain
by Amazon